THE
TRACKS
BOOK TWO

GHOST CROWN

THE
TRACKS
BOOK TWO

GHOST
CROWN

J. GABRIEL GATES
AND CHARLENE KEEL

HCI
TEENS™

Health Communications, Inc.
Deerfield Beach, Florida

www.hcibooks.com

Library of Congress Cataloging-in-Publication Data

Gates, J. Gabriel.
  Ghost crown : a novel / J. Gabriel Gates and Charlene Keel.
    p. cm.—(The tracks ; bk. 2)
  ISBN 978-0-7573-1594-7 (pbk.)
  ISBN 0-7573-1594-1 (pbk.)
  ISBN 978-0-7573-1628-9 (e-book)
  ISBN 0-7573-1628-X (e-book)
  [1. Supernatural—Fiction.   2. Magic—Fiction.   3. Gangs—Fiction.   4. Social classes—
Fiction.   5. High schools—Fiction.   6. Schools—Fiction.   7. Mexican Americans—Fiction.]
  I. Keel, Charlene.   II. Title.
  PZ7.G222Gho 2012
  [Fic]—dc23

                                                            2011036527

Publisher: Health Communications, Inc.
        3201 S.W. 15th Street
        Deerfield Beach, FL 33442–8190

Cover design by Dane Wesolko
Interior design and formatting by Lawna Patterson Oldfield

CHAPTER 1

RAPHAEL KAIN'S ADVERSARY CARTWHEELED forward and attacked with a barrage of flying fists and slashing elbows. Unable to sidestep the attack, Raphael was forced to block each blow as it came, retreating a few steps down the narrow brick alleyway. The moment he saw an opening, he lashed out, counterattacking with a front kick and a host of blazing-fast punches. He landed a few glancing strikes before his opponent managed to backflip away from him, dodging in an acrobatic fury what would have been a devastating crescent kick.

"Good thing you got out of the way of that one," Raph taunted. He wasn't even out of breath. "You'd have had a headache for a week."

As his opponent stepped backward down the alley, regrouped and came forward again, Raphael watched him closely—paying careful attention to his elbows, since he knew they would tell him what sort of strike was coming next. Raphael read his movements flawlessly and launched a perfectly timed kick—but his enemy was too fast. He cartwheeled beneath Raphael's leg, sprang to his feet, and caught Raphael's cheek with a glancing elbow as he shot past. By the time Raph spun around and struck out with a backfist, his opponent was already safely out of range.

As Raphael prepared for his next onslaught, he felt the mysterious, soul-tingling magical force his kung fu master called *Shen* filling him. It rose through his feet, traveling upward like a shiver, and it shone down on him from above, too, filling him with its unseen light. Lately, Raphael was feeling the presence of Shen more frequently, but there was still no telling when it would appear and when it wouldn't. But he felt the energy's presence now, and he used his *qigong* training to focus it.

"You're slippery," Raph conceded. "Try to slip past this!" Squinting with concentration, he willed the energy to build within him. Instantly, his chest tightened and his forehead buzzed as that familiar, electric vibration coursed through him. Then, just as his opponent was charging him again, he reached a hand out and released the power.

Instantly, his attacker was knocked backward. Stumbling, he slipped on a crushed soda can and fell hard on the dirty concrete. Raph hurried toward him and extended his hand.

"You all right, Nass?"

With Raphael's help, Ignacio got to his feet and dusted off his clothes. "Yeah. I'm good. That was crazy with the Shen, though. You're gettin' scary good with that stuff."

"You're getting a lot better too," Raphael said. "I can't believe you dodged my kick like that. How did you see it coming? Did I telegraph it somehow?"

Ignacio shook his head. "Nah," he said, "I used the knowing."

The knowing was something Ignacio was still getting used to. As he explained it to Raphael, ever since he was a kid he sometimes saw things before they happened. Sometimes he saw them only in his mind, but sometimes it felt like they were really happening and he was in the middle of the action. But no matter how it came to him, he had always been afraid of his ability. Now he was learning to embrace it.

Raphael nodded. "I think the knowing comes from Shen too," he said. "It's all connected somehow."

As they stepped out of the alley onto the sidewalk of downtown Middleburg, Raphael shivered. Winter was coming. He could feel it in the sharp bite of the wind, see it in the frosty, pale blue of the sky. He wore his dad's old goose-down parka now, over his customary hoodie, and his best friend, Ignacio Torrez, striding down the sidewalk next to him, was huddled in a frayed old peacoat he'd picked up at the Goodwill.

But despite the chill that numbed his fingers and reddened his nose on that cold Thursday afternoon, nothing could dispel the warmth Raphael felt when he thought of the awesome changes that had recently taken place in his life.

First, everyone in town knew he had rescued Aimee Banfield from Oberon. Thoughts of that day, and of Oberon, sent a chill down Raphael's spine that was worse than anything the weather could cause. In a brief mind-flash, he saw Oberon as he had looked during their battle: *sheathed in black reptilian skin with sleek, black, feathery wings jutting from his back.* He'd looked like some kind of dark, demented angel—nothing like the angels in any of Raphael's Sunday school books. Maybe it was crazy, but sometimes it was like he could still feel Oberon staring at him with his one good eye, while the other one—the glass eye—glowed a terrifying shade of crimson. The image was sobering, to say the least.

But Raphael had defeated Oberon. He had rescued Aimee. And now, people in town (even some from the ranks of his archenemies, the Toppers) were starting to show him a grudging respect—although they still had no idea about Oberon's real, horrific identity.

The whole thing had been beyond weird—and he hadn't quite recovered from it. He wondered how Zhai—the leader of the Toppers (and his long-ago best friend)—was doing with it.

Part of the overall weirdness, Raphael thought, was that he hadn't told anyone—not even Nass—about everything he'd seen, how hard he'd had to fight, and the unbelievable otherworldly creatures he'd battled just to get to Aimee. And none of the Flatliners had discussed what had happened to them—and to Middleburg—during that fateful Halloween battle.

As odd as all of it had been, it wasn't a dream—as much as he'd like to think it was. The horses in Master Chin's barnyard and the samurai helmet that sat in a place of honor on the mantel over the sifu's fireplace were proof of that.

After the Halloween battle, it seemed to Raphael that Middleburg would forever retain the peculiar, disjointed feeling that lingered for a day or so after Aimee's rescue, but in less than two weeks, it had settled into an uneasy calm as the community adjusted to her safe return—and things went back to normal.

For a Flatliner like Raphael, "back to normal" meant broke and struggling. Between their nonexistent finances and his mom's pregnancy, things were as complicated as ever in the Kain household. The only thing that got Raphael through the day was knowing he would see Aimee— even if it was just from a distance. Maybe all they had for now were anonymous notes and discreet little waves or smiles across the crowded lunchroom, and a few rare, stolen moments when they could hold on to each other and hope for better times. But it was more than either of them had ever had before. They were in love, and with that thought to keep him warm, winter had might as well give up now.

They reached Lotus Pharmacy, and Ignacio pulled the door open.

"Ladies first," he said, ushering Raphael inside.

Raph slugged him in the shoulder as he passed. It was a friendly jab, but it made Ignacio wince all the same.

"Ow!" said Nass, laughing. "How many times I gotta tell you, man— normal people can hit their friends, joking around. Kung fu masters, not so much."

"Sorry."

By that time they were at the cash register.

"You sure you want to spend this money on a cell phone right now?" Nass asked. "You don't know when your mom is going to be working again."

True, Raph thought. Since Oberon went all Lucifer-on-steroids, kidnapped Aimee, fought Raph, then plunged over the edge of that crazy temple's rooftop (hopefully to his death), his business interests in Middleburg had been in a holding pattern. Little Geno's was still open, but Hot

House strip club where Raph's mom had worked was closed indefinitely. Money was tighter than ever. *But*, Raph considered, *when you've been running around battling time-traveling samurai, a gigantic, blood-thirsty lizard and a conniving, evil man who suddenly sprouts wings—not to mention trying to keep the Toppers at bay—you kind of have to have a cell phone. You can't always count on finding a payphone so you can call for reinforcements.*

Instead, he said, "No, man. I need a phone. It'll have to be one of these pay-as-you-go things for now, but at least I'll have it for emergencies or something."

"It's about time," Nass agreed. "Imagine actually being able to call each other from anywhere. What a concept."

"Yeah," Raphael agreed. "We'll be almost like regular people now."

"All right!" Nass said. "Let's see what kind of top-of-the-line, pay-as-you-go, loser phone my pizza delivery millions can get me!"

Lydia, the pharmacy clerk who waited on them, had green hair and an eyebrow ring. She was Beet's older stepsister, and with her narrow hips and thin, almost bony frame, there was definitely no family resemblance.

"Wow, cell phones," she teased. "You're finally leaving the age of the dinosaurs. Welcome to the twenty-first century." She smiled at Raphael and Nass as she rang them up and told them how to activate their phones. A moment later, they were walking out the door again, onto the sidewalk of downtown Middleburg.

"Uh-oh," Ignacio said. "Here comes trouble."

Instantly Raphael was on guard, ready for a Topper attack. But when he followed his friend's gaze, he broke into a wide grin.

Across the street, Dalton was just coming out of Middleburg's only upscale, designer dress shop—and best of all, Aimee was with her.

Raph headed toward them, not even looking as he rushed into the street, not caring about the oncoming cars he had to dodge. He didn't care about anything except being close to Aimee.

ഔ

Laughing happily together, Aimee and Dalton exited Middleburg Couture. Everyone agreed the name was a little ironic. Although it was the only place in town to go for good labels (casual or dressy), it was far from high fashion. To get anything decent, you had to drive more than a hundred miles, but Aimee's father had proclaimed it good enough for the homecoming dance this year. Next year, he'd promised, when Aimee had a better chance of being homecoming queen, they would go shopping in Topeka.

Aimee was so glad she'd hooked up with Dalton today—funny, outspoken, fearless Dalton who had stood up for her when it counted. Neither of them had dates for the homecoming dance yet, but they were both still hopeful.

Aimee found, to her own amazement, that she was actually looking forward to Homecoming, even though her dad was pushing her to go with Bran Goheen, one of her brother's football buddies. Bran (unlike her jock brother) was actually a nice guy, but Aimee loved Raphael. And she had no intention of leading Bran on or hurting his feelings.

She might not be able to go with Raphael, but at least she would see him there and maybe even manage a couple of dances with him, and that was enough for her. She didn't need a date—but she still had to get the perfect dress. She'd found a few that fit, and that actually looked pretty good, too. Dalton hadn't been so lucky.

When Aimee saw Raphael and Ignacio crossing the street toward them, her day got even better. Raphael skidded to a halt in front of her and Nass stopped in front of Dalton.

"Hey," they both said at once, and everybody laughed.

When Aimee looked at Raphael, she forgot all her problems. She wanted nothing more at that moment than to run her fingers through his long hair, to feel his arms around her and his lips on hers. But of course that was impossible, except in secret. Raphael was a Flatliner, and Aimee's dad had spies everywhere.

As Raph and Aimee moved up the sidewalk together for a little privacy, Ignacio looked at Dalton and Dalton looked back at him. She had a playful smile on her lips, and one hand rested on her hip. Just the sight of her standing there like that—all sexy and sassy—was enough to put Nass's dignity in danger.

"What's up, girl?" He tried to be cool. As much time as he'd spent with Dalton, there were still moments when he felt completely in awe of her. She was like the sun: you could hang out in the warm glow all day, but if you tried to look directly at the light, it would blind you. Dalton was like that, he thought—not just hot, but *scorching*.

"Just shopping," Dalton said, nonchalant.

"Yeah? For what?"

"A dress for homecoming."

"Oh, yeah?" He tried to sound casual, but now he was worried. Maybe somebody else had already asked her. No surprise there. He shouldn't have waited until the last minute, but every time he tried to ask her he got nervous and chickened out. He couldn't imagine anything more terrible than seeing her dancing with someone else.

"Yeah," she said, smiling up at him expectantly but giving nothing away.

"You, uh, have a date?"

"Nope," said Dalton with an exaggerated sigh. "There's a guy I'd like to go with, but I think he's too much of a wuss to ask me."

Nass laughed in spite of his nerves. It was amazing how she could get him all twisted up like this. No girl had ever had that effect on him—not even Clarisse, back in L.A.

Dalton smiled. "Did I say something funny?"

"No. It's just . . . maybe the poor guy is just biding his time, you know?" he said. "Waiting for the perfect moment."

Dalton seemed to consider this, then shook her head. "Nah, he's had plenty of chances."

"Well if you ask me, he sounds like a loser," Nass said.

She nodded. "I guess so."

"If he never—you know—steps up to the plate, you could always go with me," he offered, a smile playing at his lips.

"Oh, you wouldn't mind?" Dalton teased, pretending to be surprised. "But a smooth guy like you—I figured you'd already have a date."

"Nah," Nass said. "I've been, uh . . . biding my time."

Dalton finally gave in to laughter. "Okay, okay—I can't take it anymore. I'll go with you—it's a date!

"Yeah," Nass agreed, grinning. "It's a date."

And he thought, not for the first time, how much he loved their little games.

℠

Raphael stood a few feet away from Aimee, carefully *not* looking at her. They were both pretending to be fascinated by the garments on display in the window of Middleburg Couture.

Neither of them had to tell the other it would be too dangerous for them to interact openly in public.

"I missed talking to you last night," he said.

"I missed you too. Sorry I didn't get a chance to call. Rick was hovering all evening."

Aimee's brother, Rick, that Topper jerk. Just hearing his name took Raphael back to the night Rick tried to burn him alive in the abandoned train yard.

Raphael took a deep breath, using his *qigong* training to center himself. *Forget about revenge,* he told himself. *Think about Aimee.* But the anger was still there. He nodded at the plastic garment bag draped over Aimee's arm. "Homecoming dress?"

"Yep. I've narrowed it down to three possibilities."

Raphael smiled sadly. "Whichever one you pick, you're going to look gorgeous. Has Bran Goheen asked you yet?" The thought of Aimee dancing with the Topper jock who was Rick's buddy sent little lightning flashes of rage shooting through Raphael, but he managed to control them.

"No," Aimee told him. "Rick said he was going to ask me and Dad has already decreed that I'm to go with him, so they're all just assuming it's going to happen."

"So, *Mister* Jack Banfield hasn't changed his mind and decided I'm perfect boyfriend material yet?" Raphael asked sarcastically.

Aimee shook her head. "Not at all. I'm afraid you're still strictly off limits."

Raphael sighed. Even though everyone agreed he'd saved Aimee's life, in her father's eyes he still wasn't good enough for her, and he never would be. But Raph just couldn't sit by and watch her go to the dance with someone else.

"If we go together it'll be a disaster—and not only because they hate me," he said. "There's actually peace between the Flatliners and the Toppers now. It would be silly to risk that just for some stupid dance."

"I know," she agreed. "Totally. You're right."

He took a covert glance at Aimee; she was gazing back at him. They both smiled and he turned away from the store window, and from her, to look up and down the block. Downtown Middleburg was, as usual, mostly deserted. Only a scowling mail carrier going into the pharmacy and a woman leaving the bank were about, and neither of them was paying any attention to him and Aimee. He risked turning back to her.

"So . . . are you going with Bran?"

"I don't want to," she said.

"That would be kind of hard to take." Raphael admitted. He was fully aware that what he was about to do was foolish. Reckless, in fact. What he had in mind would endanger Aimee, himself, and his Flatliner brothers. It would probably ignite the gang war all over again. But in that moment, he felt like he didn't have a choice.

The chill that had permeated the air before was gone now. Raph felt sharp currents of emotion coursing through him, heating his blood, and making his heart race. The words were out of his mouth before he could stop himself.

"Aimee," he said quietly. "Will you be my date to the homecoming dance?"

She glanced at Raphael, surprised, and then gave him a radiant smile. "I'd love to," she whispered. "But how?"

"I don't know yet, but if you're willing—"

"I'm more than willing," she said quickly, and her look of raw longing gave him an almost irresistible urge to sweep her into his arms and kiss her. As much as he wanted to, and as much as he could see that she wanted him to, it would have to wait until they could grab a few minutes alone.

∞

They all walked to the corner together, and then the girls headed for Hilltop Haven, and Raphael and Nass turned toward the Flats. Nass noticed that Raphael seemed thoughtful and distant, but he felt like he was moonwalking in the clouds.

"I can't wait until Saturday night," said Nass. "I've got it all planned out. Okay, I'm at her door to pick her up, and her grandma answers. I'll be, like, 'Good evening, Lily Rose. Thanks for letting me take Dalton to the dance.' And I'll give her a bouquet of flowers, just for being so cool, you know? First, we'll go to Rosa's for a nice Italian feast—I've been saving for a month. We'll eat, we'll dance, and we'll stay out all night. I'll take her up to the roof of my building, and we'll sit up there and look at the stars, just me and her. It'll be the most romantic night of her life! I'm telling you, she's not gonna know what hit her."

Nass looked at Raphael for his approval, but all he got was a wan smile.

"Sorry, man." Ignacio suddenly felt bad for him. "I didn't mean to make such a big deal about it." There was no way Raph could go to the dance with the girl he liked—it had to be rough for him to see Nass so excited.

"Don't worry. I'm good," Raph told him.

The knowing stirred in the back of Nass's mind: there was something Raphael wasn't telling him. But if his leader wasn't ready to divulge what was in his thoughts, Nass wasn't going to call him out on it. Raphael always told Nass everything—when he was ready.

Another idea stormed through Nass's brain. "Oh, I gotta call my mom," he said. "Put her on high alert for the tux, the ride, and some new kicks."

"Good luck with that," Raph said with a wry chuckle as Nass punched in the number.

His mom sounded distracted as she answered.

"*Hello?*"

"Hey," Nass said.

"*Hey, yourself. Who's this?*"

"What do you mean 'who's this?' It's your son! Calling from my brand-new cell phone, I might add. So go ahead and write this number down in case you need to reach me. Hey, listen, I have some good news."

"*Oh,* mijo*! So do I!*"

"Really? What?"

"*It's a surprise. Come home now and I'll show you.*"

"A surprise?" He shot Raph a big grin. "At least give me a hint."

"*Okay—it's for the homecoming dance.*"

Nass laughed. "All right!" he exclaimed triumphantly. "Be there in five."

He snapped the phone shut with a flourish, stuck it back in his pocket, and turned to Raphael.

"Dude, my mom has some kind of surprise for the homecoming dance. What do you think it is? I'll bet she's got me a tricked-out tux or something. Maybe she's going to rent us a limo! Man, how sweet would that be? Imagine us, cruising through downtown Middleburg in a freaking limo—like one of those big ones with a hot tub in the back! That would be ridiculous!"

The longer Nass fantasized about the perfect evening with Dalton, the more infectious his energy became, until at last Raphael was laughing and joking along with him. They parted at Raphael's apartment building (which, like all the tenements in the Flats, looked more run-down and decrepit with every passing day). Proudly, Nass held up his new phone and promised to call Raph as soon as he found out what the surprise was. Then he jogged the two blocks home, getting more excited with every step.

഼

Ignacio charged into the living room as the inviting aroma of carne asada and roasted peppers wafted out to him from the kitchen, along with the excited tones of happy voices.

"Your favorite son has returned!" Nass shouted, "I'm ready for my surpri—" the words died as he rounded the corner and looked into the kitchen.

"Surprise!" Amelia Torrez said, beaming.

She stood at the stove, stirring a skillet full of sizzling meat, onions, and peppers. But she wasn't alone. The girl standing next to her was as tall as Nass, with wavy, raven-black hair, a slender but curvaceous figure, and dark brown eyes that seemed to brim over with mirth and mischief.

"Well?" the girl asked, a seductive smile crossing her pouty, full, ruby lips. "Are you surprised, 'Nacio?"

Speechless for once in his life, Nass stared at Clarisse. *Clarisse from back home in South Central.* The girl he'd just started to get really serious about when his mom had announced that they were moving to some little Podunk town in the Midwest. The girl he'd spent hours hanging with in a parking lot on Crenshaw Boulevard, stealing kisses and watching the low-riders cruising and car-dancing by. *That Clarisse, showing up*

഼ 12 ଓ

in Middleburg. Somehow, it just seemed so wrong.

"Clarisse is going to stay with us for a while, 'Nacio," his mom said. "I was telling her mother how much you missed her and all your old friends back in L.A., and she thought it was a good idea for Clarisse to come and stay with us, at least for the rest of the school year."

"More like those mean streets were gettin' a whole lot meaner." Clarisse clarified the situation in her soft, smoky voice. "The old lady wanted to get me out of harm's way, you know?"

"Wow," Nass said. "That's . . . great." He managed what he hoped could pass for a smile. "So you're . . . staying with us for a while. *Great,*" he repeated. He knew he sounded kind of mentally challenged, but he was having a lot of trouble wrapping his head around the reality of Clarisse, in the same room with him after all this time. "Wow."

She gave him that old familiar, sardonic grin, her eyes burning into his as they used to when she'd wanted him to kiss her.

Amelia Torrez stirred the carne asada again. "And just in time for your homecoming dance, *mijo.* Now you have a date! What about that, huh? I knew you would be so, so happy about this—that's why I kept it for a surprise!"

Surprise. That was the understatement of the year, he thought.

He should be happy. If this had happened three months ago, he would have been elated. He and Clarisse had known each other for years and back in L.A. they had been best friends, inseparable *amigos,* partners in crime (sometimes literally) even before they'd started going out. But that was all back in the life he'd left behind. Now, with Dalton on the scene, everything had changed. And it was going to be a problem. Clarisse was doggedly territorial, and she wasn't the type to take no for an answer, no matter how calmly he explained the situation.

"Now," Amelia continued. "You're gonna be sleeping on the couch, 'Nacio, and Clarisse will take your room. I'll go and clean out my sewing drawers in the dining room for your shirts and socks and stuff."

His mom, Nass thought with a new respect, was a genius at squeezing the maximum space out of their cramped little apartment in the Flats. She turned to Clarisse and entrusted her with the wooden spoon, and with a sly wink at Nass, she hurried out of the kitchen.

Slowly, Clarisse stirred the sizzling meat and peppers, turned the burner down to simmer, carefully placed the spoon in the spoon rest on the stove, and then walked confidently across the kitchen in her slinky, tight jeans to stand as close as possible to Ignacio without actually touching him.

Looking brazenly into his eyes, she asked softly, "So, *mi corazón* . . . miss me much?"

"Uh . . . yeah," he said. He really had missed her, at first, until he'd met Dalton.

"Well, I'm thinkin' you should look a lot happier to see me," she said, smiling sweetly and moving closer. Before he could say anything else, Clarisse was pressed against him, her arms around his neck, and her lips on his, hot and soft and hungry.

Oh, yeah, Nass thought. *I'm in trouble. Big, big trouble.*

ဢ

"I'm serious, man," Nass said to Raphael the next morning on their way to school. "I don't know what I'm going to do."

"Two girls?" Raphael laughed. "I know a lot of guys who wouldn't mind having *that* problem."

They were walking along the stretch of railroad tracks that had always, up until Halloween night, given Raphael the creeps. When he took this route, he always got the feeling that someone (some*thing*) was walking just a step or two behind him, so close that they (*it*) could expel an icy cold breath on the back of his neck at any moment. In the days following his big battle with the Toppers and Oberon, the feeling had disappeared. But this morning, it was back—and worse than ever.

"No, man—this is sick. And not in a good way," Nass insisted. "What am I gonna tell Dalton? You don't know how long it took for me to get up the nerve to ask her and now—"

"Now you tell her the truth," Raphael advised. "You have a friend visiting from back home and your mom insisted that she tag along on your date."

Ignacio was shaking his head. "Even if Dalton will go along with it, I'll be sitting between them—Dalton on one side, Clarisse on the other— like a hunk of steak between two hungry dogs."

At that, Raphael cracked up completely. When he finally noticed that his friend wasn't laughing, he settled down. "Sorry, man—but you better not let Dalton hear you say that. Did you tell her what you used to have going on with Clarisse?"

"What? Do I look crazy?"

"And did you tell Clarisse that Dalton's your date?"

"I've been trying to, ever since she got here. But before I can get the words out, she's trying to make out with me—that's why I didn't call you last night. I'm running out of excuses not to kiss her."

"Like I said, amigo . . . such problems. Look, you're gonna have to tell her—both of them—sooner or later. But maybe you can get through homecoming first," Raph said. An idea was starting to form.

"What do you mean?"

"Okay, look. You know I want to be with Aimee at the dance, right? But we have to be careful. So this is actually perfect for you and for me. I'll go with you to talk to Dalton, and I'll ask her as a personal favor to me if we can all go together as a group."

"The four of us?" Nass looked puzzled. "Won't that kind of look like a double date? The Toppers will flip out. And what about Clarisse?"

Raphael explained that Emory was going with Myka who, with her black-and-red dyed hair, pale skin, and nose ring, was the only kid at Middleburg High who was more goth than Emory. They were riding with Beet and Natalie, a Flatliner girl who was as big and boisterous as

Beet and who, Beet never failed to remind them, was a cheerleader—part of the solid base that supported the pyramid of more petite girls at every football game.

"If Dalton can get her grandma's station wagon, Josh and Beth can go with us," Raphael said. "Benji's going solo. We can squeeze him in too, or he can go in the Beetmobile. With all you guys as camouflage, it'll be easier for me get some time with Aimee at the dance, plus it won't be weird for Dalton or Clarisse."

"I don't know," Nass hedged. "It'll still be awkward. What if one of them tries to hold my hand? Or what if I'm dancing with one of them and the other one gets mad?"

Raphael shrugged. "We don't have to go as a group. Just man up and tell Dalton you have to go with Clarisse."

"I can't! I'm crazy about Dalton."

"Then tell Clarisse you're going with Dalton."

"I can't! Clarisse is crazy. She'll kill me!" Nass shouted.

Raphael laughed, shaking his head.

"All right," Nass decided. "We'll go as a group. It'll work out some-how—right?"

It was settled. But it wasn't going to be easy, Raphael thought. Between Dalton, Clarisse, and the Toppers, the night was bound be filled with more danger than romance.

❦

Two men stood high above, on a huge boulder that jutted out from the side of the mountain that towered over Middleburg. The afternoon sun cast its rays across the landscape, gilding the little town they gazed on with a golden glow. Off to their left, the jumbled wreckage of the train graveyard stretched to a stand of dark trees. Directly below them were the Flats—block after block of rundown tenement houses with peeling paint and tattered rooftops. To their right, across the railroad tracks, was downtown Middleburg and above that, in the distance, was proud, pristine Hilltop Haven.

The younger man inhaled slowly, seeming to taste the air. He was tall and well formed with broad shoulders, a thick mane of long, black hair and a strong, square jaw. His pale complexion made his icy blue eyes even more compelling.

The other man was much thinner and not quite as tall. Bandages obscured most of his face and a pair of dark glasses covered his eyes. Leaning forward as if he had no fear of falling from the boulder and tumbling down the precipice, he was the first to break the silence.

"Middleburg," he said fondly. "A delightful little conundrum—a box within a box within a box, so to speak—and this is my favorite one of them all. From the beginning of time until the end of it, there will never be a Middleburg more ripe with possibility than this one."

"It doesn't look like much," the younger man observed.

"Appearances can be deceiving."

"And *she* is somewhere down there, in that insignificant mess?"

"Ah, yes," the older man assured him with a deep sigh of satisfaction. "She is down there. And she is the key to what we seek. She has a light like no other . . . bright. Pure. You will know her immediately."

"I'm looking forward to it."

Oberon Morrow pulled his long, black overcoat more closely about his shoulders and shivered slightly in the chill wind. "Come, my son," he said. "Take me home. We have work to do."

CHAPTER 2

Friday night.

The atmosphere in the men's room was rife with the aroma of pee and urinal cakes. Outside, drums rattled and horns blared. Chants of M-H-S, M-H-S rang through the night, and the concrete walls of the bathroom vibrated as a couple thousand feet stomped on the bleachers above, in time with the cheer. It was the fourth quarter of Middleburg High's homecoming game, and the MHS Phoenixes were behind for the first time all year. But there were bigger problems to worry about, Raphael thought, as he zipped up his jeans and joined Ignacio at the sink.

They took their time washing their hands, neither of them eager to rejoin the noisy chaos above. None of the Flatliners were too happy to be outside in the freezing cold to cheer for the football team, especially since most of them were Topper jerks they had fought in hand-to-hand combat just a couple of weeks before.

"I'm telling you, none of this is going to work," Nass said, shaking his head.

"It'll work," Raph said.

"Nothing has so far," Nass replied mournfully.

Raphael could understand his friend's concern. If tonight was any indication of how things were going to go tomorrow at the dance, Nass had plenty to be worried about. The Flatliners had met at Rack 'Em that night as usual, but Clarisse had insisted on going to the game instead of hanging out at the billiards hall.

"With four older brothers who were all tight ends, she's kind of got an obsession with football," Nass had explained apologetically. He glanced at Dalton and could see that she was about ready to blow, even though she'd gone out of her way to be polite to Clarisse.

"Me? You wait until baseball season rolls around and you'll see who's obsessed," Clarisse had announced to the group. "My 'Nacio here is a baseball star."

Dalton's expression darkened at the words *my 'Nacio,* but Raphael spoke before she could.

"Beet was thinking of going, just to support Natalie—so let's all go. We can hang at Rack 'Em any time," he said.

There was a little grumbling, but everyone could see that Clarisse was determined to go—with or without them—which meant Nass would have to go too. And if Nass went, they all had to go. The football game was big-time Toppers territory, and there was no way any Flatliner could go there alone.

Now, as they dried their hands, Nass said, "I've got to talk to Dalton and tell her what's going on."

"As long as *you* know what's going on," said Raphael.

The door swung open, and Benji and Beet walked in. "I told you," Benji was saying. "It's *by choice.* You know how many girls will be at the dance without dates? I'll just sit back and take my pick. Why would I bring a sack lunch to a buffet, man?"

"Because you've got no sack," Beet retorted, and the banter went on as Raphael and Nass headed out to the bleachers.

It only took them a minute to hike up to where the Flatliners were taking up most of a row. Emory and Myka sat with Josh and his date, Beth, a cute, wholesome-looking girl with long, straight blond hair who lived out in the country north of town.

Clarisse and Dalton were sitting next to each other in icy silence, with an open space for Nass between them. He gave Raphael a *see-what-I-mean* look and went to take his seat. Raphael took the open space on the end, next to Clarisse, just as Benji and Beet came back in from the opposite side.

"Well, well, Raphael," said Clarisse, glancing over at him. "Ralph, right?"

"Raph. No *L*. My friends call me Raph."

"You really some kind of a kung fu expert?"

"Some people think so."

Clarisse nodded, eyeing him appraisingly. "So you're not into sports?" she asked. "Real sports, I mean."

"You mean like on a team?"

"Yeah—like football, basketball, baseball. You know—the big three."

"Not really," he told her. "I used to play soccer, but school pride's not really my thing."

After a quick look at Nass, who was talking to Dalton, Clarisse turned her attention back to the field. "So who's this quarterback? He's got a great arm, and he's amazing out of the pocket."

Oh, you mean Rick Banfield? Raphael wanted to say. *My girlfriend's sociopathic brother and one of the biggest jack-holes that ever lived. . .*

But he just said, "That's Rick Banfield."

"Oh—that guy from your so-called rival gang. What do you call them?"

"The Toppers," Raphael said.

"Right. The Toppers. He got a girlfriend?"

"You interested?" Raph asked quietly.

Clarisse studied him a moment. "Don't get me wrong," she said. "Me and Nass go way back." She glanced at Nass, who was handing Dalton his phone, then back at Raph. "But we're cool, you know? He can talk to other girls," she said pointedly. "I can talk to other guys. But Ignacio is my boy. Nothing and nobody will ever change that." The look in her eyes was a complicated mixture of defiance, amusement, and flirtation, and Raphael understood at once how shrewd she was and how stubborn she could be.

She turned back to watch and clapped appreciatively as Rick picked up eight yards and a first down on a quarterback option play.

"So," she said again, nodding at the field. "He got a girlfriend?"

"Yeah." Raphael pointed down at the sidelines where Maggie was leading a cheer, her blond ponytail bouncing up and down as she waved her pom-poms. "That's her."

Clarisse looked at Maggie and laughed—a short, derisive little snort. "Well, you can't get any more white bread than that," she said, and settled back to watch the game. As she did, she reached over and casually placed her hand on Ignacio's knee. He frowned at her and pushed it off with a quick glance at Dalton, who had turned away for a moment, still on his phone. Raphael could see what Nass was talking about, now. He was in trouble with this girl. Maybe even the formidable Dalton needed to watch her back.

"Thanks," Dalton was saying into Nass's cell. "I'll be right there." As she returned it, she told him, "Well, that's what I get for volunteering to head the decorating committee. I've got to go over to the gym and make sure everything's ready for crowning the king and queen tomorrow night. They're having trouble with the balloon-drop thingy." She turned to Myka and Beth. "Come on, you guys. I have a feeling I'll need backup."

"Who wants to watch this stupid Topper loser game anyway?" Myka grumbled. Beth was already on her feet.

Clarisse tossed a quick, speculative look at them when Nass asked Dalton, "Want me to come along?"

Dalton glared at Clarisse, who turned back to the game, but she spoke to Nass. "No, thanks—I wouldn't want you to be rude to your *guest*." She snatched up her purse and buttoned her coat.

Over Clarisse's head, Nass threw Raphael a look that said, *Oh, man— she's steaming*. Raph responded with a grin and a shrug—it was impossible not to see the humor in Nass's predicament. Everyone went back to watching the game and Raphael scanned the crowd, searching for his secret homecoming date.

And there she was—on the far side of the bleachers, a couple of rows closer to the sidelines, sitting with her dad. Zhai Shao and Dax Avery, another Topper, were with them. Raphael was still annoyed that Aimee couldn't sit with him, but they both knew if they wanted to have any time together at the dance they would have to stay away from each other during the game. If Jack Banfield saw them together, she would be grounded and not make it to the dance at all. It was messed up, Raphael thought, but that's the way it was. After a moment, as if she could feel his gaze on her, Aimee looked around and saw him. She smiled and managed a discreet wave, and he longed to be with her more than ever.

The only thing going right, he thought, was the scoreboard, which read: Middleburg 28, St. Philips 35. With nine seconds left on the clock, Middleburg was backed up on their own thirty-three-yard line. A loss tonight would ruin the Phoenixes' perfect season, and might just help to deflate Rick's overblown ego a little bit. It would be even more appropriate for that loss to come on the night of the homecoming game, when the stands were more packed than usual. It was a Middleburg tradition to hold their homecoming later than any other school in the area, and this year it was the second-to-last game of the season. If they won tonight, Middleburg would be top seed going into division playoffs. If they lost, it would be a huge embarrassment, especially for Rick.

Now, it looked like that just might happen. Raphael could only hope.

As Middleburg's undefeated season had progressed, Rick had become more and more of a celebrity around town, until some of the old-timers at the Dug-Out coffee shop started wearing Middleburg Phoenixes t-shirts with RICK BANFIELD FOR PRESIDENT emblazoned across the back. The sight of the shirts had almost been enough to make Raphael puke, not to mention the horror he felt at the thought of Rick actually becoming president—of anything.

If he and Aimee got lucky, the Phoenixes would get their wings clipped, and Rick would be so pissed off that he wouldn't even show up tomorrow night. Without Rick there to harass them, they could have every dance together.

He looked at the scoreboard again. The clock was ticking down.

On the field, the offense broke huddle and lined up. The crowd hushed, tense, as Bran Goheen, the running back, lined up behind Rick. For an instant, everyone froze in anticipation and then the center snapped the ball. The linemen for both teams clashed together. Middleburg's famed gigantic Cunningham brothers barreled over the St. Philip's defensive line. St. Phil's secondary was playing way back, expecting a long pass from Rick's NFL-bound arm, but instead Bran ran a shallow slant route and caught Rick's low, dart of a pass mid-stride. The Middleburg crowd shot to their feet, cheering as Bran sidestepped one tackler and then plowed through a second.

He sprinted all the way to St. Phil's twenty-yard line, only to get hemmed in. The clock was ticking down to nothing. Raph saw how it would go down and it was beautiful. Bran would be tackled, and Middleburg High would lose the game. As one, the crowd deflated.

But out of nowhere, Rick came tearing through, running with incredible speed just a step behind Bran.

"Here!" Rick shouted, and Bran tossed the ball back to him just before two of St. Phil's cornerbacks brought him down.

Suddenly, Rick had the ball and was barreling toward the end zone. There was one man to beat, a huge safety who had planted himself on the five-yard line and seemed poised to make the tackle and end the game. Rather than trying to avoid him, Rick charged straight toward him. He blasted into the safety, running right over him. The defender hit the ground sprawling and his helmet came loose and rolled across the grass like a severed head. Rick high-stepped into the end zone, holding the ball up and yelling a triumphant battle cry.

The stands erupted into chaos, with Middleburg High's students, teachers, parents, and alumni cheering, screaming, stomping, and clapping, the band frantically playing the Middleburg fight song and the cheerleaders waving their pom-poms wildly and doing backflips and toe touches.

Raphael exchanged a glance with Ignacio and he knew they were thinking the same thing. *Terrific. The great Rick Banfield is the hero. Again.* At the same time, they noticed that the St. Phil's player wasn't moving. When the coach and the trainers couldn't revive him, they waved over the EMTs, who stood near the ambulance that was parked next to the field, to load him onto a stretcher and take him away.

But the game wasn't over yet; Middleburg was still down by one and needed to kick the extra point to send the game into overtime. The kicking squad trotted onto the field and lined up quickly, catching both St. Phil's defense and the still-celebrating crowd off guard.

Raphael watched as the center snapped the ball. The place holder—Bran Goheen—caught it. But rather than placing it on the ground for the kicker to boot through the uprights, he stood, tucked it under his arm, and sprinted for the right side of the end zone—going for the two-point conversion and the win.

It looked like St. Phil's defense was going to stop him—the entire defensive line shifted to the right and presented a wall of huge bodies to block the way—but Bran raced forward, leaped into the air and, with an amazing, acrobatic front flip, threw himself over the defensive line and into the end zone. The referee's arms shot upward, the crowd screamed once again, and the announcer's voice boomed over the P.A. system:

Two-point conversion is good! Number twenty-three, Bran Goheen, on the rush. Middleburg High wins—thirty-six, thirty-five!

Down on the field, Rick Banfield was swaggering along the sideline. Clarisse sat up a little straighter when the cheerleaders bounced over to their hero and surrounded him, and he reached out to grab Maggie and pull her close. Raphael saw the reticence in Maggie, her slight resistance to Rick's show of possession, and he wondered if Clarisse saw it too. Rick was oblivious. With one arm around his gorgeous cheerleader girlfriend, and the other raised in the air, holding up one finger, *number one*, he continued his victory strut until his teammates stampeded over and lifted him, along with Bran Goheen, onto their shoulders. Raphael noticed that Maggie withdrew, looking kind of pale, into the group of retreating, yelling cheerleaders.

Raphael caught a glimpse of Aimee, clapping and shouting happily, along with Zhai, her father, and the rest of the crowd.

She glanced up and saw him and her eyes met his. She gave him a smile and a little shrug, as if to say: *Sorry. I know my brother's a jerk, but he's a pretty good football player.* She went back to applauding, a little more subdued.

It was too bad, Raphael thought. Aimee should be happy. She should be proud of her brother. The thought that his feud with the Toppers was ruining her fun filled him with regret, and for the first time, he thought that maybe she'd be better off without him.

Everyone was filing out of the bleachers. A flood of students and proud parents poured onto the field to celebrate with the football team, and others were hiking toward their cars, trying to beat the rush out of the parking lot. Even if they weren't too big on school pride, the joyous mood seemed to have infected the Flatliners, too, as they exited the stands. Beet was carrying Benji piggyback style, and Benji was slapping him on the butt with a program and shouting, "Mush, dammit! Mush!"

Josh and Emory were in front of Raphael, talking quietly while their dates walked a few paces ahead. Ignacio and Clarisse were walking ahead of everyone.

"I'm just saying, Clarisse is smokin'," Josh commented. "Nass is doing solid work."

"Yeah, she's definitely not ugly," Emory replied. "But neither is Dalton."

They looked at each other and grinned. "It's gonna be some showdown," observed Josh. "Who do you think's gonna come out on top?"

"My money's on Dalton," said Emory. "But that little honey from the hood looks like she could do some serious damage."

Raphael saw that they were getting as big a kick out of Nass's problem as he was, and his thoughts turned to tomorrow night for probably the one-millionth time. He imagined himself pulling Aimee close, dancing with her in the shadows, trying to avoid Rick and his cronies. Even a few stolen moments were better than none, and in just a little while he would feel her in his arms again.

Above, the last pink streaks of sunset were fading from the sky, slowly giving way to a misty twilight. The wind gusted, cutting like a frozen scalpel through Raphael's coat. A snare drum was still rat-a-tat-tatting in the distance, and the Phoenixes' fight song echoed through the trees.

One thing was for sure: no matter what happened, the homecoming dance would be something he'd never forget.

૪૦

Around lunchtime on Saturday, Nass sat at the kitchen table, frantically trying to finish his pre-calc homework before he had to get over to Little Geno's. Homecoming or not, pizzas had to be delivered and he needed the money. With his mom out at the grocery store and Clarisse in the shower, he was taking advantage of the rare quiet time to get caught up. When the front door swung open, he almost groaned in frustration, but it wasn't his mom—it was only his dad getting in from work. Raul Torrez, unlike everyone else in the household, was a quiet person. As usual, he was covered in dust and wearily lugging his toolbox. Six and a half days a week at Shao Construction was no picnic, but in today's economy, Nass knew his father had little choice.

"Hey, kid. How's the homework coming?" he asked as he put the toolbox in the hall closet next to the front door.

"Good," Nass lied. Math made him want to pull his hair out. "Mail came already—it's on the coffee table. Just a bunch of junk mail—and something from the rental company." He tried to focus on the problem he was doing as his dad looked through the pile of bills and circulars.

Raul fished an envelope out of the stack and ripped it open. He was silent for so long that Nass looked up from his math book. He didn't like the worry he saw on his dad's face.

"What is it?" he asked.

"It's a notice—to terminate our lease. They're kicking us out of here." Nass jumped up. "No way!" he exclaimed. "Why? Can they do that?"

"They don't give a reason—they just say the lease we signed gives them the right to evict without cause, with a thirty-day notice. That's what this is." He put the letter back in the envelope, folded it, and put it in his back pocket. "Don't tell your mother, okay? She'll only worry."

Yeah, Nass thought. *And probably go marching down to the rental company to tell them off and make matters worse.* But he said, "What are we gonna do?"

"It's no big deal, 'Nacio. I'll figure it out. You just worry about your homework." Raul smiled and then headed down the hall toward the kitchen. His dad was awesome, Nass thought. To him everything was no big deal—but Nass didn't share his optimism. He'd seen the yellow eviction notices on a couple of Flats apartment houses, and something told him this *was* a big deal.

"Hey, Nass!" Clarisse called from the bathroom. "Nass!"

"What?" Nass put down his pencil and looked up. The bathroom door opened a few inches and he saw Clarisse peeking out from behind it, her wet hair dripping.

"Hey, grab me a towel, would you? I forgot." She flashed him a smile and opened the door a little wider to reveal a bare shoulder and part of a bare thigh—a move he was sure was anything but accidental—before shutting it again.

Nass was once again pondering the complexity of his life as he opened the linen closet, right next to his former bedroom. As he grabbed a clean towel off the stack, he heard Clarisse's phone buzzing. With a quick glance inside the room, he saw it on the nightstand next to his former bed. He grabbed it, intending to give it to her along with the towel, but the text message jumped out at him and filled him with gut-numbing fear:

```
Text from: Oscar S.
i don't care where you're hiding, you sneaky bitch.
i'll find you & if you don't have my 12 g's
i'll cut off your worthless head.
```

As far as Nass knew, there was only one Oscar S in his old neighborhood. Oscar Salazar—who was one of the most ruthless drug dealers in Southern California. What the hell was he doing texting Clarisse—and what had she done to make him so angry?

"Nass!" Clarisse yelled. "You forget about me or what? Where's my towel?"

"Got it right here," he said grimly. As he handed it to her through the door, he added. "Get dressed—hurry. I gotta talk to you."

"Sure, babe," she said. "What about?"

"Oscar S," he said quietly and held up her phone.

She was dressed and out of the bathroom, the towel wrapped around her hair like a turban, in record time. "So you're going through my stuff now?" she demanded as she joined him in the living room.

"Don't turn this on me," he said. "I heard it buzz and thought I'd hand it to her in case it was your mom or something." He held it up again. "I saw the text he sent."

She tried to grab the phone, but he was too fast for her.

"He says he's going to kill you, Clarisse. What's going on?"

"Nothing!" she flared. "He's crazy. He's just pissed because we had a little thing—nothing serious—after you left. He didn't like it when I dumped him, that's all."

"He didn't like it—twelve thousand dollars' worth? Be real with me. How come you owe him money?" It hit him then, and it terrified him. "Did you steal it?"

"Of course not. I set up a deal, okay?" she explained. "I delivered the stuff, and I was supposed to take the money to Oscar."

Nass was walking in a circle, his hands pressed to his head in frustration. "Clarisse! *Seriously*? Are you crazy? You stole money from Oscar S?"

"No! His customer wanted more, so I used the cash to do another buy, from Oscar's competition. So I could turn it over quick and make some money for myself. For *us*, mijo. But I got ripped off. So now I can't pay Oscar."

"You know he's had guys butchered for less," Nass told her.

"So what? He'll never find me in Middleburg. Now give me my phone." She made another grab for it, but Nass sidestepped out of her reach and she stumbled and hit her arm on the back of the sofa.

"Ow!" she shrieked. Raul Torrez picked that moment to come back into the living room.

"What's going on here?" he asked.

"He won't give my phone back!" exclaimed Clarisse.

"Nass?" Raul looked at him questioningly as the front door opened and Amelia Torrez walked in, her arms loaded with grocery bags. When she saw everyone standing around looking so serious, she asked the same thing:

"What's going on here?"

"Nothing," Clarisse said quickly. "I just want my phone back."

Nass grabbed the bags and put them on the coffee table. "There is something going on," he said. "And it's serious. She's not here because she missed me so much. She's hiding from a drug dealer back in South Central," he said, showing his mom the phone. "I have proof."

Amelia put her purse down beside the groceries and looked at him. "Yes, 'Nacio," she said. "We know."

Nass was stunned. He looked at each of them in turn—his mom, his dad, Clarisse. "You *know*?" They all nodded. "Was anyone going to tell me?"

"We didn't want you to worry," his mom told him.

Nass was furious—and horrified. "Well, somebody needs to worry. You know what kind of danger she's put herself in—that she's put all of us in?" He dropped the phone on the floor and smashed it with his heel.

"Ignacio!" his mother cried out. "What's wrong with you?"

"You think those punks she's running from don't know how to use a computer? Oscar Salazar has a pretty sophisticated operation—his guy has hacked into LAPD files more than once—and eventually they'll track her with her phone, right to us."

His mom went suddenly pale. "You're right," she said. "We never thought of that."

"Well, what am I supposed to do for a phone?" Clarisse demanded.

Nass whirled on her. "You'll get the same kind of prepaid loser phone I've got, and when it runs out of minutes, you'll ditch it and get another one. And maybe you can get a job after school to pay for it, like I did."

She glared at him. "Anything else, *jefe*?" she asked sarcastically.

"Yeah," he said. "Let's just get through homecoming weekend. And then next week, when you start at Middleburg High, try to get lost in the crowd. Don't be such a standout all the time. And don't tell anyone else about this," he added seriously. "I mean it, Clarisse—no one else can know."

"Okay, okay—like I would," she shot back.

"It's going to be all right, 'Nacio," his mom assured him. "Her whole family got together and figured out a plan and when they called us, we couldn't refuse. She had nowhere else to go and she's right—nobody's going to come looking for her here." She glanced at Raul and together they took the grocery bags on into the kitchen.

"Okay," Clarisse said grudgingly. "Maybe you're right about the phone. I guess it was stupid to keep it."

She moved closer, appealing to him with her big brown eyes. "Don't be mad at me, 'Nacio, *mi corazón,*" she implored, and he was surprised to see tears fill her eyes. "I'm glad you know. It makes me feel safe, with you to protect me. . . . "

And she put her arms around his neck, stood on tiptoe, and kissed him, sweet and soft and vulnerable.

But Nass felt only despair. He'd hoped that the capricious Clarisse would decide to go back to L.A. soon. Now, he knew that was impossible. She had to stay in Middleburg—her life depended on it. And whether he liked it or not, Nass was now her protector.

℠

Saturday night.

This was supposed to be the best night of Maggie Anderson's life— but all she felt was fear.

"Hold still."

"I *am,*" she said impatiently.

In her bedroom, she sat before a vanity table, staring into the mirror while her mother styled her hair. Maggie knew she looked great—spectacular, in fact. Her dress—a strapless, formfitting, floor-length sheath with a long slit up one side—was perfect; the fabric was a swirl of copper and deep purple that brought out her eyes, and the way her mom was pinning up her hair showed off the graceful curve of her neck. Maggie hadn't slept much since all the weirdness of Halloween night, but with an expert hand she was able to hide the dark shadows under her eyes with concealer and foundation. She had no trouble admitting that she looked like a homecoming queen. The problem was, she didn't feel like one. Not after what she'd been through.

She had seen too much. She'd had a lifetime of terror in just a few days, starting with seeing Rick, during the battle on Halloween night, transform into something indescribable—for an instant, he wasn't Rick, but some kind of demon. As if that weren't horrific enough, after the old kung fu teacher showed up and took her mother on some mysterious mission—*her mother*, who hadn't been out of the house in *years*—four ancient Japanese warriors invaded her home and tried to drag Maggie down her basement staircase, which had somehow turned out to be a staircase to hell. Raphael Kain had gone down into the impossible heat of that underground inferno and carried Maggie all the way back up, but the trauma had been almost enough to drive her nuts.

On top of everything, just to prove she really *was* crazy, she couldn't stop obsessing about Raphael, that hot bad boy who was, literally, from the wrong side of the tracks. Not even her most passionate fantasy about him, not even the haunting memory of the one kiss they had shared, and not even her burning desire to make it happen again could banish the brief, unbidden images of Rick's face and head morphing into some kind of monster's . . . images that flickered through her mind at night as she fell asleep. Sometimes she couldn't sleep. Sometimes she was afraid to try.

As she stared at herself in the mirror, her mind replayed that last touchdown of the homecoming game, when Rick had slammed through the St. Phil's defender and into the end zone. The crowd had been so ecstatic with Middleburg so close to winning that Maggie felt like she was the only one who had noticed that poor kid never got up. He just laid there in the end zone with coaches and trainers stooping over him, until some guys came over with a stretcher and hauled him off the field.

When Rick had smashed into him, it had happened again. He changed. After the hit, Rick looked over to the sideline and for the briefest moment Maggie saw the demon face there, behind the face mask of his helmet. Just for a moment, and then it was gone.

And if Rick knew she could see what he really was—or what he was becoming—what would he do to her?

She wished she'd had the courage to break up with him, or at least refuse to go to the stupid dance with him. But she didn't dare. He would have been furious.

She was also worried about what her mother's reaction would be. Miss three-time homecoming queen had been dead set on her daughter winning the crown for as long as Maggie could remember.

She could easily chalk up her mother's obsession with homecoming as one of the many neuroses that dominated Violet Anderson's life. The woman never left the house; she worked obsessively, designing and embroidering a series of tapestries, each one more bizarre than the one before it; and she suffered from all sorts of anxieties and sleep disorders.

Maggie shuddered. The last thing she wanted was to become like her mother.

She thought she probably shouldn't resent her mom's aspirations for her. After all, Middleburg High's homecoming celebration was all Violet had left in the world. It was sad, really. Positive that Maggie was going to win tonight, Violet had called the school and volunteered to be a chaperone. It would be only the second time she'd left the house in at least two years. As dysfunctional as the whole thing was, and as much as Maggie wished she could walk away from it all, she couldn't let her mom down now, on her big night.

"Oo ook ammayain!"

"What, Mom? Take the bobby pins out of your mouth!"

Violet dropped several bobby pins from her lips into her cupped hand and placed them on the vanity. "You look amazing!" she said. "Just one more touch . . . "

She crossed to the desk and brought over a small cardboard box that Maggie hadn't noticed before. From inside the box, Violet took a beautiful white rose, the stem of which had been cut short.

"From Lily Rose," she said, as she pinned the flower in Maggie's hair.

"It's so pretty," Maggie said, but her smile was fleeting, and her mom noticed.

"What's wrong?" she asked. "Maggie, you are so beautiful—you're going to the dance with a football hero, and you're going to be the first sophomore crowned homecoming queen since my three-year reign! What is there to be sad about?"

I'm not sad, Mom, she wanted to say. *I'm scared. I just found out my jock hero boyfriend is some kind of monster, and I can't stop wishing I was going to the dance with Raphael Kain, a sexy, troublemaking* Flatliner, *of all things.*

But she couldn't say that. "I might not even win," she said.

"You will."

"I'm not the only pretty girl in Middleburg, Mom."

A frown lined Violet's beautiful face for a moment and then she shook her head. "Nonsense! Who could even compete with you?"

"Well, Aimee Banfield, for one."

"Aimee's a sweet girl," Violet said. "And pretty—but not as pretty as you!"

"Some people think she is," Maggie replied with a sigh, her mind still on Raphael. "Anyway, it's not a beauty contest. Not strictly. It's about popularity, too."

And people don't like me, not really, she wanted to add. *I can see that now. Since Halloween night, I can see a lot of things I never saw before.*

Gently, Violet took Maggie's face in her hands and tilted it up, forcing her to look into her mother's eyes.

"Well, Rick is popular enough for the both of you," she said softly. "But none of that matters. There is such a thing as destiny, and this is yours. You are powerful, Maggie. And tonight, you *will* wear the crown."

For a moment, Maggie hardly recognized her mom. She had never seen Violet looking so calm, or felt such energy emanating from her slight form. There was so much force behind her words that if she had said, "Maggie, you can fly," Maggie could have spread her arms out like wings and soared into the air.

The effect, however, was short lived. Moments later, Violet was scampering around her bedroom, nervously fussing about her own outfit. For years, she had kept the gowns from her three consecutive homecoming wins displayed on mannequins downstairs—which Maggie had always thought truly strange. Today, she had brought all three up and laid them out on the bed. Now, she was agonizing over which one to wear.

"I always loved the pink best, but what about the lavender one?"

This is going to be a nightmare, Maggie thought, starting with her mother parading around the school gymnasium in some fancy, puffy, prehistoric dress. It was too much to bear. She dug into her mother's closet and came out with a conservative, navy blue gown with a cream-colored sash.

"How about this one?" Maggie suggested hopefully. "You're so pretty, Mom. You don't need anything fancy."

At first, Violet seemed disappointed, then she smiled. "What a nice compliment," she said. "Thank you." She took the dress and held it up, looking at it as a painter might examine her subject.

"I suppose simple could be nice . . . " she mused, a little distant. "And after all, it's *your* night. All right. Navy it is."

Maggie had never been to church in her life, but she thanked God profusely as her mother slipped the dress over her head and stood in front of the mirror, looking conservative, attractive, and blissfully normal.

Of course, two minutes later Violet was frantic again, demolishing her room in search of a pair of missing pantyhose.

The doorbell chimed and Maggie went down to answer it. She undid the half dozen locks her mother insisted upon and opened the front door to a familiar face. He was short, with a white goatee and long, sparse hair, and he wore a powder-blue tuxedo with a white rose on the lapel, and a broad smile.

"Mr. Chin," Maggie said, confused. And then a sick dread settled in the pit of her stomach. "You're here to see my mom." It wasn't a question.

The kung fu teacher smiled and nodded once.

"Indeed, I am," he said pleasantly. "I'm her escort for the evening."

Zhai rode in the back of his family's Maybach, an elegant gold box of assorted Godiva chocolates on the seat next to him, and fumbled with his bow tie, frustrated with it, and with the tuxedo, but even more frustrated with himself. He'd fallen in love with Kate the first moment he saw her. Every day for the last two weeks, he'd tried to get up the courage to invite her to the homecoming dance, and every day he had lost his nerve.

And anyway, the closer it got to the dance, the more uneasy Zhai became. He had a nagging feeling that something, somehow, was going to go wrong. He was still a little shell-shocked about all the weirdness he'd experienced when he and Raphael had faced off that night on the old railroad tracks. Ever since his harrowing quest, Zhai had been practicing his daily meditation, just as Master Chin had instructed. He could feel the *Shen*, the spirit, the magic within him, strengthening day by day. And right now, the Shen told him that something bad was going to happen tonight.

He tried to tell himself it was just his imagination, but the only thing that made him feel better was the thought of having Kate on his arm when he walked into the gym. Finally, an hour before the dance was to start, he told Bohai, the family's chauffer, to take him down to the train graveyard where the beautiful Kate lived. Incredible as it seemed, the homeless but resourceful girl had turned one of the old abandoned passenger cars into a rustic but cozy little apartment. She was awesome—he'd never met anyone like her.

As they approached the big lot where all the old train cars were stored, he realized it was too late to ask her to the dance. She probably didn't have anything to wear and would be embarrassed if he asked her. He looked at the box of chocolates again, and then he groaned and leaned his head against the glass of the window, in turmoil.

"Sir, are you getting out?" the chauffeur asked. Bohai was a kind, quiet, middle-aged Chinese man who'd driven for the Shao family for years. Ever since Zhai had known him, he preferred to go by his American nickname, Bob.

Zhai opened his mouth to answer and then closed it. He started to reach for the door handle, and then stopped. He thought longingly of Kate, her beautiful face, her sweet, musical accent, her quirky, sweet demeanor, and he groaned again.

As much as he wanted to be with her, as much as he longed to see her, he was unable to get out of the car. Memories of how she had looked right into his eyes with such complete trust—and how he'd almost kissed her—consumed him on a daily basis. Since the near-deadly Halloween battle, when he had seen all those strange, otherworldly creatures on the battlefield, thoughts of the lovely Kate, who had helped him fight off that zombie knight, were all that had saved his sanity.

Those comforting daydreams, strung like luminescent pearls throughout his day, had become his treasure trove. If he asked her to the dance and she said no, that treasure would vanish. Try as he might, he couldn't bring himself to take that risk.

Finally, he made his decision. He told Bob where to leave the chocolates and stayed in the car. When the chauffeur returned, Zhai told him to take him back to Hilltop Haven. A short time later, they pulled to a stop in front of the Banfield house, behind a long, black Cadillac Escalade limo parked at the curb.

Zhai forced a smile to his face as he rang the doorbell. Just because he was going to be the only Topper without a date didn't mean he had the right to ruin everyone else's evening.

A maid answered the door and led him through the foyer and the kitchen, to the family room at the back of the house where the whole Topper crew was gathered. Rick and Bran stood together with sodas in their hands, decked out in tuxedos, gesturing animatedly as the big screen behind them replayed the video of their football heroics from the previous evening.

Occasionally, one of the massive Cunningham brothers or Michael Ponder would chime in with a detail or two about one of the plays from their point of view, while Dax Avery, the only non–football player of the bunch (besides Zhai) stood by, grinning and nodding. Their dates were there, too, smiling or laughing at everything they said. Maggie was sitting on a couch in the corner, with her mother. Zhai hadn't seen Mrs. Anderson in a couple of years, and he was surprised at how thin and pale she had become. Even more surprising was the person sitting next to her. Zhai hurried over to say hello.

"Master Chin?" Zhai couldn't imagine what reason his kung fu teacher could possibly have for being there, dressed in such a cool, old-school tuxedo.

"Hello, Zhai. Looking good," Master Chin said. He rose to clap Zhai on the shoulder.

"What are you doing here?"

"It is my great honor to be a chaperone for Middleburg High's eighty-seventh annual homecoming celebration. And I'm going to dance, too. Believe me, I know how to get down."

Zhai laughed. "I have no doubt," he said. Master Chin was good at everything.

"Don't worry," Chin said. "Go hang out with your friends." He gave Zhai a reassuring wink, which actually made Zhai feel better. The uneasy feeling lifted a little. He was glad that his *sifu* would be at the dance.

Master Chin sat down and resumed his conversation with Mrs. Anderson, and Zhai turned to survey the room.

He'd heard from Rick that Maggie had hooked Dax and Michael up with her best friends, Bobbi Jean and Lisa Marie, but Zhai couldn't quite remember who was going with whom. Toppers and their assorted dates were sitting or standing around with soft drinks or bottled water, nibbling on an assortment of catered snacks from Spinnacle, the best restaurant in town. Even Zhai's sister was there with her friend Weston Darling.

Like Li, Wes was a freshman and he was in all of Li's honors classes. They had been working together on a science project when she had lapsed into that mysterious coma a few weeks ago and he had traveled to the hospital in Topeka several times to visit her. He had even taken her some flowers and a teddy bear. After her recovery, when Zhai teased her about a romantic interest between them, Li had merely chirped her happy little laugh as if it were the silliest thing he had ever said in his life. Still, she and Weston had been nearly inseparable at school, hanging out together between classes and always eating lunch together. And now here they were, going to the homecoming dance together.

Weston's family lived in one of the biggest houses in Hilltop Haven. The story was that his father had been a professor at Stanford, then a speech writer for one of the Presidents Bush, before leaving politics to settle in Middleburg. Wes was slender, almost willowy, with pale skin, small, sharp brown eyes, and short, blond hair that was always perfectly styled, never out of place. All the kids from Hilltop Haven dressed really well, but this kid took preppy to a whole new level. His dress pants—he never wore jeans—were always immaculately pressed, and he usually wore a sweater vest over an oxford shirt and a perfectly knotted necktie. He was the sort of kid who would get picked on nonstop in most schools, but at Middleburg High, he'd managed to fly under the radar. With things always tense between the Toppers and the Flatliners, no one had time to mess with someone as unassuming as Weston. It was probably one of the few times in history when a gang war actually made someone's life easier, Zhai thought.

Li smiled as she saw Zhai approach and his spirit lifted at the sight of her, so bright and healthy after the terrible illness she'd suffered. Perhaps he was biased, but he thought she looked even more beautiful than she did before she got sick. And he was incredibly grateful that his quest to find healing for her had succeeded.

"Hey, Zhai!" she said, giving him a quick hug. Weston nodded politely and shook his hand. "Weston, get me a Coke," Li ordered.

"Sure, Li. Excuse me, Zhai," he replied pleasantly and headed off toward the kitchen.

"Hey, where's Aimee?" Zhai asked Li.

"Um, I don't know." Li looked around. "I haven't seen her."

Rick had told Zhai he'd made sure that Aimee was going to the dance with Bran, and as far as Zhai could tell, everyone else was here. She was probably upstairs, getting ready. Zhai forced himself to relax. He would hate to have some kind of standoff with the Flatliners tonight and if Aimee was with Raphael (there were wild rumors going around school that the two were in love), he knew it would come to that.

"Zhai!" Rick called, spotting him from across the room. "What's up, man? You see the game?"

"I did. Great job. You too, Bran. You guys were awesome. Is Aimee around?"

Rick's smile dissolved. "She's getting ready over at Dalton's. My dad didn't want to let her go, but Dalton's grandma talked him into it. You know Lily Rose."

Zhai nodded. Dalton's grandmother was an exceptional woman. Aimee and Dalton had been almost inseparable since the play, and Zhai knew Jack Banfield was not happy about it—but not even Rick's dad was a match for Lily Rose. Whenever she talked to you, it was as if she was inside your head and knew all your thoughts and your innermost secrets. If anyone could convince Jack Banfield to let his daughter get ready for the dance at a house in the Flats, it was Lily Rose.

"So, she's meeting up with us when we get there?" Zhai asked, glancing at Bran.

"Yep," Bran said with his usual confident grin. "I'd look pretty silly wearing this myself." He held up a clear, plastic box with a corsage in it.

"Looks like everyone's here," Rick said, his unusually good humor continuing. "Let's roll!"

CHAPTER 3

EVEN BEFORE THE DANCE DEVOLVED INTO CHAOS, Ignacio felt like locking himself in a bathroom stall and hiding. It was almost funny and he couldn't blame Raph and the rest of the Flatliners for seeing it that way. All his life, he'd thought it would be cool to have two hot girls like him at the same time. Now that it was happening, however, it was a different story. After he got home from an afternoon of delivering pizzas, he had to wait an hour for Clarisse to get ready before he could jump into the shower. She came out looking stunning, in a skimpy black dress and smoky eye shadow, with heels that made her an inch taller than Nass and blood-red lips that looked like some kind of delicious but poisonous candy.

"Be quick, *papi*," she'd teased as he had slipped past her into the bathroom. "I'm not gonna wait for you all night."

He still wasn't too happy with her (or with his parents) for keeping such a big secret from him, but his anger had softened. She really didn't have anywhere else to hide and she was probably safer in Middleburg than any place else. Besides, he'd never been able to stay mad at her for very long.

When he was suited up and looking slick he and Clarisse walked the few blocks over to Dalton's house. Beet's car was already in the driveway, and they found the whole crew lounging in the living room, munching on the crackers and cheese that Lily Rose had set out on a big silver platter. Everyone looked pretty good except Benji, who wore a t-shirt with a tuxedo front printed on it, wrinkled black dress pants, red suspenders and a pair of clunky old Doc Martens boots. Nass started to laugh at his friend's ironic outfit, but at that moment Dalton emerged from her room, and she looked even more spectacular than usual.

She wore a close-fitting gown of dark purple satin that looked tailor made for her, and her hair and makeup were simple and natural. She was so beautiful. If Nass had tried to visualize the perfect girl, he couldn't have come up with anyone as stunning. He realized he was staring an instant before a stabbing pain shot through his foot.

He looked down to see a stiletto heel pressing down on the top of his shoe. Clarisse, pretending to be oblivious to the pain she was causing, was waving happily at everyone.

"Hey guys!" she called. "Hey, Benji—nice shirt! I love it!" Nass groaned and tapped her on the shoulder. She looked back at him, then down at his foot. "Oh—was that your foot?" she asked sweetly. "I'm sorry." She leaned over and kissed him on the cheek, close to his mouth, then looked smugly over at Dalton. "Hey, Dalton. Don't you look nice!"

Dalton managed a stiff smile. Nass could tell she was trying to make the best of the situation, and he wanted to say something to her, but then Aimee Banfield came into the room.

Nass was surprised. Aimee and Dalton had become friends and they spent a lot of time together, but he'd never expected a girl from Hilltop Haven to be hanging out in the Flats, especially with the Flatliners crew. He doubted that her dad and brother knew where she was, and he had to wonder if Raphael had lost his mind. Hanging with Aimee at the dance was one thing, but taking her into the Flats—that might be going too far. The last thing Raph should do, Nass thought, was tangle—again—with a bigwig like Jack Banfield.

He looked around for the only person who could tell him what was going on, but Raphael was nowhere to be seen.

"Hey, where's Raph?" he asked Beet, who was playing the hand-slap game with Natalie.

With Beet distracted, Natalie whacked both his hands so hard that everyone in the room winced and then laughed. "Ow," he said, gingerly rubbing his hands.

"Where's Raph?" Nass repeated, getting more worried by the moment.

"Oh, he's coming," Beet said. "Should be here any minute."

"So who's riding with us in the Woody?" Ignacio asked.

"We'll go with you guys," Emory said, and Myka, who was holding his hand, nodded.

"Josh, Beth and Benji can go with me, then," Beet offered.

"What about me?" The voice was soft, tentative. It was Aimee. Just then, a horn honked outside. Beet peered out the window.

"That's gotta be Raph," Beet said.

Nass didn't have to be intuitive to see the change in Aimee. A soft pink blush caressed her cheeks, and her eyes lit with expectation and hope, she went out onto the porch. All the Flatliners exchanged looks and crowded around the windows in Lily Rose's living room to see what was going to happen.

Outside, Raphael waved to his mom as she drove off. He was wearing a white suit and white shoes. His hair was combed and had some kind of product in it, and he had a small, red rosebud in his lapel. He walked up on the porch where Aimee was waiting for him, took her hand, drew her close to him, and kissed her slowly and tenderly.

The scene froze as an image flashed into Ignacio's mind—a vision he'd had before, not long after he came to Middleburg—a big, dark ocean wave, poised above the town, ready to crash down on it. Above the wave, ominous clouds rolled and lightning flashed. The image was there for a second or two, then gone. But Nass got the message.

Aimee and Raphael going to the dance together was a really bad idea.

Someone coughed and the world went back into motion. Emory whispered something to his date. Josh loosened his tie, as if it was choking him. Dalton seemed deep in thought. Even Benji, behind his sarcastic grin, looked a little rattled.

It was surprising enough that Aimee was in Dalton's house at all, but the fact that she was clearly and openly going to be Raphael's date—that was a twist even Nass wasn't expecting. *So much for going as a group,* he thought.

"Well, you all had better get going." The gentle voice came from behind Nass, startling him. He turned to find Dalton's grandma standing there. Her weathered, brown face looked even more creased than the last time he'd seen it but her strange, beautiful eyes were filled with just as much life. "Don't want to miss too much of your dance," she said. "Now, you children go on and have a good time. Be careful."

"Yeah, let's get a move on, guys," he said quickly. He tried to sound upbeat, but more than anything he was worried. He didn't know how much of a good time anyone would have if Rick spotted his little sister dancing with the enemy.

∞

Kate Dineen hummed as she bustled around her little train car home, putting her freshly washed dishes away, stoking the fire in her little wood-burning stove and mopping the floor. She performed these tasks automatically, but her mind was far away, on her secret admirer.

He had brought her *two* boxes of chocolates now, and sometimes at night, she would hear beautiful, romantic violin music drifting through the trees that surrounded her little makeshift home. Each time she'd tried to find the source of the music it eluded her, and each time she knew it was a blessing that she couldn't find him.

"Middleburg isn't my home, after all," she would say to herself, out loud, as if to reinforce it. "I'll be leavin' as soon as I find the way." So a romantic entanglement was impossible. That would only make it more difficult for her to go back when the time came. But the longer she stayed in this quaint little town, and the more she got to know Raphael and his friends, the more she liked the place.

And now a secret admirer.

She thought she knew who it was. That strange and wonderful boy who had fought off those dreadful, ancient knights just to find her and get a lock of her hair. Before she'd arrived in Middleburg, she would have thought such a thing impossible. Not anymore.

"And what if he *is* the one, Kate Dineen?" she lectured herself soundly. "The one who's givin' you chocolates and playin' music for you—you cannot *think* to get involved with him. Are you daft?"

But in the deepest, most secret part of her, she was dying to meet her mysterious suitor. As she thought of him, she got that feeling again. She stopped cleaning, her head tilted to one side as she listened . . . *waited*. Yes, there it was again—a tingly, self-conscious sensation, as if someone was watching her—and it wasn't the sort of warm presence her secret admirer exuded.

This feeling was cold and unsettling, and she'd had it on and off all night.

She went to the window, pulled back the curtain and peered out at the desolate landscape of overturned freight cars and battered, burned-out passenger cars that surrounded her home—the place Raphael called the locomotive graveyard. She scanned the horizon slowly but, as she expected, there was nothing there. Just moonlight, shadows, and silence. She let the curtain fall into place and resumed mopping. When she was finished with her chores, she decided, she would reward herself with a nice cup of tea and *two* of the chocolates her secret admirer had sent.

She tried to pick up the song she was humming before, but the unsettling feeling did not go away.

৪৩

Aimee had a sudden, sinking feeling in the pit of her stomach as Dalton parked her grandma's station wagon in a far corner of the crowded student lot. Going into the dance with the Flatliners was *not* no big deal, as she'd been telling herself, and now that the moment had arrived she was starting to worry. She glanced around for any sign of Rick. His car wasn't there, which was a relief—but he was sure to show up at some point. The plan was for Aimee to walk in with Dalton, Nass and Clarisse, with Raphael waiting at least fifteen minutes before going in. He took her hand briefly and let it go.

"Go on," he said. "I'll see you inside. The longer we stand here together, the more chance Rick or one of his goons will see us."

"He's right," Dalton said. "We should go in."

Raphael smiled at Aimee and she wished he would take her hand again. "Don't worry," he said. "I'll watch for a chance to dance with you—and I'll dance with you every chance I get."

Aimee smiled and started to walk away from him, but her soul cried out against the unfairness of the situation. All the others were entering the dance with their dates, and she knew none of them could possibly share the feelings that she and Raphael did. It was ridiculous. She stopped and turned back to him.

"This is wrong," she said.

"What?" Raphael looked stunned, like someone had hit him. "I mean . . . if you've changed your mind, Aimee, it's okay. We'll find a way to hang out another time."

"Dalton," Aimee said over her shoulder, "You guys go ahead. I need to talk to Raphael."

Dalton looked at her, puzzled, and Ignacio cast a quick, worried glance at Raphael.

"Really," Aimee said. "It's okay."

She knew they all thought she had changed her mind and that she was going to break up with him—she knew Raphael thought that too. He looked down at his shoes, resigned, as his friends walked away.

"I'm not going to sneak around all evening like we're doing something wrong," she said.

"Yeah. I can understand that," he said. He was already turning away. She put her hand on his arm to stop him.

"I want to walk in with you," she told him. "*You* asked me to this dance, Raphael. I'm *your* date. Why shouldn't we just go in there together and have a good time, like everyone else?"

"You know why," he said.

"Yeah—well, I don't care anymore. What's my dad gonna do? Ground me forever? I can still see you at school, which is all we have now. And it will be totally worth it."

"Are you sure about this?" he asked.

"Unless . . . you don't want to."

"I want to—more than anything."

"Okay, then," she said softly. "I'm with *you*, Raphael, and I'm proud to be with you. I want everyone to know it."

"What about Rick? He'll start something if he sees us walk in together."

"Probably," she agreed. "If he does, we'll leave. I've spent way too much time worrying about what he and Dad think about us. I've tiptoed around them long enough. It's time I stand up to them and choose my own destiny. And that's what you are." It was a liberating thought, and the moment the words left her lips, Aimee knew that they were true—right.

Raphael just stood there for a moment, looking at her.

"Well," she said, smiling up at him. "Say something."

But he didn't. Instead he gently kissed her, took her hand, and led her toward the school. They walked through the doors together.

The Middleburg High gymnasium didn't look anything like it did during the zillions of mind-numbing basketball games Aimee had watched Rick play there. Now, it was festooned with streamers and balloons and filled with flashing lights and romantic shadows. A bank of refreshments lined one wall, and a bunch of round tables stood nearby. On the far side of the room, a DJ had set up near the large, open space where a lot of kids were already dancing. The bleachers were folded back into the wall and covered with a huge, time-worn paper sign emblazoned with pictures of corn and wheat and an overflowing cornucopia.

In letters a previous generation of students had painted it read, WEL-
COME TO MIDDLEBURG HIGH'S HOMECOMING & HARVEST BALL.

Other schools may have had a different theme for every homecoming
dance, but at Middleburg High it was always the same: the harvest. It was
pretty lame, but it had been that way ever since the school was founded—
probably, Aimee thought, because Middleburg was in the middle of some
of the best farmland in the United States. Even though there weren't as
many farms as there used to be and the community was no longer depen-
dent on the harvest for survival, no one had ever thought to change it.
Usually the decorating committee just taped up some cheesy pictures of
various crops growing in fields, but this year, Dalton had made it special.

Aimee knew how hard she'd worked to stretch the small budget so
there was enough for tons of balloons, flowers, streamers and lots of glit-
ter, which Dalton had used in abundance. She'd rummaged around in
their drama teacher's props department and found some fake haystacks,
pumpkins and even a scarecrow from a long-ago production of *Jack and
the Beanstalk*. She had even procured a fog machine somehow, and the
dance floor was shrouded in mist and sparkling lights. The place had an
ethereal, almost magical quality.

Aimee looked up at Raphael, and found him already staring at her.

"You sure you want to do this?" he asked. "It's not too late. Nobody's
seen us yet."

From the look in his eyes and the way he was smiling at her, she could
tell that the last thing he wanted was to leave her side.

"I'm sure."

Their timing couldn't have been better. As they stepped onto the dance
floor, the beat changed from a bass-thumping dance track to a slow song.
As Raphael pulled her close and enfolded her in his arms, an involuntary
sigh escaped her lips, and she leaned her head against his shoulder as they
swayed together, letting the music carry them. His cinnamon-spicy scent,
his strong arms, his warm, loving energy was all around her now, as she

was blissfully, beautifully encompassed by his presence and his love.

Aimee was vaguely aware of the other dancers pulling back, stopping to watch them in a mixture of shock and horror. She could only imagine what they must be thinking, seeing the king of the Flatliners and the princess of the Toppers there, dancing together for everyone to see. But she didn't care; it didn't matter what anyone thought. Let the whole world burn up around them, for all she cared. With Raphael holding her close, she was in heaven already.

∾

The rest of the Flatliners had already found their way to the area where the tables and chairs were set up. Beet and Josh headed for the snack bar, while Emory and the girls grabbed tables where they could sit together. Benji was the first to notice Raphael and Aimee out on the dance floor. He stared for a moment, and then raised one arm and pointed. Nass turned to see what was going on and Dalton and Clarisse followed his gaze. A collective hush fell over them as they all turned to watch Raphael and Aimee moving together, looking into each other's eyes. The Flatliners exchanged looks, and Nass knew what they were all thinking.

Sure, it's cool that a girl from Hilltop Haven has selected one of our own and decided to go public—but it's going to make trouble and we'd all better get ready for it.

Nass looked around, relieved to see that none of the Toppers were there yet. If only they wouldn't show up, that would be amazing, he thought. But that was way too much to hope for, and God only knew what was going to happen when they arrived.

In the meantime, he had his own problems to worry about.

He tore his gaze from Raph and Aimee to look for Dalton, hoping to ask her to dance, but instead, Clarisse was there. She grabbed his hand and pulled him toward the dance floor.

"Come on, mijo," she said softly, with a little pout that was meant to be sexy. "It's a slow one."

Nass looked over his shoulder at Dalton, who stood alone near the refreshment table. She looked away immediately, but the expression on her face was unmistakable. A mix of emotions swept her features—at first she was surprised, then hurt, then angry, and then resigned.

And he knew that she'd suddenly gotten it. She'd realized there was something between him and Clarisse—something more than just an old friend from back home—or there had been. Nass decided it was time to put on the brakes. He pulled Clarisse to a halt. She turned back to him, confused.

"What?" she asked. "Why you look so serious?"

"I promised Dalton the first dance," he said.

Her countenance darkened. "What do you mean?"

"Look—Clarisse. I've been trying to tell you," Ignacio said. "I like Dalton. I *like* her, okay?"

"Before you left L.A., you said you *loved* me. We said we love each other."

"We also said we both had to move on, since I was moving away. We never expected to see each other again."

The pretty little pout turned into an angry frown. "Well, I'm here now," she said. "So what is it? You love me and you like her? You *like* us both? Or maybe you *love* her and you *like* me?" she finished with cold finality.

Clarisse's eyes flashed with indignation. Ignacio sighed. He had to tell her the truth, but first he had to talk to Dalton.

"We can talk about this later," he said. "But now I'm going to dance with Dalton—my date."

"You do that," she snapped and headed for the exit.

"Clarisse, come on!"

She flipped him off and stormed out the doors. He looked over to find the whole Flatliners crew watching him, grinning like a bunch of idiots. He decided to ignore them. Dalton was standing near the punch bowl watching him, but as he approached, she averted her face. He hurried to her with a hopeful smile.

"Hey, you want to dance?" he asked.

She finally looked at him, and he could see the pain in her eyes.

"Clarisse is mad at you so now you come back to me?"

"No—it's not like that," Nass began.

"I'm not going to be anybody's second choice," she told him quietly, and she turned and walked away.

"Dalton, come on!" He hung his head in frustration. Somehow, his dream night had turned into a nightmare.

He heard booming, boisterous voices behind him, and the gym doors screeched open. *Great,* he thought. *Just when I thought things couldn't get any worse.*

The Toppers had arrived.

&

Before Zhai ever stepped into the gym, he knew what he was going to find there. The power of Shen he'd felt stirring within him was growing stronger by the day, *by the minute*, and it warned him of what was coming. He was not surprised, therefore, when Rick, Bran, and Maggie came to a full stop in front of him—and stared at the dance floor, transfixed.

"I told you," Maggie whispered to Rick.

"Shut up," Rick ordered, his voice tight with anger.

Bran looked down at the corsage in his hand and then chucked it into a nearby trash can. "I'm outta here," he said, turning to leave.

"The hell you are," Rick said and stepped in front of him. "You're going to let that Flats rat punk make you look like an idiot?"

Bran looked uncertain. "Hey—you know. If that's Aimee's choice—"

"That's not the point," Rick cut him off. Then he lowered his voice and moved closer to Bran. Zhai moved closer too. "If he makes you look like an idiot, that makes all the Toppers look like idiots," Rick said, keeping his voice muted, strange, almost hypnotic, like Zhai had never heard it before. "It makes *me* look like an idiot, Bran. That's not acceptable."

Rick was clutching the back of Bran's neck with one big, meaty paw, and looking dead into his eyes. Bran straightened up, took off his jacket and tossed it over a chair.

"Nobody makes me look like an idiot," he said in a strange monotone, and started toward the dance floor.

Rick took off his coat and followed Bran. The other Toppers were crowding through the doorway now. As one, they marched forward, past Zhai, heading for Raphael and Aimee.

"Wait, guys!" Zhai shouted. "It's just one dance. I'll talk to them—"

But it was too late. The Toppers were streaming across the dance floor, toward Raphael. Students, faculty, and chaperones parted before them, moving out of the way as quickly as possible. Maggie and the other Topper girls stood together near the doorway, looking on in eager anticipation.

Zhai glanced over his shoulder, hoping to find Master Chin, but he didn't see him. Zhai was on his own.

഼

Maggie watched breathlessly as, across the room, the phalanx of Toppers approached Raphael and Aimee—who were so engrossed in one another that they didn't notice, until the last moment, Rick and Bran striding over, with Dax and the other Toppers backing them up.

Raphael stepped in front of Aimee, shielding her from whatever was about to happen. The sight made Maggie ache with envy.

Bran didn't stop until he was standing nose-to-nose with Raphael, and without saying a word, Bran shoved him. Raphael fell back a step and then raised his hands, ready to fight. Maggie thought he was going to strike back, but he waited, perfectly still, for Bran's next move.

The Flatliners, at tables in the far corner of the gym, rose and started making their way toward the dance floor. Maggie didn't think they could get to Raphael in time to help—but maybe she shouldn't worry about that. It could work to her advantage. She would hate to see Raph get hurt but if he got beat up for taking Aimee to the dance, maybe he would break up with her. And that, as far as Maggie was concerned, would be wonderful.

Rick stepped forward, now shoulder-to-shoulder with Bran and getting ready to launch an attack, when the microphone shrieked as the DJ cut the music. Principal Innis, red-faced and grinning, walked out on the little stage to stand next to the DJ.

"Hello, Middleburg High!" he exclaimed.

Grudgingly, Bran and Rick stepped away from Raphael. With the head of the school just fifteen feet away, looking right at them, there was nothing they could do. They would have to wait for another opportunity. Bran cursed and stormed off, pushing his way through the crowd. Rick took out his cell phone and started texting someone.

"All right, guys," Innis announced exuberantly. "It's time! The moment you've all been waiting for! I'm going to name this year's homecoming king and queen!"

There was some applause, and a few excited shouts. Some joker mooed like a cow and everyone laughed, except Maggie. She felt a flush of anger and vowed to get even with that person if she ever found out who it was. This was her moment, and she wouldn't stand for anyone messing it up. She felt a gentle hand touch her shoulder. It was her mother, with Mr. Chin at her side.

"Here it is, Maggie," Violet said, and Maggie was surprised at how calm, how serene she sounded. "Your time is *here*. Are you ready?"

"I guess so," she answered. It was so weird to see her mom out of the house, interacting with other people, behaving so normally.

Violet put her arms around Maggie for a moment, in a clumsy hug. Over her mother's shoulder, Maggie saw Mr. Chin smiling pleasantly, his eyes scanning the room, until his gaze came to rest on Raphael, Rick, and Aimee.

Maggie glanced at the encroaching battalion of Flatliners. They'd made their way to the edge of the dance floor and were waiting there, maybe for a signal from Raphael.

She tore her gaze from them and looked back up at the stage, feeling strangely serene. A month ago, Maggie had thought that the homecoming queen title was one she absolutely *had* to win. Not only because the thought of living with her mom if she didn't was unbearable, but also because she'd hoped it would finally make Rick appreciate her. She no longer had any such illusion. If she won today, she realized, it wouldn't be for either of them. It would be for herself.

Mr. Innis took an index card from the pocket of his ugly brown sports coat and cleared his throat—right into the microphone.

"All right then!" he proclaimed. "Without further ado, your homecoming king is . . . "

Innis paused and there was actually a drum roll and a trumpet fanfare from some band members stationed near the stage.

". . . in a landslide vote, and the hero of yesterday's epic win over St. Phil," the principal continued, "Rick Banfield!"

The crowd broke into loud applause. Whistles, shouts, and a chant of "Rick! Rick! Rick!" went up from the Topper crowd as he bounded up onto the stage. He shook the principal's hand and then stooped down a couple of inches so Innis could put the crown on his head. A couple of girls from the homecoming elections committee put a purple, faux-fur mantle over his shoulders and handed him a gold-colored plastic scepter. But Rick wasn't smiling. His mind, Maggie guessed, was exactly where hers was—on his sister and Raphael Kain.

Maggie's mom grabbed her by the shoulders and turned her around so they were facing each other. Her eyes glowing with satisfaction, Violet said, "You look perfect, Maggie. *Perfect.*" She took Lily Rose's flower out of Maggie's hair. "To make room for the crown," she explained. "Now go on. Don't make them wait once he's called your name!"

Then she gave Maggie a little shove toward the stage, and Maggie felt a surge of power rushing into her, sharp and crackling hot. She suddenly felt like she could run the world.

She was going to win.

She slipped across the crowded dance floor and moved quickly toward the stage. Principal Innis was holding another index card. Maggie watched, walking in what seemed like slow motion, as he brought the microphone to his mouth.

"Now, for your Middleburgh High homecoming queen. I have to tell you, this year it was the closest vote I can remember. Okay—here we go. This year's homecoming queen is. . ."

Maggie felt like her heart had frozen in her chest. For an instant, everything stopped. Time was suspended. The earth quit spinning and the universe screeched to a halt.

Aimee Banfield, Maggie thought with horror. He's going to say *Aimee Banfield*.

Principal Innis smiled and finished: ". . . Maggie Anderson!"

Again, the crowd cheered. As Maggie moved, almost floating, up the steps and onto the stage, she listened closely for the dreaded boos or stupid animal sounds, but she heard none. She was next to Principal Innis now, and the faces in the crowd had become black shadows, silhouetted by the lights shining on the stage.

Bobbi Jean and Lisa Marie, as her attendants, brought out a purple satin, faux-fur cape and draped it over Maggie's shoulders as Innis declared grandly, "And tonight, ladies and gentlemen, we have a former Middleburg High homecoming queen with us to do the honors."

Violet came out on stage, carrying the crown on a red velvet pillow. As she brought it forward, Maggie stared at the crown. The light glinting off its deep, golden surface seemed to draw her in. Her mother used to talk about that crown all the time—about how it wasn't some fake, rhinestone-studded tiara like the homecoming crowns at most schools.

And it wasn't like the plastic crown for the Middleburg High homecoming king, either. In the trophy case in front of the principal's office, where it was displayed year round (except for this one night) it seemed pretty ordinary. But tonight, Maggie could see why it was so special.

It was made of some kind of burnished, golden metal—maybe even real gold, she thought, and it was set with roughly cut gemstones—one that looked like it could be a diamond, centered between two red ones that could be rubies. Maggie remembered her mom saying that it was really old and was originally used for the queen of the Harvest Festival. Sometime in the early nineteen hundreds, Middleburg quit having the festival, and it became the homecoming-queen crown.

Violet set the pillow on Bobbi Jean's outstretched hands, and Maggie closed her eyes as her mother lifted the crown and placed it gently on her head. The first thing she noticed was the weight of it. It was heavier than Maggie had imagined—and a lot heavier than it looked. So heavy, in fact, that she felt her knees might buckle under its weight. It was certainly no cheap, costume crown. As she turned and looked out over the crowd, she saw that the fog machine mist and the shadows that had filled the room earlier were gone. She could see everyone clearly. She could see their faces and peer right into their eyes.

Through their eyes even, into their minds.

More of the strange, bright energy lanced through her as her mother leaned over and kissed her cheek. Maggie found Raphael in the crowd and for a moment their eyes locked. She felt as if she was falling into his consciousness, into his *soul*. Suddenly, she was awash in the sea of anger, and all the hope, sadness, passion, love, and confusion that were Raphael. She was drowning in it, in *him*. As she struggled to rise from this turbulent ocean, she saw a white lighthouse, its distant beam slashing across the fog and brine of frustration that clouded Raphael's mind. And the name of the lighthouse, Maggie somehow knew, was *Shen*.

She blinked, and the vision was over.

She was dizzy and trembling, and she felt faint and a little feverish. The crown seemed even heavier now, and she was sure the weight of it would force her to her knees. At the same time, the power coursing through her built and built. It wasn't something from outside her, exactly, nor was it something new. It was as if the energy that had been within her all the time was suddenly amplified a thousand times. She felt bigger than herself, as if her energy encompassed not just her thin body, but the entire stage, the entire room, the entire school.

"Would you like to say a few words?" she heard Principal Innis asking.

He was offering the microphone to Rick, who leaned into it and muttered: "Go Phoenixes." His hate-filled eyes, Maggie saw, were still trained on Raphael Kain.

Raphael, who was standing in front of Aimee, *protecting* Aimee. Who would be kissing Aimee later, when he took her home. Who had once kissed Maggie with more passion than she had ever felt from Rick. A new feeling of rage shot through her.

Innis was holding the microphone up for Maggie. Taking a deep breath, she fought to steady herself. She could bounce along the sideline leading cheers all night, but she wasn't so good at speaking in front of a crowd.

I can do this, she thought. *I will do this.*

She opened her mouth to say thank you, but before she could get the words out, the doors at the back of the gym flew open and a frigid wind whipped through the room with near-gale force, bringing with it dust, debris, dried leaves, bits of trash, and even a few errant, swirling snowflakes. Napkins from the snack table exploded across the dance floor like confetti. The blast of wind was so powerful that a few girls, already unbalanced in their high heels, fell over. Others took cover under the tables.

Principal Innis jumped down from the stage and hurried toward the doorway, fighting his way through the wind and gesturing wildly to the teachers and chaperones as he went.

"Did anyone see the news?" he shouted. "Was there a severe weather warning? Come on—let's get these doors closed!"

As the grown-ups rushed to secure the doors, Rick made his move. He was off the stage in a heartbeat. Bran was pushing his way across the dance floor too, shoving though the crowd toward Raphael. Maggie saw Raphael's friend Nass moving toward him, shouting and signaling for his crew to follow. The Flatliners rushed onto the dance floor, to the spot where their leader stood, backed up against one wall of the gym, with Aimee shielded behind him. Maggie could see it all: the Flatliners and the Toppers were converging at the spot where Raphael and Aimee stood, just to the right of the stage.

The crown on her head pressed into her mind, crushing it and freeing it all at once. She couldn't *think*, but she seemed to *know everything*. And she knew that Raphael loved Aimee as he would never—could never— love her. And that made her angrier than ever.

CHAPTER 4

Zhai had been pacing at the edge of the dance floor, waiting for the inevitable to happen and wondering what to do about it. When he saw his fellow Toppers moving in Raphael's direction, he slipped deftly through the crowd to try and head them off. Only a week had passed, he realized, since he and Raphael had managed to work together to accomplish the Magician's quest, and already the war was back on. There had to be some way to stop the impending fight.

Raphael and Aimee had retreated, and their backs were nearly against the gym wall near the right corner of the stage. Everyone on the dance floor, seeing what was about to happen, pulled back and formed a big semicircle around them. Bran and Rick broke into the circle first, striding shoulder-to-shoulder over to Raphael.

A hateful smile crossed Rick's face as he stared at his enemy, still standing in front of Aimee like a human shield. "Look at you two," he said. "Pathetic."

Bran said nothing, but Zhai could see him trembling with uncharacteristic rage. He knew Bran had liked Aimee for a long time and that he must feel betrayed, but he'd been ready to let it go until Rick pushed him into a confrontation.

"What's up, Rick?" Ignacio demanded as he broke into the circle with his crew right behind him. "You got a problem?"

"Don't make it yours," Rick warned, and he stepped forward and lunged at Raphael. Raphael saw it coming and quickly spun out of the way, avoiding Rick's big, powerful fist and hitting him with a hard strike to the kidneys. Bran moved in and caught Raphael in the eye with a left jab. Before he could follow up with a right, though, Raphael hit him in the face three times, in a rapid-fire, staccato burst of energy, and then tripped him and sent him to the ground.

"Guys, stop!" But before Zhai could stop them, the Toppers and Flatliners charged each other, rushing into the fray.

D'von Cunningham clotheslined Josh. Beet tackled Dax Avery while Michael Ponder traded blows with Emory. Cle'von kept trying to grab the slippery little Benji.

The circle widened as frightened students pulled back from the battle. Principal Innis bleated ineffectually into the microphone. "Kids, stop! Hey, stop it!"

Rick and Bran were both on Raphael. They had him hemmed in from both sides and were throwing haymakers at him, one after another. Zhai watched as Raphael deflected an overhead right from Bran, pulled him off balance and struck him in the temple, a blow that sent Bran stumbling. Raphael turned just in time to block Rick's fearsome left hook and hit him with a quick counter, then turned and blocked Bran again. His former best friend was doing well against two powerful opponents, Zhai thought, but even Raphael couldn't keep up that pace forever. Zhai hurried toward them, hoping to intercede—but Ignacio blocked him.

"Going somewhere?" he asked, and threw a sweep kick at Zhai's knees. Zhai moved and the strike missed. Before Zhai could explain that he was trying to stop the fight, Ignacio's foot was flying toward his face. Zhai blocked this kick, too, and the three punches that followed. When Ignacio struck him in the stomach with an intricate, graceful capoeira cartwheel attack, Zhai realized he had no choice but to fight back. He managed to land two quick, ineffective punches before Ignacio once again cartwheeled out of the way.

As the battle intensified, Zhai could feel the power of Shen building up all around them, its seething, tingling energy sizzling through his body and vibrating the floor, rattling the light fixtures, shaking the walls. He looked over and saw that Rick had broken away from his fight with Raphael. He was over near the wall between the gymnasium and lobby, holding on to his sister's arm, and dragging her toward a set of exit doors. She struggled with him and screamed, and Dalton ran over to help her. Raphael started after them.

Suddenly, a female voice, strong and rich and full of power, cut through the mayhem.

"Stop!"

With the single word, a concussion of air exploded like a bomb, and the atmosphere shifted. Zhai felt a jolt of Shen shoot through him, as if his soul had shivered.

The blast struck Rick, slamming him against the wall, and sent Aimee and Dalton sprawling to the floor as well.

Zhai looked around to find the source of the voice. Maggie Anderson was standing on the edge of the stage, the homecoming queen crown still firmly and regally on her head. Both hands were clasped over her mouth, as if she was stunned by the power her own voice had just unleashed.

The battle had ceased with her one-word directive, and Ignacio was staring at the gymnasium wall where Rick and Aimee were standing. Zhai turned to follow his gaze. There was a sharp snapping sound and a large crack suddenly formed in the cinder-block structure, from the floor all the way up to the ceiling. As he watched, a second crack appeared, then a third.

"Dalton! Look out!" Ignacio shouted, but it was too late. There was a metallic screech as one of the girders in the ceiling flexed—and then with a deafening crash, the wall fell, taking part of the roof with it.

A rush of dust instantly blanketed screaming students, teachers and alumni who all stampeded toward the exits. The music came to an abrupt stop as rubble tumbled and skittered across the polished, wooden gym floor, ending in a mass of crumbled cinderblocks and twisted iron rebar.

Ignacio was the first to move. He ran toward the collapsed wall calling desperately, "Dalton! Dalton—where are you?"

As he rushed toward the pile of debris, a sickening realization hit Zhai. Rick, Aimee and Dalton had all been right there, with Raphael only a few feet away, when the wall collapsed. Now, they were buried under the rubble.

∞

Raphael coughed and wiped the dust from his eyes. "Aimee? Dalton?" he shouted into the haze. "Aimee?"

"Here!" she called. To Raphael's relief, she was walking through the dust cloud toward him, picking her way unsteadily through the debris. He'd thought she was right under the wall when it fell, but apparently he'd misjudged her position.

He ran to her and gathered her close. "You okay? Are you hurt?" he asked as he stepped away from her and scanned her face, her head, her arms for any sign of injury.

"I don't understand what happened," she said slowly, a little dazed. "I saw the wall coming down, right at me. I was there and then I wasn't . . . I think . . . maybe Dalton shoved me out of the way."

Raphael put his arms around her again and held her as tightly as he could without hurting her, worried that she was in shock. Trembling against him, she hugged him back.

"Where's Dalton?" she asked, her lips close to Raphael's ear. "And Rick?"

They turned back toward the collapsed wall. The rubble moved and Rick emerged from beneath a pile of fallen cinderblocks. He groaned, with pain or fury, as he got to his feet and brushed the dust from his hair.

He straightened his tie and cracked his neck. Tentatively feeling one arm, he winced a little, but otherwise he seemed unharmed. The stunned crowd watched in silence, probably, Raphael knew, thinking the same thing he was: there was no way Rick could have gotten out alive. But here he was.

"Rick . . . are you okay?" Aimee asked, taking a tentative step toward her brother.

Rick looked at her and snorted. He took the red handkerchief from his coat pocket and wiped his face. "Better than you're going to be when dad gets here," he said.

"No!"

A low, anguished wail coming from the far side of the debris pile drew their attention. Raphael took Aimee's hand and they rushed toward the sound.

It was Nass. The I-beam had come down from the ceiling and had fallen across Dalton's abdomen. She lay motionless beneath it. Tears were streaming down Ignacio's face and he was heaving on the beam with all his strength. He couldn't move it. Raphael ran over to help.

A second later, Aimee and Beet joined them and then Zhai rushed over too. As Zhai grabbed the end of the beam, his eyes met Raphael's for an instant before he added his strength to theirs and started lifting. The five of them were able to move the beam off Dalton.

Using the breathing techniques he'd learned from Master Chin, Raphael calmed and centered himself, and then dialed 911 on his cell phone. As it rang, Ignacio went down on his knees beside Dalton, who still wasn't moving.

Raph's dad had worked in the metal fabrication business before he died, and Raph knew how heavy those beams were. Thousands of pounds of steel had landed on Dalton. It didn't look good.

Nass took a deep breath, covered Dalton's mouth with his and started doing CPR. Aimee knelt nearby too, and took Dalton's hand.

On Raphael's phone, the operator answered, "911, what's your emergency?"

"Yes," Raphael said. "I'm at Middleburg High. One of the interior gym walls just collapsed."

"Was anyone injured?"

"Yes."

"How badly?"

A voice in Raphael's head said: *fatally*.

But as he watched, Dalton took her hand from Aimee's and put it behind Ignacio's head. He was no longer giving her mouth-to-mouth, Raphael realized with awe. They were kissing.

Nass pulled back, obviously amazed, and Raph saw that Dalton was smiling.

"Ignacio Torrez, were you just trying to get fresh with me?" she mock-scolded him, and sat up as if nothing was wrong.

Aimee and Nass helped Dalton to her feet, and she started to brush off her dress. Miraculously, the garment was neither dirty nor wrinkled. And the part that covered her stomach, the part where the steel I-beam that should have crushed her had lain, was completely unscathed. Aimee gave Raphael a *can-you-believe-this* look.

"Hello? Sir?" the lady from 911 asked. "Was anyone was hurt?"

Raphael glanced across the room, to where the Toppers were standing around inspecting Rick's injured arm. Rick waved them off.

"I guess not," he said, and ended the call.

"You're okay?" Nass was asking Dalton.

"Yeah, I'm fine," she answered. "Why wouldn't I be?"

"The beam—it was *on you*. It could have crushed you."

Dalton rubbed her abdomen. "It does feel a little bruised," she admitted.

"Bruised!" Nass shouted wildly, relieved. "Bruised? Girl, what's that dress made of—some kind of titanium-Kevlar blend?"

Dalton ran her hands over the fabric thoughtfully. "You know, I'm not sure. My grandma made it for me. I couldn't find one I liked."

Nass laughed. "Well, if I ever join the army, remind me to have your grandma sew me a uniform, all right?"

He hugged Dalton, then pulled back to look at her, and then hugged her again. Raphael noticed Clarisse standing back in the crowd, watching, and she didn't look pleased. Dalton must've seen her too, because she quickly moved away from Nass, as if suddenly remembering she was still mad at him.

As the rest of the Flatliners went to check Dalton out for themselves, Raphael moved closer to the broken wall. A twenty-foot-wide gash now ran from the floor to the ceiling where it slashed a rip in the roof. After Raph glanced up at it, he went to the edge of the hole in the floor and looked down into it.

A pit perhaps thirty-five feet deep had opened up right where the wall fell. The bottom of the hole was littered with debris, but there seemed to be openings on either end. It wasn't just a hole, Raph realized. It was a tunnel. A chill crept slowly over him.

A tunnel ran beneath Middleburg High School. How weird was that?

"Pretty weird," Zhai said, as if Raphael had spoken aloud, and Raphael glanced over to find his old friend standing next to him. He gave Raph a quick glance and walked back toward the Toppers. Standing in the crowd behind Zhai, Raphael was amazed to find a familiar face: it was Master Chin. He gazed solemnly at Raphael, then gave him a slow nod. Raphael knew what his sifu was telling him—despite everything that had happened, he'd behaved honorably. It made him feel a little better.

Before he could go over and talk to his kung fu teacher, Aimee, Dalton, and the Flatliners approached.

"Well, I guess this scene is a bust," Benji said. "Anybody want to head over to Rack 'Em—whoa! Check it out, man." As they drew close, they all noticed the hole too.

But what Raphael saw behind them was far more disturbing.

"I think we'd better take a rain check," he told Benji, and nodded in the direction of the gym's front doors. They all looked around and Aimee groaned. Jack Banfield, her dad, had just entered. His tie was askew, his face was red, and he was heading right toward them, with Rick just a step behind him.

Aimee wished she could melt into the floor and disappear. She felt Raphael's arm go around her, and she was grateful for his strength even though she knew he should run away instead of trying to make a stand with her. It was bad enough that she was about to experience her father's wrath; Raphael shouldn't have to suffer too.

The sight of them standing defiantly together seemed to infuriate her dad even more, but she knew he would maintain careful control with so many people watching. He didn't yell at her. Instead, he grasped her arm—hard—and leaned down until his eyes were only inches from hers.

"Get in the car," he said quietly, through clenched teeth. *"Now."*

"Daddy, please. I'm sorry—"

"Now!" he snarled. "You've defied me for the last time, Aimee. You can either walk out of here or I'll drag you—but you are leaving *now*."

"Mr. Banfield—" Raphael began.

As soon as he spoke, Aimee felt the grip on her arm tighten. Slowly, her father turned his head toward Raphael, his eyes filled with fire. Aimee knew that if she didn't obey him, things were going to get a lot worse—especially for Raphael.

"I'm going, Daddy, okay?" she said quickly. "I'm going." Jack's grasp loosened and she was able to shrug it off. Slipping past him, she gave Raphael an apologetic glance, but his gaze was locked on her dad's.

As she headed for the gym doors, she felt so overwhelmed with raw emotion she was almost numb. This was supposed to be the most beautiful, most triumphant night of her life, and it was a mess. Dalton had almost gotten killed, a brawl had broken out, and now she was going to be grounded for the rest of her life. Or worse . . .

Rick stood in the center of the dance floor. He looked a little pale and his injured arm hung at kind of an odd angle. Still, he managed a mocking grin as Aimee approached.

"Well, well, well," he said, as he turned and walked with her toward the doors. "Daddy's little girl got busted big time."

"Shut up, Rick."

"You know, I think when Dad sends you back to Montana, I'm going to have him turn your room into a gym so I can move all my weights up from the basement."

"I'm *not* going back to Montana," Aimee said, and walked faster, trying to leave her brother behind, but in her high heels that was impossible.

Bran Goheen sat in a chair near what was left of the tables with his arms folded over his chest, watching her. The minute she spotted him, he turned his face away from her. He looked sad, she thought, and she felt a pang of guilt. She'd never really agreed to go to the dance with him, but she'd never refused, either. She shouldn't have left him hanging like she had.

When she reached the doors, she turned to look back at Raphael. Her dad was still talking to him. She couldn't hear the words but cold anger was carved into her father's face like he was some kind of ice sculpture. She pushed her way out the exit doors and walked out into the night.

The Flatliners crew was gathered around the flashing lights of an ambulance. Dalton sat on the tailgate while an EMT guy pressed on her stomach. When Dalton saw Aimee with Rick, she seemed to understand the situation at once. Waving, she gave Aimee a sympathetic smile as Rick opened the car door, shoved his sister into the backseat, and then slammed it. Aimee leaned her head against the window and closed her eyes. Part of her wanted to kick off her heels, get out of the car and run away before her dad got there, but there was no point. There was nowhere to go. And the person she wanted to run away with was still trapped inside.

◦◦

Maggie sat on the edge of the stage and watched as the gym cleared out. *So much for my glorious reign as homecoming queen*, she thought. She'd worn the crown for all of five minutes before a fight broke out, the school collapsed, and the dance ended. She'd lived long enough to know that things in life rarely turned out as she imagined they would, but this couldn't get more ridiculous. And then she saw her mom and Mr. Chin approaching.

"Right," her mom was saying to him. "This is from three tapestries ago. You know what's coming next."

Chin shook his head. "It can't be. It's too soon."

"My darling, look at you!" Maggie's mom took her hand, and the look of worry that had been on her face a moment before vanished. "Every inch a queen."

Maggie laughed bitterly. "It was a disaster," she said. "Literally."

"But you were beautiful," her mom said. She gently stroked Maggie's hair, and checked to make sure the crown was sitting properly on her head. "And such power. With *one* word . . . such power."

What do you mean? Maggie wanted to cry out. *What are you talking about? What kind of power? I didn't do anything.*

But she knew exactly what her mom was talking about. One word. That's all it took from her to bring that wall down.

On top of Aimee.

She had been angry, seeing Raphael and Aimee together on the dance floor, seeing his arms around her, his lips pressed against her hair. Seeing how Raphael protected Aimee when Rick and Bran attacked.

Maggie wanted Aimee out of the way, for sure. But she didn't want her dead—did she?

The thought was appalling. Again, she told herself that it was impossible. No matter how angry she was, there was no way she could have caused what happened. She knew she had a little magic in her—there was that little trick where she could touch a person's temple and make them do what she wanted them to, but that was nothing compared to this.

She noticed that Mr. Chin had gone over to the spot where the wall had collapsed. He was staring at something down in the hole, near the foundation of the building.

Jack Banfield had finally walked away from Raphael and was heading for Principal Innis when he glanced over at Maggie and stopped. He just stood there a moment, staring at Maggie's mom. Slowly, as if trying to think of what to say, he made his way over to them.

"Violet?"

She turned to find Jack Banfield staring at her. A blush rose to her normally pale cheeks. "Jack . . . " she murmured.

"Where on earth have you been?" he asked. "I haven't seen you in—years."

"Oh," she said slowly. "I don't get out much these days."

Understatement of the year, Maggie thought.

"You still look beautiful," he said.

"Thank you," she replied softly. "And you're as handsome as ever, Jack."

"It wasn't so long ago that you and I were on this stage ourselves . . . king and queen. Do you remember?" Jack almost smiled at the recollection.

"I remember every second of all three years, Jack," she said softly.

He seemed to lose himself for a moment, staring at Violet. Then, he got himself together. He glanced at Maggie. "Congratulations," he said, and with a final glance at her mom, he turned and walked toward the exit.

The moment he was gone, Chin hurried up to Violet. "There's a tunnel beneath the wall," he said softly.

Violet's already pallid skin grew a shade lighter.

"Someone's been digging," Mr. Chin said darkly.

"Just like in the tapestry," Violet said, and Maggie noticed that she shivered as if the temperature had suddenly dropped twenty degrees.

&

Aimee and her dad rode back to Hilltop Haven without a word spoken between them. It was a hostile silence, as constricting as a straitjacket. Aimee knew what *that* felt like, courtesy of Mountain High Academy.

They pulled into the garage and Jack shut the car off. They both got out and headed for the door leading into the house. As soon as they were inside, he grabbed her arm and dragged her toward the stairs. His hand was around her arm like an iron clamp, on the same spot, already bruised, he had grabbed during the dance.

"Ow! Dad, stop! That hurts!"

Not even looking at her, he pulled her up the stairs and down the hall, and then shoved her through the doorway of her bedroom.

It was too much. Her father stood on her threshold blocking her exit, which made her instantly claustrophobic. Her heartbeat quickened, doing flips in her chest like it used to when she felt a panic attack coming on, and it was getting harder to catch her breath.

"Dad, stop. Please. It was just a dance!"

Her father stared at her, his eyes as cold as a snake's.

"I asked you to do one thing: to stay away from that boy. And you couldn't do it."

She took a deep, measured breath, as her shrink at Mountain High had taught her to do, and tried to remember the quote he'd given her—the little mantra that was supposed to help her stay calm. But her mind was blank. She took another steadying breath and looked up at her father.

"He's nice to me, Dad! Nicer than anyone else has been since I got back to Middleburg." Aimee was trying to stay calm, but her voice got louder and sharper with every word she spoke. She felt trapped, and she was having trouble breathing. "He saved my life!"

"You know how many times that kid has slandered me around town, calling me a murderer because his stupid father was careless and got himself killed in my factory? You know how many times he's attacked your brother?"

"Well, how many times has Rick attacked him?" she shot back, disgusted. "You don't even care that he got me back from Oberon?"

"That doesn't give him the right to ruin your life," he said. "And I'm going to see to it that he doesn't. I have been to hell and back because of you, Aimee—including losing your mother—and I will not allow you to throw yourself away on some loser from the Flats!"

"He's not a loser!" she shouted, finding her voice and her courage at last. She was trembling. "Rick is the loser—and you, because all you know how to do is hate. You use people and when they're all used up, you hate them for it! That's why my mother left! It wasn't because of me."

He looked as if she'd slapped him. He went instantly and eerily calm. "You believe that, Aimee," he said quietly. "If it helps."

"All I'm saying is, give him a chance. If Mom were here, she would."

"Your mother is gone. Whatever her reason for leaving, she let her family down—just like you did tonight."

Aimee recoiled from the sting of his words.

"The Kain boy is out of chances," he continued. "And so are you. Get packed. You're going back to Montana tomorrow."

"No," Aimee said, but her dad had already stepped out of the room and slammed the door. "No, Dad—I'm not going back!" she shouted through the door, pounding on it with her fist. She tried to open it, but it was locked. From the outside. She was trapped.

The claustrophobia descended on her like a dark, suffocating cloud.

"Dad!" she screamed. "Dad!" But there was no answer.

CHAPTER 5

TYLER'S PARENTS WERE OUT OF TOWN. *Aimee told her mom she was stay-ing over at Maggie's house (Aimee and Maggie were friends back then, in another life), and that was all it took. But instead of going to Maggie's, she walked down the hill to Tyler's, near Hilltop Haven's back entrance. He opened the door for her as she headed up the walkway and when she reached him, she jumped into his arms and kissed him. Hand in hand, he led her to the kitchen where he had two glasses waiting, filled with ice and a funny-tasting, sweet liquid. Tyler laughed at the face she made when she first sipped it. Vodka lemonade.*

"Seriously, you never drank before? I thought you were kidding."

She wasn't kidding. She was a good girl—back then.

Three vodka lemonades later and the world was spinning. She was in the hot tub with Tyler, and for some reason they started talking about the tunnels. The four Middleburg tunnels through which no trains ran anymore and into which no Middleburg child was ever supposed to venture. Tyler was fascinated with the tunnels and had been ever since she could remember, and she'd known him pretty much all her life.

He pushed a wet tendril of her long blond hair behind her ear and teased her with the warning every kid in Middleburg had heard growing up:

Keep out of the railroad tunnels
And stay off the tracks
Don't go into the Train Graveyard
Or the Middleburg Monster will break your back . . .

Tyler bragged to her that one day he would go into the South Tunnel, the one by the old train graveyard, find the spot where the tracks crossed and take a picture.

They made out in the hot tub for a while but when the heat got to be too much, she pulled away from him and sat on the edge, her feet dangling in the water, his too-big t-shirt (her makeshift bathing suit) clinging to her skin. When he moved close again, she shook her head and took a sip of her booze-laced lemonade.

"What were we just talking about?" she asked. She couldn't remember how many drinks she'd had.

"Going up to my bedroom?" He said it with a charming, hopeful grin on his face.

She laughed and struggled to bring reason to the situation, but her brain was in chaos. She liked Tyler a lot, maybe even loved him, but she wasn't ready to go upstairs with him. Not now. Not like this.

"No . . ." she said. "We were talking about the tunnels."

Tyler nodded, laughing. "Right. You believe your big, tough brother wouldn't go down there with me? Rick—Mr. Big Tough Quarterback. And he actually wants to be the leader of the Toppers some day? Like that'll happen." Tyler laughed and then his eyes fixed on Aimee's. "Come on," he coaxed, his words a little slurred. "Come upstairs with me."

The world was still spinning. Aimee had to grab on to the edge of the hot tub to keep from falling off. Tyler's hand was on her thigh, moving up.

"Let's go down there," she said suddenly.

Tyler looked confused. "Down where?"

"To the tunnels."

His grin wilted a little.

"You said you could go in and find the spot where the two tracks cross, right? The spot that's supposed to be cursed or whatever? Let's go down there and you can go in and take your picture. You could blow it up and stick it on the wall at school. That would be awesome."

"I don't know," he said. "I don't think I should drive right now."

"Oh," Aimee said, playfully. "Not scared, are you?"

"I'm not scared, it's just . . ."

"Wuss!" Aimee teased, her face an inch from his.

Tyler's fear hardened into resolve before her eyes. "I'll get my camera," he said, and climbed out of the hot tub.

The next thing Aimee knew, she had dried off and dressed and was in Tyler's car. Treetops passed by the window in a wavy blur. Then, they were walking down the train tracks. Every time she stumbled, Tyler caught her and they laughed—and she stumbled a lot.

At last, the tunnel entrance rose up before them, black, like a window that looked out on outer space. Tyler stood with the flashlight in one hand and the camera in the other, staring into the darkness. Aimee stopped giggling. Suddenly, they were stone-cold sober.

"You don't really have to do this," Aimee said.

"No, I'm going in," he said. There was something strange in his eyes.

"Come on—I'm sorry I called you a wuss. It was a stupid idea."

"Too late to apologize now," he said, and winked at her. "I'll show you who's a wuss." And he was walking forward, into the tunnel.

She took a few steps off the train tracks and was looking for a place to sit down and wait for him (and maybe a good place to throw up) when she heard it. A faint hiss, and beneath it a low and distant humming sound.

She looked into the inky darkness of the tunnel. Tyler was pretty far in by now—at least two hundred yards away. She could just make out the feeble glow of his flashlight beam. For a second, she thought she saw something else in the beam, too. A hint of movement in the deepest part of the tunnel, a rippling of shadow.

A scream ripped from the tunnel mouth, but it cut off abruptly, replaced by a strange, empty silence. As she watched, astonished and terrified, a weird, reddish glow illuminated the tunnel and a great, black shape, growing and *swelling, rose up, taking Tyler with it. Suddenly, the dark, churning mass shot forward with lightning speed until it was only a few feet from her and—this she found impossible to believe later (the police hadn't believed her when she told them)—Tyler's limp body was dangling in front of her, held aloft by a shadow. Or a monster. Or a monster made of shadow. It was long and black, thick and massive. It had legs one moment that morphed into squirming tentacles the next. Its eyes were like bowls of liquid fire.*

And its teeth . . .

The creature held Tyler, caught in its mouth, high above her, silhouetted against the black, nighttime sky, its two giant fangs running straight through him. But Tyler wasn't dead. Not yet.

"Aimee," he whispered hoarsely, his jaw trembling with shock and with his effort to speak. There was blood on his lips. His hand quivered as it reached out to her. There was blood on his fingers, running down from his fingers, dripping onto the tracks.

Aimee knew she should do something, go for help, call somebody—something. But she stood frozen in place, staring up at the beast, and at Tyler, as he writhed in excruciating pain. And as she watched, the creature bit down on him. His final scream choked off and ended in a breathy wheeze.

The beast's eyes were on Aimee's now, red and blazing, staring at her, into her, and the old nursery-rhyme warning echoed through her brain, burning into it like a brand, repeating over and over, ". . . the Middleburg Monster will break your back.*"*

The thing opened its jaws and Tyler's lifeless body slid down its fangs like a piece of meat sliding off a skewer. It landed with a thud on the ground at Aimee's feet.

The monster turned away and slithered slowly back into the tunnel, disappearing into the suffocating darkness.

Poor Tyler was staring at the sky, his eyes as vacant as two pieces of broken glass.

Why didn't it kill me? *she wondered vaguely. That was her last thought before she started screaming, her voice stabbing through the heart of that silent autumn night.*

She didn't stop screaming for days.

℃

Aimee stared out her bedroom window at the beautiful nightscape view of Middleburg, nestled below her at the base of Hilltop Haven. Then her focus shifted to her own dark reflection in the glass. It had been more than a year since Tyler's death, and this was the first time she'd let the memory of that terrible night wash over her fully in all its excruciating detail. Although it had been horrible to relive it, it was also liberating. She was no longer too terrified to let herself remember. She'd used her mental exercises to calm herself when her anxiety started to rise and this time, it was different. This time, she didn't cry.

It was as if her old, fragile self had been wrapped in a cocoon for the last year, and now that she had emerged, she was different. She wasn't a butterfly, though. She knew now that she was tougher than that, almost indestructible. Whatever life threw at her now, she would not cry again. And she would *not* go back to Montana, no matter what.

℃

Looking around to make sure he was unobserved, Orias Morrow levitated an inch or two in the air, floated up the steps to settle on the porch of the old Victorian house, and let himself in the front door.

The house had been in his family further back than he or anyone else could remember. A broad veranda wrapped around the imposing structure, which was large enough to accommodate a ballroom on the third floor. Most of the bedrooms and a small parlor were on the second floor. On one corner of the house, a round tower with a pointed roof stood watch over the thick, lush garden that filled most of the backyard. Below the tower, which Orias had thought of as a child as the Castle Tower, round attic windows peered out beneath the gables. The paint on the exterior of the house—a deep, muted red with dingy, faded brown trim—was peeling in places. Despite its size, the place looked just as plain and unassuming as he remembered it from his last visit to Middleburg, thirteen years before. Of course, they could afford to repaint the house any time they wanted. If they wanted to, they could get the whole place gold plated. But Orias had learned the importance of living in shadow, feigning humility, and, above all, biding his time.

Yes, he had learned his father's lessons well, he thought bitterly. For years Oberon Morrow had played a role in Middleburg, posing as the modest owner of a couple of shabby businesses, living in a beautiful but rundown house a block over from Main Street. In all the years Oberon had lived in Middleburg, no one had an inkling of his power. It had been important, he always told Orias, to keep it that way.

Two days before, Orias had brought him down from the mountain-side and taken him home. As they'd stood together at the front door, Oberon had said, "It's locked," and reached into his pocket for his keys.

"You underestimate me, sir," Orias had told him pleasantly. "I've honed my skills since I saw you last." He opened his left hand and passed his palm in front of the doorknob, and there was a click as the latch retracted. Then he'd moved his hand slowly up the door until they heard the sound of the deadbolt sliding back. Orias had waved his hand then, as one might swat a gnat, and the door had swung open.

The house was dark and smelled musty from being shut up, as if Oberon had been absent for years instead of just a few days.

Orias had glanced briefly around the shadowy foyer. The elabo-rately carved wooden banister he'd slid down as a boy looked smaller than he remembered, but he supposed that was the way of things when one had no choice but to age—albeit more slowly than other mortals. He took a few steps and glanced into the main parlor. The antique chaise was still there, and Orias had a vague recollection of seeing his mother sitting on it, holding her arms out to him. The memory filled him with an aching sad-ness. Even after all these years, the pain of her death still tormented him.

"You'll have to get me up to the Tower Room, Orias," his father had told him. "As long as the police are looking for me I can't take any chances. I'll have to stay up there until Dr. Uphir arrives."

"When will that be?" Orias asked.

"Who can tell with his kind?" Oberon grumbled, as he groped his way along the wall, toward the staircase. Orias tried not to take too much pleasure in seeing his father in his pathetic, handicapped state.

"Wait, Father," he said kindly. "Let me help you."

Laboriously, tediously, Orias had helped Oberon climb up to the tower. He could have levitated with him, but he was not yet ready to share with his sire how well developed his skills were. Opening a door was one thing, but the ability to levitate two men up the stairs would have taken some explaining. He'd helped his father get unpacked, put fresh linens on his bed, and made a note to himself to call whatever cleaning service Oberon used.

It wasn't long before boredom had set in and Orias became restless, so tonight he'd gone looking for her.

After a couple of false starts—an old movie house, a coffee shop— he'd had dinner at the little Italian restaurant a few blocks away, and there he'd heard a group of kids, all dressed up in gowns and tuxedos, talking about their high-school homecoming dance. And he'd wondered . . .

So after he'd paid for his meal and a glass of substandard wine, he'd strolled over to Middleburg High, taking his time, getting a feel for the town. Gaining admission to the dance had been no problem. Orias had learned, at an age much earlier than usual for his kind, how to camou-flage his appearance and blend into any background, whenever he chose. When he no longer needed to hide, he simply took one step forward and, chameleon-like, his disguise fell away.

And he had found her there—in a high-school gymnasium. His father was right—she was impossible to miss. She shone like a star, bright and pure. Radiant. He'd gotten only a brief glimpse and a whiff of her elusive, tantalizing scent as she glided by in the arms of the boy who had taken his father's sight. But even that became unimportant in the moment. Because Orias had known.

He'd known she was the one.

And just as he was about to step forward and ask her to dance, all hell (at least a high-school human's version of it) broke loose. That asinine jock had picked a fight, then the homecoming queen had lost control of her puny magic and knocked the wall down.

Orias had lingered long enough to see the girl walk out of the dust and debris, unharmed, and then he'd mingled with the crowd and made his way home, thinking of her all the way. He would have his chance with her, but not tonight. Tonight, he would have to content himself with thoughts of her, dreams of her. Tonight, he would sleep blissfully, drunk on the possibilities she represented. Because she existed, the world would never be the same again. Yes, there was no doubt about it, he thought, unable to repress a grin—she was definitely the one.

❧

Raphael awoke with a start, the remnants of a dream still clinging to his mind . . . a clackity-clack-clack of train wheels and the slow howl of a spectral whistle approaching down a set of dream-world train tracks. Almost instantly, however, the nightmare faded and the shrieking of the whistle dissolved into an insistent beeping sound. He looked around, groggy for a moment, before realizing it was his cell phone.

Grabbing it off his bedside table, he looked eagerly at the caller ID, but it wasn't Aimee. There's no telling what kind of hell her dad had put her through after he dragged her out of the dance. His threat had been so ominous that Raph had hardly been able to sleep last night.

"*You're never going to see her again,*" Jack Banfield had proclaimed softly, his voice a cold monotone. Nothing in his expression indicated that he was furious, but Raphael saw it in his eyes. "*Never.*"

Maybe everyone else in Middleburg thought Jack Banfield was an upstanding citizen, but Raphael knew better. The picture of his dad still sat on his bedside table. He had his arm around Raph's mom, and they looked amazingly happy. The photo was taken only a few months before the so-called accident in Jack's factory took his father away forever. If Jack Banfield said you were never going to see someone again, you had to take him at his word. He didn't have any concrete evidence that Jack Banfield and his partner, Cheung Shao, had murdered his dad, but he knew it was true. The way birds know which way to fly in the winter, the way flowers know when it's time to bloom. *He knew*.

Raphael blinked, rubbed his eyes and looked down at his phone, still waking up. His caller ID said EMORY, and it was about to go to voicemail.

"Yo, Ems. What's up?"

"Bad stuff," Emory said. He usually sounded mellow and upbeat on the phone, but not this morning.

"Why? What's going on?" Raph said, getting up.

"Just come over to my place, okay? And hurry."

Still pulling on his long-sleeved t-shirt as he charged through the living room, Raphael searched frantically for his sneakers. He was surprised to find his mom lying on the couch, her expanding belly clearly visible now beneath a thick, purple sweater. As she yawned and sat up, he wondered if it was normal for a pregnant woman's stomach to get bigger every single day. Despite the extra passenger, Raphael thought his mom looked as pretty as ever as she stretched and smiled at him.

"Morning, Raphy," she said sleepily. "Where you off to so early?"

"It's not that early. Emory has some kind of problem. I'm going to see if I can help him out. What are you doing out here?"

"The bed was killing my back," she said as she swung her legs around and put her feet on the floor. She was wearing a pair of his thick wool socks.

"And the couch is better?" Raphael asked, skeptical.

"Yeah. Don't ask me why. There are a lot of things about being pregnant that seem to defy the laws of physics."

Raphael finally found his shoes under the coffee table. He pulled them out.

"How was the dance?"

He sat down in the chair and put his sneakers on, trying to figure out how to sum it up for his mom. "It was weird," he said finally.

She laughed, "You and your friends wearing suits? I'm sure it was." When he didn't respond, she asked, more seriously, "Did something happen?"

"Well, one wall of the gym collapsed, for starters."

She gaped at him. "Was anyone hurt?"

"No." The image of the steel beam lying across Dalton flashed through his mind. She should have been hurt—killed, maybe—and he didn't know how to explain to himself, much less to his mom, the fact that she was miraculously unscathed.

"So did you have a date? You never even told me."

"I gotta go, mom. Emory's waiting."

"Dalton?"

"No, I didn't take Dalton."

"That girl from your science class you liked last year?"

Raphael sighed. "Okay. You'll hear about it sooner or later, I guess. I took Aimee Banfield. And her dad wasn't too happy about it."

A crosscurrent of different emotions played over his mom's face as she processed his revelation. "Why wasn't Jack happy about it?"

Raphael looked at her for a moment, surprised that she had to ask. "Come on, Mom," he said. "Why do you think?"

Look where they live, he wanted to cry out, his heart heavy. *And look at our home sweet home. Even worse, you and Aimee's dad have been seeing each other and—although you won't say so—he's probably the father of my new little baby brother or sister. Why the* hell *do you think?*

Instead, he shrugged. "Aren't you going to tell me to stay away from her like everyone else has?" he asked.

"That depends," his mom replied, getting awkwardly to her feet. "Do you like her, or are you dating her just to piss Jack off?"

"I like her," Raphael whispered. He heard a vulnerability in his own voice that made him uncomfortable, but his mom only smiled and embraced him.

"Then she's a lucky girl," she said.

He hugged her back, incredibly grateful for her presence. But Emory was still waiting, and he hadn't sounded good on the phone.

"I gotta run," Raphael said, pulling away.

On her way into the kitchen, his mom called over her shoulder, "What about breakfast?"

"No time."

She grabbed a banana off the counter and tossed it to him. "Love you, kiddo."

"Love you, mom."

And he ducked out the door.

෨

Raphael was stunned by what he saw as he jogged up to Emory's apartment building. It was a big, old Greek-revival mansion that had been divided into six apartments. It had four columns on its front porch, none of which were straight. Half the windows were filled with particle-board in place of missing or broken glass panes, and the whole structure was covered with ugly scabs of dark blue paint that had largely peeled away to reveal the old, gray wood beneath. But that was normal for the Flats. The surprise was all over the skimpy, patchy front lawn.

It looked like someone had thrown everything in the whole building outside. Furniture, rugs, tables, chairs, couches, lamps, and TVs littered the yard. As Raphael watched, a couple of burly men came down the front steps with an old, beat-up entertainment center, which they carried down the walkway and deposited near the curb. All the while, an old lady followed them in a flowered mumu, her hair a ball of tangled white fluff on her head, cursing them out in what sounded to Raphael like some Eastern European language. He scanned the strange scene for a moment before he spied Emory on the far side of the yard, pacing furiously.

"Hey, what's going on?" Raphael asked as he approached.

The words exploded from Emory's mouth. "Look! You can see what's going on! They're throwing us out! All of us!"

"Throwing you out? Of your apartment, you mean?"

"Yeah! Look, everyone's being evicted. Every family in the building."

Raphael put a hand on his friend's shoulder. "Okay, Emory. Calm down. First of all, they can't just evict somebody. Now without giving them a notice or something."

Emory shrugged in agitation. "They did give us a notice. My dad went to talk to the realty company three times, and they just kept putting him off. He didn't think they could really do it, but look—they're already changing the locks. All our stuff is going to get ruined." Emory gestured accusingly at the sky where a host of storm clouds was indeed sweeping in. "We're screwed."

"Like getting all hysterical is going to help," a sarcastic voice said. Raph looked over and saw Haylee, Emory's eleven-year-old sister, sprawled in a recliner, playing an old-school Game Boy.

"Shut up, Haylee," Emory said with disdain. "You don't even understand what's going on." Raphael had never seen Emory look so serious—or so worried.

"Oh, right. Because I'm eleven? I get better grades than *you*."

Emory looked like he was about ready to strangle his sister, but Raphael put a hand on his shoulder again.

"Let's focus, man. We'll figure this out. Where's your mom?"

"She's inside. They let her pack up some of the plates and stuff."

"And your dad?"

"He went down to the rental office, but I think they're closed. That's probably why they waited until Sunday to throw us out. There's no one to complain to."

"Did you get the summons to go to court?" asked Raph. Every family in the Flats knew the drill. You didn't pay your rent on time, you got threatened with eviction. But that threat came in the form of a three-day notice that heralded the summons to appear, with a date.

"I think we got a thirty-day notice, then a three-day notice," Emory said.

"That can't be legal."

Emory laughed, bitter and harsh. "Yeah, well. They know once they get us out we can't fight it. It's not like we're going to worry about hiring a lawyer when we're living in a cardboard box."

Raph nodded. He was angry, but not surprised. Some rich property owner living up in Hilltop Haven had decided to throw six families out of their homes for no good reason. It was just another day in the Flats.

He took out his phone, scrolled down to the name NASS and pressed TALK.

"Nass, it's Raph. Call the crew. Get everyone down to Emory's place, right away. It's an emergency."

When Raphael ended the call and looked back at his friend, he could see that Emory's face was stiff, his jaw clenched, as he tried to hold back tears.

"We have no place to go, man," Emory said quietly.

"Don't worry. We're going to figure it out."

Above, the storm clouds continued to roll in.

so

Maggie snuggled deeper into her big, fluffy, pink comforter and pulled it up over her head. She'd woken up three times already, and three times she'd drifted back to sleep. Still a little hazy from lying comatose for so long, she had no desire to get up. There was no reason to leave her bed. Her life was a wreck. She had a dad who'd skipped town years ago, a mom who was nuttier than squirrel poop, and a hot boyfriend who didn't love her and who, if the lighting was just right, kinda looked like he might actually be a demon. The boy she really liked was in love with her ex–best friend, Aimee—and now, on top of it all, what would be known forever as "the homecoming dance incident" would follow her through the rest of high school. She had worn the homecoming crown for all of five minutes when that wall had collapsed.

When she had brought that wall down.

It was crazy, she knew, but that's what happened.

Sure, maybe there was some kind of a hole under the gym that helped make the wall crumble, but she had done most of it. *How* she had done it she had no idea. All she knew was that she had felt some kind of power surge through her, and that she'd never felt anything like it. Her confidence had started growing from the moment her mother had told her she was powerful (although she had never really cared what her mother thought). When her mom had placed the crown on her head, she'd felt like something really important had clicked into place in the universe— and that was just plain weird.

But it had. And whatever it was, some kind of awesome power came with it. Even after Principal Innis took the crown from her and placed it back in the trophy case, even now, lying in bed, she felt the weight of it on her brow, like a ghost crown.

She wondered if that could be what was heightening her perceptions. It was as if she could feel every single thread of her sheets resting against every skin cell on each of her arms.

She didn't know where the power came from, but she knew what had unleashed enough of it to demolish a wall: it was seeing Raphael with Aimee, protecting her. Loving her. Seeing them together like that infuriated Maggie. The closeness, the sweetness—that was something she would never have with Rick, something she would give her soul to have with Raphael.

Maggie hadn't really wanted to hurt anyone. She had just wanted Aimee gone, out of the way. And if the look on Jack Banfield's face was anything to go by, that just might be happening. Maybe he would send Aimee back to boarding school. More awake now, she wondered if anything had spread over the gossip grapevine yet, and she fumbled on her nightstand for her phone. Then she remembered it was in her purse. She'd been so tired last night that she hadn't even bothered plugging it into the charger. It was all the way across the room.

And I have to go all the way over there to get it, she thought, wishing it would somehow come to her. But it was really time to get up anyway. Arching her back, catlike, she stretched, yawned, and threw back her duvet cover.

And froze.

Her cell phone was hanging in midair, next to her bed, suspended as if by an invisible hand, as if merely wishing for it had brought it to her.

She screamed and it dropped to the floor.

Scrambling backward against the headboard, she bunched the covers up in front of her like a barricade. Then slowly, cautiously, she peered over the end of the bed. The cell phone was lying on the plush rug.

It occurred to Maggie, for the first time in her life, that she might be inheriting her mother's madness.

"Maggie? You okay up there?"

"Yeah, Mom! Fine!" Maggie yelled back. Her mom sounded way more mellow than usual. And something else was weird too. Her mother was downstairs already, which meant she'd begun the next phase of her work, transferring her sketches to the fabric she would embroider.

But that didn't make sense either. When her mom was working on a tapestry, nothing could draw her away from it. Maggie could scream her head off while the house burned down around them and her mom would still be sitting there sketching or stitching away with the speed and intensity that only the truly deranged could manage. So if she was downstairs and she wasn't working on the tapestry, what was she doing?

"Maggie, come on down and have breakfast."

Now she knew something really strange was going on. Her mom barely ate the breakfast Maggie served her every day—and Violet Anderson certainly didn't *make* breakfast.

"Coming!" She shouted and climbed out of bed, careful not to touch her possessed cell phone. She hurried downstairs, still in her pajama pants and tank top.

She headed into the kitchen, but there was no sign of her mom, and no evidence that any cooking had taken place.

"Mom?" she asked, getting a little worried.

"In here, honey!"

Maggie followed her voice into the dining room. There, beneath the crystal chandelier, a beautiful breakfast was laid out complete with her mother's best silver and the nice china. And her mom, looking healthier and more vibrant than Maggie had seen her in years, stood next to the table in a pretty knit dress, her hair neatly brushed for once. Maggie stared.

"What's going on?" she asked.

"Breakfast," Violet said brightly. "It's ordered in—from Spinnacle. I didn't trust myself to cook such an important meal. It's been a while." She pulled a chair out for her daughter and gestured for her to sit.

"Important . . . why?" Maggie moved closer to the table.

"It's tradition. You're homecoming queen and this is the first day of your reign."

"Mom—get a grip," Maggie said. "It's a title and a picture in the yearbook. And wearing that stupid crown." But even as she said it, she was sorry. Her heart did a funny lurching thing, and she realized she *missed* it. She missed the crown as if it were a living, breathing thing. "It's no big deal," she finished halfheartedly.

"No," her mother said firmly as Maggie took her seat. "It *is* a big deal." She pushed the chair in for Maggie and sat down next to her, at the head of the table.

"Okay." Suddenly ravenous, Maggie decided to humor her—it was so much easier when her mom got something fixed in her mind and couldn't let it go. "Whatever. But you didn't have to do all this."

She grabbed a strip of bacon, and as she took a big bite of it she studied her mom, who was just sitting there, looking at her so seriously. Violet held her back straight and her head high. Bathed in the pale morning light, she looked regal. Like she was a queen herself, Maggie thought. Like the years she'd spent as a frazzled slave to her own idiosyncrasies—compulsively checking the doors to make sure they were locked, obsessively designing and stitching her tapestries, harping on Maggie about the importance of being homecoming queen—like it had all been a bad dream from which she had now awakened.

"Maybe it's just a title for now," her mom said as she poured coffee for both of them. "In time you'll see that it's much more. All you need to know for now is that with the queenhood comes great power and great responsibility."

Maggie managed not to laugh at her mother's corny terminology. "After last night, it looks like all I'm going to be queen of is a big hole in the ground."

"Oh, no, my daughter. You have a great destiny before you. Last night was part of that destiny."

"Oh yeah?" Maggie retorted cynically. "When do we get to the good part?"

Again she thought of Raphael Kain, and remembered his lips on hers one night not so long ago, his arms around her, holding her close, as they slid together down the wall to the floor of the abandoned railroad car.

✼

Instead of rain, it was snow that fell from the steel-colored sky as Beet and Josh hauled the last piece of Emory's family's furniture—a faded and tattered brown plaid couch—from the back of the pick-up truck toward the old, rundown garage that stood behind Beet's dad's auto body shop.

The rest of the Flatliners were hard at work too. Benji was running two extension cords across the cracked concrete between the shop and the garage, one to run the electric heater they'd borrowed from Dalton and Lily Rose, and the other to run a clock radio and a little microwave. Mr. Van Buren, Emory's dad, had gone up to a gas station to pick up ice for the cooler, so they could keep their food from spoiling. Mrs. Van Buren was inside, thumbtacking old towels over the garage's three windows so that the family would have some privacy at night, and Raphael and Nass were arranging the furniture and supplies so that everything would be accessible, but still leave room for the family to move around in the cramped two-car garage.

Beet's dad had been kind enough to move the two old cars he normally stored there, and had let Beet take the company truck to move all the furniture. Josh and his family were avid campers, and they had donated some sleeping bags.

Raphael was proud of the way his crew had come together to help their friend. It wasn't the perfect solution—it was illegal to live in a garage, Raphael knew, and if city officials found out about it, Emory's family would have to move again. But at least they'd have a roof over their heads until they found a more permanent solution. They had no relatives in Middleburg, and none of the other Flatliners had enough space in their small, cramped apartments to take them in.

At Raphael's request, Emory was rifling through some papers in the boxes, looking for their lease. His sister, still wrapped up in her Game Boy, was sprawled on her bed, which was pushed against the wide, metal garage door.

"Haylee, why don't you do something useful instead of playing that stupid game?" Emory asked her irritably.

"Why don't *you* do something useful, instead of going through that stupid *box*?" Haylee mocked.

"Whatever," Emory said.

Raphael finished stacking a pile of heavy boxes in the corner, then pulled out his phone. It was noon, and still no call from Aimee. He wished he could call her—he just wanted to hear her voice and know she was okay—but it was impossible. If he called, it would only get her in worse trouble.

"Hey, Raph," Nass said, and he gestured for Raphael to follow him outside.

In the driveway, scattered snowflakes drifted lazily in the frigid air. When Nass spoke, Raphael could see his breath crystallizing in front of him.

"I didn't say anything before because I didn't want to freak everyone out," Nass said quietly, "But we got a lease termination notice too. It says we have thirty days to get out."

Raphael nodded gravely. "Also illegal. You were right not to tell the others, though. Let's find out what's going on first."

At that moment, Emory emerged from the side door of the garage, holding a packet of papers up in one hand.

"Found it," he said triumphantly and handed the document over to his leader, who scanned it.

"Look," Raphael said, pointing at the first page. "Banfield Realty manages the building. The owner is listed as 'Middleburg Property Group, herein referred to as MPG, Incorporated.'"

"What does that mean?" Ignacio asked.

"Middleburg Property Group is a corporation owned by two investors," Raphael said, looking up from the document. "They own three-quarters of the property in the Flats."

"Two investors," Nass said. "Jack Banfield and who else?"

"Cheung Shao," Raph said quietly. "Zhai's dad."

Emory groaned.

Rick's dad and Zhai's dad. As if the Flatliners needed another reason to hate the Toppers.

"Are you sure?" Nass asked. "How do you know?"

"Study your enemy. That's one of the most important things Master Chin taught me," Raphael said, and he handed the lease back to Emory. "And I've done that."

"So what do we do now? We can't live in a garage forever," Emory said.

"We find out why they're trying to push us out," Raphael said. "And we put a stop to it."

CHAPTER 6

ZHAI RAISED THE VIOLIN TO HIS CHIN and rested the bow gently on the strings. Sometimes, this was the moment he loved the best: the instant before he played the first note was always filled with anticipation, excitement, possibility. He glanced up at his family—his father, Cheung, smiling at him from the couch as he sat with his arm around Zhai's beautiful stepmother, Lotus. Lotus was smiling too, her beauty as fragile as a glass snowflake, as if she might shatter with the slightest mischance. Zhai's sister Li sat in a big leather chair near the warm glow of the fireplace, texting someone, her legs folded under her. When she saw Zhai looking at her, she put the phone down, suddenly attentive.

The concert he gave for his family every Sunday since he was ten years old was a tradition that had long been sacrificed to his dad's obsessive work schedule and his stepmother's endless social engagements. But since Li had miraculously recovered from her mysterious illness, their dad was doing a lot more of his work at home. At first Zhai thought it was because Li's illness had reminded him of his own mortality, a perfectly natural reaction. But then Zhai noticed his dad had become hypervigilant, frequently looking at his cell phone to check his caller I.D. but answering almost no calls. He seemed anxious and tense. It was almost as if he was afraid to go into the office—so Zhai had suggested the concerts again, as a way to help his father to relax.

Lotus objected—she had so much to do with the pharmacy, and she was on the school board now, too—but Li liked the idea, so it was settled. Their father doted on Li more than ever after she came home from the hospital.

Zhai played for them every Sunday after breakfast.

He had just begun his first note, a high, clear A flat, when the doorbell rang and spoiled it. He lowered the violin and bow, frustrated at the interruption, and listened as the maid answered the door. He could hear her muffled greeting and the low, clipped response of a male voice, followed by footsteps in the hall outside the music room. The maid entered and hurried over to Cheung Shao. She leaned between him and Lotus and spoke quietly to them.

The expression of his father's face was no longer relaxed, and Lotus went suddenly pale.

"It can't be," she whispered anxiously, but her husband silenced her with a glare. He rose from the couch and headed for the foyer, with the maid and Lotus right behind him.

It wasn't unusual for the Shaos to have weekend visitors, but none of them showed up unannounced, and none of them had ever elicited this sort of response. With one look at Li, Zhai knew she was thinking the same thing. Zhai put his violin back in the case and, with his sister, crept toward the half-open door, hoping to catch of glimpse of their visitors.

Both men were Chinese, which he thought unusual since there were not many Chinese families living near Middleburg. They each wore a black suit topped with an overcoat. They both had close-cropped hair and each wore a black derby hat. The two men could easily have been brothers; the only difference between them was their height—one was about six inches taller than the other—and the color of their ties.

"Just more corporate wonders," Li observed dismissively and went back to the fireplace.

But Zhai felt compelled to stay in the doorway. He tried to keep out of sight but as they approached, but the taller guest glanced over, and for a second he and Zhai locked eyes. Zhai felt a jolt of recognition. It was the same feeling he got upon waking up from a dream he couldn't quite remember, only this was a thousand times more insistent. He had seen this man before. He *knew* him. And somehow, he knew that the man knew him, too. It was an uncomfortable feeling... unsettling.

An instant later, his father's two visitors were past the doorway, tramping their way up the stairs. But even in their absence, the unsettled feeling did not abate. Zhai was on the verge of something—some incredibly important realization—but the harder he tried to figure out what it was, the further away it slipped. He wiped one hand across his forehead and realized that his brow was covered with clammy sweat. His knees were shaking.

"... some of my friends are going—Weston, and Amanda, maybe Lucy. It should be fun. *Hello?*"

Zhai realized Li had been talking to him.

"Are you going with me to Spinnacle tonight, or not?" she repeated, annoyed.

"Yeah. Sure," he said. "I'll take you. Sounds good."

"Are you okay?" Li asked, taking a step closer to him. "You look like you're going to be sick."

"I'm fine," he said, his voice constricted. "Spinnacle for dinner. Sounds good."

And he turned and hurried out of the room. He raced up the steps, taking them two at a time, and jogged down the hallway, his footsteps falling silently on the thick, plush carpeting.

He stopped in front of the door to his father's study and leaned closer, placing his ear gently against the wood.

From inside, he heard Lotus shouting until his father yelled at her to be silent. Zhai could hear words but couldn't make out what they were saying. After a second he realized they were speaking Chinese. He cursed himself for slacking off on his Chinese lessons.

Giving up and turning away from the door, Zhai saw Li in the hallway, looking at him quizzically.

He raised one finger to his lips, silencing her, then pointed to the door. As usual, she understood exactly what Zhai wanted. She crept up to the door next to him and put her ear against it, her face next to his just as the shouting erupted again. She listened for a moment, concentrating, then finally stepped back.

"What are they saying?" Zhai whispered. Lotus had made sure her daughter stuck with her Chinese lessons, and Li had a natural flair for it.

"It doesn't make any sense."

"Tell me anyway," he said.

"Something about a scroll. The Scroll of the Wheel, I think. Then . . ." Confusion and worry lined her face.

"Tell me, Li," he said. "Word for word."

"One of the men told Dad, *'Remember, Cheung Shao, who it is you serve. You are our slave.'*"

℥

By the time Lily Rose answered the door, Maggie had stopped crying, but when she saw the tender concern in the old woman's eyes more tears threatened.

"Maggie!" Lily Rose exclaimed cheerfully. "I thought you might come by today."

The comment struck Maggie as strange; she'd only been to her housekeeper's home once when she had dropped Raphael off there, after he'd battled samurai warriors in her kitchen. She had the address—her mom had taped Lily Rose's business card to the refrigerator door years ago, and it was still there. It was plain, simple, completely unembellished:

Lily Rose's Cleaning Service
We put things right.

Maggie hoped with her whole heart that Lily Rose's slogan was true—because she desperately needed someone to talk to. She couldn't talk to her so-called friends—all they were interested in were clothes and boys. Rick was a demonic psycho. Her mom was—well, her mom. Raphael was too wrapped up in Aimee to know Maggie existed. Everything in her life had suddenly become so bizarre, and she felt like she was drowning in confusion. There was no one in the world she could turn to—no one, except Lily Rose. Maybe.

The old woman was already leading her inside. "Come in, come in," she said. "Oh, child—I can see you're vexed something awful. Come on now. Let's go into the kitchen and see what we can find."

Lily Rose's kitchen was as clean and shiny as it must have been the day she'd had the cabinets installed, which had to be some time in the 1950s, unless the old lady was into retro chic. But these looked original. Maggie knew about home décor. She planned to support her pursuit of a modeling career in New York with some kind of interior-design job. Black-and-white checkered tiles covered the floor, an immaculate, plastic lace-patterned tablecloth adorned the small kitchen table, and there was a tallboy filled with elegant, gold-trimmed dishes and little glass figurines. Lily Rose steered her to the table and sat her down, then crossed to the kitchen counter and opened several glass jars filled with what looked to Maggie like herbs.

"What you need, Maggie, is a nice, warm cup of tea. Lucky for you, I make the best tea in town."

Maggie was about to object that she didn't like tea, but the aroma of the herbs and crushed flowers Lily Rose was scooping into a little, slotted metal ball was amazing. Lily Rose filled the teapot with water from the tap and put it on the stove while Maggie slouched forward on the table, her chin leaning on her hands, staring down at the plastic lace tablecloth. She'd never known her grandparents—they had all died before she was born—but she guessed that this must be what it felt like to be a little kid at Grandma's house. It was wonderful, after all the time she'd spent trying to help her mom keep it together. It was nice to be taken care of for a change.

"Grandma, what—" Dalton walked into the room and stopped short when she saw Maggie.

"Dalton, sweetie, look who's come to see us."

"Why is she here?" Dalton asked, glaring at Maggie.

"We're having a cup of tea," Lily Rose said, as if it were the most natural thing in the world. "Why don't you join us? We can have—what do you children call it—we can have us a little girl talk."

"I'll pass," Dalton said and stamped out of the room.

Lily Rose sighed and took a little silver plate out of the cupboard, placed it on the table and started arranging cookies on it. "Please forgive Dalton," she said. "She's having a tough time right now." She leaned closer to Maggie and whispered, "Boy troubles, I think. I bet you know something about those, don't you?"

Maggie nodded glumly. "Yeah," she said, her voice low and tremulous as she thought of Rick. *Or whatever he was.*

Lily Rose smiled as she set cups on the table. "Well, what girl your age doesn't have boy troubles?" she asked philosophically. "I try to tell her that all these worries will pass with the season and everything will work out in the end, but she won't listen. I guess I wouldn't either, at her age."

But Maggie knew why Dalton didn't want her there. Dalton was Aimee Banfield's new best friend. Maggie started to wonder why she'd come here in the first place.

"Maybe I should just go . . ." she mumbled.

"Nonsense," said Lily Rose. The teakettle was shrieking, and she turned off the stove and filled an elegant old teapot, into which she had placed the little silver ball, with steaming water. "You haven't told me what's on your mind yet."

Again, the old woman's strangely colored eyes bored into hers, and Maggie had an overwhelming urge to tell her everything that had ever hurt or frightened her throughout her entire life. She just had to figure out how to do it without sounding like a lunatic. They waited in companionable silence for a few seconds as the tea steeped in the pot. Lily Rose poured for them, and Maggie took a tentative sip. To her surprise it was delicious—sweet and refreshing and soothing all at once. She felt the tension melt from her body as the warmth of the drink slid pleasantly down her throat.

"You know what happened at the dance, right?" she asked. Everybody in town probably knew by now.

"You mean when that wall fell down?"

"Yeah." Maggie bowed her head and blinked away the tears that made her feel so weak. "Yes, ma'am," she amended softly.

"Yes, baby girl. I know what happened. What do you have to say about it?"

"I think . . . I did it."

Lily Rose studied her for a moment, as if trying to decide something. And then she looked into Maggie's eyes. She took off her glasses, cleaned them with a corner of her apron, and put them back on. At last, she spoke.

"Now what makes you think you could do something like that?" she asked.

Maggie was almost hypnotized, just looking into Lily Rose's eyes. They were two different colors—one amber and one blue—and Maggie's secrets were defenseless against them.

"Weird things have been happening," she said. "For a couple of weeks. Since Halloween." She dropped her voice to a whisper. "I've been seeing things."

Lily Rose sat up a little straighter and took a sip of her tea. "What kind of things?"

"It's like I can see . . . what's *under* people. You know, what's under their skins. Like their truest selves—what they are inside."

Which is why she knew she could trust Lily Rose. When Maggie looked at Lily Rose, she saw paradise. She saw flowers and rainbows and birthday cakes. She saw glorious sunsets and great forests with waterfalls and birds and fawns and bunnies. She saw a tiny woman with a lap big enough to hold a troubled teenage girl. And sometimes, when Lily Rose turned away from her, Maggie thought she saw the faintest, transparent outline of big, white wings.

"That might be a good kinda sight to have," mused Lily Rose. She nibbled at a cookie. "What troubles you about that?"

"Some people are really ugly underneath," said Maggie. She wasn't ready to tell anyone about Rick, not even Lily Rose.

"Like I said, good sight to have. It lets you know who you got to keep an eye on. What else, baby girl? What else is scaring you?"

And Maggie realized it wasn't just her eyes that made the old woman so amazing. It was also her voice. When she spoke, it was musical, mesmerizing, and filled with pure love. Maggie knew Lily Rose could probably talk anybody into doing just about anything.

"I'm afraid . . . " Maggie began, and then tears really did start to flow. She wiped them away with the paper towel Lily Rose had given her to use as a napkin. "I'm afraid I'm going to end up like my mom," she said, choking back a little sob. "She's really crazy, isn't she?"

Lily Rose reached across the table and patted her hand. "No, she is not," she declared. "Your mama is as sane as you and me."

"Then what's wrong with her?"

Lily Rose gave her that look again. *Like she's deciding how much to say*, Maggie realized.

"She's got a job to do," said Lily Rose.

"What kind of job?" Maggie scoffed. "All she does is work on those stupid tapestries."

"Exactly. Those tapestries are important. They tell the history of Middleburg."

"Oh, who cares about that?" Maggie said. "Middleburg is a great big nothing, in the middle of a great big nowhere. Nothing important ever happens here."

Only, it does, Maggie thought. The battle between the Toppers and the Flatliners the night she'd first seen Rick change into a demon—that was important. The wall collapsing in the high-school gym was important. The crown she'd won and worn so briefly—that was important too. She didn't know why, and she didn't know how she knew, but it was.

"Now you know that's not true," Lily Rose observed. "But whether people think your mama's job is important or not, it is her destiny. You'll find your own soon enough."

"She's got it into her head that mine is to be homecoming queen of Middleburg High . . . forevermore."

"That could be part of it, I guess."

"Anyway, I don't believe in destiny," said Maggie. "I mean, I think you make your own destiny. You have a choice, right? My life can't just be predetermined."

That has to be true, she thought. *I can't end up like my mom, alone and unappreciated in a miserable, decaying little town.*

"Well, maybe it's a little bit of both," said Lily Rose. "Think of destiny as a road running along the side of a mountain. Most people are born into a certain life, and that's where they stay—on that road. It's the easiest path, after all, and so they move through life pretty smoothly. Some fail to meet their responsibilities, and they fall into the valley below, where it's rough and rocky. The path is tough down there; it's slow going, and it's hard to climb back up where you belong. But a few, a very few, choose the highest path of all. It's slow and treacherous, climbing up to it. I tell you, it's mighty rocky and hard, but once you reach that mountaintop, once you're moving along that ridge, child, the sun is on your face. It's so nice, you feel like you might just sprout wings and fly."

"That's what I want to do, Lily Rose," Maggie said, suddenly filled with hope and conviction. "I want to fly. I don't want to be like my mom. Will you help me?"

Lily Rose dabbed the corner of her mouth with her napkin and stood. She went to the china cabinet, opened a drawer, and took out a book, which she offered to Maggie.

It was surprisingly heavy. The cover was thick, made of some kind of gold leather. Embossed on it in black letters were the words *The Good Book*. It was secured with a small gold lock.

"Oh, we're not really religious," Maggie said quickly.

"You don't have to be for it to work," Lily Rose told her with a little smile. She pulled on the thin gold chain around her neck and drew it up from the collar of her blouse and used the tiny gold key that hung from it to open the lock. Inside, Maggie expected to find the microscopic print of a Bible, but the first page was blank. The paper was thick and weighty, and had a pearlescent sheen to it that seemed to swirl and sparkle as the light played off it, but there were no words. She flipped ahead. All those pages were blank too.

Lily Rose laughed. "Not what you were expecting?" she asked. "*The Good Book* only shows you what you're ready to read. I tell you, half of mine is still blank, and I been thumbing through it since you were knee-high to a grasshopper."

Maggie tried to give the book back to her, but Lily Rose waved her away. "Keep it, baby girl. It's yours." She took the key on the gold chain from around her neck and handed that to Maggie as well. "But I want you to do something for me, you hear?"

"Yes, ma'am."

"Look at the book every day, and when it shows you something, I want you to come and have tea with me again. Will you do that?"

Maggie nodded. "Thank you, Lily Rose," she said, rising from the table, "I mean, seriously. Thank you."

Lily Rose smiled, her beautiful dark skin crinkling up around her eyes. "Now don't you worry. When one person helps another, the helper often gets even more benefit than the helpee. But you'll get to that chapter soon enough!"

As Maggie stepped out onto Lily Rose's front porch, she felt more at peace and more alive than she had since—since she could remember.

More aware, more alert. It was still only noon, and she supposed it was the chill in the air that made her feel so awake, so vibrant, and somehow much more *real*. The heavy book tucked securely in the crook of her arm seemed to give her weight, to anchor her to the earth.

Again she felt the crown, as if it were still there, sitting heavily on her head, pressing against her brain, but it was no longer creepy and mysterious. It was actually starting to feel . . . pleasant.

The ghost crown.

As she hurried up the sidewalk toward her car, eager to get out of the Flats, she thought about what Lily Rose had told her. Some people could escape their destiny, then sprout wings, and soar above and beyond it. Maggie wasn't sure if that was true or not, but she desperately wanted to try.

෯

Aimee woke on Sunday around noon and she knew exactly what she was going to do. It was as if someone had whispered the plan to her in her sleep. On her way to her bathroom, she spotted two granola bars and a note on the floor near her door, as if they had been shoved underneath it from the outside. The note read:

> Aimee,
>
> Rick's arm is still bothering him so I'm taking him to the hospital in Topeka. We'll be back for dinner and if you behave yourself we can go out to Spinnacle for a nice family meal. Still waiting for a call back from Montana.
>
> DAD

Aimee laughed bitterly, wadded the note up, and tossed it across the room. She tried the doorknob, but, as she had guessed, it was locked. She rattled it once, furiously, and then struck the door hard with the bottom of her fist. There was a hollow thud and her hand throbbed, but the door was undamaged.

All the time, all the effort she'd put in at Mountain High Academy trying to find a way to deal with the horror of watching Tyler die, and then trying to get over her subsequent panic attacks—and now her father had locked her in her own room. Didn't he know that was about the cruelest thing you could do to a person with anxiety problems?

He knew, she thought; he just didn't care. He would do anything to keep her from seeing Raphael, even if it made her go completely crazy.

Crazy. The word snapped her back to her first night in Mountain High Academy. The place was nestled in the mountains, designed to look like a French chateau, but it reminded Aimee of the hotel in *The Shining*, and she tried to escape the first chance she got. Big mistake. They had caught her before she got outside the gates.

She had screamed as two huge orderlies held her arms while another tried to put the straitjacket on her, treating her like the insane person they thought she was, pinning her down to the cold tile floor. A woman in a pantsuit came forward with a hypodermic needle that looked at least six inches long. Eventually they got the straitjacket on her, and they posted a young nurse at her bedside to watch her all night.

And now, it was as if something—some malevolent energy—was draining the air from the room. And if she didn't get out of there soon, she really would go insane and break everything in sight, until she smashed her way out. Slowly she paced back and forth, calming herself as her counselor had taught her. When the panic started to subside she went into the bathroom to brush her teeth. As she squirted the paste onto her toothbrush, she forced herself to think calmly and logically about her situation. She had come too far, she had fought too hard, to let her dear old dad push her back into that nightmare.

Locking her in her room was just one more example of how her father dealt with the world. He controlled his businesses, he controlled the city council, the mayor, the police—he controlled the whole town. And he ruled with fear. Everyone in town did exactly what Jack Banfield wanted because they were afraid of what might happen if they didn't. They could get fired, arrested, or run out of town. Aimee knew all this, because her dad bragged about it. Winning at any cost was his prime objective. When people were afraid, he boasted, everything fell into place for him to get what he wanted.

"But I'm not going to be afraid," she said to her reflection in the mirror. "Not anymore."

Back in her bedroom, she pulled on her heavy parka, slid carefully out her bedroom window, walked across the roof of her porch, and climbed down the trellis. She knew it would never occur to her dad that she would dare do such a thing. He had no idea how many times she'd done it in the past to meet Tyler.

Instead of going down the driveway in front of the house, she went to the back and pulled a lawn chair over to the back fence so she could climb over it to the service road that ran behind the property. Then she hiked down to Hilltop Haven's back entrance, where no security guards were stationed, and left by the pedestrian gate.

Her plan was simple. She was going to find Raphael and be with him every minute that she possibly could, until her father shipped her to Montana or did whatever he was going to do.

She hurried on, skirting around downtown Middleburg, staying away from the main roads and close to the forest. In twenty minutes, she'd be in the Flats.

❧

By two in the afternoon on Sunday, Emory and his family were settled into their makeshift home, and Raphael was able to call a Flatliners meeting inside one of the bays of the body shop. A calendar featuring a bikini-clad woman leaning on the hood of a car hung above a cluttered old desk in one corner, next to a map of Middleburg. The place was littered with tools and smelled of grease. The big bay door was open, letting in the occasional gust of cold air and an influx of pale, wintery light, but it was still warmer than being out in the open.

"All right," Raphael said to his crew. "We have a problem here. We're not going to stand by while Emory and his family lose their home. And I'm afraid they're not the only ones."

"Yeah," Benji piped up. "When I told my mom what was happening, she said the people in the building next door to us got eviction notices, too."

"I saw one on the door of the little house across the street from us," Josh said.

Raphael and Nass exchanged a glance. "Nass and his family got one," Raphael said gravely. "And they just moved here a couple of months ago."

"We gotta hit 'em back!" Benji said.

Raphael nodded, "Right. But first we have to find out what's going on, and we have to know who to hit. They're not just targeting Flatliner families, so this isn't a gang thing."

"How can they just throw people out on the streets like that?" Beet asked.

Raph sighed. "I read Emory's lease. There's a clause giving the landlord the option to end the lease any time with a thirty-day notice. Although I'm sure that's not legal."

He went to the map and pointed to the Flats. "Whatever's going on, it's happening building by building. I want all of you to keep an eye out for anything weird going on in the Flats. Ask your neighbors if they've heard or seen anything. Nass, Emory's building is across from yours, so I want you to keep an eye on it."

"For what exactly?" asked Nass.

"For anything you've never seen before—anything that doesn't belong."

Josh spoke up. "I've seen something. Couple of trucks parked in front of that old abandoned boarding house on the corner of my block about a week ago. Logo on the truck was some kind of demolition service out of Topeka."

"What's unusual about that?" asked Benji. "That place has been empty for years, so they're tearing it down."

"Yeah," Raph said. "But for what? What are they going to put there? Who in his right mind would build anything in the Flats? There's something going on. I *feel* it. And that hole in the gym—there's a tunnel on one end of it—and I want to know who made it and why. I want to see where it goes."

Nass cleared his throat and gestured toward the open bay door. Raphael was amazed to find Aimee there, in jeans, running shoes, and a thick, light blue parka with a fur-lined hood, smiling at him.

"Hi. Hope I'm not interrupting," she said.

"It's okay," he said. "We were just finishing," he turned back to his gang brothers, who all stood there, amused, waiting to see what would happen. "Remember, keep your eyes open," he said.

In keeping with their Wu-de code of conduct, Raphael gave them a small bow, which they returned, signaling that the meeting was adjourned.

Benji glanced from Aimee back to Raphael, "You two want us to give you some privacy?" he teased with a theatrical wink.

"Forget you guys," said Raphael. He zipped up his jacket, grabbed Aimee's hand, and led her out to the front of the shop.

"This is a nice surprise," he said, smiling at her. "I thought you were grounded."

"I am. Forever. My dad is threatening to send me back to school in Montana."

Her words made Raphael feel like he'd just been hit in the chest with a brick. "When?"

"I don't know. He took my cell phone last night and locked me in my room this morning. I climbed out the window."

"You sure that was a good idea?"

"I could be on the next flight out of here, Raphael. I had to see you."

He knew they should be careful, even with their relationship now out in the open, but when she looked up at him with such longing he forgot about being careful. He put his arms around her, drew her close, and kissed her, long and slow. When it was over, she smiled at him.

"Until I have to go I'm spending every minute with you," she declared.

Raphael tried to smile and he mostly succeeded, but the thought of losing Aimee filled him with a sorrow that made his soul ache.

෨

Zhai watched from the window of his father's second-floor library as, below, the two Chinese strangers walked slowly down the walkway, toward the long white Cadillac that waited at the curb for them. The taller man went to the driver's side. He opened the door and glanced up at the house, perhaps even at Zhai, and then he got into the car and closed the door. As they pulled away, Zhai sat down heavily in a chair near the window, his knees suddenly weak.

He had seen those men before, he was certain of it. But he couldn't remember where or when. And why did the sight of them fill him with such foreboding? He'd begun having these feelings . . . intuitions . . . during the Halloween battle, and they had grown stronger every day since. As much as he tried to ignore them, he could not deny that they heralded some real event—and somehow, he was sure these men were a part of it. He had to find out what was going on.

Zhai stood, crossed the hall, and went to the door of his father's study. He could hear his father and Lotus inside, behind the thick cherrywood door, yelling at each other in Chinese, which worried Zhai. In all the years they'd been married, he'd never heard them exchange anything more spirited than a few impatient words. This sounded like an all-out battle. He knew it would be rude (and perhaps imprudent) to interrupt them, but he had a deep, driving need to learn the truth. He knocked on the door. Instantly, the shouting stopped.

"Yes?" Lotus said, the tension in her voice suddenly replaced with melodic courtesy.

"I'd like to speak with my father, please."

There was a moment of silence behind the door, followed by a few softly spoken words, then the sound of footsteps. Lotus emerged from the room, slipped past Zhai without so much as glancing at him, and departed down the stairs.

"May I come in?" Zhai asked politely, observing his father's need for respect. Cheung Shao nodded and looked away.

Zhai crossed the threshold and closed the door behind him. Instead of his usual place behind the desk, his dad occupied a brown leather loveseat. His normally erect posture had deflated, and as Zhai drew near, he was dismayed to find his father looking older, wearier than he had ever seen him.

"Please," his father said, and gestured for Zhai to sit on the couch next to him.

Zhai sat, folded his hands in his lap, and looked down at them, wondering where to begin. For some reason, the prospect of discussing the two strangers seemed frightening. But some force—Shen, perhaps, compelled him. There was nothing to do but be direct.

"Those two visitors," Zhai said. "I've seen them before. Who are they?"

His dad looked at him for a moment, studying him, and then again averted his eyes.

"Ah . . . old business associates," he said softly, almost to himself. "From China."

"How do I know them, Father?" Zhai asked. "Where have I seen them? Have they ever come to the house before?"

Cheung Shao shook his head. "No. Not until now."

"Then when did I see them?"

His dad looked at him again, his expression resolute, as always, giving nothing away. "You don't remember?" he asked. There was a strange, almost hopeful tone in his voice.

"No," Zhai said.

His father exhaled, and the worry in his eyes seemed to abate a little. He seemed relieved. "They helped us when we came here," he said. "To America."

"On the boat?"

His father nodded. Zhai knew the story: they had come over from China on some sort of cargo ship when he was about three years old, shortly after his mother died, but he didn't remember the journey.

"So they're just business associates?"

His father nodded again.

"How long will they be in town?"

Cheung Shao rose and went to the bar. He poured some water into a tall crystal glass and drank half of it down before he answered. "I don't know. They're working on a project."

"What kind of project?"

Zhai's father looked at him curiously. "You've never shown such an interest in my business dealings before," he said. "Why now? We've had many visitors in this house, Zhai. These are just two more."

But it wasn't that simple, Zhai knew. The two strangers made his father nervous and his stepmother angry. For the first time in his life, Zhai knew his dad was hiding something from him.

"I just feel like . . . there's something about them I should remember," Zhai said.

Cheung looked at Zhai for a long moment and then gave what Zhai thought was a forced chuckle. "Forget them. They are not important."

Cheung Shao went back to his desk and Zhai knew the conversation was over, but as Zhai walked out of the office and down the hallway, he replayed it in his mind. In his room, he closed the door and immediately sat down cross-legged on the rug near the window. Closing his eyes, he took seven deep, slow breaths and allowed himself to sink into meditation. If his father wouldn't reveal the truth about those two mysterious men, perhaps Shen would.

CHAPTER 7

RAPHAEL STOOD WITH AIMEE OUTSIDE the entrance to the Middleburg High School gymnasium. There was yellow police tape blocking the doors. Above, the gray sky cast a dreary pallor over the world. He pulled a flashlight from his backpack.

"You all right?" he asked. "You really don't have to do this, you know."

It was the third time he'd made that offer since she'd met him at the auto body shop, and each time she'd declined. When she asked him what he was planning to do today, he should have said something a little safer—folding laundry, maybe, or hanging out at Rack 'Em. But the truth was, he was planning to investigate the hole beneath the school, and as soon as he mentioned it to Aimee, she had insisted on coming, too.

"No—I'm going with you," she said again, squeezing his hand. "I'm just wondering how we're going to get in."

He laughed. "You really don't have a clue, do you?"

"About what?"

It was one of the reasons he loved her. She wasn't all tough and edgy like the Flats girls. She was innocent. Soft. He leaned down and kissed her velvety cheek. "About what it's like to be a Flat's rat."

He led her around to the back of the building to a little trailer that served as the janitor's office, explaining that the first time he got detention at Middleburg High, he'd been assigned to help old Mr. Simmons mop the hallways. There was a row of potted plants along the front of the trailer, and Raphael went to the one on the far end and pulled the fake plant out of its pot and withdrew the key that was under it.

"Come on." He grabbed her hand and looked around to make sure they were alone. Then he led her back to the door to the janitor's office, opened it, and reached inside for the master key that would unlock the gymnasium. "Old Sims keeps his key ring hanging right next to the door," he explained.

When they were inside the school, Raphael switched on the flashlight, holding it low and keeping it pointed down until they got through the lobby and into the main arena. The gym was just as they'd left it last night. He guessed that no one would clean it up until the police, school board, and city fathers were done with their investigation into what had caused the cave-in. Raph wondered if his old nemesis Detective Zalewski would be on the case.

The hole was roped off, but he ducked under the police tape and held it up for Aimee. Together, they made their way around the rim of the crater to a spot where the rubble made a natural ramp to the bottom and carefully climbed down. They didn't waste much time looking at what the cops had already trampled all over. It was a hole, nothing more, and all that was in it was dirt and clay and pebbles, and the collapsed cinderblock of the wall. But that wasn't what interested Raphael. He shone the light around, and then down to the end, where the hole opened into a passageway.

"Look," he said. "It's dry, so it's not a sewer or a storm drain. And the walls are just dirt. Someone dug a tunnel under here."

"Why would they?"

"I don't know—but I'd sure like to know where it leads. I mean, what if it isn't only under the school? What if it's under the whole town? Come on—let's see how far it goes."

Cautiously, they edged their way into the tunnel, and Raphael swept the flashlight beam from side to side. It was square, probably carved out by some tunnel-boring machine with cutter heads that could chew through rock and deposit the gravel directly into a holding bin. In the seventh grade, Raphael had done a report about Middleburg's mining past, when that kind of machine was used. But this wasn't some old abandoned mine shaft; it still smelled of freshly dug earth.

The passage headed away from the gymnasium toward the main building. At first they saw rocky, soil walls shored up with logs, but soon the walls were sturdier, carved out of solid granite, the floor littered with loose gravel. In the beam of his flashlight they saw odd objects scattered here and there, probably dropped through carelessness, he thought. There was a shovel, a forgotten work light hanging from a bracket overhead, some cigarette butts, candy and sandwich wrappers, and soda and beer cans. In some places the air was okay; in others, it reeked of stale tobacco and sweat.

Several minutes passed and he realized he and Aimee were no longer beneath Middleburg High. The tunnel stretched out before them as far as his light could reach. It was an amazing feeling—the two of them together in the dark, exploring. Scarred walls scrolled along on either side of them, but they didn't pause to look. They kept on walking, holding hands, talking quietly. He had no sense of dread in this tunnel, as he'd had in the North Tunnel on Halloween night, just curiosity. But Aimee suddenly grew quiet.

"You okay?" he asked, stopping for a minute to put his arms around her. "You want to go back?"

"No. I'm good. It's just that . . . "

She hesitated, a frown crossing her lovely face.

"What?" he said gently.

He waited, and after a moment she said, "I never told you about the night Tyler died."

"No."

"It was just outside the North tunnel," she said quietly, her voice echoing eerily through the black catacomb. "The Middleburg Monster killed him. I . . . I saw it. That's why everyone thinks I'm crazy. But I'm not. You probably think so too. It does sound insane when I say it out loud, even to me."

"Not to me. I saw it when I was looking for you and Oberon."

"You did?" Aimee asked, clearly surprised. "You never told me that."

He sighed as the reality of their situation hit him again. "It's not like we've really been able to talk much, you know. But yeah—big, black, shadowy snake-worm-centipede thing with three-foot-long fangs?"

"Right, exactly!"

"Yeah. I hate that thing. I rode on its back and it almost ate me."

"So . . . you don't think I'm crazy?" Even in the darkness, Aimee's eyes shone with a hopeful light.

"Only about me," he said with a grin. Then he added more seriously, "I don't think you're crazy, Aimee. I never did."

She moved into his arms and hugged him. "Thank you," she whispered, her face pressed against his coat.

As he returned her embrace, his eyes traced vague outlines of the shadows around them; talking about the monster had put him on edge.

They kept on walking, moving from solid granite walls to log-reinforced dirt and rock and then sandstone, until Raphael estimated, from the direction they were traveling and the distance they'd gone, that they had probably passed Golden Avenue and were approaching the edge of town, near the locomotive graveyard.

Then the tunnel they were in opened into a huge, dark, cavernous space. They both recognized it: the North Tunnel.

"This is so weird," he whispered to himself. "What *is it*? What's it for?"

"Do you want to keep going?" she asked tentatively, sounding a little afraid.

"No. Not today. Let's get out of here." He didn't have to remind her what they'd gone through in the tunnels, not so long ago, when Oberon had dragged Aimee off into some strange, foreign world where he intended to keep her. Raph didn't want to do *that* again.

"We'll come back tomorrow," he said. "Bring reinforcements and more flashlights."

That's when they heard it.

*"Aimee . . . "*Faintly. Whispering. And again, *"Aimee. . ."*

Aimee stopped walking. "Raphael—that's my mom!"

Raphael froze in place too, listening. "Are you sure it's her? You told me Oberon tricked you before, right?"

"But Oberon's gone," she said. "Why would I hear her voice if she's not down here somewhere? You heard it, right?"

"I heard it. But—"

"Aimeeeee . . . " Plaintive. Sad.

"Raphael, we have to look." Aimee's eyes filled with emotion. "What if it is her? What if she's down here?"

Raphael studied her for a moment. He would much rather come back tomorrow with lots of reinforcements, more flashlights, and a longer stretch of daylight ahead of them, but he knew Aimee was right. If there was even the slightest chance her mom was down there, they couldn't just walk away and leave her.

"All right," he said. "But stay behind me—and stay close."

And he led the way forward. Ahead, somewhere in the dark, was the big X where the two railroad tracks crossed, and beneath it, the mysterious Wheel of Illusion.

⋙⋘

"Mom?" Aimee called again.

Nothing.

But she had heard her mother's voice in this tunnel, the same as she'd heard it before, when Oberon had abducted her.

And it was real.

Her mother was close.

She tried to clear her mind of everything else. She squeezed her eyes shut, concentrating until she had a picture of her mom in her head, and then she held on to the image. She saw her mother as she'd looked when Aimee was getting on the plane to go to Montana, her face streaked with tears, waving good-bye. The vision made her heart ache, but she held on to it anyway.

"Mom?" she called hopefully. Nothing.

Together, she and Raphael pressed on.

"We're close to the X where the tracks cross," she said. "If we use the Wheel of Illusion, I know we can find her. She's close—I can feel it."

Already she could make out the faint amber glow that she knew illuminated the Wheel's control panel. In just minutes, they found it—the site of the old underground roundhouse where, back in the day, railroad workers could switch locomotives to pull a different load, or turn them around to go back the way they came. But this was no ordinary roundhouse, she knew. It was the Wheel of Illusion, a massive piece of ancient machinery filled with some mysterious power that allowed its user to travel through time. The last time she was here, Raphael used the Wheel to bring her back from the terrifying jungle world that Oberon had dragged her into. She could feel the wheel's energy all around her now, throbbing, humming, singing through every cell of her body and making the little hairs on her arms stand on end.

Aimee put one hand on the control panel's heavy, brass lever and looked back at Raphael. He groaned, and she could see the worry on his face.

"It might be dangerous, Aimee," he said. "Look, I'll go. You wait here and—"

"I'm going," she said, giving him her best determined face. There was no way she was staying behind.

"Okay," Raphael relented, after a moment. "But we have to be careful. And if wherever we wind up seems dangerous, we'll leave and get help. Deal?"

"Deal," she agreed, her tension growing.

He dug into his pocket and pulled out Lily Rose's gold pocket watch. "I tried to return this to her a few days after we used it to get home from Oberon's alternate world," he told Aimee. "You know what she said?"

"What?"

"She said, 'It doesn't just tell time, Raphael—it tells time what to do,' and she made me keep it. It shouldn't surprise me that she'd know we might need it again. Are you ready?"

Aimee nodded, and Raphael carefully fitted the watch into the face of the control panel as he did the first time he'd used the wheel.

"Okay, Aimee—try to get a good image of your mom in your mind," he said. "Then pull the lever."

Aimee took a deep breath, closed her eyes, and thought of her mom puttering around in the kitchen, singing softly to herself. *Take me to her*, she thought and she pulled the lever.

There was a heavy metallic clinking sound and, just as it did the last time they used it, the wheel rumbled to life. Massive machinery groaned and clacked beneath their feet. Then the huge turntable beneath them began to rotate, slowly at first and then faster and faster.

The wheel was going at super speed now, and Aimee was dizzy, disoriented. It felt like she was free-falling, plummeting to her death. The image of her mother fled from her mind as, panicked, she opened her eyes and looked up, expecting to see herself tumbling downward, away from the tracks. Instead, she saw only the stark, black dome above them. Her hand felt numb from the vibration, but she managed to release the lever. It swung upward, clicked into place, and the massive, unseen machinery ground to a halt. The wheel beneath them slowed and stopped. But she couldn't quite shake that terrifying, plummeting feeling.

"We're here," she whispered. Where ever *here* was . . .

෨

As soon as the tunnel exit came into view, Raphael knew something was very wrong. It was dreary when they'd entered the school to explore the tunnel, but the light that came through the great, arched exit now was even dimmer, and it was tinted with the ghostly reddish brown of a sepia photograph. Wind howled across the opening in a mournful, endless moan.

Instinctively, Raphael pulled Aimee close for a moment as he shut off the flashlight. He stuck it in his backpack and then they walked several yards up the tracks before they stopped, squinting into the lashing wind at the strange, unfamiliar world before them.

Everything was gone. There were no trees, no bushes—not even a single blade of grass. The earth was a sickly rust color, and so parched it was riddled with deep cracks. The dark clouds of swirling, blowing dust swept across the sky, behind which the sun hung, crimson and small, no larger, brighter or warmer than a stoplight. To Raphael, the landscape looked exactly like the NASA rover's pictures of the surface of Mars that he'd seen online. But this was no alien planet; the railroad tracks on which they stood stretched out across a barren plain all the way to the horizon.

"This doesn't look anything like Oberon's kingdom," Aimee said. "At least, not the part we saw."

Raphael led her out of the tunnel, into the open. The wind hit them so hard Raphael had to widen his stance to keep from falling over, and Aimee was having trouble staying on her feet. Even wearing his parka, he shivered in the frigid air. It had to be at least twenty degrees colder than it was when they'd entered the tunnel. Already, his nose and cheeks were aching from the harsh wind. He led Aimee a few more steps into the open and then looked around, taking in the lay of the land.

"What is this place?" Aimee asked.

Raphael stared into the distance, at a hill. A familiar hill.

"Middleburg," he said, his voice almost lost in the wind. He pointed to the hill and saw recognition dawn in Aimee's eyes, too. Perhaps a half a mile away was the rise on which Hilltop Haven normally sat. Although the shape and location were exactly the same as the Hilltop Haven they knew, there were no more beautiful mansions. The structure that now sat upon the hill looked more than anything like a pile of trash, but Raphael could tell that there was an order to the seemingly jumbled pieces of wood and metal. It was a fence, a battlement. Some kind of a fort.

Staring up at it and squinting into the icy gale, he took a few steps off the track and almost tripped on something. Looking down, he saw part of an old weathered aluminum can protruding from the hard soil. He loosened it with the toe of his shoe and then pulled it out. The green paint had almost faded to nothing, but he could still make out the word *Sprite* written across it. He glanced at Aimee.

"You think this is really Middleburg?" she asked.

"Or at least, it used to be."

Fighting through the wind, she bent next to him and pulled something else up from the soil. It looked like a shard of smooth, white pottery with a hole in it. Maybe, he thought, it had been part of a large, round jug for holding liquids.

She turned it over in her hands. "What do you think it was?" she asked.

Raphael saw another shard sitting nearby and picked it up. It fit with the first shard like a puzzle piece and what it formed made Raphael feel suddenly sick.

"A skull," Aimee whispered. She dropped the pieces and wiped her hands on her jeans just as a sudden scream pierced the air, answered shortly by another, more distant call. The eerie shriek seemed distorted in the blasting wind.

Raphael looked around. He saw nothing—no one—that could have made that unearthly sound. He looked up at the ramshackle fort on the hilltop, and he and Aimee headed in that direction, through what he thought had to be hurricane-force wind, with gusts so strong they had to lean forward at a forty-five degree angle just to stay upright. In the cold, even with his hands in his pockets, Raphael's fingers were entirely numb.

They walked for perhaps five minutes without talking; there was no sound except for the howl of the wind and the faint scuff of their feet on the dead earth.

"What do you think this is?" Aimee shouted over the gale, breaking the silence. "Some kind of parallel dimension?"

"Yeah—maybe," he said. "The Magician told us that time is an illusion, that all time exists at once, but we're able to perceive only the present. I think the Wheel somehow breaks down the illusion that separates different times, allowing us to travel between them, from the present to the past or the future."

"So that last time we used the Wheel, when we fought Oberon?"

"The distant past, I think."

"And this is the future?" she asked sadly.

Raphael nodded. "I think so."

To their right, the rusted, skeletal frame of an old car was half buried in the earth. It looked like a weird piece of modern art.

"What do you think happened?" Aimee asked, "Nuclear war? An asteroid strike? Maybe overpopulation created some kind of environmental disaster?"

"Looks to me like all of the above."

Suddenly, he put a hand on Aimee's shoulder, and they stopped walking. He pointed ahead. Three triangular shapes were coming toward them across the barren landscape, from the direction of the fort, moving fast.

"Down," Raphael said, and he pulled Aimee with him to the ground.

"What the heck are those things?" she asked.

"Don't know. But whatever they are, they're heading right for us. Come on."

They hurried back to the rusted car frame and ducked behind it. When he looked out again, he could see that the brown triangles were much closer now. At their current speed, they would arrive in a matter of seconds.

He gently pushed Aimee back against the car. "Crouch here, okay?" he said. "I need you to stay safe until I find out what we're dealing with." She gave him a quick kiss and took cover beneath the rusty car frame.

Raphael looked out again, just as the first of the three triangles shot past. It was a windsurfer that somebody had put together, Frankenstein-like, from an array of scrap wood and metal, with a sail made of what looked like a multitude of filthy rags stitched together. But that wasn't what worried Raph: it was the creature riding it.

It looked like a man, slightly taller than average and so sickeningly skinny that it was just a skeleton with skin stretched over it. A few long, wispy hairs clung to its otherwise bare scalp. It was almost naked save for an oily-looking leather loincloth, and its skin was so pale it was almost blue. It shrieked, the piercing sound of a baby in pain, showing as it did it a mouth full of sharp, elongated teeth. To Raphael, it looked kind of like Golem from *Lord of the Rings*—Golem, in desperate need of a suntan.

The other two triangles shot past too, moving at incredible speeds. As Raphael watched, all three swung around to make another pass, and he could see wicked-looking metal weapons in the hands of the riders.

"Stay here, Aimee," he said. She nodded, and he stepped away from the car.

The first sail-rider raced toward him, his windsurfer board skittering smoothly across the blasted earth.

"Hey!" Raphael shouted. "We don't want to hurt you. We're looking for someone."

The rider hissed, adjusted his sail, and shot forward. He was upon Raphael instantly, lashing out with some kind of crude saber as he ripped past. Raphael managed to sidestep the blow, but the blade slashed his jacket open in an explosion of feathers.

"This coat was my *dad's*!" he shouted, furious. He dove and rolled just in time to dodge the second attacker. The third caught a big gust of wind and jumped, pulling his desert-skimmer into the air and attacking Raphael from above.

Raphael deflected the attack, slapping the flat of the blade away just in time. It sliced so close to his face he could feel the stirring of air on his skin. He had no time to regroup; the first surfer had already turned and was heading back to make another pass.

Raphael looked around for something to use as a weapon. There was nothing but dirt and large, half-buried stones. Not so much as a stick anywhere.

Breathe, Raphael told himself, *focus. Harness the Shen.*

But his body was so clenched up with the cold that he couldn't relax, and before he could even draw one deep breath, the next sail-rider was on him, hacking at him as he sped by. Raph felt a sharp sting in his shoulder and glanced down to see a small gash, just beginning to bleed.

"Raphael!" Aimee called.

"I'm fine!" he shouted. "Stay there."

But it was too late. She had already emerged from beneath the car frame and was running toward him. One of their attackers saw her, swung his sail around and shot toward her. She tried to change her direction to avoid him, but he kept coming, swinging something over his head. It was a bola, Raph realized, a cord with a rock tied to both ends. He threw it at Aimee, and it wrapped around her legs in mid-run, tripping her and sending her tumbling.

Raphael ran toward Aimee but at that moment another sail-rider swooped in. Raph tried to sweep him off his board with a leg kick, but the rider hopped over his attack and struck back, slashing Raphael's coat once more. The third rider was close behind, but this time Shen responded when he called on the power. It sizzled through every nerve in his body and exploded from his outstretched hand. The scorching blast of lightning knocked Raphael's enemy from his sailboard and sent him sprawling to the dirt. Instantly, Raphael was on him. The hideous maggot of a man squirmed violently beneath Raphael, struggling with super strength to shove Raphael off him, but Raph concentrated all his energy on his enemy's wrist, on the hand that held the weapon. First he pinned it, then twisted it. The creature growled and chomped at him, trying to bite him with those creepy, sharp teeth, but Raphael kept twisting and finally made him let go of the weapon. The rider gave a shout of pain as Raph seized the weapon and brought the handle of it down on his head three times, knocking him out cold. The weapon, something like a crude sword, was an oddly shaped piece of rusted metal. It looked like a salvaged piece of machinery someone had sharpened on a rock, with a grip that was nothing more than a length of dirty fabric wrapped around bare metal, but it would have to do.

The other rider was sailing in for another pass. Calmly, Raphael watched and waited as he approached. At just the right moment, he feigned a high strike then quickly crouched and chopped at his enemy's legs, catching him solidly in the back of one knee. The man-thing shouted pitifully and crumpled, falling face first to writhe on the hard earth. His board stayed upright and shot across the empty desert for about fifty yards before it finally hit a rock and tipped over.

Raphael looked around for Aimee. He didn't see her anywhere.

Just when his concern was becoming desperation, he spotted it: the triangle of a sail, far away now, and moving fast, toward the fortress on the hill.

"Crap," Raphael murmured.

As fast as he could, he stooped over the windsurfer belonging to the rider he'd knocked out and pulled it upright. The raging wind almost jerked it away from him.

He'd skateboarded for a while in Middle School, until kung fu had become more important to him. And he'd never sailed or surfed in his life.

I'd better learn fast, he thought, watching his enemy's windsurfer fading into the distance, taking Aimee with it.

He stepped onto the board. Instantly, the wind gusted and blew him over. He righted himself and tried again, pulling back against the wind this time, and in a moment he was moving fast, skimming across the desert floor, toward Aimee.

CHAPTER 8

AIMEE FOUGHT WITH ALL HER STRENGTH until her muscles ached, but escape just wasn't going to happen with the bola wrapped tightly around her legs. They were gliding over the desert on some kind of sail-sand-surfer thing, and the man (if that's what it was) was holding her firmly in front of him. He had tied her hands with a strip of leather, and one of his arms was clamped around her neck in a fierce headlock. She never would have guessed such a skeletal limb could be so strong, but it felt like a steel band; no way could she break a grip like that. With his other hand, the pale creature steered his sailboard expertly across the flat, empty land, toward the hilltop fortress.

Aimee managed to look back over his shoulder twice, hoping to see Raphael in pursuit, but there was nothing behind them but the howling wind, blowing furiously in a gritty, brown tempest. The thought that one of the other pale riders got Raphael was too horrible to contemplate. She tried to look back a third time, and the creature's breath on her face was so rancid she had to turn away—but not before she saw him grin and run his tongue over his sharp teeth. She couldn't tell if he was hungry or if it was some kind of invitation to hook up. His voice raspy and hollow, he whispered in her ear as he pulled her more tightly against his scrawny chest.

"Tahw-wheeeeeat," the vile thing rumbled.

Aimee struggled more fiercely against him. His grip on her neck tightened.

"Towah-*eeeeeit*," the creature wheezed, more insistently, and suddenly she felt a spark of pain on the top of one ear.

"Ow!" Angrily, she jerked her head away. The skeleton thing grinned at her, blood glistening on its sharp front teeth.

"To *eeeeat*," he said again and grinned.

Aimee shuddered as images of this pale, skinny thing ripping her apart with its sharp teeth and devouring her one limb at a time crowded in. She shook her head, banishing the vision—and then, chaos erupted.

Something slammed into the board, sending it careening to one side. It tipped over and Aimee tumbled across the hard sand and skidded to a stop a few yards away. And then she was on her back, staring up at the brown, dust-choked sky. From behind her came the sound of clashing weapons, and she turned to see Raphael and her captor dueling with primitive, roughly made swords.

She sat up, pulled her wrists out of her now-loosened bindings and then started unwinding the bola from around her ankles, keeping an eye on the battle. The lanky, pale warrior was an inch or so taller than Raphael and moving with practiced precision as he swung his scythe-like blade at Raphael. Raph easily parried the strike and countered, slashing his enemy's shoulder, which only made the creature more furious. It lashed out at Raphael, swinging hard—too hard. Raphael moved slightly, letting the blade go past him as his enemy followed through, its arm crossing over its body. Raph quickly stepped forward and pinned its arm against its chest with one hand. With the other, he swung his weapon at the creature's neck in a decisive blow. When Aimee saw the blood start to spread across its pale chest, she looked away.

They were now at the foot of the hill; the fort was only a few hundred yards away. *My mom could be in there*, she thought. *In two minutes, we could be together again.*

And she heard it again. "*Aimee . . .*"

Sad. Afraid. Pleading. And it was coming from the direction of the garbage-dump fort. She picked up the bola—though she had no idea how to use it—and with renewed energy, she charged up the hill. Something was pulling her forward. Something that was making her unafraid.

Raphael's voice came from behind her, faint in the roar of the wind. "Aimee, wait! Aimee!"

She heard his footsteps coming up behind her, but she could see a break in the fortress wall. She headed for it, slipping on the powdery earth and then regaining her footing and charging onward. At last, she reached the top of the hill and burst through the opening in the fortress wall.

Instantly Raphael was next to her, breathing hard, his weapon raised to protect her from whatever enemies were lying in wait. But there were none. Aimee moved forward, making a slow circuit around the inside of the fortress wall. Bones littered the ground all around them: small bones, from the rodents that the skeleton-men probably ate, and larger bones that looked frighteningly human. A number of human skulls lay around too, half-buried in the soil. *They look like stepping stones*, Aimee thought, *from some horrific fairy tale.*

On one side of the fort, a lean-to structure stood erratically against one wall. Its roof was a cracked, plastic Shell gas station sign. Together, Raph and Aimee peered inside. There were a few soiled rags, some sharpened sticks, and more bones. A ring of stones surrounded a pit of dark ashes, but it looked to Aimee as if there hadn't been a fire there in a long time. Unless the men wanted to start tearing down their fort, there was nothing to burn—at least nothing she could see on this devastated landscape. An ancient-looking M-16 assault rifle leaned against one wall, but it was covered in dust, its barrel bent. It was clearly unusable. The smell inside the lean-to was bad—like rotten meat marinated in sweat, and Aimee couldn't stay in there for long. Raphael followed her back out into the icy wind.

"She's not here," Aimee said, her voice barely audible over the gale. Raphael put an arm around her. "It's okay," she continued. "I'm glad she wasn't in this place, with *them*. But I heard her voice. You did too."

He nodded.

If she's not here, then where is she? The question echoed through Aimee's mind. "If Oberon brought her through the Wheel, she could be lost in some other time," she said.

"Or even some other dimension," Raphael said gently. "We'll figure it out, I promise. But for now, let's get out of here. There might be more of them, and we don't know when they'll be back."

She took Raphael's hand and together, they walked out of the fortress. As they made their way down the slippery hillside, she asked, "What do you think happened—to make the world like this?"

Raphael only shook his head. "It could have been anything," he said. "Some natural disaster. An asteroid. But . . . I think it was war."

"If this is the supposed to be the future, do you think it has to turn out this way, or can we change it?"

"I sure hope we can change it," he said.

He picked up the windsurfer from where it lay tipped over on the desert floor and gestured for Aimee to get on it with him. A second later, they were skimming across the cracked, ruined ground at an unbelievable speed. They made it back to the tunnel mound in what seemed to Aimee like no more than two minutes.

As they headed up the tracks, into the mouth of the tunnel, Aimee hazarded one more glance over her shoulder and noticed something she hadn't seen when they first arrived. What she had taken for a boulder was in fact the top of a tank turret, almost completely buried in the ground.

"It *was* a war," she said.

"Hmm?" Raphael asked. He was digging through his backpack, looking for the flashlight.

"Nothing," Aimee said. "Let's get out of here. This time sucks."

☙

Aimee experienced a barrage of conflicting emotions on her walk back to Hilltop Haven. She was relieved and disappointed that they hadn't found her mother in that weird alien world, but she still worried that wherever her mom was, she might be in terrible danger. If Raphael was right about the Wheel, and about traveling through time, then her mom could be trapped in one of any number of alternate worlds.

But knowing that Raphael loved her and that he was willing to fight anyone or anything to keep her safe was a feeling Aimee had never experienced, and it filled her with a giddy, feverish warmth. That made the thought of losing him even harder to bear.

He was always thinking of her best interest, too. Though she'd insisted on staying with him in the Flats until her dad showed up and dragged her onto the Montana-bound plane, Raph had convinced her to go home.

"It'll work out somehow," he'd assured her as they walked out of the tunnels together, hand-in-hand. "But if you run away with me now, your dad is going to find you, and he might do something even worse than send you to Montana. I can't let that happen, Aimee. I think you'd better go back, at least for tonight, until we can come up with a better plan."

She protested at first. Deep down she knew he was right, but that didn't make the idea of leaving him any easier to stomach.

By the time she got back to Hilltop Haven, her dad would probably have the plane ticket all lined up to send her back to Mountain High Academy—tonight, for all she knew. She spent the rest of her walk concocting an elaborate escape plan. If her dad insisted on sending her away again, then fine, she would leave. But she wouldn't go to Montana. She'd go someplace her dad would never find her—and somehow, she'd find a way to take Raphael with her.

As she came around a row of bushes, she saw her dad's car pulling into the driveway. She ducked back behind a hedge, praying he hadn't spotted her.

She watched as the garage door slowly lowered, obscuring her dad's custom license plate, and then she came out of her hiding place. She ran as fast as she could up the side of the house, to the trellis, trying desperately to make it to her bedroom before he did. The first thing he would do the minute he got inside, she knew, would be to go upstairs and check on her.

She clambered up the trellis like a monkey with a sugar rush. Near the top, one of the wooden slats snapped beneath her foot, but she clung to the vine it supported and managed to keep from falling. Crawling up onto the rooftop, she shot across it in a crouching run, all the while listening for her dad's voice calling up the stairs to her. She slid her window open and dove inside, headfirst. She could already hear his footsteps coming up the stairs.

"Aimee?" he called.

She fought to disentangle herself from her curtains and yanked the window shut.

"Yeah!"

He was outside the door now, his hand on the knob.

"You decent? I'm coming in."

She fought to pull her coat off, but the zipper was stuck. She yanked it up over her head, thrashing.

She could hear the doorknob turning as she frantically pulled the coat free and stuffed it under her bed, and then she grabbed a book and flopped down on her stomach on top of her duvet. She opened the book a microsecond before her dad opened the door.

"What have you been up to today?" he asked, already suspicious.

"Nothing," she said. "Reading, homework. You know."

"Not thinking about your actions and how they affect this family?"

"Oh. Yeah, I did some of that, too."

He nodded, his brow furrowed. "We got the news on your brother's arm, in case you were wondering."

"Right. Sorry. What did the doctor say?"

"It's a break," he said solemnly. "He's out for the rest of the season."

Karma's a bitch, huh, bro? she thought. Out loud she said, "Oh—that sucks." For a flash, she almost felt some sympathy for Rick. Football was pretty much the only thing in life he cared about; the news today must have been devastating for him.

"It sucks all right," her dad agreed, and then his eyes narrowed. "What happened to you?"

Panic threatened. "What do you mean?" she asked tentatively.

He pointed to his own ear, and she reached up and touched hers. It stung, and her fingers came away bloody. The memory of that desert rider biting her ear flashed in her mind for a moment. The skeletal thing hadn't taken a chunk off or anything, but he'd perforated it through and through.

"Oh, it's just . . . I was trying to pierce my ear. It didn't work." She shrugged and added, "I was bored."

He only shook his head, the look on his face a mixture of bewilderment, annoyance, and disgust. "Pizza's on the way. Be down in five."

"Wait—what about Montana?"

"It's all set," he told her. "We're just waiting for a space to open up—and that could happen any day." He started to leave her room and then turned back. "And one more thing," he said with exaggerated patience. "If you don't stay away from that Kain kid, I'm going to ruin his life. And it'll be your fault."

He shut the door behind him, but his words hung in the air, as black as a flock of crows.

Aimee flopped back on the bed and let out a deep, pent-up sigh. For now at least, she was safe. But her father's final words echoed through her mind again and again.

I'm going to ruin his life. And it'll be your fault. . . .

☙

Nass stared out the window, through the heavy purple of twilight, at the apartment building across the street. Earlier, he'd taken a walk around the block with Clarisse tagging along (even though he'd tried to discourage her), and he'd seen a Shao Construction pickup truck parked in the back. Since then, workers had put cardboard over all the first floor windows so it was impossible to look inside, but now Nass could see lines of yellow light around the edges of the cardboard. The construction guys were in there, and they were working on something.

"Hey, 'Nacio," Clarisse called from the kitchen. "Come help us with dinner."

Nass rolled his eyes. Was there no escaping her?

"Coming," he said.

Little Geno's Pizza Oven closed unexpectedly for the day, for some kind of meeting with the new owner, and Nass had hoped to head over to Dalton's house to try to patch things up. But he'd had no such luck: Clarisse was following him around like a shadow. Raph was off with Aimee, and the rest of the Flatliners were at their weekend jobs or having family time. So with nowhere to go and nothing to do, he'd been stuck in the house all day while his mom and Clarisse prattled away together in Spanish.

Nass's mom was born in Mexico, in Monterrey, so Spanish was her first language. But his dad was born in Arizona, so Nass grew up hearing a mix of the two languages—but mostly English. And although he knew some rudimentary Spanish, he couldn't follow the rapid-fire dialogue his mom exchanged with Clarisse—who was fluent.

Half the time they'd look over at him and laugh happily, and when he would irritably ask them what they were saying, his mom would respond with something like, "Relax, mijo. We're just talking about how cute you are," and she and Clarisse would burst out laughing again. Now they were in the kitchen, giggling and making dinner together.

The inside jokes weren't really what was bugging him, he thought as he glanced down at his cell phone. *No missed calls.* In the few private moments he'd found today, he had called Dalton three times. Each time he'd left a message with Lily Rose, who told him that Dalton would have to call him back; except she hadn't. He knew she was mad at him, and he totally understood why, but that didn't make it any more bearable. Not being able to talk to her about it was torture.

At least he had his lookout duty to keep him occupied, he thought as he shoved his phone back into his pocket. Ignacio wandered back to his post at the window. Just as he leaned against the frame, a pair of headlights drifted up the street outside and stopped in front of Emory's building. It was a big, new, white Caddy, and the two guys who got out of it looked to Nass like a couple of 1930s gangsters, complete with funky old-school derby hats. They slammed their car doors and headed up the driveway, toward the back of the apartment building.

The knowing crept into Nass's bones again. Whoever these guys were, they had something to do with why that building had been cleared out. A *big* something.

He started for the door.

"Hey," Clarisse said, poking her head out the kitchen doorway. "You helping or what?"

"Yeah, yeah. Just a sec. I just—forgot something in the car," he said.

Clarisse wrinkled her nose up and threw a black olive at him. He caught it in his mouth and winked at her as he chewed it up, and she blew him a kiss. As he slipped out the door, he could hear her laughing. Conflict rippled through him as he remembered all the fun they'd always had together. But Dalton was so . . . so *Dalton*! He couldn't imagine being without her. And he couldn't tell her why Clarisse had suddenly come back into his life and why she had to stay there for a while.

He dialed her number again as he hurried down the stairs.

As it rang, he stepped out the front door of his apartment house, crossed the street and stopped to lean against a thick tree trunk. From this shadowy vantage point, he could keep an eye on the building without being seen.

Dalton's phone was still ringing. Finally, Lily Rose's ancient answering machine picked up. His brain churned into overdrive, trying to come up with something to say, but when the beep came, he was still pretty much blank. He cleared his throat to buy himself some time.

"Hey, uh, it's me, Ignacio. Nass," his voice sounded unnaturally low and serious and he wished he could start over, but that would be really stupid, so he continued. "Dalton, if you can, call me back, all right? I need to talk to you. Um—it's Nass. Okay. Bye."

He shut his phone and sighed, pretty sure he'd just made an ass of himself.

"Important call?"

He jumped and turned to find Clarisse standing behind him, her keen eyes watching him.

"Your mom sent me out to see what you're doing. She's worried about you."

"Oh. I was just—" Suddenly a low, rumbling hum seemed to vibrate up from the ground, through the soles of his feet. Actually, he thought, it wasn't so much a sound as a feeling. "You feel that?" he asked.

Clarisse nodded. She was frowning, as if concentrating on the sensation. "You have earthquakes here?"

"I don't think so," he said. But that's what it felt like. A tiny, sustained tremor. He turned back to stare at the apartment building a moment, and then he started walking toward it. With each step he took, the vibration beneath his feet grew more pronounced. Clarisse came up next to him.

"I think it's coming from over here," she said, moving closer to the building, but Nass grabbed her arm.

"No, don't go in there—it might not be safe," he said quickly, and wondered why he'd said it. Probably, whoever was renovating the building just had some heavy equipment running.

But no, the knowing told him—it was more than that. "We shouldn't go snooping around," he finished.

Clarisse slipped out of his grasp. "All right, fine. Let's go home, then— your mom will wig out if the food gets cold."

As Clarisse took his hand and pulled him back across the street, a host of emotions assailed Nass all at once. He felt worried and loved and confused—but most of all he felt trapped.

℘

Raphael, Nass, and Clarisse stood atop Raphael's apartment building, passing around a pair of old hunting binoculars that had been Raphael's dad's. When Nass called to report the activity at Emory's old building, Raphael had invited him to come over. He had guessed that his building's view of the back of Emory's apartment would be more useful than Nass's view of the front—and so far, he'd been right. From their high vantage point, leaning cautiously on the rickety iron rail of the rooftop widow's walk, they had been able to see half a dozen men going in and out of the back door of the building. Several of them were Asian—special employees of Shao construction, Raphael guessed, and the rest looked like regular, all-American construction-worker types, though Raphael didn't recognize any of them. He guessed they were probably day laborers from Benton.

"What do you think they're doing in there?" Raphael wondered aloud.

"Just renovating, I guess," Nass said with a shrug. "It sucks that they kicked everyone out to do it, though."

Clarisse gave Nass a look. "They're not renovating," she said.

"No? Why do you say that?"

"Come on," she responded impatiently. "Your dad worked with my dad in renovation for the last eighteen years—and you don't know anything about it?" She turned to Raphael and explained. "The first step of any renovation project is demolition. So if they're doing renovations, why aren't we seeing them come out with old toilets, sinks, buckets full of debris? There'd be a huge Dumpster someplace to put all the junk in. There's none of that here. Just a couple guys coming out to make phone calls or smoke cigarettes, then going back in."

"True," Nass agreed.

"So what *are* they doing?" Raph asked.

As if in response to his question, two of the Asian workers came out the back door of the building and walked over to the bed of the pickup truck. They pulled back a heavy black tarp and carefully unloaded a large contraption. It had a big T-shaped metal handle and there was a white disk, about three feet wide, suspended from the bottom of the T. At that moment, the two men in the derby hats came out the back door and stood on the stoop, watching the workers as they set the T contraption upright. One of them was holding a briefcase.

"Those are the weird-hat guys I saw going in!" Nass said.

As they watched, the two workers removed a black, rectangular plate that was attached to the T and gave it to one of the hat guys. The way he was handling it, it seemed to Raph like an iPad or something. The two workers each grabbed one side of the T handle and methodically carried it back and forth across the yard, sweeping the disk over tufts of wilted grass. The man on the porch gazed intently at the screen of the iPad thing.

"It looks like a big metal detector or something," Nass said quietly.

Raphael nodded. "Or sonar. Something like that." He lifted the binoculars again and kept them under surveillance.

The shorter of the two derby-hat guys opened his briefcase, took something out of it, and walked down into the yard. At first, Raph couldn't make out what it was. Then it caught the moonlight and he understood—sort of. The item the man was holding was shaped like a big Y or more accurately, a wishbone. Made of some sort of highly polished silver metal, it glittered in the starlight and from the way the guy was holding it—delicately, with one tip of the wishbone between the forefinger and thumb of each hand—it was also very light. The man waded down into the weed-filled backyard and slowly marched along behind the workers with the sonar device, holding the metal "Y" parallel to the ground and watching it intently.

"What's he doing?" Clarisse asked, leaning forward over the rail, straining to see.

Raphael handed her the binoculars. "It's a divining rod. Back in the day, people believed if you walked around holding a Y-shaped twig or branch like that, it would dip down if there was underground water beneath you. That's how they knew where to dig their wells. Some people still do it, I think. That's a pretty fancy one." He wondered if it worked better than a simple wooden stick.

"You think they're looking for water?" Nass asked.

Raphael shook his head. He didn't know what they were looking for, but he was pretty sure it wasn't water. "Nass, I want you and the guys to take shifts watching this building. As soon as they leave, as soon as it's unguarded, we're going in. We need to find out what's going on in there."

☙

As she waited for history class to begin on Monday afternoon, Aimee struggled to stay awake. She'd hoped that the school would be closed today—maybe when the gym wall collapsed there had been structural damage and they'd get to stay home for a while, she'd thought. But there was no such luck, her dad informed her over breakfast. The building inspectors had been at Middleburg High on Sunday. Gym class would be cancelled for a couple of months, but aside from that, school was proceeding normally. It was depressing. To make matters worse, everyone around Aimee was still talking about homecoming, Rick and Maggie getting king and queen, a fight nearly erupting, and the wall crashing down. To Aimee, it seemed like it had all happened a lifetime ago, her weekend had been so emotionally and physically exhausting. And she had no interest in rehashing the drama.

She yawned and let her head slump onto her arms on top of her desk, not even trying to pay attention as she allowed her thoughts to drift to Raphael. She had to find a way to see him despite her dad's threats, but how? Sleep almost came before an answer did. Just as she was drifting off, the staccato clack of high heels announced Mrs. Dupris's arrival. The conversations dwindled, and Aimee hoisted herself upright in her chair and managed to open her eyes. Only the woman standing at the front of the classroom wasn't Mrs. Dupris, who was short and wide, with straight, almost colorless blond hair and a broad, plain face, and who was also very pregnant.

The woman standing in front of the class now was quite a contrast. First of all, she barely looked old enough to be a teacher. She had short, curly dark hair, bright, playful eyes and the upright, lithe carriage of a dancer. She was wearing a cute gray knit dress and a pair of beautiful black leather boots. Aimee loved the outfit, but she doubted she could pull it off the way this woman did.

The new teacher waited patiently while the last conversation wound down to silence, and then she smiled.

"Good morning, everyone," she said. "My name is Miss Pembrook. Mrs. Dupris had her baby yesterday—a healthy little girl, I hear—and she'll be on maternity leave for the rest of the year. So you guys are stuck with me."

There were a few whistles and catcalls and two boys sitting in the front of the class exchanged a high-five. Everyone laughed and Miss Pembrook smiled graciously and continued.

"A little about me: I'm a graduate student at DePaul, in Chicago, with a degree in education. I'm going for a doctorate in history. My thesis is on the history of this region with an emphasis on Middleburg. I don't know how much you know about this charming little town, but I can tell you it's fascinating. You live in a truly unique place."

"Yeah, uniquely boring," somebody mumbled, and everybody laughed again.

"Only boring people get bored," Miss Pembrook countered, which elicited another round of laughter. Aimee could tell they liked her. She liked her too.

"I assure you," the teacher continued, "the history of this town is extraordinary, and there are pieces of the story that haven't been uncovered yet. Trust me, we'll be talking a lot in this class about Middleburg's past and by the end of the year, I guarantee you won't find it boring."

Oh, it's anything but boring, Aimee thought. *We have secret tunnels running under the whole town, our very own terrifying monster and a passageway to some kind of alternate universe. Not boring at all.*

"Which brings me to my next point," Miss Pembrook was saying. "I could use some help in my research, so if there are any history buffs in here, I'm thinking of starting an afterschool history club."

A few people groaned—obviously, studying history after school was their idea of torture—but Aimee felt as if the stars had just aligned. She needed a reason to get out of the house and a way to meet up with Raphael, and this was it. Her hand shot into the air.

Miss Pembrook looked at her, that warm smile of hers deepening. "Yes?"

"I'll do it," Aimee said. "I'll do the club."

Several of her classmates, including Maggie Anderson, looked at her as if she were nuts. It was understandable. In the three months since she'd returned to Middleburg High, Aimee had hardly uttered a word in class—until now.

Miss Pembrook looked surprised too, but pleased. "Great," she said. "If anyone else would like to volunteer I'll have a sign-up sheet after class. Meanwhile, let's get down to business, shall we? If you would please open your books to page 343 . . . "

Aimee felt a little pang of dread as she flipped through her book, looking for the right page. She might've just signed up for a lot of excruciatingly boring afternoons, but if it allowed her just a few moments with Raphael, it would be worth it.

∞

Monday after school, Raphael opened his locker and found a note from Aimee stuck inside. *Instant relief.* He hadn't talked to her since their near-disastrous detour into the future, and he hadn't seen her in school all day. He'd been worried that her dad had already shipped her off to Montana. When he opened the note and saw her handwriting, he felt like he could breathe again.

Call me. Block your number.

LUE

Raphael smiled. L.U.E. Love you eternally. He'd said it to her one night on the phone and the phrase had stuck; now they said it to one another all the time. It was the perfect way to sign a note like this too. If Rick or somebody got a hold of it, there was no way they could prove that Aimee wrote it.

He thought, not for the first time, how grateful he was to be going out with such a smart girl.

Grabbing his coat and cell phone from his locker, he hurried out of the school. When he stepped outside, the frigid wind bit into him but he pressed onward, out into the courtyard beneath a canopy of gray clouds that were heavy with the threat of snow.

Aimee was standing on the other side of the courtyard, smiling at him. As soon as he saw her and nodded to acknowledge the smile, she looked away, in case anyone was watching. He also turned away and, after he'd blocked his i.d., he called her. She picked up instantly.

"Raphael," she said, soft and low. He loved the way her voice got a little catch in it when she said his name.

"Hey, beautiful—I was starting to think I'd have to go and rescue you from Montana."

"No, not yet. They have to wait for a bed to open up."

"That's good news." Raphael was leaning against the brick wall of the school, and he tilted his head back in silent thanks. "Let's hope it takes forever."

Aimee laughed. God, how he loved the sound.

"Also, I'm going to be doing a history club thing after school. I can use it as an excuse to get out of the house."

"I could join too, maybe," he offered, but across the courtyard he could see her shaking her head.

"Too obvious. We got away with that during the play. There's no way my dad will stand for it this time."

"You're right," he agreed.

"The history thing will be my cover, so we can meet up. And maybe go look for my mom again?"

Raphael was hoping she would let that go. "About that," he said. "I don't want you using the Wheel with me anymore."

He was pacing now, and out of the corner of his eye he could see Aimee frowning.

"What do you mean? We have to find my mom."

"We will," he promised. "But first I need to learn more about how to use the thing. There are infinite points in time that it could take us to, and we have no idea which one your mom is in or exactly how to get there. It's too dangerous, Aimee. I'm not going to risk you getting eaten by a saber-toothed tiger or falling into a primordial volcano or caught up in a civil-war battle or something. We just found each other. I can't lose you."

"I can handle myself."

"Like you did with skeleton boy and his wind board—when you were supposed to keep down and out of sight?"

"I was trying to help," she said solemnly. "If something happened to you, Raphael, I couldn't stand it. I can't lose you, either." He could hear frustration rising in her voice. "And I can't lose my mom. If there's even the ghost of a chance she's in those tunnels somewhere—I have to find her. And I don't care who or what I have to fight to do it." A tense silence hung between them for a moment.

This could easily turn into their first fight, Raphael realized, and he wanted it to be their last. It gave him an awful feeling in the pit of his stomach. But he'd thought about it a lot and it was just too dangerous to keep taking her through the Wheel. Somehow, he had to convince her.

"You can't fight," he said finally. "You don't know how."

"Then I'll learn," she said, and she sounded pretty determined. "I'll learn how to take care of myself and fight at your side. I'll go ask Master Chin to teach me."

"It's not that easy," Raphael warned her, but he couldn't help smiling.

"Why, because I'm a *girl*? You don't think I can learn to fight?"

He chuckled. "I like it when you get all spunky on me like that. It's pretty hot."

"Stop it. I'm serious."

"All right. First of all, you should know that Master Chin never takes on new students. Zhai and I are the only ones he's had since—well, since I can remember. And even if he *did* take you on, it takes years of hard work to get really good. I'm sorry, Aimee." And he was. He hated to see her disappointed in any way. "It just won't work. Let me find out more about how to use the Wheel, and then I'll go in and find your mom. Me and my crew. You have to trust me on this."

Raphael glanced across the courtyard. Aimee was looking directly at him. It was a risk, he knew, but he looked into her eyes too.

There was pain in them, a pain he understood all too well. He'd also lost a parent, and he knew exactly what that agony was like. She had the opportunity to get hers back, and he understood why she would be willing to do whatever it took, even if it meant she might die in the process. He understood completely—but there was still no way he was going to let her risk her life.

"I know it's hard," he said. "But please, just be patient."

"I can't," she said softly.

A few snowflakes drifted down between them. He wanted more than anything to jump over the picnic tables that separated them, run over to her, wrap his arms around her, and hold her as close as he could. In front of everybody.

And someday he would.

"We better go back in," Aimee said. "Rick's going to be looking for me." The distance that had crept into her voice impaled him like a blade of ice.

"LUE," he said softly, but she'd already ended the call. He watched as she turned away from him and headed inside, leaving him alone with the slowly falling snow.

CHAPTER 9

Zhai sat at his customary table in Spinnacle, stirring the ice in his cranberry juice with his straw. Almost the whole Toppers crew was present, even Maggie and her friends.

She sat next to Rick, looking, Zhai thought, a little uncomfortable and tired. She was as beautiful as ever, except for the shadows under her eyes and the anxious look in them. Lisa Marie sat next to her, telling some elaborate story about a shopping trip she and her mom had taken to Chicago. Michael and Dax listened intently and nodded in all the right places. Bran looked on, a pleasant but distant smile on his face, his mind clearly elsewhere. D'von and Cle'von Cunningham sat at the far end of the table, engrossed in a flirtatious conversation with the waitress, and Rick sat brooding next to Maggie. Occasionally, he would let go of her hand and rub the shoulder of his broken arm. He stared down at the white linen tablecloth with a lethal look in his eye, as if he were trying to set the fabric on fire with his mind. And Zhai wondered why he'd even thought that. Rick was a bully and he was big and mean and strong—but there was no way he had any of the raw magical power Zhai had experienced on Halloween night, and that he'd seen in Raphael, as they had battled each other on the tracks.

The news that he was out for the rest of the football season had to be a terrible blow to Rick, Zhai knew, especially since Middleburg was ranked first going into the postseason. Michael Ponder would be taking over the role of quarterback, but everyone knew he wasn't half the athlete Rick was. Rick had taken the news hard. Like a huge, fiery star collapsing to form a black hole, Rick's rage seemed to have condensed to form something darker and deeper, but perhaps equally dangerous, Zhai thought. But certainly not supernatural.

"And I was like, seriously, you have got to be kidding. I am going to *murder* you!" Lisa Marie said shrilly. Michael and Dax, who had actually been listening to the story, laughed, and everyone else took that as their cue to laugh too. Zhai glanced away from their table into the bar area, and he was shocked to see the two Chinese guys who'd been to the house earlier to visit his father.

The shorter man finished his drink, and the taller one took out his wallet and put some bills on the table, and then they both stood and headed for the door. If either man noticed Zhai staring at them, they gave no indication. The minute they were gone, Zhai rose to his feet.

"Whatsa matter, Kung Pao?" Bran drawled, using his own little nickname for Zhai. "You leavin' us already?"

"Yeah, for a few minutes. I, uh—forgot something. Hey, Rick, can I borrow your ride?"

Wordlessly, Rick dug into his pocket and tossed Zhai his keys.

Zhai stepped into the parking lot just in time to see the white Cadillac pulling out of its parking space. He moved quickly down a row of cars toward Rick's silver Audi SUV, trying not to be seen, opened the door, and jumped into the driver's seat.

Carefully keeping his distance, Zhai followed the Caddy down Golden Avenue. It went left on Main Street and then right on River Road before pulling off onto a rutted trail that led down to the locomotive graveyard. Following them into the woods in Rick's SUV would be way too obvious, so Zhai pulled to the side of the road and got out. On foot, he waded into the deepening, late-afternoon shadows of the forest. The leaves had long since fallen, leaving the trees gray and barren. The ground was brown and parched. Even the sky looked depleted, its customary blue faded almost to a dull shade of nothing. As he moved cautiously up the trail, he heard the sound of distant voices. Ahead, he saw several parked cars including the white Caddy and two Shao construction trucks.

What are my dad's workers doing in the train graveyard? Zhai wondered. *And what if they find Kate?*

There were plenty of decomposing old train cars there, but as far as he knew there weren't any houses in need of renovating, no concrete slabs that needed to be poured. He passed the cars and hurried forward, taking a winding, narrow trail that sloped first up, then down, into the train graveyard itself. The terrain was covered in sticky, slick mud, and he groaned as he looked down at his shoes—a pair of fairly new Lacoste sneakers, now covered in sludge.

He finally reached the end of the trail and stopped, leaning against a tree. From here, he could look down and see much of the huge junkyard full of abandoned rail cars. And what he saw perplexed him even more. There were two construction workers there carrying around a strange device that looked to Zhai like one of the big, round, flat radar antennas from his dad's yacht, turned upside down. The two workers were walking together, sweeping it over the ground while one of the men who had made that surprise visit to Zhai's father looked at a flat monitor. It had to be some kind of sonar device, he thought. They were looking for something buried underground. But what?

He wondered what his dad knew about this.

And, he wondered with sudden alarm, where was his dad's other Chinese guest?

"You are curious, I see."

The thick accent told Zhai that his question had been answered.

He turned around slowly, bracing himself in case the man rushed him. It was the shorter of the two visitors, and he stood a few yards away, gazing calmly at Zhai.

"You're Cheung Shao's boy, aren't you?" His voice held no expression.

"Yes, I'm Zhai. I saw the Shao Construction trucks. What's my dad's company doing back here?"

"Oh," the man said, faintly mocking. "*Your dad's* company?"

Zhai nodded. He had no idea where this was going, but he had a feeling it wouldn't be good.

The stranger's voice took on a darker, deadlier tone. "Did your father send you to spy on us?"

"Of course not."

"How much has he told you about the project *his* company is working on?"

"Nothing," Zhai said.

"Really," the man sneered. "He was always a clever man, your father, and ruthless. I wouldn't like to think he is ruthless enough to risk his own son."

"I should be getting back," Zhai said quietly as he struggled to understand what was happening. He was starting to think he was in trouble.

"No," the man said pleasantly. "You should stay."

With incredible speed, he reached into his coat and pulled out what appeared to be a short stick. There was a metallic click and something silver and shiny sprang from it. It was a knife, with what had to be an eight-inch blade.

Before the man could strike, Zhai made his move, dashing to the left where a large tree trunk would screen him from his adversary. But when he got there, the man was on the other side waiting for him. How could he move that fast, Zhai wondered? It seemed impossible.

The man spun the dagger in his hand and leaped forward, clearly intending to bash Zhai in the head with its pommel. Zhai blocked his strike, slipped to the side and struck him in the face with one quick, hard backfist. The man stepped back and turned to Zhai, a look of surprise on his face. He reached up, completely composed, and dabbed a spot of blood from the corner of his mouth with one finger.

"Ah, you've been trained," he said. With a click, the knife blade retracted and the man slipped the weapon back into his coat. Then he bowed to Zhai. Automatically, Zhai returned the gesture, then watched as his smiling adversary assumed a fight-ready position he'd never seen before.

Zhai felt his insides light up with the amazing, energized calm that always filled him before a fight.

"Well, go ahead, boy," the man said evenly. "Let's see what you can do."

Without hesitation, Zhai shot forward, intending to use a move called a *Bong Sau* to jam up his enemy's lead arm, but the man moved out of his way as fluidly as water, and Zhai took three quick strikes to the side of the head before he was able to block the counterattack. The man stepped back, laughing, and Zhai took the opportunity to strike again. This time, he led with a punch. As soon as the man tried to block the first punch, Zhai threw a second into what should have been an opening in his opponent's guard. Instead, the man grabbed his arm and, using the momentum from Zhai's strike, pulled him forward and gave him a solid elbow to the face. Zhai stumbled away, reeling. He had to grab a branch for support to keep from falling over.

"You have talent," his challenger said, sounding a little amused as he adjusted the derby on his head. "A few more years, and you might be pretty good."

Zhai's ears were ringing from the blows he'd received, but he shook it off and assumed the ready position again.

"Really? More?" the Chinese man said. "Very well, then—come on."

Zhai didn't move.

"Oh, you've decided you can't attack me," the man observed. "Do you think you can withstand my attack?"

Zhai didn't respond; he remained still, motionless . . . ready.

The man smiled. He moved toward Zhai with incredible grace and speed, almost seeming to glide across the forest floor, and then he struck, throwing six punches in quick succession. Zhai had been tempted to look at his enemy's face, to see if the mocking smile was still there, but he kept his eyes, instead, on his enemy's elbows—just as master Chin had taught. By staying focused, he managed to block all six strikes.

"Not bad," the man said.

And Zhai struck back. He threw ten of the fastest punches he'd ever put together. The last one actually made it through the man's guard, skimmed off his cheekbone and caught the brim of his hat, knocking it off his head. He turned away from Zhai with blurring speed and caught the hat on his foot before it hit the ground.

"Oops," he said, and kicked it back up.

The second while the hat floated in the air seemed to last an eternity. Zhai, sure that he had the advantage, struck with all his strength, aiming for the back of his enemy's neck. At the same time, his opponent spun around toward him, intercepting Zhai's punch and somehow pinning both his arms against his body with one hand. He shoved Zhai back against a tree with both of Zhai's arms twisted painfully against his chest, and snapped one fist up, holding it half an inch away from Zhai's nose. As he stood frozen there, the hat landed neatly on his head.

Un-be-freaking-lievable, Zhai thought. *This guy is my idol.*

"Give your father a message," the man said, his thick accent steeped with dark humor. "Tell him that he will get his reward only after we find what we seek. Tell him there is no place in heaven or on earth where he can escape the Order. Now, you belong to us—as he does."

In that instant, the fist hovering in front of Zhai's face blasted forward, plunging Zhai into unconsciousness.

❧

As he watched Maggie and her friends pull out of Spinnacle's parking lot, Rick called Zhai's cell again. Again, there was no answer. He swore under his breath.

"Why don't you ride up to the Haven with me," Bran said, leaning against his brand-new black Camero. "Zhai can bring your car back to your place when he's done with it."

Rick considered, and then shook his head. He'd had to sit it out at football practice today (even jogging killed his arm), and he felt like he had so much pent up energy that if he didn't do something with it, he'd explode. And the frustration of being stuck without a car wasn't helping him feel any more relaxed.

"I'm gonna walk downtown or something," he said, and without waiting for Bran to respond, he headed off across the parking lot. He'd gone through times like this for as long as he could remember—dark moods that nothing but a fight or some violent collisions on the football field could curb. Now, with this stupid injury messing up his whole life, he had more anger than ever and nowhere to put it.

As he wandered through the few partly residential, partly commercial blocks between Spinnacle and downtown, he fantasized about turning a corner and finding one of those Flats rats wandering around alone—that fat-ass they called Beet, maybe, or that little queer Emory. He imagined the look they would get in their eyes as they realized what was about to happen to them, and then he imagined chasing them downtown and into a blind alleyway. He imagined the feel of their faces on his fist, the sound and smell of blood splattering on brick, the whimper as they went still and silent, helpless against his fury.

He was so caught up in the ecstasy of his daydream that he was startled when a voice called to him.

"Looks like quite a boo-boo you have there."

Rick turned to find a young man standing on the broad porch of a house, leaning casually against a wooden column. He was big and muscular, maybe a couple of years older than Rick, with long, dark brown hair, weird blue eyes and a smartass grin on his face. And he was one of those pretty boys that girls like Maggie and her stupid friends would drool over. Rick disliked him instantly. He also disliked the disquieting fact that when he'd passed the house just a second before, there'd been no one standing there. It was like the guy appeared out of nowhere. In fact, Rick thought as he looked up at the huge, battered three-story Victorian structure, he'd never noticed the house before, either. And he'd been down this street plenty of times.

"What are you looking at?" he challenged.

"Your arm," the guy said, nodding toward Rick's cast. "What happened to it?"

"What's it to you?"

Gracefully, the guy hopped down from the porch and walked across the lawn and right up to Rick, who was surprised to find him every bit as broad shouldered, and even a little taller than he was. His face only inches away from Rick's, the guy stared at him for a moment.

"I could fix it for you," he whispered.

Rick took a step back. "Yeah, right. Are you a doctor?"

"Not exactly."

"Well, you don't know what the hell you're talking about," Rick said. "I've already seen two doctors—that's why it's in a cast, in case you didn't notice."

"I noticed." The young man smiled at him. "But you can get rid of that cast in time to play in the game on Friday." His voice was magnetic, and Rick wanted to believe him.

"That's impossible," he said, still resisting. "The doctor said I just have to be patient and sit out the season."

"But you don't, Rick. What would you do for me, if I could heal your arm today?"

Rick looked into those sharp blue eyes, and somehow he knew this guy was telling the truth. He felt the world go dim around him. He didn't even wonder how the guy knew his name. For a second, it felt like everything around them disappeared and it was only the two of them and no one else—no one else in the world.

"I'd do anything," Rick said. "I swear."

∽

The instant Zhai regained consciousness, he lashed out. Instead of striking his mysterious Chinese attacker, however, his hand slammed into some sort of pan. It fell to the ground with a clatter. Someone gasped. Zhai was on his feet now, spinning left then right, looking for the enemy. Instead, he found a long row of windows, a weird and eclectic collection of pictures, stuffed animals and cooking implements, and a beautiful, petite red-haired girl, staring at him with wide-eyed concern.

Kate.

"It's all right," she was saying, her adorable Irish lilt so soothing. "There, now. It's all right. You're goin' to be fine."

Zhai squeezed his eyes shut and opened them again, trying to clear the fog and figure out how he'd gotten there. His shirt was off. There was a shallow pan lying on the floor of the railroad car beside him, and soapy water all over the floor. He felt something running down the bridge of his nose; when he touched the spot, his fingers came away bloody. He had terrible pain in both his hands, as if he'd stuck each of them in a hornet's nest. They were both wrapped in thick, white gauze.

He was totally confused, but as Kate approached him he relaxed a little and allowed her to help him up and lead him toward her little cot.

"What happened?" he asked as he sat down, his voice thick and his mind groggy.

"I thought perhaps you could tell me. I was on my way to the market and found you lying in the middle of the tracks with your face all bruised and bleeding, so I brought you back here to look after you."

"How?" he asked. She was such a little thing he didn't see how she could have carried him.

"You made it most of the way on your own—well, leanin' on me a bit. And then I had to drag you. You don't remember?"

He shook his head. "Those guys—in the derby hats. Did you see them?"

"Two Chinese men?" she asked, and he nodded. It made his head hurt. "I saw them walking around earlier with a couple other fellows, but they've all gone now."

Zhai exhaled, trying to steady himself, to get his bearings.

He'd been fighting with one of his father's mysterious visitors, who had punched him in the face and knocked him out. Apparently, they'd dragged him into the middle of the tracks and left him there. That explained his headache. What he didn't understand was what was wrong with his hands—why they were bandaged and why they ached so much. He looked down at them.

"Do they hurt?" Kate asked.

"Yeah." Zhai began unwinding the bandage on his left hand, with a sudden pang of dread about what he might find there.

"Your poor hands," Kate said. "I hope this doesn't make it hard for you to play your fiddle."

"No, I'm sure I'll still be able to play," Zhai said, then froze, the strip of gauze still between his fingers. For the last couple weeks, he'd come down to the train graveyard with a little gift for Kate, every time hiding among the trees and playing his violin for her. So far, he hadn't gotten up the nerve to reveal himself. Now, he realized with horror, he'd just given himself away. The thought that she might be disappointed to learn he was her secret admirer made him want to shrink into the fetal position, but when he looked up at her, she was beaming.

"I hope so," she said. "I adore your music."

Hoping she wouldn't see him color, Zhai again started unwinding his bandages. When he'd pulled the last bit of gauze away, he stared down at the back of his left hand, utterly bewildered. Frantically, he pulled the bandages off his right hand, too. On the back of each of his hands, someone had tattooed a Chinese symbol.

"What do they mean?" Kate asked slowly, a note of apprehension in her voice.

Zhai stared down at his stinging skin, his head swimming with confusion. "I don't know," he whispered.

ဢ

Rick wondered how things had ended up this way: he'd gone out looking for a fight, and wound up sitting on a dusty, antique-looking couch in some random guy's dimly lit living room, sipping a glass of the best wine he'd ever tasted, and waiting for this stranger who wasn't even a doctor to fix his broken arm.

The long-haired guy had poured the wine for Rick and then disappeared up the stairs. Meanwhile, the sun had gone down, and in the dying light, the house that had seemed eerie and dead to begin with was starting to get even creepier as twilight settled in. It was weird—everything looked a little fuzzy. Now and then, out of the corner of his eye, he'd think he saw something move in the shadows, but when he looked there was nothing there. He didn't mind that, necessarily. Being a little scared gave him a dose of the adrenaline he loved, something he craved beyond everything else. But now he was starting to get bored.

He looked at his Movado watch, also starting to get pissed off, then he tipped the glass up, swallowed the last of his wine, and stood. It didn't make any sense for him to be there in the first place.

Screw this guy, Rick thought. *I'm out of here. This whole idea is stupid.*

But Pretty Boy was leaning against the arched doorway leading to the hall. Rick hadn't heard him enter.

"Leaving so soon?" he asked. He was smiling, but there was no amusement in his tone. He moved gracefully into the room, almost gliding, Rick thought, like he was wearing those skate-sneaker things. Only he wasn't—he was wearing expensive leather boots. The light of the dying day faded even more, and shadows seemed to be clustering around the stranger, as if trying to hide him from the light.

"I've never seen you around before," Rick said, growing more nervous by the minute—and that made him angrier. He wasn't afraid of anything, but all he wanted to do at that moment was get the hell out of there. "Are you from around here?"

"No. I did visit a few times, as a child."

Rick heard the click of a lighter and a small flame lent an unnatural luminescence to the shadows. The young man took a candelabrum off the mantle and lit the five candles it held and then put it on the mantle again. A giant shiver raced down Rick's spine and he felt like he was about to break out in goose bumps. Pretty Boy reached out to shake Rick's hand and Rick found his grip surprisingly strong. His hands were broad but soft and well groomed. Not a laborer by any means. On one hand he wore a large onyx ring.

"Now, let me introduce myself properly," he said. "I am Orias."

"Yeah? Cool," said Rick. "How did you know my name?"

"Ah—no mystery there," said his host. "You're Middleburg's one claim to fame, I hear. I've read about your prowess on the sports page of the *Middleburg Chronicle*. Now tell me, Rick. What happened to your arm? Were you injured in a game?"

"No," Rick said. "A damned wall fell on me."

"A shame," said Orias and his sympathy sounded genuine. "And just at the end of a very important football season."

"You said you could fix it?" He was hopeful, even though he was starting to think this guy was running some sort of scam.

"What you said before—that you'd give anything to finish out the season. Did you mean that?"

"Damn right, I did."

Orias stared at him a moment, a strange light in his eyes. "Well then. Let's get started. Would you lie down on the sofa, please?"

"Hey—wait," Rick said. "No offense, but when I said I'd do anything, I didn't mean—look, bro, I'm straight."

Orias laughed and the sound was deep, rich and full. "None taken," he said. "So am I."

"I mean, not that I have anything against them, you know," Rick said. But he did. He hated queers with a passion. Almost as much as he hated Raphael Kain and the rest of those Flats rats. But for some reason he didn't want to admit it to this guy.

"Neither do I," Orias assured him with a broad smile. "Now, do you want me to fix your arm or not?" He gestured to the couch.

Rick lay down, wincing as his arm shifted positions.

Orias reached into his pocket and withdrew a small leather pouch. "Open your mouth," he commanded.

"You sure you can fix my arm?" Rick asked. He was growing more uneasy by the minute.

"I can fix just about anything," Orias said. "Now open your mouth."

This time, Rick obeyed and Orias dumped the contents of the pouch—a chalky powder—down his throat. Instantly, Rick felt like he was choking. He coughed, and a little puff of dust came out of his mouth.

"Keep your mouth closed," Orias ordered, suddenly sounding fierce.

The stuff tasted horrible, like Rick imagined the guts of a piece of old roadkill would taste. He wretched and tried to spit it out, but his lips seemed to be plastered shut. The paste solidified into a thick, rubbery mass that expanded to fill his whole mouth. He felt a moment of panic, and then Orias reached over and touched his injured arm.

Rick heard a dull cracking sound and the cast fell away. From another pocket, Orias took a small, glass vial filled with red liquid. To Rick, it looked like blood. Orias pulled the little stopper out and then he dipped his fingertip into the tiny bottle. With the blood or whatever it was, he drew something on Rick's forehead.

This is all way too freaking weird, Rick thought. Whatever was in his mouth was still expanding, moving down his throat, constricting his airway, and he couldn't spit it out. He couldn't open his lips at all; it was like they were superglued shut. He tried to sit up, planning to run away, but when he rolled over he realized there was nothing beneath him!

The couch was at least a foot below him; then two feet, then three. He was *floating*, suspended in midair. He could feel hands on him, holding him up, but when he looked there was nothing there. Then, his broken arm started to burn and then to twitch. The pain grew until it was almost unbearable—a hard, cold ache that went through him and threatened to snap every bone in his body into a thousand pieces, like some kind of human jigsaw puzzle. He looked at his broken arm and to his horror, he saw movement under the skin, like the pieces of bone were twisting, grinding, rearranging themselves. The pain was beyond anything he'd ever felt or imagined. He was screaming with all his might but all that came out of his choked airway was a pathetic, high-pitched moan.

Orias was standing in front of the sofa, his arms spread wide, his eyes closed. His long hair floated up and away from his face as if it were also levitating. His brain starved for air, Rick felt himself sinking into a hell of darkness and soul-rending agony.

I blacked out, he thought a moment later as he sat up on the couch. Orias was looking down at him, smiling.

The substance in his mouth was moving now, loosening, and he could feel hair on his tongue and scurrying little feet scratching against his teeth. At last he was able to get his lips apart and he opened his mouth as wide as his jaw would go.

A fat, black rat scrambled out, tumbling from his saliva-soaked chin down to his chest.

Rick screamed, and the disgusting rodent leaped to the floor and took off into the shadows. He leaned over the edge of the couch and retched until his eyes felt like they would pop out of their sockets. And then he jumped up and grabbed Orias by the front of his shirt.

"You think that was funny?" he shouted and he cocked back to punch Orias in his smug, pretty face. But when Orias looked directly into his eyes, Rick forgot why he was angry.

"Ah . . . are you going to hit me with that fist?" Orias asked calmly. "I thought your arm was broken."

Rick blinked. He opened and closed his hand and then he stretched out his arm. The cast now lay on the floor beside the couch, split in two. His arm didn't hurt at all. He made a motion, like he was throwing a football, and there was no pain. His arm felt stronger than ever. He was completely healed.

"I can't believe it," Rick said. He could hardly wrap his mind around what had just happened. "This is awesome. How much do I owe you?"

Orias put a brotherly arm over his shoulder. "For now, let's call it a favor between friends," he said as he led Rick toward the door. "When the time comes, you'll do any favor your friend requires—won't you? Just like you promised."

"I will," Rick said, and he meant it. "Whatever you ask, man, it's yours."

CHAPTER 10

THE FOLLOWING AFTERNOON, Raphael stood in Master Chin's *kwoon,* practicing his attack approaches. There had been flurries the night before, and they'd left a thin layer of powdery snow on the grass and the trees, but Master Chin had stoked the wood-burning stove that sat in one corner of the barn, filling the place with a comforting warmth.

Raphael's training was going well—he had even caught his normally invincible sifu with a few good strikes. This time when he went in for the attack, though, Master Chin easily intercepted him and countered, rapping him on the forehead with one knuckle. Raphael stepped back, rubbing the spot.

"Ow," he said.

"Ow is right. Imagine if I had a knife, then you'd be saying more than *ow*!" Master Chin laughed good-naturedly. "Break time. Sit."

He pointed to two beanbag chairs near the wood stove. Raphael walked over to one of them and plopped down, wiping the sweat from his forehead with the back of his hand. As he watched, Master Chin poured some apple cider from a plastic jug into a saucepan and put it on the wood stove to heat up. Warm apple cider had been a wintertime tradition in Master Chin's kwoon for as long as Raphael could remember; it was the reward for a long day of hard training. But when Chin came over and sat down opposite Raphael, he didn't look entirely pleased.

"On the last attack, your mind was elsewhere, Raphael," he said. "Is there anything you'd like to talk about?"

Raphael nodded, but he wasn't sure how to respond. Ever since the Flatliners had battled the Toppers a few weeks before, he had wanted to talk to his sifu about some of the weird things he and Zhai had seen—and fought—that night, but he hadn't known how to bring it up. Sure, he and his kung fu teacher had discussed Shen and magic and the All—primarily, Raph suspected, so Chin could prepare him for that fight.

But since Halloween, things had settled into a comfortable, complacent normalcy and the events of that night felt less real, less believable, even to him. And Master Chin seemed more committed than ever to keeping Raphael focused and centered, wasting not one moment of their training sessions, which didn't leave much time for questions.

If Raphael had been waiting for the right time to talk to him, this was it.

"Yeah," he said. "I was thinking about something. But it's kind of strange."

Chin chuckled. "I would be surprised if it were otherwise."

The old kung fu master poured their warm cider into mugs and added a stick of cinnamon to each. When he rejoined Raphael at the chairs and gave one of the cups to him, Raph spoke again.

"Well, first—I went back to the gym the other day and took another look at the hole that opened up when that wall collapsed."

"What did you find?"

"Aimee went with me. We went down there and looked around. There are tunnels under the entire town, Sifu. Man-made tunnels, like some kind of excavation."

"Interesting," Master Chin said. As usual, Raph couldn't tell whether he was surprised or not. "How far in did you go?"

"Far. The one we were in went under Middleburg and all the way to the North Tunnel."

"And then?" his sifu prompted.

"Then we heard Aimee's mom calling out to her—she's been missing for eight months, you know."

Master Chin nodded.

"We followed her voice toward the Wheel of Illusion. She has to be lost in one of the worlds—or times—that the Wheel connects, we figured. That must be why we could hear her. But the place the Wheel took us to . . . it was horrible." Raphael shook his head, remembering it.

"And Emily Banfield wasn't there." Master Chin surmised.

"No," Raphael said. "I promised Aimee I'd help her get her mom back, but if we keep winding up in random places—or times—sooner or later we're going to get ourselves killed. I need to learn how to use the Wheel, to get it to take us to the right time. I was hoping you could help me."

Master Chin went to the stove and refilled their mugs. He gave one to Raphael and then sat down again.

"The Wheel is a manifestation of Shen, the All," he began.

"Wait," Raphael said. "You mean Shen and the All are the same thing?"

"They are," Chin agreed. "Shen exists constantly, in all things. It is a purely good, creative force. Those who move with Shen, in the direction it leads them, will reap its blessings. Those who follow it perfectly, with perfect purity of heart, will be filled with its power, and become invincible. Those who depart from it, or who oppose the pure goodness of its ways will reap suffering, and, in the end, death. That principle is sometimes called the law of nature, the law of karma, or the law of sin. Cause and effect. What you reap, you sow. This is why I teach you and Zhai the Wu-de. It is the part of the law of Shen that applies to martial artists. Follow this law, and you are protected. But even if you are the most powerful warrior in the world, yet you oppose the pure and good will of Shen, you will ultimately meet your destruction. Does all that make sense?"

"Yes, Sifu," Raphael said. "I mean, I understand but I still don't see how that will help me work the Wheel." As he blew on his cup of hot cider and took a tentative sip, he noticed Chin's smile.

"I think 'work the wheel' is not quite the way to approach it," said Chin. "You don't work it. You tap into the power, the power of Shen, so Shen can work through you. Then you will be able to control the Wheel—instead of having the Wheel control you."

"How do I learn to do that?" Raphael persisted.

"Meditation," Master Chin said, and slurped his cider.

Raphael nodded. He'd tried to meditate every day since his battle with Oberon, but with everything going on in his life, getting his mind quiet, tranquil, and receptive seemed almost impossible. "Okay," he said. "I can do that. So how long will it take until I'm able to control the Wheel?"

"How long does it take for a caterpillar to become a butterfly? Or to make a lying man honest? How long does it take for a miser to become generous? Answer those questions and you will know how long it will take."

Raphael sighed, sat back in his beanbag, and took a big sip of his drink. Sometimes he hated it when Master Chin started getting all Zen and wise, especially when all he wanted was a simple answer. Besides, if the only way he could learn to use the Wheel was to meditate every day until someone like Jack Banfield decided to start being honest and give all his money to charity, he'd be waiting a long time.

The lesson was clear enough, though. If he was going to learn to tap into the power of the Wheel, he'd have to develop his connection with Shen. And to do that, apparently, he'd have to learn patience. Not the greatest thing for a guy like him, whose favorite thing in life was throwing punches and kicks at the speed of light. But if that's what he had to do to help Aimee, he'd do it. "All right," Raphael said. "I'll meditate every day. But I have to wonder if it was really Aimee's mom's voice we heard . . . last time Aimee heard it, Oberon was using it to lure her into the tunnels. What if he comes back?"

"Raphael, you cannot live your life on what-ifs. The truth is in you— you can feel it. What do you believe? Is Mrs. Banfield lost in one of the tunnels, or somewhere beyond?"

Raphael hesitated. "Well, I heard the voice too. And Aimee believes with all her heart that it was her mom."

"And is hers a heart you can trust?" asked his teacher.

"Yes," he said, finally understanding. "It is. We'll find Emily Banfield. I'll meditate every day."

Chin nodded, satisfied. "A wise man's questions surpass the answers of the fool, but the silence of the enlightened is divine. Meditation is the key."

"I understand," Raphael said, setting down his cup of cider. "Oh," he added eagerly as he shot to his feet. "I think I might have figured out the Strike of the Immortals. You want me to show you on the punching bag?"

But Chin was already shaking his head. "Nope," he said. "That's not it."

Raphael frowned. "But I haven't done anything yet!"

His sifu only gave him an enigmatic smile. Raphael sat down again and finished his cider. Then, feeling renewed and focused, he stood and bowed to Master Chin. Afterward, he called Beet to come pick him up and headed out into the snow.

৪৩

Not long after Raphael left, Chin heard a knock on the thick wooden door of the barn. His eyes were closed and his mind was distant, lost in the deep folds of a meditative journey. It was with some reluctance that he ended his session and opened his eyes. He already knew who was knocking, and he stood to greet her.

"Come in," he called, and the door swung open.

She wore a puffy white vest with a fur collar, designer jeans, and leather boots that came up to her knees. Her hair was short and dark, her frame petite—a bit too thin, perhaps—but there was an unmistakable gleam in her eye that Master Chin liked instantly.

"Hi, Master Chin? I'm—"

"Aimee," Master Chin said with a smile, "I know who you are. Raphael has told me a lot about you. Welcome."

At the sound of Raphael's name, a lovely blush swept across Aimee's cheeks, but she continued. "I've come to ask you something. A really big favor."

"Yes?" he replied.

"I . . . I'd like to train with you. To learn kung fu. Please."

Chin stared at her blankly, waiting to see how she would respond to his intransigence.

"Pretty please?" she said.

Chin couldn't help but laugh, but before the girl's confidence deflated, he said quickly, "Now, now. I'm not laughing at you because of your request, only because I've never had anyone ask me quite that way before. Tell me, why is it you'd like to learn my art?"

"Well . . . " She looked away for a moment, but Chin saw the pain in her eyes. "I guess everyone knows my mom is missing. Raphael promised to find her for me, but I can't let him do it alone. I mean, she's my mom, not his. I have to help him, but there's no way I can do it unless I get stronger. So I thought maybe you could show me a few things."

Master Chin nodded slowly, taking the girl in again. It wasn't just the light in her eyes—there was an unmistakable depth about her too. A depth of which she was not yet entirely aware. And her sorrow and longing for her mother were genuine and haunting.

"Well," he said. "Your request is certainly sincere, but I have reservations. First, learning kung fu the way I teach it is not something to be taken lightly. I cannot simply *show you a few things*. This is an art. A lifestyle."

"I understand," Aimee said. "I'm totally committed. I already went through a lot to be here. I had to sneak out of my house, walk all the way downtown, get a taxi, and follow Raphael out here because I didn't know where you live. Then I had to hide outside, freezing my butt off until he left. And if my dad finds out I'm not at home, he's probably going to kill me—literally. Trust me, I'm committed."

Chin's smile faded. He could see that she had potential, but she wasn't ready for training. Not yet. "You're very small, even for a girl," he observed. "You really think you can learn to be a formidable fighter?"

"I know I can."

Chin looked into her eyes, and he knew she believed it. She might not know if she could fight, but she was willing to die trying. Maybe too willing.

Chin turned away from her, looking around the barn.

"I can pay you," she said quickly. "Whatever you normally charge, you can double it. I have a trust fund from my mom and when I turn sixteen, I'll have access to some of it—a lot of it. If you can extend credit until then."

Finding what he was looking for, Chin crossed to an empty horse stall beneath the hay loft. "I'll tell you what," he said, returning with a board that was about an inch and a half thick. "If you can break this board with your fist, I'll train you."

The girl looked at the board, her eyes wide. "Right now?" she asked meekly.

"Right now. You break this board, I'll train you—for free. We'll start today."

Pensively, Aimee looked at the board, clenching and unclenching her right fist.

"What do you think?" Chin asked. "Can you can do it?"

"Yeah," Aimee decided, unzipping her vest and removing it, revealing a soft, cashmere sweater beneath. "I can do it," she said.

Chin watched with mild amusement as she stretched out, hopped up and down, and paced back and forth across the barn's worn floorboards, psyching herself up.

"Whenever you're ready," Chin said, smiling.

"Okay," she said. "Now."

He held the board out in front of her, gripping it solidly in both hands, and she stood in some approximation of a martial-arts ready position and took a few deep breaths. She bared her teeth, looking truly savage for a moment, and cocked her arm back. Then, she struck with all her strength.

There was a *tock* sound like a rock being thrown against the side of a house, and Aimee pulled her little fist away, wincing in pain.

Master Chin looked down at the board in his hands. There was a tiny dent where one of her knuckles struck, and a small smear of blood. Otherwise, the board was completely undamaged. Aimee was cradling her hand.

"Let me see," Chin said.

He took her hand and looked at it. A couple of her knuckles were raw, swollen, and red, but nothing was broken.

"I can do it," she said quickly, trying to hide her pain. "Let me try again."

Master Chin chuckled and patted her on the shoulder. "It was a very good attempt," he said. "I'm glad to see you have spirit."

"So . . . does that mean you'll train me?"

"No, I'm sorry. A deal's a deal. But when you're ready, the board will be here."

❧

Aimee took a taxi back into town. Feeling empty and sad, she stared out the window at the ghostly outlines of snow-covered trees. She had thought Master Chin might not be willing to train her, but the possibility had at least given her something to hope for. Now she felt powerless. She'd felt that way her whole life, and she was sick of it. She knew Raphael was only trying to keep her safe, but no one was doing anything to keep her mom safe. And if she had to go back to Mountain High Academy without knowing what had happened to her mother—especially after hearing her voice in the tunnel—well, she would go crazy for real.

The knot of frustration in her stomach seemed to shift suddenly, and she realized it was more hunger than nerves. She was ravenous—she hadn't eaten anything since breakfast and then it had only been a slice of toast and some juice.

"Hey—excuse me," she said to the driver. "Would you pull over in front of Little Geno's? Just wait outside for me. I want to get some food."

She'd already been gone for hours; her dad or Rick had had probably found out by now and she was already in big trouble, but she was too hungry to care. The cab stopped at the curb and as she crossed the sidewalk, she realized there was something different about Little Geno's. She paused, staring at the yellow and red sign and the plate glass of the storefront, perplexed, until she realized that it wasn't Geno's that was different; it was the building next to it.

It was a six-story, brick-fronted structure dating from sometime in the eighteen hundreds, like most of the buildings in downtown Middleburg. It had been vacant for most of her life, and her dad had inquired about buying it several times, only to be told by some out-of-town lawyer that the owner—whoever it was—had no interest in selling. For a while, her dad had grumbled about it every time they drove past, until finally he'd given up on the place.

Now there was a brand-new, modern-looking sign above the door. MORNINGSTAR INC., the shiny, silver letters read. Aimee walked slowly toward the display windows and looked through them. Someone had redone the place, and it was beautiful. The floors were slate, the walls exposed brick. Several modern-looking desks made of some sort of sleek, dark wood—ebony, maybe—were arranged artfully around the room. Each desk had a cool-looking new computer and a vase of fresh flowers on it. In the center of the room was a statue of an angel, carved of some sort of dark stone. It rose up from the center of the floor almost to the ceiling, and had to be at least eleven feet tall. She looked closer and saw that the statue was a fountain. Streams of water were coming out the angel's eyes—two rivers of tears that ran down her cheeks, down across her breasts and the stone tendrils of her hair and into a small pool of water below. Her outstretched arms reached toward the ceiling, and her face was tilted pleadingly upward. It was a gorgeous piece of art, but it gave Aimee the creeps.

She wondered suddenly how the place had been redone so quickly—and why. She and Rick passed this storefront every day on the way to school, and she hadn't noticed any activity here at all. It was as if the place had been completely renovated overnight. Aimee didn't know much about construction, but she was pretty sure it would take months to do this kind of beautiful work. It was certainly the most lavish office in town, even more luxurious than her dad's.

As strange and beautiful as the furnishings were, something else caught Aimee's eye. There was someone—a young man—sitting in the back corner at a desk larger than all the others, wearing a perfectly tailored gray pinstriped suit. He looked just a little older than Rick and he was writing something with a thick, black pen—like the fancy one her dad showed off when he signed important documents. His hair, the same dark color as the wood of his desk, reached to his shoulders. As he leaned over the document he was reading, a thick strand of it fell across his face. When he brushed it away to reveal his perfect features, Aimee was momentarily captivated. He was stunning—prominent cheekbones, a strong square chin—but it was more than that. The light above his desk was the only one on in the office, and he sat under it as if it was a carefully placed spotlight. He seemed to Aimee like a work of art—like a living sculpture or a painting come to life.

Without meaning to, she stepped forward and cupped her hands against the glass, staring in. At that moment, he looked up from his paper and his gaze met hers. Even from this distance, she could tell his eyes were a deep, piercing blue. The smile he gave her was strangely serene as if, Aimee thought suddenly, he knew some divine secret he wasn't about to tell.

A bit of the old panic seized her briefly and she backed away from the window, slipping on the ice and almost falling as she hurried to the cab, just managing to keep her footing and make it safely. As she closed the door behind her, she could have sworn she heard her own heart, beating fast in the silence.

She didn't understand her reaction to the sight of the handsome young man. She was in love with Raphael and nothing would change that. But she felt so strange—awkward at being caught in such blatant voyeurism, yet intrigued by the thrill she'd felt for one brief moment as he looked up and stared right into her eyes.

"What, no pizza?" the driver asked.

"No," she murmured. "Just take me home, please—Hilltop Haven." She wasn't hungry anymore.

As they pulled away from the curb, she couldn't help but glance once more at the office of Morningstar Inc. The lights, now, were all off.

I'm in love with Raphael, she thought. *I am.*

But all the way home, she couldn't stop thinking about the handsome young man with the piercing blue eyes.

ॐ

Bright, clear strains of music soared through the room, painting the walls, the ceiling, the floors with shafts of warm, invisible sunlight. Zhai had mastered many of the most difficult violin solos ever written, and for the past few months, he'd been experimenting with improvisation. But he'd never dreamed of making up a piece on the spot and playing it for someone—until now. He almost always kept his eyes shut when he played, but now he ventured to open them just for an instant.

There was the beautiful Kate, sitting on the bench at the foot of his bed, watching him with a rapt, dreamy look on her face. For a moment, it was hard for him to believe that she was really there with him. It seemed much more likely that she was some sort of beautiful delusion conjured up by the music—but there she was, as gorgeous as ever. He felt his heart beat faster and his music sped up with it, as he played a soaring run that peaked at a high A then plummeted back down again—but as the beautiful piece (*Nocturne for Kate*, he would call it) reached its glorious conclusion, something bizarre happened. The backs of his hands began to burn terribly. The bow felt heavy and strange between his fingers, and the notes he was playing started to go off pitch. He looked down at the violin in horror. He was dragging the bow back and forth across the strings now, grinding out a terrible atonal, groaning sound. Kate winced and looked confused, but still he could not stop. His hands moved of their own accord, in twitches and jerks as the awful noise filled the room. He fought with all his strength to resist, but it was impossible. The horrible music continued for what seemed like forever, until at last whatever force was causing Zhai's hands to move disappeared. Immediately, his arms dropped to his sides. The bow fell from his hand onto the carpet and the neck of the violin slid through his fingers. The whole world seemed suddenly to go dim and his mouth filled with saliva as if he were about to vomit.

"Zhai? What was that awful scream?"

He rolled over and opened his eyes.

Li was standing in the doorway, with her friend Weston. Zhai got out of bed and stood, but when he tried to walk to her, he started to go down.

"Weston, help!" Li shouted and hurried to Zhai. They caught him before he hit the floor and got him back to bed. The strange feeling slowly dissipated. Zhai looked at his sister, confused for a moment, and then he looked around.

Kate wasn't there. It had been a dream, but the stabbing ache in the back of his hands was real. And it was real that he wouldn't be able to hold his violin properly for a while, although he could remember every note of *Kate's Nocturne*. As soon as he could, he would write it all down, and he would play it for her some day. He shuddered as he also remembered how it had changed to hellish, devil music.

Li sat down on the edge of his bed and Wes paced the room. They both looked worried.

"Zhai, what happened?" Li asked. "Should I get Mom to call a doctor? I'm calling her." She pulled her phone out of her pocket but Zhai put his hand over hers.

"No," he said. "I'm fine. It was just a dream."

"One of the bad ones?" The sympathy in her voice was genuine.

"No. Actually, it was a pretty good one—at first." He smiled, remembering how Kate had looked at him as he played for her.

"But you never take naps, Zhai. And you almost fell. And . . . " She took Zhai's hand. "What's with the gloves?"

Zhai looked down at his hands then up at Li. Yesterday, after he had discovered the tattoos, he had stopped off at Lotus Pharmacy where he'd picked up a pair of black leather driving gloves, the kind with little holes on the knuckles and no tips on the fingers. They looked like something the leader of a motorcycle gang would wear, and they didn't exactly go with Zhai's rugby shirt and khaki pants, but he'd figured the gloves would be easier to explain to everyone than the weird tattoos on his hands. And, as it turned out, none of his friends had even asked about the gloves. He thought they probably just assumed it had something to do with his kung fu training.

"I know you, brother mine," she said fondly, using her old childhood name for him. "What are you hiding?"

Quickly she pulled the glove off his left hand, held the hand up and stared at the tattoo on the back of it. Then, she pulled the glove off the right hand and looked at it, too.

"Zhai . . . " she began, her voice scarcely more than a whisper. When her eyes met his, the fear he saw in them sent a chill through his whole body.

Weston shifted on his feet uncomfortably and pushed his drooping glasses back up the bridge of his nose.

"Do you know what they say?" Zhai whispered, almost afraid to ask.

"They're both the same," she said quietly, her hands trembling against his. "They say *slave*."

CHAPTER 11

MAGGIE SAT IN BED, the copy of *The Good Book* propped against her knees, her fingers toying with the little key on the gold chain around her neck.

Her mom had been surprisingly lucid again today. When Maggie got home from school and cheerleading practice, she'd found her mother cooking. It was just spaghetti, and it was kind of mediocre, but she had actually taken time away from her precious tapestries to do something useful. When dinner was over, Violet went back to her little breakfast-room studio, which was fine with Maggie. All she wanted to do was go upstairs and take a shower. And she wanted to be alone.

Her bedroom was probably her favorite place in the world, the one spot on earth where she didn't have to worry about looking pretty or sounding smart or acting cool. In there, with the door shut, surrounded by all her familiar things, she could just relax and be herself.

Everyone seemed to be getting on her nerves more than usual today, even Bobbi Jean and Lisa Marie. She no longer had the patience to listen to their gossip or their pointless conversations about boys and cheerleading and football players. And Rick.

She knew they had crushes on him—they had crushes on all the jocks, but Rick was the real prize. Maggie had once thought so too.

Well, they're welcome to him, she thought. It's not like she had a relationship with him anymore. They hardly ever talked and he only called her once in a while to tell her where and when they were going on their next date, in plenty of time for her to look gorgeous.

She took a deep breath and unlocked Lily Rose's book, hoping that when she opened it this time she'd see a page full of words of wisdom about how she could soar above her destiny and make her own choices. But the pearlescent pages were still blank. She had opened it several times since she'd gotten it, and each time she'd been disappointed. But, she thought now as she considered the problem, she had been opening the book in the middle. Even if the book was magic, it was probably best to begin at the beginning. *Especially* if the book was magic.

She flipped back to the first page, enjoying the silky feel of the paper against her fingers. She was disappointed again. It was blank.

She thought, not for the first time, what an idiot she was for believing all this magic stuff anyway, but as she started to close the book, she felt a pressure, a slight constriction on her head, as if the harvest crown—the ghost crown—was still there and pulsing away, trying to send her a message. Maybe it was.

She looked down at the page again and after a moment or two of staring at it she realized something was different. The whiteness of the page was not static at all as she'd first thought. It was like staring out an airplane window while passing through a cloudbank, with wave upon wave of thick white vapor slipping past. Something was moving—something *inside* the page. As she stared, the ghost crown constricted again, and the feeling was painful but also satisfying, and suddenly she was able to see something coming toward her out of the roiling clouds that were somehow trapped inside those mysterious pages. Words started to form, at first distant and milky, then growing nearer and more distinct, until finally becoming perfectly clear:

> Vision not of light
> Eyes not required for sight
> Close them, and see right

Maggie stared at the words, transfixed, as they fluttered in the center of the page like a flag in a breeze. She read them over and over, trying to process exactly what they meant. All the while she could feel the invisible harvest crown pulsing against her brow. The pressure of the crown and the hypnotic movement of the letters drew her toward sleep. Her eyelids drifted slowly downward and she sank into a comforting darkness.

But she wasn't asleep. In the silence of this relaxed state, she heard footsteps coming up the front walkway. Then the doorbell rang. She heard her mother's footsteps crossing the marble floor of the downstairs foyer as she moved to the door. Maggie felt herself falling deeper into the darkness behind her eyelids. There was a strange feeling inside her head, then a subtle *click*, like when someone flipped a light switch, and her eyes snapped open.

The words on the page were still there, and they were no longer wavering. They were fixed, printed, like the words in any ordinary book.

Before she had time to figure out what it could mean, she heard her mom at the foot of the stairs, calling up to her.

"Maggie—come down. You have company."

She carefully closed the book, slipped out of bed, and started down the stairs and then abruptly stopped. There was someone at the foot of the stairs, where she thought her mom would be standing, someone with porcelain skin that glowed with a shimmering, golden light, and where it encircled the woman's head, the glow was tinged with red, and it was more pronounced. The figure did resemble her mother, she realized. Or a younger version of her mother. *No, not younger,* Maggie corrected. *Ageless.*

As she watched, the halo around her mother's head pulsed, grew brighter for a moment and then diminished again. When the light ebbed, the halo looked different, like a golden crown. Like the harvest crown. It pulsed once more, with its own peculiar light, before it diminished, then pulsed again.

"Maggie, are you coming or not?" Violet asked. "How long are you going to keep your guest waiting?"

Feeling dizzy and a little weightless, Maggie slowly made her way down the stairs and into the foyer. She walked carefully past her mother's glowing, surreal form to the front door, which was ajar. She pulled it the rest of the way open and froze in horror.

The thing on the stoop was colossal. Its dark face was twisted, grotesquely deformed. Its shoulders were broad and sublimely muscled, and its eyes were black, with irregular, crimson pupils, like stars made of blood. Its left arm was not made of flesh and bone but some kind of filthy, rusty metal, and at its end was a claw.

"Maggie . . . " It said her name softly, seductively. "Maggie, my love." Its hideous face was twisted into a mad grin.

"No . . . " she whispered, terrified.

She started to slam the door but the monster chuckled—a snorting little laugh—and stuck its foot in the doorway.

"Maggie, what are you doing?" Violet asked. "What's wrong with you?" She turned solicitously to their horrific guest and opened the door wider. "Rick, dear—how are you?"

Maggie watched in stunned silence as the thing opened its mouth, wiped away the saliva drooling down its chin and growled a few distorted words. "Fine, Mrs. Anderson. How are you? My dad sends regards."

"Sorry not to invite you in," said Violet. "I'm just in the middle of cleaning. You understand."

"Sure," the thing said and leaned over and kissed Maggie, its foul breath hot on her lips. "Just wanted to see if Maggie would like to go out to the lake and collect pine cones and stuff for the Thanksgiving display for the trophy case at school. We're on the committee again this year."

"No," Maggie said quickly. She squeezed her eyes shut and opened them again, but the thing still didn't look like Rick. "I—I've got a headache. I think I'm coming down with something. See you at school."

And she slammed the door shut in its face, ignoring her mother's protests as she slid all the deadbolts home and fumbled with the chain locks until she had them all in place.

There was another "click" feeling in her brain, and the next thing Maggie knew, her mother's hands—surprisingly strong—were gripping both her wrists and she could hear her own ragged breathing. Violet was staring into her eyes. She was no longer glowing, and the aura that had encircled her head was gone.

"Maggie, what's going on? Why were you so rude to Rick?"

"Rick," Maggie said vaguely. She was still terrified and wondered if she was going into shock.

"Why did you close the door in his face? Are the two of you fighting again?"

"Yes," Maggie said.

"What on earth about?"

Maggie only shook her head as she pulled away from her mother's grasp. Her brain felt like all the circuits were overloaded.

"Well, whatever it is, that's no way to treat a boyfriend if you want to keep him. It's not like Middleburg is brimming over with handsome starting quarterbacks."

"Mom, I know, okay?" Maggie said. "I'm really not feeling well. I think I'm just going to bed."

She slipped past Violet and headed for the stairs.

That thing on the stoop had been Rick—looking the same as he'd looked during his last big battle with the Flatliners. Hulking, twisted, demonic. She'd thought then—had been horrified, in fact—that she was going insane, only she wasn't. Everything she was seeing was really there. She was seeing things—people—not as they appeared on the surface, but as they *really were*.

Because, like the book said, she was seeing *right*. And that, she thought as she slipped back into bed and pulled the blankets up over her head, was more terrifying than insanity could ever be.

The feel of her soft, sensuous lips pressing lightly against his pulled Nass reluctantly from a dream in which Dalton was kissing him and moving closer . . . closer. It was dark in the living room and quiet in the apartment. A slim, feminine hand ran down his chest, then down to his waist, and on down. Coming fully awake, he pulled away from the kiss and pushed himself up against the armrest of the sofa.

"I was just getting started." The voice, always seductive, was even more so in the dark. But it wasn't Dalton. It was Clarisse.

"What are you doing?" Nass whispered, confused, nervous, and frustrated all at once. Every kiss he and Clarisse shared would make for another painful confession when he and Dalton finally reconciled. *If* they ever reconciled, he thought bleakly.

"Oh, don't get so excited," Clarisse said. "What do you think—I came in here to have my way with you, with your mom right in the next room?"

"What's up, then?" Nass asked with a huge yawn. The clock on the end table said three-twenty-four in the morning and that made him feel even more tired.

"You're supposed to be keeping an eye on the building across the street, right?" she asked, snuggling closer.

"Yeah—so?"

"Well, the workers just left. I was up messing around on the Internet and I looked out the window. The lights are off and all the trucks are gone."

"All of them?"

"All of them. Weren't you supposed to call Raphael or something?"

Nass turned on the lamp and fumbled for his phone. He was about to call, then decided he didn't want to wake up Raphael's pregnant mom, so he just sent a text.

workers left Em's building. orders?

"Let's go see what's going on in there," Clarisse said, an adventurous gleam in her eye.

Nass laughed. "You're not going anywhere. If anyone goes in, it'll be me."

Clarisse gave him a look. "You think you're going without me, mijo? Think again."

Nass sighed. He and Clarisse had been friends for most of their lives, and up until they turned thirteen or fourteen she could always run faster, throw further, and hit harder than he could. Once eighth grade rolled around, Nass finally got his long-awaited growth spurt and Clarisse shed her tomboy jeans and high-tops in favor of skirts, halter tops, and high heels. But Nass remembered all too well how for years Clarisse had been the alpha dog of their little pack, and he knew that once she latched onto something she wasn't about to let it go.

"Come on," she urged. "Let's do it."

"Sorry, not this time. This is Flatliners business."

"So?"

"So you're not a Flatliner."

"I'll join."

"You can't," Nass told her. "You're not from the Flats."

"Neither are you. We grew up on the same block, remember?" She crawled up his body, nestled against his chest again and teased his earlobe with the tip of her tongue.

Nass let his head bang back against the sofa's armrest in frustration, which only made Clarisse laugh. Seeing her there like that, her wavy hair falling around her shoulders with a smile on her face, wearing a cute little blue tank top, it was easy to remember why he'd always loved her so much.

Man, life was confusing. Times like these he didn't know what he wanted—but he knew he had to get out of there if he was ever going to get Dalton back. If he didn't, something bad was going to happen. Or something really good, which would be even worse.

"Okay, okay," he gave in. "You can come. Let's go." He slipped out from under her and grabbed his jeans off the chair. "But we're not going in there alone. Either we get some of the guys to go with us, or we wait until morning."

℘

Twenty minutes later, Nass, Clarisse, Josh, and Benji stood in front of Emory's old building. Nass had managed to get Josh on his cell and then he'd thrown little stones up at Benji's window until he finally got up and snuck out via the fire escape. Beet's phone went straight to voice mail, and there was no way Nass could call Emory in his makeshift garage apartment without waking up his whole family. Raphael never texted back, which had to mean he was asleep with his phone off.

"Should we wait for him a little longer?" Josh asked.

Nass stared at the darkened building for a minute and then shook his head.

"We don't know when those workers will be back," he said. "This might be our only chance to find out what's going on in there."

Benji nodded and Josh shrugged.

"Let's do this," Nass said, and he led the way up the driveway to the back of the building. They found the back door locked.

"Crap," Nass said. "We have to find a way to—"

But Clarisse was already slipping past him. She'd pulled a screwdriver from one of her coat pockets, and in one smooth movement she slipped it in between the door and the frame. Looking up at Nass, she smiled, all sexy and sweet.

"Come on, *papi*," she coaxed. "Give me some of that boy muscle."

Nass came forward and slammed the butt of the screwdriver with the heel of his hand and leaned on it, prying until the doorframe made a cracking sound. Then, together, he and Clarisse shouldered the door open.

"Just like old times," she said softly. With mock courtesy she added,

"Gentlemen, after you," and stepped aside so they could enter first.

Nass smiled in spite of himself as he stepped past her and turned on his flashlight.

"You are amazing," Benji told Clarisse worshipfully. "I love you."

"Sorry, shorty, you're not my type," she said and then amended, "but you're kinda cute. Maybe I'll keep you around for a spare."

"I am so there," Benji quipped.

Nass was already forging ahead into the tenement's hallway. On his left was a door with the number three on it—Emory's old apartment. Nass grabbed the knob, expecting it to be locked, but it opened easily. What he found inside was bizarre.

"What the .. ?" Josh murmured behind him.

Clarisse and Benji piled in behind them, also stopping at the doorway to stare into the apartment, perplexed. It was filled, floor to ceiling, with dirt.

"Dude, this is trippy," Benji said, but Nass was already heading down the hallway, opening the door to Apartment 2. When it opened, a tiny avalanche of dark soil slid out onto his feet. This apartment was also crammed with dirt—so much of it they couldn't even see past the doorframe.

"Okay, seriously," Clarisse said. "This is weird, right?"

Nass ignored her and hurried next door, to Apartment 1. He knew the couple that had lived there with their three little kids. It was the largest unit in the building. He tried that door. It was locked.

He stepped back and kicked the door once, then a second time. On the third kick it cracked and fell inward, swinging half off its hinges.

"Ooh, tough guy," Clarisse teased, her voice low and inviting. Nass ignored that too (although it *did* register). He was already hurrying into the apartment. This one had some dirt in it too, piled up in the corners, but much less than in the others. And something else was different. In the center of the living room there was a huge hole cut into the floor.

Cautiously, he edged closer and aimed his flashlight down into it. It was about forty feet deep, and he could see tunnels opening out of it in at least two directions. On the far side of the crater someone had propped an aluminum ladder, leading down into the pit. Next to it was a jackhammer.

"Hey, what do you think *this* is?" Benji asked. He was standing over a steel plate that was bolted to the floor. There was a round opening in its center. Nass swept the flashlight beam over the floor and saw three more of them around the edge of the hole.

"Mounting brackets, maybe?" Clarisse suggested.

"Yeah," Nass agreed. "For whatever heavy machinery they used to drill the hole. That must've been the vibration we felt the other day. Remember—when you asked me if we have earthquakes here," Nass said. "They would have had to mount the machine to the floor there so it wouldn't move while they drilled or dug or whatever."

"Yeah, but why dig here in the first place?" asked Josh. "You think they're looking for oil or gold or something?"

Nass was already skirting around the hole, heading for the ladder. "Only one way to find out," he said, and started climbing down.

A second later, his feet hit the soft dirt. "I see four tunnels," he called up. "How much you wanna bet one of them runs all the way underneath that wall at the school?"

There was no answer from above.

"Guys?"

The knowing kicked in suddenly, and a wave of dread shot through him. Something bad was going on up there.

"Guys!" he shouted again.

Nass looked up just in time to see Benji falling toward him. He landed in the dirt a few feet away and rolled onto his back, his wide eyes trained upward. Clarisse's scream was shrill enough to slice Nass to the bone as she, too, plummeted down and rolled to a landing in the soft soil. Nass hurried over to her.

"You okay?" he asked. "What's going on?"

Above, he could hear sickening thuds as fists struck flesh, and Josh cried out in fury or in pain. A moment later he was dangling over the rim of the hole. Then whoever or whatever was holding him let go and he landed in the dirt, face first and unconscious.

While Benji hurried to Josh's side, Nass aimed his light upward, looking for some sign of their attacker—but all he saw was the jagged edge of the hole and the blank white ceiling of the apartment above.

"You messed with the wrong people today, *hombre*," Nass shouted up. He wanted to sound defiant, but he could hear the tremor in his voice. "You think you're so tough? Show yourself!"

And a figure wearing a black tank top stepped up to the rim of the hole. He was lean yet terrifyingly muscular, his face gaunt, stern and mostly concealed in the ever-changing shadows.

Nass felt the hairs on the back of his neck stand on end as *the knowing* kicked in again. They should have waited for Raph. Now, they were in trouble.

Without further warning, the figure leaped down and attacked.

CHAPTER 12

NASS BACKED UP QUICKLY as their enemy landed as softly as a puma in the center of the hole. His eyes flicked to Clarisse, and he saw his fear mirrored in her eyes. Josh was lying on his back now, awake but still dazed, and Benji was scrambling to his feet, raising his small fists into a ready position.

The enemy crouched as if preparing to strike, his face still cloaked in shadow, and it struck Nass how strangely he moved. Each motion was graceful, yet twitchy, unnatural, like . . . a marionette. With a shout, Benji rushed him, but the mysterious combatant spun and nailed him with a kick that crumpled him.

Clarisse attacked now, too. She'd picked up a heavy rock and she threw it at their attacker, full force, but it was a futile attempt. The powerful stranger deflected the stone the same way Nass had seen Raphael block so many punches in the past, with a simple *Pak Sao*. Now Clarisse was charging, her wicked-long nails aimed like spears at the enemy's eyes, but he grabbed her by the throat and, with his longer reach, kept her slashing claws away from his face. With a quick kick, he swept her legs out from under her and she landed on her back in the dirt, the breath knocked out of her.

Josh was sitting up now, his eyes unfocused, trying to take in what was happening. Nass could see that he was stunned and too confused to defend himself. But instead of going for Josh, the attacker turned toward Nass. Quickly, Nass raised the light to his enemy's face—and his mind went in to a tailspin.

It was Zhai Shao—but the expression of twisted rage on his face was something Nass had never seen, not even when Zhai was in the throes of battle. And there was something else. He had what looked like Chinese characters tattooed on the back of both hands and—Nass thought he must be imagining it, but it almost looked like the symbols were glowing red.

But there was no time to wonder what it meant. Between one heartbeat and the next, Zhai was upon him, faster than Nass had ever seen anyone move.

All he knew then was the coppery taste of blood in his mouth, just before his face went in the dirt. His head throbbing, Nass looked up, blinking the soil out of his eyes, and saw that Josh, Benji, and Clarisse were on their feet. They all rushed Zhai at once—and Zhai, moving like a mad puppet, destroyed them. Josh was in the center, and Zhai blasted him with a punch right between the eyes, knocking him backward. With one fluid kick, he swept Benji and, with his follow-through, cracked Clarisse on the side of the head.

Nass was standing now, and he sprinted at Zhai in a blind rage, jumping forward with what he thought was a perfectly timed superman punch. With preternatural speed Zhai spun, grabbed the front of Nass's shirt and used his own momentum to flip him against the dirt wall. Nass felt his back hit and then he fell, head first and straight down, into the ground. It was just like the pile-driver wrestling move his cousins practiced on him when he was a kid—but ten times worse. The world was spinning, and streaks of white, like little shooting stars, fluttered across his field of vision as he stared upward. It took a second for him to register what he was seeing.

Zhai stood above him, the rock Clarisse had thrown at him raised above his head, ready to bring down on Nass's face. And, Nass knew instantly, a blow like that would kill him. But when he tried to move, he felt like he was in slow motion.

"Zhai, please," Nass begged. "You don't want to do this. Come on, man."

Even though Zhai was their enemy, Nass never thought of him as a killer. But there was no sympathy, no hint of mercy on his face now. All Nass could do was close his eyes as Zhai rocked forward to hurl the stone at his head.

He heard the sound of the impact, but he felt nothing—and he wondered if that meant he was dead. There were more sounds—thudding and grunting—and he reached one hand up and touched his face to assess the damage, expecting to find nothing but a crater where his nose had been.

But he seemed unhurt. When he opened his eyes, he understood why. The rock was sitting on the ground next to him—and Raphael was fighting Zhai. By the time Nass managed to stand, Raph had blood running down the side of his face, but he was holding off Zhai's unorthodox attacks—barely.

"Nass," Raph shouted desperately. "Get everyone out of here. Now!"

The urgency in Raphael's command squashed any hesitation Nass might normally have felt, and he obeyed without question, rushing to Clarisse, pulling her to her feet and helping her up the ladder. Benji followed. Josh stumbled toward Raphael, intent on helping their leader, but Nass grabbed his arm.

"He ordered us up the ladder," Nass reminded him. "Remember the Wu-de."

Wordlessly, Josh reversed his direction and mounted the ladder.

"You go too!" Raphael shouted at Nass now, just as he ate a hard kick to the gut. He retaliated with three quick strikes, but Zhai blocked them all. "Go up and pull the ladder up behind you."

"But—" Nass started to object and then he shut his mouth. Raphael was the leader of the Flatliners, and the Wu-de was their code. It required him to obey, not to question. Reluctantly, he limped to the ladder and climbed up. Then, with Benji's help, he pulled the ladder up behind him.

Now, Raph and Zhai were trapped in the pit together. The only way out for either of them was through one of the pitch-black tunnels.

"What do we do now?" Clarisse asked. "Sit here and watch until they kill each other?"

From the looks of it, they just might do that, Nass thought. They were both bloodied, and their pace showed no sign of slowing. But something was different about the way Zhai was fighting. Nass had seen him and Raph duke it out before, and their styles had been identical; today, the way Zhai moved, attacked and defended himself was completely different. More relentless, more determined. *More dangerous.* Raphael took another fist to the side of his head, and Nass knew he wouldn't be able to stand up to that kind of pounding indefinitely.

"No," he told Clarisse, looking around the room for an answer. And he spotted it. "We help. Josh, Benji!" he shouted as he pointed. "Grab that jackhammer."

Meanwhile, he orbited the crater. On the far side, there was a spot where the hole in the floor was larger than the hole in the ground beneath it, leaving a flat section of dirt jutting out. Nass headed for it.

It was obvious that there was something crazy going on with Zhai; there was no way even Raphael could beat him in a regular fight. The best they could hope for, Nass thought, was to stop him.

Benji and Josh met him on the far side of the hole with the jackhammer, and Nass lowered its tip so that it was digging into the soil at the rim of the hole, about two feet back from the edge.

He gave a shrill whistle, and Raphael, barely avoiding one of Zhai's lethal strikes, managed to glance up at him for a second. The grin Raphael gave him told Nass that he understood the plan.

Expertly dodging and weaving, Raphael retreated, backing his way around the circumference of the hole while Zhai methodically attacked him, circling, all the while, toward the spot where Nass waited.

Nass had never used a jackhammer before, but he sure hoped it wouldn't be too hard.

As he watched, Raphael lured Zhai closer.

Finally, Raphael stood with his back against the wall, right beneath Nass. Raph waited there for an instant in tense stillness, the bait for Nass's trap. Zhai hesitated, and Nass thought for a second that their plan might not work at all; then, Zhai struck. Just as Zhai's fist hit the earth behind him, Raphael dove and rolled clear.

"Now!" he shouted.

Nass pulled the trigger on the jackhammer and the thing sprang to life in his hands, giving him a jolt that made his teeth rattle. Instantly, the loose dirt below gave way and the jackhammer fell downward, almost taking Nass with it. He managed to let go at the last second and Benji and Josh grabbed the back of his jacket to keep him from falling into the hole. There was a cloud of drifting dust, and everyone stared down into the chasm, waiting breathlessly for the air to clear. When it finally did, they all sighed as one, relieved. The plan worked. The jackhammer had caused a little landslide, and Zhai was now buried up to his neck in dirt. He twitched violently, trying to get free, but for the moment at least, he was stuck.

"Grab the ladder," Nass said. "Let's get Raph out of there."

Raphael was sitting on the ground, in the same spot he'd landed when he rolled out of the way of the trap, staring at Zhai. When the ladder came down next to him, he glanced at it, as if startled awake from a dream. Then he slowly rose and started to climb up.

A thin trickle of blood ran from the corner of his mouth and he had a cut above one eye. He was bruised and filthy—but the worst part for Nass was the worry in his face.

"Thanks, guys," Raphael said weakly and then he looked down at Zhai, who was still struggling to get free. The rest of them looked, too.

"What the hell is up with him?" Nass asked. "Is he on some kind of super steroids?"

Raphael shook his head. "I don't know."

"Why didn't you use Shen on him?" Nass asked.

Raphael shook his head. "I tried but it didn't work. I don't know why." He finally tore his eyes away from the pit and looked at his crew. "Let's get out of here before the rest of the Toppers show up," he said.

Everyone followed Raphael outside, into the cold night air. He didn't stop until they had crossed the street and gathered on the stoop of Nass's building.

"Well, now we know what they're doing with the apartments: digging big-ass holes in them," Benji said, with his usual sarcasm. "Makes perfect sense."

"Yeah," Josh agreed. "Digging holes and using kung-fu-master gang leaders to guard them. That's normal for a real-estate company, right?"

"It's normal for Middleburg," Raphael said, a glint of humor finally returning to his eyes.

"There was something weird about Zhai, though—right?" Nass said. "About the way he was fighting."

"Yeah," Raphael admitted. "He kicked my ass."

"What do you think is going on—with Zhai and the holes and everything?"

Raphael gazed across the street at the empty apartment building and shook his head. "I don't know, Nass," he said. "All I know is I've had enough fun for one night. Let's get some sleep. I'll catch you guys at school."

∽

Zhai felt a strange, plummeting sensation and his vision came into focus. His left cheek ached and he tried to reach up and touch it, but he was unable to move his arm. He looked down and saw that he was buried up to his collarbones in dirt. His tank top was filthy and spotted with little drops of blood. His eyes closed as he struggled to remember, to understand why he was here, what was happening, but the place in his mind where the memories should have been was glaringly, painfully empty. He remembered doing his nightly meditation, putting his homework away, and zipping up his backpack, then climbing into bed and switching off his bedside lamp. The next thing he knew he was here, buried chest deep at the bottom of what seemed like an indoor pit. It was dark, but above him he could see the ceiling of what looked like a normal room. What he couldn't see was any way to get up there.

After a few frustrating minutes, he managed to extricate one of his arms from the dirt. His hand hurt, and he paused for a second to stare at the tattoo on the back of it. It was throbbing and stinging now, like the insistent pain from a burn. But worse than the pain was what the words meant.

Slave.

That's what Li had told him. She seemed terrified for him when she saw those marks on his hands.

But that was crazy. He wasn't anyone's slave—was he? What had he done while he was blacked out, and on whose behalf? And whose blood was on his shirt—his or someone else's?

Growing more claustrophobic by the second, Zhai worked fast, shoveling dirt away from himself with his free hand until he was able to get his other arm loose. After another few minutes, he managed to get his body and his legs out of the dirt. He rolled down the slope of the little avalanche that had buried him and stood, brushing the black, sticky soil off his clothes as he looked around.

Four tunnels radiated out from the pit, each with an entrance wide enough for four people to walk through side by side. He looked up. The hole he was in was deep, and there was no way he could climb the slippery, crumbly walls. He looked at the tunnels again, and spotted a yellow extension cord strung down one of them. Far back in that tunnel, he could see a faint glimmer of light. He hurried toward it.

It was hard to know how much time elapsed as he moved through the barren corridor. He passed numerous work lights—single bulbs enclosed in protective metal housings—affixed to the extension cord. Each of them offered a small oasis of illumination on his journey through the darkness. Once, he almost took a step forward when a sudden rush of cool air coming from below warned that there was no floor beneath him. He reversed his momentum at the last second, falling backward; then he eased forward and stared down over the rim of what appeared to be a downward leading shaft. There wasn't much light so it was impossible to tell how far it might go, but Zhai was thankful for the superior sense of balance Master Chin's training had given him. If not for that, he would be at the bottom of another pit. He leaped over the chasm, moving forward more carefully now. As his journey progressed, he found three more down shafts, all of them so deep he couldn't see the bottom. He hopped each of them and continued on, his unease growing. What if there was no exit the way he was heading? What if it was just a dead end? What if he didn't see the next pit in time and fell in? What if somebody unplugged the extension cord and the lights went out, stranding him in darkness?

At last, he saw a jumble of debris ahead, and heard the rustle as a snarl of yellow caution tape crinkled in the breeze. He hurried forward and found himself in yet another pit, this one strewn with broken cinderblocks and shattered concrete. He looked up and to his left, he could see the ceiling of the Middleburg High gym, complete with a faded MIDDLEBURG PHOENIXES—1980 STATE BASKETBALL CHAMPIONS banner hanging from one of the girders. To his right was open sky, clear and black with a surprising array of stars, where a little section of the gym roof caved in when the wall fell. Zhai easily scaled the debris and pulled himself up, then followed the red glow of an exit sign across the gym to a doorway. He pushed through the doors and stumbled onto school's lawn, still white from a dusting of snow. He had no idea what time it was, or what he'd been doing, but he was completely exhausted. All he could think about was taking a shower and getting back into bed.

Automatically, his hand went to his pocket and came out with his phone—whatever state he was in when he left home, at least he'd remembered that—and called his family's driver, who sounded confused and sleepy. Bob responded to Zhai's request for a ride with what Zhai was sure had to be a curse in his native Chinese, but soon the Shao's huge, regal-looking car pulled up in front of the school.

Zhai jumped into the backseat and cranked up the heat. Whether he was chilled from waiting out in the winter night in only a tank top and jeans, or from the fear of what was happening to him, he didn't know—but either way he couldn't stop shivering.

A few minutes later, he hurried gratefully into the house, entering from the garage into the kitchen. He slipped out of his shoes, not caring what the maid would think when she found them there, caked in filth, the next morning. He hurried across the moonlit tiled floor and passed through the foyer. Suddenly a hand reached out of the darkness and grabbed his arm. Instinctively, he spun and struck out, just managing to stop his fist an inch before it struck his stepmother's face.

"Lotus?"

In the shadows, he could barely make out her features. He was surprised to find her downstairs in the middle of the night. He was even more amazed that when he'd almost hit her in the face she hadn't even flinched.

"Did I startle you?" she asked, her voice as even and pleasant as ever.

As Zhai lowered his fist, she caught his hand and turned it over, examining the mark on the back of it, along with his bloody knuckles. He expected to see some fear or concern when she raised her eyes to his again, but she remained perfectly placid.

"Well," she said. "Perhaps those fighting lessons your father has been paying for all these years haven't been wasted after all."

She knows, Zhai thought. *She knows something about what's happening to me.*

"Those men who came over the other day—who are they?" he asked.

"They are from the *Hei She Bang*," she responded. "The Order of the Black Snake."

"What's that?"

"Nothing you have to worry yourself about, my son," Lotus said. It was the first time Zhai could ever remember her calling him that, and he thought he detected a trace of sarcasm in her tone.

"What are they doing in Middleburg?"

"The same thing they do in China," she said with a cynical smile. "Whatever they want."

"What is it they want?" Zhai pressed. "What are they doing to me? Why did they call Dad a slave?"

"That I can't say—but I will tell you this." She spoke quietly but her tone was serious. "Best to stay away from them. But if you can't, whatever they ask, do it. Whatever they want, give it to them. There's a saying: those who poke at snakes get bitten." She stared into Zhai's eyes for a moment longer and then dismissed him. "Good night, Zhai," she said. "Pleasant dreams." And she turned and gracefully ascended the stairs.

"But—wait," Zhai began. There were so many questions he needed answered, but Lotus didn't turn back.

Silently, she disappeared into the shadows.

శి

Orias Morrow had a solitary meal at Spinnacle but he did not eat as mere mortals did to sustain life. He ate because it was delicious and, because no matter how much he gorged himself, he didn't have to worry about gaining weight. He ate to fill the emptiness in his soul, the lonely void that permeated his life—thanks to his father and his very human mother. It was a void that would be with him for all time, no matter how much he ate, how many houses he owned, how many designer clothes and cars and motorcycles he bought, or how many beautiful women fell at his feet, ready to give him anything he wanted. He ate to spite all the miserable souls in the world who had no appreciation for the gifts God extended to them on an unlimited basis. But most of all, he feasted for the same reason he did everything: because he wanted to.

After his dinner he walked, sometimes rising an inch or so above the sidewalks and gliding around Middleburg until midnight, when he was sure Oberon had consumed enough wine to pass out. Only then did Orias go home where he drifted, a few inches above the carpet, up the attic staircase to slip into the hidden tower room, a new Sharpie marker in his hand. He had discovered that his father was normally in a deep sleep at this time, so he could slip in and out undetected. Tonight was no exception. Oberon lay on his back on the bed, a quilt pulled up to his chest, the scarred sockets of his ruined eyes staring sightlessly upward at the water-stained ceiling. But water stains weren't the only things on the cracking plaster; there were words, too. Three words written over and over and over again across the walls, the windows, the door, the floorboards, all in the same broad, angular script. Orias's handwriting.

Though the words were perfectly clear to him, they were written in a language that no human on earth could read. It was a language that began in the Celestial City, but this was a corrupted version of it. The tongue of the Dark Territory. And although it lacked its original beauty, it contained all the power of Celestial speech—and then some.

Of all the surfaces in the room, only the bottom half of the door had not yet been covered; Orias stooped in front of it now and began writing. He knew he had to work fast. Three words:

SHALL NOT PASS

His father could read in that tongue too, of course—if his eyes worked. Weeks had passed since Oberon had summoned Dr. Uphir. If Orias's work wasn't finished by the time he arrived, there would be no way to contain Oberon.

As he wrote, his mind wandered to the life he'd left in New York City. He had thrived there, and he missed it. The press of Manhattan's crowded sidewalks, the honking of the taxis, the shouts of the angry and the insane (who roamed freely), the sheer energy of the place: all these fed his desire for chaos. It was like the Tower of Babel just after it fell, all those people clashing and contending with one another, struggling with one another, competing with one another, building and destroying and building again. New York was home for him—or at least, the closest thing he could find to home on this earthly plane of existence—and he had been loath to leave. But Middleburg was completely different.

In New York, the veil between worlds was thick and solid—a metaphysical stone wall that kept everything earthly and material in and everything supernatural out. But in Middleburg, the veil was thin, frayed, as insubstantial as a sheet of tattered gauze. With only a little force, he knew, one could punch through it altogether. It was a prospect that made his mind reel with possibility. But that wasn't all. There were souls here that were greatly prized by God—souls that could, if properly developed, be nearly invincible in His service. How delicious it would be to cause their fall!

Then, of course, there was the treasure. He could feel it now, throbbing, thrumming, singing across the mountains and valleys of time and space, its voice filled with power beyond comprehension, calling to him.

Orias, come! Use me! Possess me! Corrupt me, and become mighty beyond all reckoning!

At last he understood why his father was so fascinated by this miserable out-of-the-way place. It had the potential to be a wonderland of abomination, the epicenter of all annihilation. And if Orias could not find peace in a decaying world that he was cursed to wander for generations (seventy times seventy, times seventy thousand, times seven of them, to be exact), why should anyone?

The crossing of the tracks was like the crosshairs of a great gun sight aimed at all of humanity, and with a little luck and a lot of cleverness, he could be the one to pull the trigger. It would be incredibly amusing—and he wasn't about to share the fun with his father. If the mad old bastard hadn't lost his one good eye in a battle with a *kid*, he never would have called on Orias in the first place. They'd never had more than a cursory relationship, yet his insufferable ego had convinced him that his son would rush to do his bidding, as he'd done as a child. But once Orias was finished writing on every inch of the walls, floor and ceiling, the incantation would be complete. His father would be sealed in this room forever.

With Oberon out of the way, Orias would get Aimee Banfield to fetch the treasure for him. With the treasure, he would be able to open the door to the Dark Territory. And with that door open, the world would be his.

His father stirred on the bed in a great screaking of springs.

"Orias?"

Yes, you pathetic old man?

"Yes, Father. I'm here."

"What's that I smell? It smells like a marker."

Pathetic, but still as cunning as ever—and as dangerous.

"It's paint, downstairs," Orias said. "I was painting my bedroom. I just came up to get your dinner tray." Silently, he recapped the marker and slipped it into his pocket. He had a little more to do, but it would have to wait.

"Any word from Uphir?"

"Not yet, Father. I'm sorry. You know how it is. The doctor's priorities are not always of his choosing—it's that business on Mount Hermon, I think."

"Conclave of the Seventeen Prefects. Yes—and usually a bad business," mused Oberon.

Orias laughed. "So . . . what? He's on call in case they start hurling thunderbolts at each other?"

"Don't make jokes," Oberon said sternly. "That's exactly what they'll do if things don't go well."

Orias went to his father's bedside, and when he bent down to pick up the tray, Oberon reached out with incredible speed and grabbed his wrist. As lean as his father was, Orias felt bone-crushing strength in his grip.

"Are you attending to the family business—all of it?" he asked.

"Yes, Father. I am."

"Have you encountered any problems yet—from either faction?"

"Don't worry," Orias assured him. "The Toppers and the Flatliners—one group operates from greed, the other from need, both equally easy to manipulate."

Oberon nodded, satisfied. "And what about the girl? Have you decided how you'll meet her?"

Orias forced himself not to pull away from his father's grip. "I'm giving a talk at her school tomorrow," he said.

Oberon laughed. "Excellent. You are your father's son, Orias. Make me proud."

"I will, Father." *You sick, crazy, impotent creature.*

At last Oberon released him and sat up, his back against the ornate headboard of a bed that had once belonged to a king. He was gloating, a wide grin on his face. "Ah, yes . . . *Aimee.* Spin your web carefully for her, my son. She must not slip away from us. And those Oriental wizards, the snake-men—what of them?"

"They're still searching."

Oberon chuckled darkly. "Fools. They don't know that only the Banfield girl can retrieve it. She is ours, and soon the treasure will be too."

No, old man. It will be mine. But he quoted the old Dark Territory lullaby. "Good night, Father. May the ruin of your enemies fill all your dreams."

"The doctor will be here soon, and I'll be as good as ever," Oberon said. "Maybe even better."

"Of course you will."

As Orias left, his gaze drifted to the bottom left panel of the door. One last section to cover with his writing and his father would be his prisoner until the end of time.

CHAPTER 13

AIMEE FOLLOWED HER CLASSMATES as they filed into the school auditorium. She was normally half asleep during morning announcements, so she had no idea it was career day until teachers passed out worksheets and told everyone to take notes on all the professions the various guest speakers would be presenting. To Aimee, it all seemed like a major waste of time. She had no idea what she wanted to do in life, and she doubted that having some people come in and talk about their lame jobs would help. She'd enjoyed acting in the play, but somehow she couldn't see herself moving to L.A. or New York and going to a million auditions, hoping to be discovered. It would be cool to be a painter, or some kind of artist, but she could barely draw stick figures. She liked music, but she couldn't play any instruments, and singing in front of people made her so nervous she felt like she would hurl. And after years of watching her dad strut around in his stupid suit on his stupid cell phone, the thought of having some corporate job made her feel equally ill. So, she wasn't very excited about career day.

A row of steel chairs lined the stage behind a single microphone and podium. The kids took their seats, and Aimee automatically scanned the audience for Raphael. She found him in the front with all his friends, up near the stage, and they exchanged a quick smile before he turned away and sat down. Someone gave her the elbow, and she turned to see Dalton sliding into the seat next to her.

"What's up, hot thang?" Dalton asked playfully.

"Finding a career, apparently," Aimee said with an apathetic shrug.

As Mr. Innis took the stage, the general commotion around them wound down to silence.

The principal nervously spun his key ring on his finger a few times as he stepped up to the mic, then stuck his keys back into his pocket and cleared his throat.

"Uh—hello? Can you hear me?"

"*Yes.*" A few kids yelled back. They sounded bored and annoyed already.

"Good. Great. Okay, so welcome to Middleburg High's twenty-seventh annual career day! I have a wonderful bunch of guests here to talk to you about their various jobs. They've taken time away from their busy schedules, so I know you will all pay close attention and give them the respect they deserve. First, please welcome Cheung Shao . . . "

Zhai's dad stepped out from one wing of the stage in an expensive-looking suit. He gave a stiff little nod to the audience who responded with polite applause.

"Mr. Shao is the owner, part-owner and/or president of several companies, including Shao Construction and Middleburg Materials Corporation," Innis announced. "Thanks for joining us." Mr. Shao shook the principal's hand, then took a seat in the row of chairs. The process was repeated with each of the guests. "Next we have Dave Ingram—most of you know his son Beet."

Aimee could see Beet sitting next to Raphael—probably turning red as Innis continued.

"Mr. Ingram owns Body Builders Auto Repair, and he's going to talk about something many of you boys will be interested in—careers in automotive maintenance." He glanced, just for a moment, at the row where the Flatliners were sitting, and Aimee was sure it wasn't his intent to single them out so blatantly, but there was some rude laughter in the audience. She looked over to her right. Of course, it was Rick and some of his buddies. She shrank down in her seat, embarrassed to be related to such a jerk. Oblivious to their derision, Mr. Innis shook Mr. Ingram's hand and directed him to his seat on the stage.

There were also a realtor from Banfield Realty, the new pharmacist from Lotus Pharmacy, a foreman from Middleburg Materials, a hairstylist from Solomon River Salon, a manager from Middleburg Couture, the bank manager and his secretary, and one of the waiters from Spinnacle. Just when Aimee felt her eyes starting to glaze over, the principal introduced his last guest.

"Now, I'd like a big welcome for a newcomer to Middleburg. I met this amazing young man recently, and he made quite an impression on me. He's only a bit older than some of you, but he's already gotten himself a degree in business from Cornell, and he's just arrived back in town after a long absence to manage his father's, um . . . "

Innis paused and cleared his throat, suddenly uncomfortable.

"To handle his father's estate. He has also started a new business venture downtown, Morningstar Inc. Please welcome Orias Morrow."

As the young man took the stage, Aimee sat up straighter in her chair. It was him—the guy she'd seen through the window, the guy with long, dark hair and piercing blue eyes.

Next to her, Dalton was shaking her head. "Well, well. I thought the stories I heard about him were exaggerated. I guess not."

"Why? What did you hear?" Aimee asked, unable to stop looking at him.

"Just that he's like, tall and *way* beyond hot. You know Myka, Emory's girl? She just got a job at Morningstar as a part-time receptionist. She said she feels like she's going to faint every time he walks in. I can see why."

Aimee shrugged. "He's all right," she whispered. But she couldn't take her eyes off him. His hair was tied back in a neat ponytail, and he looked comfortable in his white business shirt, open at the collar, designer jeans, and a sport coat that hung perfectly on his broad shoulders. And his countenance (and oddly, that's how she thought of it) was heartbreakingly, breathtakingly beautiful.

"Aimee?" Dalton elbowed her again.

"What?" She came back, as if waking from a pleasant dream.

"Were you even listening? I said, do you know who his dad is—or was?"

Aimee shook her head and reluctantly turned away from the young man to look at Dalton.

"Who?"

"Oberon."

Oberon. She could still see his chiseled face turn all creepy, the way he'd looked at her just before he abducted her. And she remembered the way he looked when he changed, too—those great, dark wings, the glowing red eye, the black, leathery flesh.

"I told Myka not to take the job," said Dalton. "I told her to stay as far away from him as possible, but she says he's paying so much she couldn't pass it up."

Slightly lightheaded, Aimee only nodded. She looked at Orias again and then forced her gaze back to Principal Innis, who'd finished the introductions and turned the mic over to his first guest.

Mr. Shao stepped up to the podium and started speaking, but try as she might to resist the pull, Aimee's gaze wandered constantly back to Orias Morrow. She heard nothing the other speakers said, but when it was Orias's turn, his words touched her heart.

He spoke of his childhood and told them, a haunting sadness in his eyes, how his mother had died when he was very young, after which he and his father became estranged. How he'd been to Middleburg only twice before and had always remembered it fondly. He told a few funny stories about his college years, eliciting delighted laughter from everyone in the crowd, and then segued to the present day. His voice was rich, warm and sincere when he told them how, after receiving word of his father's death, he'd come back to settle his business affairs, with no intention of staying.

"But," (and Aimee could have sworn he looked right into her eyes as he said this), "I fell in love . . . and found I could not leave this quaint, charming little village."

He finished by telling them about his plans for Middleburg—that in addition to looking after his father's investments, he was starting some new ventures that would create many new jobs within the community. He took his seat again to thunderous applause.

When all the guests had finished speaking, it was lunchtime. Most of the kids filtered out the back doors of the auditorium, heading for the cafeteria, but some stayed behind to ask questions. Already there were at least two dozen students—most of them girls—lining up to talk to Orias. Aimee stared at them with a vague sense of unease.

"You coming?" Dalton asked. "Grandma packed me some peach cobbler today—you play your cards right, you might just get a bite."

Aimee glanced at Dalton and gave her a distracted smile. "Okay," she said. "I'll catch up. I just need to . . . ask someone a question."

Dalton gave one of her trademark, squinty-eyed looks of concern, but Aimee was already making her way down the aisle, toward Orias.

∞

Everyone else had left the auditorium, but Maggie remained in her seat, her hands gripping the armrests until her knuckles turned white.

Even now, she didn't trust her eyes, didn't believe what she had seen, what she was *still seeing*.

The moment Orias Morrow stepped onto the stage, Lisa Marie and Rhonda Marris had started whispering to one another about how hot he was. That was Maggie's first impression, too, but as she stared at him, his figure began wavering like a mirage. It took a moment for her to register what was happening.

His shoulders grew even broader, his height even greater. His perfect face and arresting eyes, already stunning to behold, became terrible in their beauty. And behind his head, a shape formed, round and roiling and dark, like his own private black hole—one that had the power to draw a multitude of souls into its void. A halo, the color of a moonless midnight, encircled his head.

Maggie had blinked. She'd closed her eyes, she'd looked away, but each time she looked back at the handsome young man she saw the same thing. And then she ventured a glance at Rick. He looked the same as he had on her doorstep, with the twisted form of some dark, grotesque beast. The students sitting around her looked different too. There were shapes around them, little swirling clouds of color. She'd looked through enough of her mom's stupid new-age books to know that what she was seeing were their auras. Lisa Marie and Rhonda Marris's were both a matching shade of pink. Principal Innis's was a bright, sunny yellow. She didn't know if there was a name for what she saw when she looked at Rick and Orias Morrow, but Lily Rose's words came back to her.

"Good sight to have. Lets you know who you got to watch out for."

So Maggie made herself look at them. And again, she felt the invisible presence of the harvest crown surrounding her head, compressing it, caressing it, swimming around it, lap after golden lap, a circle of electric energy.

As crazy as it was, she couldn't deny what she was seeing. It was real. And it meant something. She knew Lily Rose was right. If she paid attention, and waited and watched as she adjusted to this strange new gift of hers, she just might be able to figure it out.

Maggie heard scarcely a word of the career presentations. She only realized they were over when half the girls in the school descended upon Orias, like insects drawn to a bug zapper.

She felt a sudden pity for all of them. With terrible certainty, she knew he could make any of them do whatever he wanted.

Aimee Banfield was the last girl in line, and she was impossible to miss. Her aura was twice as big as anyone else's. It swirled close to her head, a chaotic mix of pink and yellow and deep violet, but further out, it was a pure, bright white. The more Maggie stared, the brighter it became, until she had to squint just to look at it.

As Maggie watched, Aimee stepped forward to stand in front of Orias, but she didn't say anything, not a word. Neither did Orias. He simply looked into her eyes and extended his hand, and Aimee took it. To anyone else, Maggie knew, it would have looked like an innocent handshake, but she saw the black halo that surrounded Orias throb and swell, diminishing the healthy colors surrounding Aimee. The swirling black shadows from Orias's dark halo polluted Aimee's radiance, swarming into her aura like a flock of bats.

Orias stared at Aimee for a second longer, his eyes locked on hers, and then he released her hand. Still silent, she pulled her hand back from his—a little too quickly, perhaps, as if his touch had burned her. Without a word, she turned and walked up the aisle, away from him, toward the back doors.

Slowly, Orias looked up, his glance sweeping the auditorium until it came to rest on Maggie. And she heard, inside her head, as clearly as if he were sitting right next to her:

You see me, Maggie Anderson? Well, I see you, too.

She shrank back in her seat, trying to escape the scathing beauty of those hypnotic eyes, and inside her head, she heard him laughing. The ghost crown contracted again, painfully this time, as if trying to expel the horrible, ringing laughter, but the sound became louder, more maddening. Desperate to escape it, Maggie got to her feet and hurried up the aisle, almost tripping as she ran up the steps in her high heels. She burst out the doors and into the hallway, her hands clamped over her ears. Only then did his mocking laughter fade.

Maggie sighed in relief and lowered her hands. She looked up, ready to head to the lunchroom, but what she saw made her hesitate.

Aimee Banfield stood near the window, staring vacantly out at the white, swirling snow. And within the glow of her aura, there remained a groping, seething blackness.

Maggie knew that some kind of connection had happened between Aimee and the newcomer, and she knew that would be bad—very bad—for Aimee. Maggie's conscience dictated that she say something to her former best friend, to warn her. But then she thought of Raphael, remembered his kiss, the feel of his lips pressing against her own, and how badly she wanted that feeling again.

Maggie glanced at Aimee once more and then hurried away.

≈

After school, Aimee and Dalton went to Miss Pembrook's classroom for the first-ever meeting of the Middleburg High School History Club. They sat at a long table in the back of the classroom while, up at her desk, the teacher was explaining a homework assignment to her last straggling student; the rest were outside in the hallway, yelling and slamming lockers.

"Well," Aimee said, smiling at Dalton. "This is it. History Club. We're officially nerds."

"Speak for yourself," Dalton said. A shadow of her old, mischievous smile crossed her face, then disappeared again. "Remind me, how did you talk me into doing this again?"

"It was easy—because I'm your best friend and you *looooove* me," Aimee joked.

Dalton laughed, but it was hollow. It broke Aimee's heart to see how depressed she had become since things got weird with Ignacio. Dalton had already confessed to Aimee how hard she was falling for Nass—and then his old girlfriend or whatever she was had to show up. It was obviously a complicated situation, and it wasn't Nass's fault. Even Dalton didn't blame him. Still, it wasn't easy for Aimee to watch her best friend get her heart stomped on.

Miss Pembrook finished with her student and came over to their table, smiling over a huge stack of books she was holding. She set them down with a weighty thud, and Dalton coughed at the little puff of dust they expelled and gave Aimee a dirty look.

≈ 203 ≈

"Well," Miss Pembrook said. "Look at us! Three beautiful historians. I'm so glad you two decided to sign up. We're going to have a blast."

She handed a big, antique-looking book with a worn cover of embossed leather to Aimee and another to Dalton, then took a third for herself and sat down.

"So . . . what are we supposed to do?" Dalton asked, making a face as she tried blowing some of the dust off the book.

"Sorry about that." The teacher said. "Just go through the book and look for any mention of Middleburg." She reached into her book bag and took out a stack of index cards, which she placed on the table with a few sharpened pencils. "Whenever you find something, copy down the quote, the book title, author and page number—write it all on an index card. If the quote is too long to fit, just write the book title and page number."

"And why are we doing this exactly?" Dalton asked.

"Well, this is research for my college dissertation on the history of Middleburg."

Dalton crossed her arms. "Oh. So we're doing your homework for you?"

Aimee winced. She knew that look, and she braced herself for a battle, but Miss Pembrook remained as cool and sweet as ever. "You'll get something out of it too, I think," she said.

Dalton was skeptical. "Such as?"

Miss Pembrook's smile widened as she took a heavy book from the middle of the stack and put it on the table in front of the girls. It looked to Aimee like it had to be about a thousand years old. Its binding was cracked, and the leather had become dark and brittle with age. Carefully, the teacher opened it to a page she'd marked.

"Do you recognize this building?" She asked, pointing to a drawing of a church on one of the fragile, ancient pages.

"Sure," Dalton said. "It's Middleburg United Church."

"Wrong," Miss Pembrook replied. "This church was built in the late twelfth century in Israel, near the Sea of Galilee. It's unlike any of the other churches constructed at that time, and historians have no idea who built it."

"But . . ." Dalton's brow furrowed. "That's impossible. It looks just like our church."

"You're right," Miss Pembrook said. "But I've been there. I've studied them both. They're exact replicas. Same floor plan, same everything. Now look at this."

She opened a folder and took out a modern, color photograph of another church. This one, too, looked exactly like Middleburg United, but Aimee could tell the landscape surrounding it was different. It seemed to be built on a broad, sloping hill, with misty green mountains in the background. A caption at the bottom of the picture read: CHRIST TEMPLE, ANXI, FUJIAN PROVINCE, CHINA.

"No way," Dalton said, and Aimee could tell she was getting interested.

"Way," Miss Pembrook assured them and took out more photographs. "And there's more. These symbols were found in each of the churches."

Aimee stared at the pictures. They looked like Chinese symbols. "What do they mean?" she asked.

The teacher shrugged. "They predate modern Chinese. The only people I've been able to talk to think it's some kind of unusual regional form of Cantonese."

Dalton was squinting at the pictures, as if by staring hard enough she might be able to unravel their mystery. "So these things are in all three churches? Three churches that all look alike?"

"Yes, all three. They're chiseled into the stone around the top of the interior walls, so it's hard to see them unless you climb up with a ladder. No one even noticed them in the Middleburg church until they were restoring the stained-glass windows a few years back."

Dalton set the pictures down but continued looking at them, with a mixture of fascination and distrust.

"But I haven't told you the most interesting part yet," Miss Pembrook went on, almost bubbling over with excitement. "My old professor had the wood beams in each of the churches tested. They're all made of cedar from Lebanon—the same material used to construct Solomon's temple in ancient Jerusalem. Radio-carbon dating done on the wood confirms that they were all built within fifty years of each other."

"When were they built?" Aimee asked. The whole thing was starting to give her a funny, excited feeling and she was catching the teacher's enthusiasm.

Miss Pembrook leaned close. "Approximately 1200 A.D.," she said and then sat back in her chair, looking smug and satisfied that she'd piqued their curiosity.

Aimee started to ask a question, but then stopped as she tried to process the impossibility of what she'd just heard.

"There were no Christians in North America at that time," Dalton protested. "So who built it? Native Americans?"

"How would they get wood from the Middle East?" Aimee asked.

"Well," Miss Pembrook said quietly. "That's one of the things I'd like to find out."

Dalton raised her eyebrows and gave a little nod. Without another word, she took a stack of index cards, opened her book, and got to work. Aimee did too.

CHAPTER 14

FRIDAY AFTER SCHOOL, ZHAI SAT in Kate's train car, sipping root beer from a glass with blue flowers painted on it. He'd swung by Master Chin's house first, but when he found the kung fu instructor wasn't home, he told Bob to take him to the train graveyard. He wasn't sure exactly what had prompted him to seek out Kate of all people, to decide he wanted to confide in her. True, he was thinking about her more and more these days, and when he tried to think of someone to tell what was going on with him, she was the first one who came to mind. He'd never felt comfortable sharing his most secret thoughts with anyone, not even Li, but he trusted Kate—and he had to talk to someone.

As he sipped his soda he couldn't suppress a smile, despite his worry. Kate was wonderfully levelheaded and had a practical, no-nonsense way of looking at things—and besides, seeing her again just made him feel good. Being in her presence was not only intriguing and intense—it was comforting. And comfort was exactly what Zhai needed.

His strange encounter with Lotus last night had shaken him. Although he believed she loved his father, Zhai had always seen his stepmother as basically self-serving. Her warning about the Order of the Black Snake had left Zhai feeling hemmed in on all sides by something he didn't understand, and he had to figure it out.

He stared into his glass for a moment, wondering how to uncover the mystery surrounding his father now. How did he know those men in the hats? What was the Order of the Black Snake, and how did Lotus know so much about it? Now Zhai felt like he didn't even know *himself*.

He tipped the glass to his lips, drained it and set it down on Kate's little makeshift table. And again he stared at the marks on the back of his hands. *Slave.*

He'd tried to research the Order of the Black Snake, but there was only a small amount of information on the Internet—in English, anyway (and "Translate this" didn't help much). He'd printed one page—a single blog entry from a journalist in Hong Kong. Kate was reading it now, her beautiful brow furrowed in concentration. Zhai had read it so many times he could remember it almost word for word. The journalist had written about a friend of his who'd met a man who claimed to be a defector from the organization. This defector planned to write a book about the Order and expose what he claimed were terrifying secrets.

. . . It was four years ago when my friend, who I'll call Peng (not his real name, of course) first met with an operative who claimed to be a defector from the legendary Order of the Black Snake. At first, Peng was skeptical. After all, most Chinese view the stories of the Order as mythology, a fairy tale meant to scare children into doing their chores and going to bed on time. According to legend, they were a cult of sorcerers whose supernatural abilities included necromancy, divination, and mind control. They were also purported to have their own deadly martial-arts style, Venom-of-the-Fang, which was a closely guarded secret.

At various times in history, the state media used the Order as political propaganda, associating it with revolutionary liberal intellectuals, the Democratic Movement and Japanese spy services.

According to Peng's defector, all the outlandish claims people have made about the Order's paranormal abilities are true—and then some. He claims they are bound together in purpose by a prophesy laid out in an ancient, secret Taoist text, The Scroll of the Wheel, of which the Order possesses the only known copy. Though the defector had never seen the scroll himself, he'd heard his superiors discussing it and had pieced together enough to know that it told of a war between light and darkness and a potential end of the world as we know it. There was also a certain location described in the scroll, a hill that was once a temple, or a temple disguised as a hill (his description of it was vague and muddled) that the Order had been seeking for nearly a millennium. At first, everyone had believed it was located in China, but now the Order's leaders were convinced it was somewhere in North America. This hill (or temple) was, according to the scroll, a nexus of great heavenly and earthly metaphysical importance where a profound alchemical event was destined to take place. The primary goal of the Order was to find its location. What was to happen next, the man either didn't know or didn't want to tell Peng.

He was frightened of the Order, and repeated often that he was risking his life by talking. He advised Peng to be careful, and frequently set their meetings in remote areas under the cover of darkness.

As terrified as the defector was that the Order would find him, he seemed to be even more frightened of what they would do when they found the mysterious temple. His purpose in contacting the journalist through Peng was to secure a publisher for a book he'd written that he claimed would expose the real purpose of the Order and its connections within the upper echelons of the Chinese government. The revelations it contained, he claimed, had the potential to change the world on a spiritual level, and to avert what he called, "the impending desolation of humanity."

Unfortunately, on the day Peng was supposed to meet with the mysterious defector and pick up the manuscript, he arrived at the assigned meeting place, a hotel room in Hong Kong, and found that firefighters had cordoned off the hallway. Using his press credentials, he got inside and learned someone had set a fire in the room and burned its contents. All that was left were ashes and the charred, unidentifiable remains of a man. The manuscript, Peng guessed, was burned as well.

Four months later, Peng died of a heart attack at the tragically young age of thirty-six. Even in my grief, I remembered the strange stories he'd told me about the Order and I had to wonder if they had found him and killed him, too. I'll probably never know for sure, and even if I did I wouldn't be able to prove it.

Still, I can't help but wonder what was in that lost manuscript, and what effect the Order of the Black Snake might one day have on the destiny of humankind.

Kate's eyes were wide as she handed the printout back to Zhai.

"So those men in the hats—you think they belong to this Black Order?"

Zhai shrugged. "That's what my stepmother said. I don't know much about her past, only that she knew a lot of people back in Hong Kong. It's possible she knows more than she's saying."

Kate glanced at Zhai's hands, then back to his face. "Well, it certainly seems like some sort of sorcery, doesn't it? There was a time I never would have believed in such things, but . . . that was before I came to Middleburg."

"So you feel it too?" he asked. "Things in this town are just weird?"

"Yes, I do feel it," she admitted.

"I'm sorry to lay all this on you. I just don't know who I can trust, or who would understand, and you're . . . you're easy to talk to." He smiled, feeling suddenly, deliciously light-headed. He couldn't believe he was finally sitting here at last, talking to her, being with her, as if it were the most natural thing in the world.

"Well, I dare say you're easy to listen to," Kate returned warmly, answering his smile with her own, and the touch of a blush on her face. "But I think we should get those marks off your hands."

"Soap and water doesn't work—I tried it," Zhai said absently. "Anyway, I've got to head out." He took his phone out of his pocket and glanced at the time. Six-thirty exactly. "The football game starts in a few minutes and I promised my friends I'd go. Maybe, uh . . . would you like to come along?"

"Well," Kate said brightly. "I thought you'd never ask! It would be my pleasure, indeed."

With a clatter, she gathered up their empty glasses, put them into her little dish tub and grabbed her shawl from a hook on the wall. As Zhai watched her, he marveled once again at how different she was from every other girl he'd ever met. Of course she wasn't from Middleburg, but the difference was much deeper than that. Even her clothes were different—and although faded or well mended, they were spotless. The way she looked, spoke, thought, and acted was just so wonderfully—different. And for perhaps the hundredth time, he said a silent prayer of thanks that she'd come into his life.

∞

A look of shock registered on Kate's face as she sank into the luxurious Nappa leather seat in the rear of the Maybach.

Zhai laughed. "I know. It's comfortable, right?"

"Why—only the softest thing I've ever sat on in all my life! It's . . . it's . . . " she scrunched down in the seat, wiggling her behind and sighing happily as the driver headed down the dirt road leading to the main street. "It's the closest thing I've found to heaven on earth," she finished.

"Hey, Bob. The football field, please," Zhai instructed, and then he raised the partition between him and Kate and his driver. As they went, Kate gazed out the window at the last departing rays of sunshine slanting through the forest and glittering off the snow.

"What a beautiful evening!" she exclaimed.

"Look up," Zhai said, and he touched a button on the car's center console. As he did, the glass ceiling above, opaque and black, suddenly became clear, revealing the first few timid stars, beginning to peek out through the deep blue of dusk.

Kate gasped. "It's like magic!" she said.

"That's what the salesman told my father, anyway. It is pretty cool, I guess. We have TVs, too."

Kate stared at him blankly.

"Right here," he said, pointing to the black screens built into the partition in front of them. She still looked confused, and Zhai laughed. "Haven't you ever seen a television?" he joked.

"Well, of course I have!" she exclaimed. "Through people's windows, and some of the wee ones on display at the Lotus Pharmacy. I even have one—I just don't know how to get the moving pictures to come on it."

It was incomprehensible to him that she'd never enjoyed the wonders of the Syfy Channel, MTV, endless reruns of *Two and a Half Men*, and news and weather reports at the touch of a finger. It was also intriguing and refreshing. Where had she been, never to have watched TV?

"Would you like to watch now?" he asked, delighted that he could show her.

"Oh, aye—I would indeed." She looked eagerly at the screen.

Zhai picked the little remote from its place in the center console and turned it on. It was a cop show, with some young detective chasing a perp down a beach in Hawaii while they exchanged gunfire.

Kate stared at the screen, wide-eyed, then reached forward and tentatively touched the glass just as the camera angle cut to a wide shot of Waikiki beach.

"It's so beautiful," she whispered. "And so real." She watched for a moment and then asked, "Do you think you could get my little TV to work?"

"I'm sure I can," he answered, adding silently. *I'll buy you a new one, and a generator to run it with, too.*

But how, he wondered, could an amazing, intelligent girl like Kate never have been exposed to television? Even if she came all the way from Ireland, she would know about TV, unless she'd grown up in a convent or something. Before he could ask her about it, the car slowed to a halt in the parking lot of Middleburg High.

"We're the Phoenixes, we rise from flame! We're the Phoenixes—remember our name! We're the Phoenixes, yeah, yeah! We're the Phoenixes! Woooo!"

Maggie did a toe touch and shook her pom-poms in the air, but it was only habit. No real sense of school spirit drove her actions. With everything else going on in her life, it was almost impossible to concentrate on the normal stuff like cheerleading and school work. Slowly she'd started getting used to the strange things she was seeing—the auras around some people and the weird, inhuman forms others took, that no one else seemed to see. But after a while, it all gave her a sort of mind overload, kind of like the brain freeze you got when you chugged a Slurpee. Several times, she'd consulted Lily Rose's *Good Book* hoping to find a way to shut it off, but no new writing appeared. Nothing since *Vision not of light . . . Eyes not required for sight . . . Close them, and see right.*

Now, it seemed even the football game would be ruined. Usually, she thrilled at the roar of the crowd, the feeling of all those eyes on her as she did her little dances and toe-touches and flips. She loved the smell of the grass, the plastic snap as players' helmets clashed together, the electric drone of the PA system as the announcer recapped the last play. But not today. Lisa Marie was next to Maggie and every time she moved, her thick pink aura bobbed up and down uncertainly, which Maggie found annoying, and there was a host of dark, semiformless figures gathering between the woods and the chain-link fence on one end of the field. They seemed to Maggie like snooping, ill-tempered ghosts.

The crowd hushed as the players lined up on the field for kickoff. Everyone stomped on the bleachers and yelled as the opposing team's kicker got ready to start the game. He ran forward, and as he booted the ball, the crowd erupted into applause. The cheering got even louder when Bran Goheen broke a tackle and ran the kick all the way back to the fifty-yard line.

"Woo-hoo! Go, Bran!" Lisa Marie shouted, her voice shrilly and grating. She'd had a crush on Bran for as long as Maggie could remember—almost as long as Bran had had a crush on Aimee Banfield.

The PA squealed to life. "Bran Goheen on the return. And taking the field for the Phoenixes, starting quarterback Rick Banfield."

Maggie's pom-poms dropped to her sides.

"Wasn't Michael going to start?" Lisa Marie asked, her nose all crinkled up as if it were the mystery of the decade. "I thought Rick's arm was broken."

It is broken, Maggie thought. Everyone knew it. She'd noticed at lunch that he wasn't wearing his sling but assumed he was just being macho.

"Well, how did it *heal*?" Lisa Marie persisted. "It's only been a week!"

Maggie was looking out at the field, staring at Rick as he lined up to take the snap. She knew it was him in that familiar number 13 jersey with BANFIELD on the back. Even the way he swaggered out of the huddle was one-hundred percent Rick.

He took the snap, dropped back three steps, and launched a long pass up the center of the field, right into Michael Ponder's chest, and the opposing team took Michael down on about the nineteen-yard line. Now, the players were lined up in front of Maggie and her squad of cheerleaders. Everyone else was facing the spectators, going through the normal cheer routine, but Maggie ignored them, her eyes glued to the game. She could see the colored aura hovering around each player—except Rick. The only light coming from him was a strange, reddish glow, like a flicker of firelight emanating only from his face mask, where his eyes were. His body seemed unnaturally large and powerful, and it seemed to be pulsating beneath his uniform and pads.

The center snapped the ball again, and this time Rick pitched it to Bran on a sweep. Bran raced to the corner and then up the sideline. There were too many defenders there, so he changed direction, cutting back inside. For a second, it looked like he was going to make it to the end zone and a cheer went up from the crowd, but a safety on the other team caught him at the last moment with a solid hit that knocked the ball loose. The spectators groaned as one of the defensive players scooped it up and returned it, weaving past the stunned Middleburg team in just a few strides. Rick was the only one left to stop him.

The furious yell that came from Rick as he sprinted toward the defender made Maggie shudder. At first it looked like there was no way he would be able to get from the center of the field to the defender who was at the near hash mark, but somehow he did. There was a terrible sound—like cars crashing into each other—as Rick slammed into him. The defender went limp before he even hit the ground—clearly unconscious—and landed in a heap with his arms and legs at odd angles. D'von Cunningham fell on the ball, and the Middleburg fans roared their approval.

Maggie was aware of the other cheerleaders jumping up and down ecstatically, but she stood frozen, staring at the boy lying on the grass and the orange aura that drifted slowly upward, away from his body.

"No," she whispered, still finding it difficult to believe what she was seeing. If that light left him, she knew it would mean only one thing. She watched in horror as the ball of light drifted upward, into the night sky. A fissure opened above, incredibly high up, a tear in the blackness that revealed, just for a moment, a world of pure illumination waiting behind it. A shaft of blazing white light shone down, catching the aura in its rays. The aura moved up, following the light.

And Maggie knew the boy was dead.

"No!" she whispered, focusing her energy on the aura. "Go back! Go back down! Don't leave!"

Several trainers gathered around the kid, trying to revive him. As Maggie watched, the aura slowed its ascent. It drifted downward, then up again, as if undecided about which way to go. After a moment, the tear in the sky slowly closed, healing like a wound before her eyes, and the ray of light disappeared. The aura pulsed for a second and then shot back downward, into the body of the injured player, and Maggie saw his leg twitch. A moment later the coaches had him on his feet, helping him to the sideline.

Maggie looked around to find the whole cheerleading squad staring at her. It was only then that she realized she had tears running down her face. She wiped her cheeks quickly and forced a smile.

"Are you okay?" Lisa Marie asked.

"Yeah. Sure. Of course," Maggie said, snapping into full bitch mode. "Why wouldn't I be?"

She gave Lisa Marie a look, daring her to say another word, but she only gave Maggie a conciliatory smile.

The next play, Middleburg scored a touchdown with the twenty-seven-yard pass Rick completed to Michael Ponder in the back of the end zone. The pass was a bullet. Rick's throwing arm was stronger than ever. Maggie stared at her boyfriend as he exchanged a chest bump with Bran and then trotted off the field. She remembered the way he'd looked on her porch the other day—a twisted beast with one arm made of steel—and a sour taste suddenly invaded her mouth as if she was about to throw up. Maybe everyone else in town would hail Rick's amazing recovery as some kind of a football miracle, but not her. Something was going on with Rick—and whatever it was, it was most definitely evil.

❧

While the rest of Middleburg was at the high school worshipping Rick and his Topper cohorts, Raphael was doing what he did most Fridays—working at Rack 'Em Billiards Hall. As hard as his job was—bussing tables, washing dishes, taking out trash, hauling in new kegs and cases of beer and buckets of ice—he was grateful for it. His friends were all gathered around the two pool tables in the back—Beet, Emory, Josh, Benji, Dalton, Myka, and Beth. Nass was doing his gig at Little Geno's (Raph could only guess where Clarisse was—probably riding shotgun with Nass in Geno's delivery vehicle), and Natalie was cheerleading. Beet looked a little forlorn without her, but the game was over by now, and it wouldn't be long before customers started pouring in to Rack 'Em to celebrate or commiserate.

"Hey, you missed a spot," Benji joked, pointing at the table Raph was wiping down. Raphael flicked the cloth at him, sending a spray of table disinfectant his way. Everyone laughed as Benji made a show of spitting out the drops.

"Uck. Tastes like cat pee," he said.

"Yeah? How do you know what cat pee tastes like?" Josh asked.

"Your mama old me," Benji retorted.

"Hey, Raph!" Raphael turned to see his boss, Rudy, standing behind the bar holding up the phone receiver. "Phone call."

Raphael's first thought was that it could be his mom—something to do with the baby, maybe. He abandoned his bus tub and hurried over.

"Hello?"

"Hey there. How's your night going?" The voice was sweet, sultry, and familiar—but it wasn't Aimee's.

"Who is this?"

"Meet me out back, okay?" said the voice. "Right now." The phone line went dead, and Raphael handed the receiver back to Rudy.

"Everything okay?" Rudy asked.

"Yeah," Raphael said distractedly. "I'll be right back, okay?"

As Raphael hurried through the kitchen, wondering what the call was all about, his muscles tensed and he automatically took a cleansing breath, preparing himself for whatever was to come. Opening the back door a crack, he peered out to make sure there was no ambush waiting for him before he slipped out into the parking lot. A single car was idling there, its bright, blinding headlights trained on the door. Raphael squinted in the glare and they shut off. He recognized the red Mercedes immediately.

Maggie Anderson.

She was waving him over to the car. He glanced around the parking lot once more to make sure he wasn't walking into a trap, but he saw no one else. It was just him and Maggie.

He went to the passenger side and the window came sliding down.

"Get in," she said.

Settling warily into the seat beside her, he looked at her inquisitively and braced himself for trouble. But her smile seemed innocent enough—like she was relieved to see him. Raphael thought once again that she was probably the most baffling person he'd ever met.

"So, how's work going?" she asked, as if they were best friends. She looked like a model, sitting there with her fur-trimmed coat over her short, cheerleading skirt.

"Uh, fine," he said, knowing that she didn't give a damn about his job. He decided to play along. "How was the game?"

"Brutal, as usual. But we won." There was a brief, comfortable silence, and then she asked, "Do you get off soon? Maybe we could take a drive—"

He cut her off. "I don't think so. I'd rather not take the chance of being burned alive, if you don't mind."

"I'm sorry about that, Raphael. Really."

Either she was a really good actor (and he had seen her in the school production of *Grease* so he knew that wasn't the case) or she was truly sorry.

"Rick made me do that train car thing," she went on. "He's a monster."

"So break up with him," Raphael said, a little irritably.

A flicker of what looked like hope lit Maggie's eyes at his words, but it quickly faded. "I wish I could," she said.

"Then why don't you?

Maggie was silent for a moment, staring at the steering wheel in front of her. At last, she looked at him.

"I'm afraid of him," she said. "Because he really *is* a monster."

Her eyes locked onto his, and he could see genuine terror in them. "You saw him change, didn't you?" he asked. "When?"

"Halloween night," she said. "I was hiding in the woods when you guys were fighting. He threw his head back and howled and he turned into something—wait. You saw it too?"

"Yeah. I saw it."

"Well, that's what scares me," she went on. "Not so much what he's done, but who he is. *What* he is."

And Raphael saw it again—for a lightning-flash moment—Rick transforming from a muscle-bound high-school jock into a twisted, howling demon.

"What is he?" Raphael responded quietly, surprised to see that her big, brown eyes looked different now than they had in the past. They seemed to stare right into him—*through* him.

"I was hoping you could tell me," she whispered. "Raphael, I don't know what the hell is going on in this stupid town. All I know is I'm leaving as soon as I'm out of high school. In the meantime, I've got to figure out how to stay away from Rick. If he knows I've seen what he really is, I don't know what he might do."

"Why me?" Raphael asked. "Why are you telling *me*, Maggie?"

Her gaze faltered. "Because you're strong. Because you weren't afraid of those samurai warrior things, or going down into the basement to bring me back up. And . . . " Choked with emotion she finished softly, "And I don't have anyone else."

Her words struck Raphael almost as much as her vulnerability. He'd always thought that popular Toppers like Maggie were awash in a sea of friends and generous, doting parents. Was it possible that she felt just as tortured and lonely as he sometimes did?

"Well, you can't stay with him," he said at last. "Not knowing what you know. It's too dangerous."

"So what do I do? He'll freak if I break up with him. Unless . . . " she hesitated.

"Unless what?"

"Maybe . . . if I had some kind of backup."

"What—you want me to go with you to break up with your boyfriend?"

"Would you? I mean, just to be nearby when I tell him. If he tries to hurt me, I think you're the only person in Middleburg who could stop him."

Raphael hesitated briefly and then said, "All right. Any excuse to kick Rick's ass is good in my book. You can count on me."

"Thank you." And before he knew what she intended, she slid closer to him and threw herself against his chest. He put one arm around her, meaning it as a comforting move. She looked up at him, her lips slightly parted. He knew she expected him to kiss her—and he would have a month or two ago. But now he had Aimee in his life, and he wouldn't risk losing that for anything. After a moment, Maggie sighed softly and kissed him on the cheek.

"I'd better get back inside," Raphael mumbled. "My boss . . . "

"Sure," Maggie said. "No problem."

Raphael opened the car door and started to get out, but Maggie caught his sleeve.

"So—are we friends now?" she asked. He knew she caught his look of astonishment because she quickly added, "Oh, I know what you're thinking. But I don't really—have many friends. Not friends I can talk to—not about all this stuff."

He could see that she was sincere. He didn't have many people he could talk to about all *this stuff* either. And she was part of it, just like the basement in her house was part of it.

"Okay," he said and gave her a little grin. "As long as you keep the handcuffs away from me and we stay out of boxcars."

She laughed and her relief was genuine. "You got it," she promised, but her smile was sad. He had to admit that she looked more beautiful than he'd ever seen her, painted with the pale hues the moonlight cast on her through the windshield.

Before he got out of the car, he gave her his cell number in case Rick gave her any more trouble. As he hurried across the parking lot and back into Rack 'Em, he wondered what he'd gotten himself into.

CHAPTER 15

AIMEE SPENT SATURDAY MORNING in the library with Miss Pembrook, poring over musty old books. It was just the two of them, since Dalton's grandma had roped her into helping set up a church bake sale. It was kind of tragic, Aimee thought, that she was giving up her Saturday morning sleeping-in time, but at least the teacher had brought in some delicious cinnamon rolls for breakfast. And Aimee was meeting Raphael afterward, though just for a few minutes—and that made it all worthwhile.

She and Miss Pembrook sat in a quiet corner of the big, terrazzo-floored, high-ceilinged library, flipping through the books. She hadn't expected to, but Aimee found herself enjoying the work. It was like being a detective, sifting through page after page hoping to find some important clue. She wondered if she could be a historian when she finished college. The idea would have been laughable only a few weeks ago. She thought of historians as stoop-shouldered, balding old men with reading glasses perched on the ends of their noses and hair growing out of their ears, but Miss Pembrook, with her beautiful blouse, tailored slacks, expensive shoes, and a chic, cute hairstyle made history seem almost glamorous.

Aimee finished writing on her note card, flipped forward to scan the last few pages, and then closed the book with an authoritative thump. Miss Pembrook looked up and smiled.

"Anything good in that one?"

"A few descriptions of the railroad being built," Aimee said and then picked up one of the index cards. "But this was kind of crazy. Did you know the tunnels through the mountain were already there when the first railroad crews came through? All they had to do was shore them up. Weird, huh?"

"One more Middleburg mystery," Miss Pembrook said cheerfully. "It looks like you might have a knack for this."

Aimee shrugged. "It's kind of interesting."

Miss Pembrook grew serious. "Aimee," she said quietly, "Can I trust you with a secret?"

"Sure," she said. "I guess so."

The teacher glanced around to make sure no one was looking at them—which was silly, Aimee thought. There was no one at any of the tables within earshot, and the huge bookshelves all around them created a concealing screen. Besides, at nine-thirty on a Saturday morning, the reference section of the library was totally devoid of people. Still, she leaned close to Aimee and whispered.

"You have to swear you'll never tell a soul."

"I swear," Aimee agreed.

Miss Pembrook hesitated. "I haven't told anyone else about this. But have you ever had a secret that just burned inside you, so much that you felt like you'd die if you didn't tell someone?"

Aimee nodded. Miss Pembrook had her full attention now.

"Besides," the teacher continued, "for some reason I feel like I can trust you." She took a deep breath, glanced around the room once more, and then reached into her book bag and pulled out a long, lacquered box with an inlaid symbol on top that looked like it was made of jade. Next, she took out a yellow legal pad. She placed the box on the table in front of Aimee, but didn't open it immediately. When she spoke, it was little more than a whisper.

"The man who was overseeing my doctoral candidacy—Professor Donovan—was a great man, a genius. He was digging around in the state archives a few years ago, and he discovered this box."

She undid the clasp and slowly opened the box, and Aimee leaned forward to look inside. It held what appeared to be an ancient scroll, all rolled up, with writing on it that looked like Chinese characters.

"When he started examining it, Donovan initially thought that it was an heirloom brought over by one of the rail workers," the teacher continued. She grabbed one of the big books and opened it to a page she had marked. It was a black-and-white picture of several men wearing wide straw hats shaped like the cymbals on a drum set. They had shovels and pickaxes resting on their shoulders. "Most of the railroads across the Western U.S. were built by thousands of low-wage Chinese laborers," Miss Pembrook continued. "Little more than slaves, really. When Donovan started researching the text on the scroll, he found it was written in an ancient, obscure Chinese dialect. It took him years, and three trips to China, but he finally managed to translate it. It goes on and on, but here's a little bit of it." She looked down at the legal pad and read:

> "... From the place at the heart of the eagle,
> Within the mountain where the steel roads cross,
> There ascends the hope of man,
> Jacob's ladder, Babylon's loss,
> There will the blood of ages rise as a tide,
> As the souls of brothers contend,
> The making of the end of an age,
> Or the start of an age without end.
> In the town at the heart of the eagle
> Seek you there treasure most grand
> More gold than the leaves of an autumn day,
> More silver than moonlight expends,
> More diamonds than the dew of the morning,
> More sapphires than all of the seas,
> More rubies than all the blood spilt in man's wars,
> More emeralds than the grass of the spring.

He that brings forth from black depths of the earth
That joy which each soul desires,
No longer shackled by age shall he be,
Nor from walking of miles shall he tire,
But he shall travel o'er nations on the wings of the wind,
And through history as quick as he please,
The terrible Wheel will stop spinning for him,
And the ending of every disease.
This is the treasure that wise men have sought,
Since the day that the earth came to be,
With this treasure alone are you rich beyond words.
With this treasure alone are you free."

Miss Pembrook snapped the box shut again and slipped it back into her bag.

"Wow," Aimee said, her voice hushed with awe. "Town at the heart of the eagle? What does that mean?"

"Middleburg. Our national symbol is the eagle, and Middleburg is at the center of the contiguous United States."

"So you think there's some kind of crazy treasure buried here?"

"That's what Professor Donovan thought. He was planning to come here and do more research, maybe start some excavations. But at the end of last semester . . . " Her words choked off with emotion. She closed her eyes for a second, collected herself, and then continued, "He was murdered."

"What?" Aimee was horrified, but somehow not surprised.

"Someone broke into his house and went through all his stuff. And . . . he was tortured. The week before, he'd made some vague comments to me about how someone in China was trying to persuade him to sell the scroll to them. When he refused, they threatened him. When I found out he was dead, I knew exactly what had happened. Whoever broke in was trying to find the scroll. What they didn't know was that I had it." Her voice changed and her grief was evident. "Professor Donovan chose to die rather than tell them that I was working on translating the rest of the text. That's why I left my last job and came to Middleburg."

"Whoa," Aimee said, taking the whole story in. "So if anyone finds out you've got it—"

"It could cost me my life," Miss Pembrook finished for her. "So you have to promise not to tell anyone. I mean—*anyone*."

"You can trust me," Aimee said. "I swear. But shouldn't you tell the police or something? What if whoever's looking for it comes after you?"

"There's no one I can trust," Miss Pembrook said. "I don't know much about the people who killed Donovan, only that they're very powerful, and they have a knack for getting what they want, even from police. Besides, if word gets out that there's a treasure hidden somewhere in town, it's going to be pandemonium. We have to keep it quiet so we can find it ourselves and make sure it ends up in a museum, where it belongs."

Aimee thought suddenly of everything Raphael had told her in their secret, hurried phone conversations, about all the evictions in the Flats and how someone was digging holes in the basements as soon as they got the tenants out. It all made sense now. Whoever was buying up all the buildings knew about the treasure—and they were looking for it too.

"You all right?" Miss Pembrook asked.

"Oh—yeah," Aimee said, distracted. It was almost time for her to meet Raphael. "I just . . . there's somewhere I have to be after this."

Miss Pembrook glanced at her watch. "Well, we should call it a day anyway." She started gathering up the books. "Thanks for listening, Aimee, and for helping me with this. It's nice to be able to share it with someone, you know?"

"Thanks for telling me," Aimee said. "And don't worry, I won't tell anyone."

Except maybe Raphael, she amended silently. *If anyone could help them keep the treasure out of a murderer's hands and protect Miss Pembrook, it would be him.*

The moment Aimee walked out the back door of the library, she felt a hand clasp hers, pulling her off the sidewalk, along the side of the building, behind the book-return bin and a wall of overgrown hedges, and around a corner. They stopped beneath a window that looked out on nothing but woods. Then, Raphael's lips were on hers. She moved closer, within the circle of his arms, unable to resist feeling his body melded to hers, warming her against the chill of the winter afternoon.

"I'm supposed to be mad at you," she chided, pulling back reluctantly, flushed with the expectation he awakened in her.

"That's funny," Raphael said. "I'm supposed to be mad at you, too."

She frowned, wondering what reason Raphael would possibly have to be mad at her.

"You went to Chin behind my back," he finished.

"Okay, I'm sorry," she said. She'd hoped Master Chin wouldn't tell Raphael. "I didn't mean to get you in trouble or anything. But I have to get my mom back, Raphael, and I can't let you go on your own. It's too dangerous. Besides, I *want* to be there. I want to be the one to bring her back. I feel like it's something I'm supposed to do."

He looked at her seriously for a moment. "Well, you're in luck, then," he said.

"Why?" Aimee asked, hopeful. "He decided to train me?"

Raphael shook his head, smiling now. "No. He gave *me* permission to train you."

"You?" She felt a strange mix of excitement, fear, and confusion. Training with a stranger was one thing, but with Raphael? What if she couldn't do it and ended up looking like a total loser? And what if her dad found out?

But if they could manage it . . . Aimee nodded, letting the prospect sink in.

"So if I train with you, how long before I'm ready to go with you to find my mom?"

"If you work hard, a few months maybe."

"A few months!" Aimee exclaimed. "I can't leave my mother God-knows-where for that long!"

"I know," Raphael said. "If someone told me I could get my dad back by going into those tunnels, I'd want to go now too. But we have to be ready and that's how long it takes. I have to learn to use the Wheel anyway, and that's going to take some time."

Aimee wanted to argue the point, but she knew he was right. "Okay," she said. "It really means a lot that you want to help me."

He drew her close again but just as he started to kiss her, she pulled away. "Wait—I have something to tell you. Something that might help the people in the Flats." And she told him about Miss Pembrook's scroll and the lost treasure. When she finished, he only nodded, his face a mask of determination.

"You think that's what's going on?" Aimee asked. "Someone's looking for the treasure?"

Raphael nodded. "I'm sure of it. It makes total sense. Once again, the people in the Flats have to suffer because of someone else's greed. Because of your father's greed, Aimee—and Cheung Shao's."

It broke her heart to see his anguish, and she squeezed his hand. His anger was always seething and sometimes it was so close to the surface it frightened her. Suddenly an idea came to her.

"So, what if we find it before they can?" she asked. "You could use the money to buy back the apartments. Once the Flatliners own the land, no one can mess with you anymore—not even my dad."

Raphael's tortured expression changed instantly to a smile. "You're a genius," he said, "That's exactly what we're going to do." He leaned closer, but before he could kiss her again, her phone rang, jarring her back to reality. She dug it out of her bag and looked at the caller ID.

"It's my dad," she said. "If I don't answer it, he's going to kill me."

"But if you don't kiss me again, it'll kill *me*," Raphael teased.

She kissed him once more, quickly, and forced herself to move away. "Hey, dad."

"*I'm picking you up now. Be out front in one minute.*"

"Okay."

"*And please don't make me wait. I have things to do this afternoon.*"

"I won't. I'm coming out now. Bye."

Aimee hung up and looked at Raphael regretfully. She was already backing away, along the side of the building. His eyes were on her the whole way.

"One more kiss?" he asked quietly.

"Yeah, right—one more kiss and I'll never leave. Then I'll get grounded forever, and I'll never see you again."

"Well," Raphael said playfully, "we can't have that."

"No," Aimee agreed. "LUE."

"LUE."

She looked at him once more, storing an image that would carry her through until she could see him again, and then she slipped around the corner of the library without looking back.

Now she just had to get rid of the silly, blissful grin on her face before her dad arrived and figured out what caused it.

⁊

When the old woody station wagon rattled its way into Lily Rose's driveway, Maggie opened her eyes. After the football game on Friday night she'd made an excuse to skip hanging out at Spinnacle with all the Toppers so that she could avoid Rick. She hadn't known then what had made her go to Rack 'Em to see Raphael, but after he'd asked her why she didn't break up with Rick if he scared her so much, she realized that Raphael was the only person in Middleburg, besides Lily Rose, who made her feel safe. Talking to him had made her feel better. It had given her hope, although their meeting ended without the wished-for kiss. He was so amazing. Even the dazzling violets and reds of his aura were beautiful.

Maggie had driven straight home, charged up the stairs, and flopped down in bed—except she couldn't sleep. Even with her eyes closed, too many images crowded her mind. She saw Raphael, how awesome he looked as he sat in her car, telling her she could talk to him anytime. She saw Orias, his black halo churning like a forbidding vortex as he shook Aimee's hand on Career Day. And she saw that football player's body lying still as his aura—his *soul*—drifted skyward. When she did finally doze off, dreams of Rick's demonic face jarred her back awake.

First thing this morning, she'd taken the car and hurried over to see Lily Rose, but no one was home. Determined to wait, she'd sat down on the porch swing and, despite the cold, had apparently fallen asleep, her head resting on her backpack.

Now, Maggie heard the Woody's doors slam and footsteps approaching, and she quickly sat up and ran her fingers through her sleep-tousled hair.

"The old hymns are nice, but it would be good to have something modern, too," Dalton was saying.

"Modern? In church?" Lily Rose laughed. "Sweetie, you know there ain't nothing new under the sun."

"There is in music," Dalton replied.

They mounted the porch steps and then they both stopped to stare at Maggie. Lily Rose smiled and hurried to greet her; Dalton did not.

"Well, if it isn't Miss Maggie!" Lily Rose exclaimed. "Fancy seeing you here on this fine Saturday. Come by for some more tea, I imagine?"

"That would be nice, actually," Maggie agreed. She realized she was freezing.

Lily Rose opened the front door and gestured for Maggie to go inside, but Dalton remained rooted on the top step.

"Aren't you coming in, sugar?" Lily Rose asked her. "You're going to freeze solid, glowering out there in the cold like that."

"If you don't need me anymore, Grandma, I think I'll go see how Kate's doing," Dalton said.

"That's a good idea," Lily Rose told her. "Right neighborly. But remember you got chores later."

"Okay." And Dalton marched back down the steps.

"Don't worry about her," Lily Rose told Maggie as Dalton got in the car and slammed the door. "Come on inside now, before you catch pneumonia."

Unwinding her scarf from her neck, Maggie stepped gratefully into the warmth of Lily Rose's cozy little home. It felt amazing, like she imagined a sip of water would taste if you were dying of thirst.

Maggie smiled, glad to be in Lily Rose's comforting presence, but she felt bad that Dalton had left because of her. And that, she thought, was weird. She'd never cared about Dalton's feelings before.

"Sorry," she said as she hung her coat and scarf on the coat rack next to the front door. "I don't think Dalton likes me much."

"Well, she has her reasons, I guess," the old woman said, but not unpleasantly. She led Maggie into the kitchen. "Just have a seat," she said. "Make yourself at home. We don't stand on ceremony here." She filled the kettle, turned on a gas burner, and put the kettle on the stove.

When Lily Rose looked at her again, Maggie *felt* the kindness in her eyes as if it were a tangible thing. There was something about those eyes. Whenever they were on her, it made Maggie feel so vulnerable, so exposed, and yet so loved. And every time, it almost brought her to tears.

"I won't stay long," Maggie said quietly. She opened her backpack and took out *The Good Book*. "I just wanted to give this back to you."

Lily Rose looked at the book, but made no move to take it. "Now why would you want to do a thing like that? That was a gift. Didn't it work for you?"

"Oh, no," Maggie said quickly. "It worked. It worked fine. I stared at it and some words appeared . . . only I didn't understand what they meant. I was seeing all this weird stuff—I told you—and I thought the book would help. Maybe make it go away or something—but it didn't work. It made me see even more. Anyway, I don't like it so I want to give it back."

Lily Rose gave her a sympathetic smile just as the teapot howled. After she joined Maggie at the table and poured their tea she said, "If I gave you a mirror, and you looked into it and saw yourself but you didn't like what you saw, would you give it back to me?"

Maggie considered the question. "Maybe. I guess. If I thought I was ugly, I guess I wouldn't want to see myself."

"Here's the thing with people," Lily Rose told her. "Some moments we're ugly and some moments we're beautiful. If we were always beautiful, we wouldn't need to be here, learning and growing. We'd already be up in heaven—we'd never have had to leave heaven in the first place. But a mirror helps us see when we're beautiful and when we're not—that way we can fix ourselves up a little, right? *The Good Book* is like a mirror for the world. Lots of people go through life not seeing it the way it really is. Some ugly things—if you look close enough—are really beautiful. Some beautiful things are really ugly. And *some* things—" she paused and took Maggie's hand. "Some things that look completely ordinary are brimming over with magic. Now you could go through life not seeing any of that—most people do. Nobody would blame you. Sometimes seeing the truth is hard. Sometimes it's scary. But it's always better."

Maggie sipped her tea, enjoying the reassuring warmth radiating through her chest, through her whole body. "I just feel like I'm going crazy, seeing all these things," she said. "Like I'm not normal."

Lily Rose laughed. "Well, baby girl, *normal* is a tricky word. If everyone on earth walked around with a stack of pancakes on their head, would that make it normal? The magic that comes from goodness that lives in your heart *is* normal. It's the inheritance meant for every son and daughter of the All. The problem is, most folks these days don't have enough faith to see the magic that's all around them. These days, normal means confused, fallen, lost."

Maggie took another slow sip of her tea. There were lots of times she'd sensed magic lately—the ghost crown, pressing into her forehead at the most unexpected times, her mom's crazy drawings and tapestries that seemed to have a life of their own, whatever they had locked away, down in their basement . . . but she was afraid to believe in it. *Believing* would make her just as crazy as her mother.

As if she could read her mind, Lily Rose said, "I know a little something about your mama's fate and how it came about, and you're going to have to be strong if you don't want to end up like her. Mighty strong."

"What do you mean, my mom's fate?" Maggie asked. "You mean her agoraphobia, or her obsession with her high-school glory days?" But even as she said it, she knew the old woman was talking about something much more profound.

Lily Rose shook her head. "Now, it's not my place to talk about your mama's past, but between you and me, her past has a pretty strong bearing on your future. But you got to ask her. She's the only one who can tell you."

"As if my life isn't upside down enough already? No, Lily Rose. I can't talk to my mom. Questions like that would only upset her and I have enough to deal with just making sure she takes her meds."

"Well, you do what you think best. Just know that your life might seem even more upside down for a while yet, before it starts going right side up again. You might even end up inside out, backwards, and head over heels, too. But most of all, you got to find your faith. Could be in yourself, or others, or something greater, but you got to have it. And you will."

"I guess I'll keep the book, then," Maggie decided. "I'm just worried about what it's going to say next."

The old lady swallowed the last of her tea and set the cup down on the saucer. "I think you might be ready for the next chapter," she declared, and opened *The Good Book* to the next blank page and set it in front of Maggie.

As Maggie watched, the swirling whiteness coalesced as it had before, forming letters. Maggie read the words aloud.

Eat not meat, grain, cheese,
On manna alone subsist.
Ambrosia holy
Spirit feeds on this.

She glanced up at Lily Rose as she finished. "What does it mean?" she asked.

"Well, it doesn't do for someone else to interpret *The Good Book* for you; it's better if you do it for yourself. But I'll give you a hint. If I were you, I'd fast for three days and drink only water."

"Fast?" Maggie said. "You mean not eat?" She normally ate pretty small meals anyway, but the idea of eating nothing at all sounded awful.

"Three times a day, when you would normally take a meal, sit in your room and close your eyes. And meditate. You will be fed by the All—spiritual food. Meditation, not starvation. And when it's over, your powers will be increased."

"My powers?" Maggie asked, bewildered, not at all sure that she wanted them to increase. "Won't I starve?"

"Not if you meditate."

"How do I do that?"

Lily Rose sat back in her chair and thought for a moment. "You get quiet and comfortable. Clear your mind and breathe slow and steady. Find a word or phrase that makes you feel good . . . safe . . . and concentrate on it. Then let each breath carry you up to a higher power. Don't matter what you call it—God or Light or Love or The All. It could even be strong faith in yourself, in who you really are, the light that's within you. Next thing you know, you'll be getting answers to questions you never thought to ask. Seeds of magic will be sown within you, and you'll reap a harvest of power like you've never imagined."

"Really?" Maggie said, thinking of Raphael . . . longing for him . . . and wondering if the magic would help her get any closer to him. "Okay. I'll do it." And on her forehead, the ghost crown throbbed in assent.

CHAPTER 16

Outside, a cold wind howled, but inside the train car it was cozy and inviting. Kate sat, bright-eyed and lovely, washing the last bite of her English muffin down with a bit of orange juice. When she realized Zhai was watching her, she smiled at him and dabbed at the corner of her mouth with her napkin.

"Thank you for breakfast," she said. "It was amazingly sweet of you to think of it."

Zhai smiled. There was something about the way her lips curled and the corners of her beautiful eyes crinkled when she was really excited or happy. It was positively adorable, and the look of joy on her face was addictive—something he was finding it difficult to get through the day without. That was what had made him head straight over to Spinnacle this morning and pick up a three-course breakfast for two, to go. Going to the football game with Kate the night before had been like a dream come true; conversation and jokes had flowed between them, and the few silences were relaxed and easy. Around most people, Zhai felt a need to show that he was knowledgeable and cool and funny and confident. But it was different with Kate. When he was around her, he didn't even have to try. He was completely comfortable, completely himself.

Maybe, he thought, it was because they had something in common. Kate was an outsider in Middleburg, and although he'd lived there most of his life, he felt like an outsider too.

"Penny for your thoughts," Kate said, smiling at him over her juice.

"I was just thinking about the game last night. It was fun."

"Yes, it was!" she said. "What a wonderful sport—not like football back home, o' course. And the band, and the girls dancing in the skirts with the—what were they?"

"Pom-poms," Zhai supplied.

"It was all wonderfully spectacular."

"Back home," Zhai repeated, growing more serious. "Ireland, right?"

"That's right," but she looked away, as if she didn't want to talk about it.

"You know you can tell me anything, right? You can trust me."

"I know," Kate said.

"Okay, so I want you to trust me with this. How did you get here, all the way from Ireland? And why Middleburg?"

Kate stared down at her hands, folded in her lap. "I'd rather not discuss it," she said quietly.

"I just want to understand."

Kate shrugged. "What's to understand? I was there and now I'm here." She looked up at him and smiled. "Anyway, the past is in the past. For now, let's just enjoy the present. Because soon enough it will be the future, and who knows what the future holds?"

"I just want to know you," Zhai said. He suddenly felt very alone. There were so many things going on in his life that he didn't understand—he couldn't even control his own actions anymore—and he didn't know who he could trust.

She reached out and took his hand, as if she sensed his isolation. "You *do* know me," she said. "What you're seein'—this *is* me. Even if you knew the whys and wherefores of how I came to be here, I'd still be me. I'm Kate. Your . . . your friend. Nothing can change that. But some things I have to keep to myself. I'll ask you to respect that, and promise not to ask me questions I can't answer. If you do, I won't be able to spend time with you. And I love spending time with you."

"Okay," he said with a smile. "Me, too." He looked down to see her hand in his and it gave him a wonderful, secure feeling to see their fingers entwined—until he noticed the symbols on the back of his hand. *Slave.*

"Well," he said grudgingly. "I'd better get over to Master Chin's. I'll see you soon, though?"

"Yes, I'd like that," Kate said, walking him to the door. They both stood on her little makeshift stoop, and as the cold wind whipped around them, they moved a little closer together to ward off the chill. Her face was tilted up toward his, her eyes gleaming and warm, her lips soft, delicate, and inviting. Zhai let his imagination go crazy. He saw himself taking her in his arms and kissing her with all the passion he felt when he was with her, just like a scene out of a movie. But just as a rising flood of emotion threatened to carry him away, every muscle in his body tensed at once. His smile faded.

"Good-bye," he said quickly and hurried away.

He walked along the train tracks silently cursing himself for being such a coward. He'd never wanted anything in his life more than he'd wanted to kiss her, but that wall, that blockade that had stifled his emotions for as long as he could remember had risen up once again to imprison his dreams.

More than anything, he wanted to run back, take her beautiful face gently in his hands, and press his lips to hers. But it was too late. What if he went back and tried to kiss her, and then froze again? *That* would go over really well.

So he continued walking up the tracks, gazing up at the leaden winter sky, wondering what was wrong with him.

∽

Zhai stood nervously on the front porch of the old farmhouse, gazing out at the snow-blanketed cornfields and forests. From inside, the music blared—Jimi Hendrix—and it grew even louder when Master Chin opened the front door.

"Zhai! I'm glad you came early," he exclaimed with a big smile. "I'm making BLTs. You're just in time!"

Zhai followed his sifu into the living room of the quaint farmhouse while Chin grabbed a remote off the coffee table, turned the music down and then led the way into the kitchen.

"You like BLTs?" he asked. "I have plenty of bacon."

"Thanks, but I just ate," Zhai said. "I have something I need to talk to you about."

"Oh?" Master Chin slathered some mayonnaise on a piece of toast. "What's that?"

"The Order of the Black Snake."

The toast slipped from Master Chin's fingers, but before it could hit the floor—before it dropped even a foot—he impaled it in mid-air with the knife and slipped it back onto the plate. "The Order of the Black Snake?" he repeated slowly.

"Have you heard of them?" Zhai asked.

Master Chin's hesitation told him a lot, but Zhai knew his sifu couldn't lie to him. It was against the Wu-de.

Chin forked a few pieces of sizzling bacon out of the frying pan, drained them on a paper towel, and stacked them on the toast, along with the lettuce and tomato. Then he answered. "I have heard of them, a long time ago. Tell me, Zhai—how do you know of them?"

"Lotus," Zhai said simply. At the mention of Lotus's name, the sifu's gaze rested on him for a moment before drifting back down to his sandwich.

"Lotus. . ." he said. "What does she know about this Order?"

"I don't know. We had these two guys come to town to see my dad. Lotus was pretty shaken, and Li heard one of them call my father a slave. Then when I asked Lotus about them, she told me they're from the Order of the Black Snake and that I should stay away from them."

"That sounds like good advice," Chin said, and took a bite. Zhai had a feeling he was more concerned than he was letting on.

"What do you know about the Order?" Zhai asked.

"A lot."

"So, tell me about them."

"Your stepmother told you to stay away from them. Don't you think you should respect her wishes?" He took another bite of his sandwich.

"I would, except they gave me this." Zhai showed Chin the backs of his hands.

Chin almost choked on his BLT. He set it down, took Zhai's hands, and looked at them. He tried to rub the marks away with his thumb.

"They're permanent," Zhai said. "Tattoos or something. I saw the same two guys in the woods by the train graveyard. They were scanning the ground, like they were looking for something. One of them saw me and challenged me to a fight and—oh, Sifu, you wouldn't believe how he could fight. He smoked me. Knocked me out. When I woke up, I was lying on the tracks, and I had these marks. Then, a night or two later, I blacked out and woke up half-buried in a hole, and my knuckles were all skinned up like I'd been fighting. And these marks—they burned like crazy."

Chin let go of Zhai's hands and leaned back on the counter again, momentarily lost in thought. "Start at the beginning," he said. "Why were you following these men into the woods in the first place?"

"See, that's the thing," Zhai said. "I've seen them before. I can't remember when or where, but I've seen them—when I was just a kid."

Master Chin nodded. "Come with me."

"Where are we going?" Zhai asked.

"To learn the truth. Come."

§

On the way from the library to the Banfield house, Aimee sat in the passenger seat, messing around on the Internet with her cell phone. Her dad was on his Bluetooth, ignoring her as usual, and as usual, she was ignoring him back. As soon as his call ended, however, he did take the time to ruin her evening.

"We're having an important guest over for dinner and drinks tonight, so when we get home you need to get ready and be downstairs by five o'clock. Understood?"

Aimee rolled her eyes at his bad news. "Why do I have to be there?"

The car paused at the Hilltop Haven guard gate, and Jack turned to her, his expression like stone—cold and blank. After a moment he spoke. "Because your mother is not here—and that is mostly on you."

She wanted to protest, but she was afraid he might be right. What had happened to Tyler, and to Aimee because of it, had just been too much for Emily Banfield.

"So, in her absence, you will act as hostess whenever I entertain at home."

"You mean until you banish me to Montana?"

"Exactly." He glanced at her with an exasperated sigh. "Have you ever considered that if you'd just cooperate for a change, we could forget about that?"

She didn't answer. She couldn't promise she would stop seeing Raphael. She couldn't even think about not seeing him.

"Fine." Her father glowered at her. "But until they get a space for you, you *will* cooperate. It's time you start doing your part for the family. Is that clear?"

"Pretty much."

"And if I were you, I'd watch my tone."

She didn't respond to that, but as soon as the car stopped in the garage, she was out the door. She said hi to Lily Rose, who was at the stove stirring something that smelled delicious, and went straight up to her room, cranked up her stereo and hopped in the shower. All the while she thought eagerly of her coming kung fu lessons with Raphael, and when she got out, dried off and into her underwear, she did a few awkward kung fu punches in the mirror. When she'd done her hair and makeup and slipped into her little black dress and high heels, it was almost time to go down. She glanced once more at her reflection in the mirror and was amazed to find that she looked pretty good. Despite all the drama that had happened since she got back from boarding school—drama with friends and family, falling in love, and an evil, winged guy abducting her into some alternate reality—she was still somehow looking a little healthier and a lot happier every day. Even the bite marks on her ear were healing nicely.

Now if only she could find her mom . . . but that was going to happen, too. Raphael was learning to use the Wheel and he was going to teach her to fight so she'd be ready when they went back into the tunnels. Until then, she was determined to be the soul of cooperation so her father would get off her case and keep his attention elsewhere—even if it meant she had to be gracious and hospitable to his boring business associates. Downstairs, the doorbell rang and she took a deep breath and plastered a bright, beauty-queen smile on her face.

She took another moment to freshen her lip gloss and, in a better mood than when she got home, she almost skipped down the stairs. But when she walked into the living room, she stopped short, her smile disappearing.

"There's my girl!" her dad said, in the phoniest voice she'd ever heard him use.

Rick was there too, in a dark blue shirt and tie, and Maggie was with him, wearing a form-fitting silver dress and staring down intently at her fingernails. But Aimee's gaze moved from Maggie to the guest of honor, who sat in a big leather chair at the far end of the room, next to the fire crackling in the hearth.

"Hello, Aimee," he said and rose to meet her, a warm smile spreading slowly, lazily, along his full, inviting lips, his impossibly blue eyes probing into her own.

It was Orias Morrow.

Chin dug into the top drawer of an old bureau sitting in a corner of the barn that served as his kwoon. He took out a leather bag, and from it, he fished an old, bronze Chinese coin. Zhai sat in a straight-back wooden chair in the middle of the old barn, now filled with flickering candlelight. Chin took the other chair, facing his student.

"Is it going to be painful or anything?" Zhai asked.

Chin hesitated. He'd learned to love the Wu-de with all his heart, but the most difficult part of the code was its prohibition against lying, even when it was a merciful deceit. "Not physically," he said, and he held the coin up before Zhai, pinched between his thumb and forefinger. "Hypnosis is an ancient and natural practice."

As Chin spoke, he expertly flipped the coin between the fingers of one hand. It travelled from his index finger to his pinky and then back again, glinting dully in the candlelight. "You know, Zhai, I have always loved you as a son. Trust in that now, and let yourself relax, knowing that I will never let any harm come to you. Keep your eyes on the coin and you will feel them grow heavy . . . so heavy you cannot keep them open . . . and finally, they will close. Good. Now you feel your mind growing heavy . . . heavier . . . heavier . . . sinking into the quiet, into yourself, into the past. You feel yourself sinking back in time, in age. See yourself at fourteen, now twelve, now ten. Imagine yourself falling back to the age you were when you first saw the men you described to me. Are you there now? Go to the moment you first see them. Are you there?"

Zhai, his eyes closed, mumbled, "Yes."

"Good. Where are you?"

"In a box."

"A box?" Chin was sure he'd misheard his student. "Where are you?"

"In the box," Zhai repeated. "It's cold."

"Tell me about the box."

"It's dark in here. The walls are metal. It smells like sweat . . . "

A dark foreboding entered Chin's heart, but he still didn't understand what Zhai was talking about. "How did you get into the box?" he probed gently.

Zhai's eyes snapped open, and there was terror and pain in them. Veins stood out on his forehead. Suddenly, all his muscles seemed to contract at once.

"Zhai," Chin said. "You okay? Zhai?"

Zhai's gaze was trained on the floor, then, when he tilted his face up, he was looking at Chin through someone else's eyes.

"You!" Chin whispered in horror.

He barely got his hands up before Zhai attacked. He blocked the first strike, but he hadn't been ready for the onslaught and Zhai's second punch slipped through his defenses and sent his world spinning. If Chin had struck back at that moment, he could have regained the momentum, but it was against the Wu-de to harm his own student. Anyway, he would never deliberately try to hurt Zhai.

He stumbled backwards, trying to retreat, but Zhai—or the power possessing Zhai—didn't let up, and Chin lost count of the blows pounding his face. When he opened his eyes again, he was lying on his back with Zhai standing over him, holding a chair over his head. The marks on both of Zhai's hands glowed a sizzling crimson.

"Hello, Chin," Zhai said, in a low, guttural voice that belonged to someone else.

The last thing Chin saw before blackness claimed him was the chair coming down.

CHAPTER 17

AIMEE SAT AT ONE END OF THE LONG DINING TABLE and her father sat at the other, with Rick and Maggie on her left and Orias on her right. He had stood to greet her when she'd entered the living room and after he and Jack finished their cocktails, he'd offered her his arm and escorted her in to dinner. His easy, impeccable good manners seemed to have a positive effect on the Banfield men. When Rick started to give Maggie a hard time about being late, one curious glance from Orias was enough to settle him down.

Aimee had to admit, Orias had a charismatic presence, a quality of power and strength that was intoxicating. She had never seen her dad so agreeable and charming, and she wondered what he wanted from this intriguing stranger. At least she wasn't sitting across the table from him. She could not have tolerated those arresting eyes on her for very long.

"Well, Orias, you certainly impressed my business partner at that career-day event," her dad was saying. She forced herself to pay attention. "He came away raving about you—and Cheung Shao does not rave about anything."

"Thanks, Mr. Banfield," said Orias. "It's nice to be back in Middleburg."

"I find it odd that Oberon never mentioned having a son. And please—call me Jack."

"My father and I have been estranged for many years, Jack," Orias said. "I grew up in New York, in my mother's home, but I came here for a couple of summers. I used to love playing down by the tracks. Probably because there were all those signs telling us not to," he added with an appealing chuckle. Jack and Rick laughed too, and Aimee toyed with her shrimp cocktail. Her stomach was in knots again for the first time in weeks, and she had yet to take a bite.

"Well, Orias, we owe you a debt of gratitude," Jack was saying. "I've never heard of an ointment that can fix a broken arm."

Orias glanced at Rick. "Perhaps it was a simple misdiagnosis."

"The x-rays showed a break—I saw them myself," said Jack.

"Maybe the technician accidentally switched them with another patient's," their guest responded politely. "I believe that happens more frequently than we know."

Jack looked at him speculatively for a moment before he agreed. "You're right, of course. That's got to be it. All the same—if you hadn't cracked that cast off and used your ointment so Rick could see it was okay, he would have been sidelined for the rest of the season."

"And word on the street is he got a win Friday night." Orias reached across the table and gave Rick a high five. "Good work, man."

Aimee couldn't believe it. He'd been in the house for less than an hour, and he was already more a part of the family than she had ever been. How could her dad and Rick forget what Oberon had done to her?

"And now, Jack, if I may, I have something to say to Aimee." Vaguely, she was aware of her dad nodding, as Orias looked at her, drawing her eyes toward his, it seemed, against her will. When at last he had captured her gaze in his own, he said, "What my father did to you was reprehensible, Aimee." The regret and sympathy in his voice sounded genuine. "It was unforgivable, even though he was not well, obviously. But I hope you won't hold me responsible for his actions."

"I'm sure you know," Jack put in quickly. "There's been no love lost between me and your dad, even before that. But we Banfields are not the type to hold a grudge. Are we Aimee?"

Aimee wanted to scream at him and run away from the table, but she thought of Raphael. She knew the only way she'd get her father to relax his guard so she could continue to sneak out was to do as he said and cooperate. And she supposed it wasn't fair to blame Orias for the things Oberon did. She wouldn't like it if anyone blamed her for the things *her* father did.

"Of course not," she said at last, her voice tight and thin.

Lily Rose came in then to clear away the appetizers. Aimee noticed that as she reached for Orias's plate, he looked up at her and her hand stopped in mid air as she studied him, her wrinkled brow more deeply furrowed as if she was trying to remember something. Jack cleared his throat.

"Lily Rose," Aimee said. "Are you all right?" She also noticed that neither the old woman nor Orias was willing to break their locked stare.

"Have you met Middleburg's newest mogul?" Jack asked. "Orias, you must excuse Lily Rose. We don't have guests often—"

Lily Rose stopped him. "Oh, that's not it, Mr. Jack. I know how to serve a formal dinner. So," she said to Orias. "You're Oberon Morrow's boy."

"I am."

"Then you do know him," Jack said.

"Oh . . . I've seen him around," Lily Rose replied slowly. "Long time ago—when he was just a little boy. Didn't recognize him at first."

"I've changed a good deal since I was a child," Orias said pleasantly. "It's refreshing to see, Lily Rose, that you have not."

She stared at him for a moment, and then looked at Aimee. "You all right, honey bun?" she asked. "You need anything?"

"No, Lily Rose, thanks," Aimee replied, touched by her concern. "I'm fine." She glanced at her father and said, as elegantly as her mother would, "You may bring in the main course now, please."

Lily Rose turned her attention back to Orias. "It's notable how much you favor your father," she told him, and with another look at Aimee, she took the tray full of dishes back to the kitchen.

Orias sighed deeply and turned to Jack. "When I was a child I tried to love my father, as all sons must love their fathers." He glanced at Rick, who gave a small nod. "Unfortunately, I never got a chance to know him. But perhaps that was for the best."

His words and the almost imperceptible break in his voice held so much sadness. Aimee had never heard such sadness—and she felt bad for him.

"Have they found his . . . ah, his remains?" her dad asked.

"Not yet. The final word from the DA's office is that they probably never will. Perhaps that's for the best as well."

"What if he's still alive?" Aimee asked. "What if he comes back?"

"Then I'll make sure he doesn't hurt you," Orias told her. "And I'll get him the help he needs."

"The help he needs?" Aimee exclaimed, unbelieving. "He's not a puppy with a broken leg. He's a—a monster."

"Aimee—" her dad warned.

Aimee regretted her words instantly. Rick and her dad were glaring at her. Orias was looking at her too, and she was surprised by the pain she saw in his eyes.

"No, she's right," he said, and he gently put one of his large hands over her small one. His touch was soft, but she could feel his tremendous strength—and although his hand was warm, when his flesh made contact with hers, it sent a chill through her whole body. "I owe you an apology," he told her. "Coming here tonight with no warning—I should have known how that would upset you. It was very inconsiderate." He took his napkin from his lap and put it beside his plate. "I should go."

"You'll do no such thing," Jack said. "Aimee is fine now, and she knows Oberon's crimes have nothing to do with you. Right, Aimee?"

"Yes," she answered tonelessly, becoming more aware of how difficult it was to breathe with Orias looking at her, appealing to her, drawing her inexorably into the infinite blue depths of his eyes. "Please . . . you don't have to go."

"Good—then that's settled and we'll talk no more about it," Jack declared. "Cheung said you mentioned during your presentation, Orias, that you have some plans for new ventures here in Middleburg. I'd love to know what they are. Will you reopen Hot House?"

It was a moment before Orias replied. "I'm implementing some aggressive growth strategies for my father's investments, which do not include Hot House. I'm not a fan of that particular type of entertainment. If I open it again, it will be something else." A mischievous gleam shone in his eyes. "But I am interested in that real-estate deal you're pursuing in the Flats," he said. Aimee glanced at her dad who suddenly looked a little pale. "Now, Jack—don't think I haven't heard about it. If we're going to do business together, I think it's only fair you give me a little taste."

Jack laughed. "Sorry, kid. The Flats deal is strictly hush-hush."

"Come on. You can tell me something," Orias pressed with a charming smile. "Is it a development scheme? Mineral rights? What?"

Jack shook his head again. "I'm just handling the real-estate end of it, buying and freeing up the properties. My partner is the man with the plan. Cheung Shao hasn't even given me all the details."

"Really? Do you normally enter into multimillion-dollar deals with no idea what's going on?"

Jack grinned and took a sip of his wine. "I do when Cheung Shao is involved," he said. "I've been in business with him for more than ten years now. The guy is like King Midas. Everything he touches turns to gold."

Lily Rose came in then with the main course. After she set a magnificent rack of braised lamb on the table, she looked around the room and her eyes came to rest on Maggie, who Aimee suddenly noticed, was staring at Orias, which was no surprise. But Aimee realized there was no fascination, no rapture in Maggie's eyes as there was in the eyes of other girls who stared at him. There was fear.

"We'll have plenty of time after dinner to talk business," Jack said. "Until then, a toast. To new friends." He raised his wine glass to Orias.

"To new friends," Orias agreed, and he clinked glasses with her dad, then Rick, then Maggie, then finally Aimee. To her dismay, her glass crashed into his, sloshing his red wine on the white tablecloth.

"Oh—sorry," Aimee said. "I didn't get it on you, did I?"

"No," Orias said, still smiling. "I'm fine."

Aimee took a sip of her sparkling water, but her gaze kept drifting down to the stain on the tablecloth as it spread, wicking through the linen like spilled blood.

℁

Maggie had not wanted to have dinner with the Banfields, and when Rick called and told her what time he would pick her up, she'd tried to get out of it. As his irritation with her grew, she noticed that his voice changed. It got deeper, darker, more guttural with every word, until he sounded like the demon he truly was. Quickly, she told him it was only because she had to do something for her mother—and then she would drive herself over. It was a stalling tactic, and she'd hoped that something would actually transpire with her mom to prevent her going at all.

But Violet encouraged her to go, to have fun while she was young and still could. "Never miss an opportunity, Maggie," she'd said. "The next couple of years at Middleburg High will be the most exciting time of your life. Grab every bit of it you can, store it up so you'll have wonderful memories later . . . " and before Maggie could ask her what the heck she meant by *that*, Violet drifted back to her little studio and picked up her paintbrush. The design for her new tapestry was finished—she had taped up page after page from her sketchbook, chronologically as the story unfolded, on the walls of the breakfast room where she spent every day and almost every night. Now she was filling in the colors. She wouldn't know whether Maggie was there or not so it was Maggie's choice.

She could stay home and have a TV dinner with her mom or do as Rick said and go have one of Lily Rose's delicious meals and hope that her boyfriend's devil side would not make an appearance.

So far, it hadn't. She'd arrived late, just as they were finishing cocktails, already bracing herself for Rick's anger, but he was so intent on making a good impression on Orias Morrow that he quickly lost interest in her. Maggie was grateful that most of the attention was on Orias and she wasn't expected to contribute much to the conversation. She wondered why Jack Banfield wanted her there at all. She had no interest in business ventures in Middleburg since she was planning to leave the minute she graduated and cashed in her college fund. The only thing that sparked Maggie's interest was watching Aimee respond to Orias.

At first, Maggie had kept her eyes down, in her lap or on her plate, not wanting to see a demon's face where Rick's ought to be. But gradually she raised them and looked around the table. Tonight—so far—she was seeing only auras.

Jack's was a bleak, iron gray surrounded by a burgundy the color of dried blood, and it was jagged, with little hook shapes on the outside of it. When she looked beneath his surface self, she saw him as old, weary and lonely—and she somehow understood: that's where his ambition, greed and self-centered nature would take him. By comparison, his guest of honor had a brilliant, colorful aura. It contained all the shimmering colors of a peacock, and it was crowned with a spinning black star—and she understood that Orias knew his power and wouldn't hesitate to use it to achieve his purpose. Rick's aura (when she finally had the courage to look) was just as she expected it to be—blood red with ugly streaks of brown and dark green that reminded her of the scum that formed on Macomb Lake after a heavy rain. But at least he still looked like Rick.

The most interesting aura at the table, Maggie thought, was Aimee's. It was still bright and white, with swirls of pink and yellow and violet near her head, but the black shapes that had appeared around her the moment she shook hands with Orias on Career Day were still there. And, Maggie noticed, every time Orias looked at Aimee, those dark shadows grew larger and fluttered faster, causing the rest of her glow to dim and pulse with red. In spite of Aimee's reticence, Maggie could see she was attracted to him—just like every other twit at Middleburg High.

And that, Maggie knew, was something she could use to her advantage. She wondered if Raphael knew just how interested his beloved was in the son of her abductor. Raphael deserved to know and Maggie would make sure he found out, as soon as she figured out a way to do it.

When she looked at Orias again, he was studying her. She quickly looked away, until she heard him call her out.

Maggie.

Her head whipped back around and she heard him again, even though his lips weren't moving.

Oh, I know you can hear me.

She squeezed her eyes shut for a moment and looked again.

Think you're so clever, don't you? he asked. *Just because you can see what lies beneath the fleshly disguises we all wear. Why don't you go home and look in the mirror and see what's under your own skin before you go around judging others? And if you look deeply enough, maybe you'll even see your destiny.*

Orias smiled at her and took a sip of his wine, but he continued to talk to her—inside her head.

I will warn you only once, Maggie. Stay out of my way.

Lily Rose came into the dining room again, and Maggie was grateful for the excuse to break away from Orias's chilling gaze. The old housekeeper's aura was amazing—calm, peaceful, steadying. She had a halo of rich, golden light around her head, and extending from the light were layers of undulating whiteness, pure illumination, wrapping in concentric circles all around her, encompassing her like a protective cocoon. As she refilled Maggie's water glass and set it back in front of her, part of her aura enveloped Maggie for a moment, and Maggie could have sworn Lily Rose threw Orias a warning look before she headed back to the kitchen. Maggie lost track of the conversation until Jack suggested they go into the living room for coffee. She ventured one more glance at Orias and found him gazing at her, amusement twinkling in his icy blue eyes.

&

After dinner, everyone moved into the living room. Rick was outside, saying goodnight to Maggie, and Jack excused himself to take a phone call in his den. That left Aimee sitting with Orias in front of the blazing fire.

"And here we are," he said softly. "Alone at last."

Aimee blushed. "Ha, ha," she said sarcastically.

"I'm serious, Aimee. The truth is, my main reason for coming tonight was to see you."

A strange wave of panic surged through her. "Me? Why?"

"I saw you outside my office window the other day, looking in at me."

"I'm sorry. That was rude."

"It was intriguing," he said. "I tried to catch you, but you got away. Then I saw you at the school. You shook my hand and then ran away from me again."

"Yeah," Aimee said with a touch of contempt. "*High* school. I'm in high school, in case you didn't notice."

"Ah . . . " he said, his voice low, compelling. "Yes, I noticed."

"Well, I'm too young for you. Not that—I didn't mean—you know, not that you're trying to ask me out or anything. I'm just . . . how old are you, anyway?"

"How old do you think?"

"Well, you graduated from Cornell, so you've got to be—I don't know—maybe twenty-two or three."

He flashed her his brilliant smile again, and again she felt that odd shortness of breath, like she always got when she caught Raphael looking at her—only more intense. She tried to force herself to keep thinking of Raphael, but then Orias leaned closer to her.

"I finished high school at fifteen, Aimee, and college at seventeen," he said. "I was *very* quick—they called me a gifted child. I'm nineteen—not that much older than you." He looked into her eyes, his lips curving into a smile.

"Well, it doesn't matter," she said. "I didn't mean to imply that you're interested in me—you know, in that way."

"What if I were?"

She forced herself to lean back in her chair, away from him. "Why would you be? I'm just an ordinary high-school girl and you're some kind of genius corporate mogul—"

He put one long, slender finger gently to her lips to interrupt her. "You are anything but ordinary, Aimee." It was soft, almost a whisper.

But she was (she knew it better than anyone) quite ordinary. She thought of Raphael with his kung fu and his Shen magic, blasting Oberon with his supernatural power. She thought of Dalton, who could sing like an angel and had a magnetic personality, Rick with his incredible athletic talent, Miss Pembrook with all her historical knowledge, her dad with his business sense, her mom with her faith in God. She even thought of her ex–best friend Maggie, beautiful cheerleader-turned-homecoming-queen. All of them had something special about them; she had zilch. She wondered suddenly why Raphael even liked her.

"Well, you're wrong," Aimee said. "The only thing I'm good at is getting in trouble."

Orias's laugh was quiet . . . intimate. "That's a wonderful talent," he teased. "If I'd spent more time getting in trouble and less time with books, I might not have become a boring—what did you call me—genius corporate mogul."

"I didn't call you boring," she said. "I don't think you're boring."

His smile widened and she felt weak. "You're not giving yourself nearly enough credit," he told her. "There is something about you, Aimee. An energy that's very special. We just have to unlock it."

She ignored his reference to *we*. "And how exactly do I do that?" she asked, finally getting the courage to raise her eyes to his. It was a mistake.

"I could teach you," he said.

They remained frozen like that for a moment, with Orias leaning close to her as the fire snapped and popped. Quick footsteps striding across the marble floor announced her father's return.

"Anyone up for dessert?" he asked, as Aimee tried to steady her breathing.

"Well, I probably shouldn't," Orias said. "But what fun is life if you don't get into trouble once in a while?"

∾

"You were perfect tonight," Rick said as he walked Maggie to her car. "Orias likes you."

"What?" She hadn't really been listening until she heard Rick say his name.

"Orias—he can see what good taste I have. He likes you. You made me proud tonight, Maggie my love." He took her hand and drew it to his lips.

Dreading what she might see, she made herself look at him. He still looked like Rick.

"Oh," she said. "Good."

"So . . . maybe I'll take you out to Macomb Lake," he offered. They hadn't been out there in a long time, and a couple of months ago, she would have been thrilled. "How 'bout it—I'll follow you home to drop off your mom's car. We'll go up to our spot and take a blanket out of the trunk and—"

"No," she interrupted, and she saw him frown. "I'm . . . I don't feel so good. Something I ate, maybe. I'll see you tomorrow." The food was churning in her stomach and the ghost crown was throbbing against her brow—and then she felt it start to spin around her head, a tornado of energy that was ripping her thoughts to shreds even as she fought to put them together.

"Okay, then," he said. "Your loss." He leaned over to kiss her, and it took every ounce of strength she could muster not to pull away from him. When it was obvious he didn't want to stop, she put up one hand.

"Seriously, Rick. I think I'm going to be sick."

And she put her hand over her mouth.

He looked at her with contempt. "What the hell good are you, then?" he said. He stared at her again, and for a horrifying moment, she thought she saw a glimmer of red in the pupils of his eyes. Then, mercifully, he turned and stalked back into the house.

She exhaled in relief. He was angry, but she didn't care. She had something important to do. She jumped in the car and locked the door. When she got home she raced up to her room without checking on her mother, shrugged out of her coat, threw it on the bed, ran into her bathroom, and flipped on the light.

How could Orias know about her destiny? Would she really be able to see it, she wondered—and see beneath her own surface self—just by looking in the mirror? If she could see beneath the surface of others, maybe it would work for her, too.

She stared at her reflection in the mirror over the sink. In her room behind her, she could see her posters, part of her bed, and her pajamas over the chair in front of her desk where she'd left them that morning. And then the background behind her image in the mirror began to blur and fade and her room disappeared. All she had left to look at was herself.

And she looked deeply into her own eyes. She'd heard somewhere that if you did that long enough it would make you go crazy, but for this she was willing to take a chance.

And it worked. First she saw the past—snippets of her life . . . early, half-remembered images from her childhood that flickered in her subconscious in the moments between sleeping and waking, memories that she had convinced herself were the products of her imagination. Like when she was very small, sitting with her mother in the backyard and hearing Violet whistle a strange, shrill tune. To Maggie's delight a dozen sparrows had swooped down from the sky and landed on her arms and shoulders.

Another time, when Maggie was about eight, she was convinced there was a monster under her bed and wanted to sleep with her mom and dad. Instead, Violet went into Maggie's room, knelt down beside the bed, reached under, and pulled out the monster—a black, two-headed, eel-like thing—and dragged it away.

And there was the time Maggie had peeked into the keyhole of her mother's locked bedroom door. It was incredibly bright in the room, so bright that Maggie could hardly keep her eye on the keyhole, and she wondered what kind of light bulbs her mother used to create such an intense glow. But when she looked closer, she realized the light was coming not from a lamp but from Violet herself, who was sitting cross-legged on the floor, her pale skin glowing, enclosed in a cocoon of blazing white iridescence.

Maggie closed her eyes. All these years she'd dismissed those memories as her imagination. Now, she knew they were real.

But that was Maggie as she had been, as a child. She wanted to know what would happen in the future. She wanted to know her destiny. She opened her eyes again. Her reflection had changed.

The child Maggie was gone and the woman looking back at her now was old Maggie—the Maggie she would be some day, after she had lived a long and happy life. But then the fog blew away and the background to her reflection in the mirror was her house again, but not her room. It was her hallway—the long, long hallway in her house that led down to the basement. And then her scope of vision increased, as if the camera that had been taking the shot pulled back to a wider angle, and she could see herself—as old Maggie—sitting on a chair in the hallway, next to the door to the basement. She had *The Good Book* on her lap, and she knew she had been there for years, as her mother had. Sitting there, growing old, guarding the basement door. Alone.

Guarding the doorway to hell. That was Maggie's destiny.

The ghost crown throbbed on her head, and a voice, maybe her own voice, whispered, *Unless you change it. . .*

And she had to change it. She couldn't end up like her mother.

CHAPTER 18

EMORY'S PARENTS SAT ON THEIR BED in their temporary garage-house, watching an old black-and-white movie on a DVD player they'd managed to rig up to their outdated TV. Haylee sat on a rug on the floor, leaning against a chest of drawers, playing her ever-present Game Boy. The place looked surprisingly cozy this evening, and they seemed more comfortable than Raphael had expected them to be.

"So," he said to Emory, who was standing in the doorway with him. "How are you guys holding up?"

"About as well as anyone living in a garage and having to go into an auto-body shop to pee and brush their teeth," Emory said with a scornful laugh.

Raphael was glad to see his friend could still make a joke, at least. "Yeah, I hear you," he said. "Let's head out. The others should be getting here soon."

"You guys leaving? The party just started," Emory's dad joked.

"Raphael, thanks again for all your help," Emory's mom said.

"No problem. You guys just hang in there," Raphael replied. "Everything's going to work out."

"I'm going too," Haylee declared, turning off her Game Boy and rising from her place on the rug.

Emory groaned. "No, you're not."

"Yeah, I am. I'm going," Haylee replied stubbornly.

"Mom, please tell Haylee she's not going out with me," Emory said, his voice dripping with contempt.

"Haylee, leave your brother alone," their mom said absently, engrossed again in the movie.

"I'm tired of sitting in this stupid, smelly garage!" Haylee shouted.

"We're lucky to have it!" Emory yelled back. "Would you rather be sleeping outside?"

"Guys, guys," Raphael said calmly and stooped down to the little girl's level. "Haylee, look—I'm sorry, but you can't come with us, okay?"

"Why not?" Haylee challenged.

"Because it's going to be dangerous," Emory said.

"So?"

"Because," Raphael paused for a second, strategizing. "Because we're trying to find a way to get your house back," he said. "You're old enough to understand that we've got some serious stuff to do, and we need you to stay here and look out for your mom and dad. Okay?"

She looked at him skeptically for a moment before she agreed. "Okay," she said slowly. "Bring me a surprise?"

"You got it." He ruffled her hair. To Emory, he said, "Let's go."

"Thanks, man," Emory said as they headed across the parking lot. "She's driving me nuts."

"I know. Just hang in there a little longer, and we'll find you guys a place where you can have your own rooms again."

"Meanwhile I have to deal with her."

"It's not that hard," Raphael said. "You just have to figure out how she thinks."

"Yeah, right. The day I understand what's going on in her psychotic little brain they'll have to lock me in a psych ward."

By now, they'd walked around to the front of the body shop, where the rest of the Flatliners and Clarisse were assembled under the glow of a streetlight. Every time one of them exhaled, Raphael could see little silvery plumes coming out of their mouths in the frigid air.

"S'up, fearless leader," Benji said. He threw a playful punch at Raphael, which Raph easily blocked and countered with what would normally have been a finger strike to the eye. As it was, his fingers jammed into Benji's forehead, leaving him rubbing his brow.

"That's a little snake style for you. You can take out somebody's eyeballs with that," Raph said.

"Ow!" Benji laughed. "Nice."

Everyone else greeted Raphael and Emory and followed them into the relative warmth of the body shop. They all seemed to be in a good mood, Raphael noticed, except Nass. He didn't look too happy standing there with Clarisse, but Benji had informed Raph that she had some breaking-and-entering skills that might come in handy for tonight's mission, so Raph had instructed Nass to bring her along. It might have been a mistake, he thought—if that was really what had Nass on edge.

"All right, guys," Raphael got down to business. "I've gotten some intelligence about what's going on in the Flats with all the digging Shao construction and those guys in the derbies have been doing all over the place. I found out what they're looking for." Raphael paused, unintentionally heightening the drama of his news. "Treasure."

"Bad*ass*," Beet said, beaming.

"What kind of treasure?" Josh asked.

"I don't know exactly," Raphael admitted. "Whatever it is, it's supposed to be worth more than gold, or silver or rubies or sapphires. It has to be worth a lot, or Shao and Banfield wouldn't be trying so hard to find it."

"So what's the plan?" Nass asked.

"First, we need to sabotage their equipment every chance we get—anything to slow them down and disrupt their search," Raph said. "Then, we find the treasure first."

Everyone nodded, excited, but Nass frowned. "Wait," he said. "If they haven't been able to locate it with all their high-tech equipment, how are we supposed to find it?"

Raphael grinned. "You're going to lead us to it."

"Me?" Nass said.

"That's right."

Everyone was looking at Nass now, puzzled.

Raphael hesitated. So far, he and Nass hadn't talked to any of the others about the bizarre experiences they'd had since the Halloween battle, and if the rest of the Flatliners were dealing with any kind of supernatural stuff, they hadn't mentioned it. But they couldn't live in denial forever. It was time to start bringing it out in the open.

"When I was handcuffed in that train car and Rick tried to kill me, you knew something was wrong. When we're sparring and I try to hit you, you know what's coming."

"That's . . . that's different," Nass said, and he glanced at the other guys and at Clarisse, clearly feeling uncomfortable.

Raphael shook his head. "No it's not. It's all the same. It's *the knowing*. And you're going to use it to help us find the treasure."

"It doesn't work like that," Nass protested. "It's just a feeling. It's not even always right."

"The knowing? What's that?" Josh asked, but Raphael stayed him with a gesture and turned back to Nass. Clarisse remained uncharacteristically silent.

"Here, sit down," Raphael instructed. Ignacio sat down on the curb. "Now close your eyes. Breathe slowly through your nose and relax your whole body. Everybody—keep quiet," he added. "Nass, keep breathing deeply, slowly. Clear your mind. Imagine a light coming down from the sky, from heaven, and filling you up. Imagine another light rising from your toes all the way to your forehead to meet that light. You might feel a little vibration in your body, or a little fuzzy in your forehead. That's good. Hold on to that feeling—hold on to the light. That's the feeling of Shen."

Nass sat there breathing slowly, looking serene.

"Do this every day for five minutes, and it will help develop your abilities," he said, and then looked at the rest of his crew. "That goes for all of you. If you open yourself up, who knows what abilities might be unleashed?"

"Where did you learn that? Master Chin?" Emory asked.

Raphael nodded. "*Qigong* is a part of my kung fu training. A big part, these days. And there's not really time to get into it now, but I've had a lot of experiences with Shen magic. Supernatural experiences—ever since Halloween. Well, actually, since a couple of days before. Any of you feel anything weird that night?"

"The whole thing was weird," said Beet. "Surreal, even."

"Yeah," Raph agreed. "Well, I have a feeling things are going to get weird again—and we have to be ready." Josh and Benji exchanged skeptical looks. "I'm not asking you to believe me," Raph said. "I'm just asking you to do what Nass is doing now, and have a little faith."

Nass opened his eyes. He looked much calmer now, less distressed.

"Could you feel what I was talking about?" Raphael asked, and Nass nodded. "Hang on to that feeling of Shen. It'll help you as we look for the treasure."

Josh still looked skeptical. "I don't know," he said, "You think that stuff really works?"

"I can prove it," Nass said suddenly, and everyone looked at him. "I had a feeling earlier today—a *knowing*. If we go out tonight, Zhai will attack us again."

His words hung heavy in the air for a moment. Everyone was silent. After what had happened the last time they saw Zhai, no one was eager to fight him again.

Emory was the first one to speak.

"Maybe we shouldn't go out, then," he suggested, a shadow of fear crossing his face.

Everyone looked at Raphael, waiting for his orders.

"We'll go," Raphael decided. "If Zhai shows up, we'll be ready for him." With a glance at Josh, he added, "And if he does show up, then none of us will question Shen anymore."

∞

The Flatliners had done a good job keeping an eye on the various projects Shao Construction was doing in the Flats. A small apartment building on Third Street was now empty, a high privacy fence surrounded a vacant lot on Second, and Middleburg Property Group had evicted tenants from a house on Fifth and Golden Avenue. Raphael's crew had seen Shao Construction trucks at each of the locations.

The Flatliners hit the vacant lot first, since it was close to the body shop. Raphael posted Beet, Josh, Benji, Clarisse, and Emory at various points outside the perimeter as lookouts while he and Nass scaled the fence. As Raphael anticipated, the lot looked like it had been the site of a bombing raid; it was riddled with ten-foot-deep holes, and a yellow backhoe sat in one corner, looking lonely under the streetlights.

"You picking up anything?" Raphael whispered to Nass. "Is the treasure here?"

Nass hesitated. "I don't know," he said. "I'm not sure I could tell if it *was* here. Maybe they already found it."

"Just tell me what you feel—your gut instinct. Here or not?"

Nass stared into the distance for a moment, and then he shook his head. "No," he said. "It's definitely not here."

Raphael nodded once, "All right then. Let's take care of this backhoe."

Dodging the holes, Raphael and Nass hurried up to the big machine. While Nass uncapped his bottle of soda and poured it onto the control panel, Raph opened up an engine compartment and started ripping out wires. Together they found the battery, pulled the heavy, plastic brick loose, and hauled it to the other side of the lot, where they dumped it in one of the holes and threw dirt down over it.

When they were done, Raphael glanced at Nass and gave him a nod that said, *nice work*, which elicited a little smile from his friend. If nothing else could cheer Nass up, Raphael knew the possibility of getting into trouble would always do the trick. They ran back to the fence, scaled it, and landed safely on the other side.

At the apartment building, the Flatliners repeated the process. They found two massive holes in the basement, but no sign of any treasure. Nass ripped a bunch of wires out of an air compressor, Emory hid a jackhammer in a crawl space, and Benji peed in a toolbox.

The mission went off smoothly, but Raphael was still worried about Zhai. He'd come to trust Ignacio's feelings—even more than Ignacio did. And the fact that Zhai hadn't shown up yet made it more likely that he would show up soon. Raphael felt his tension increase as he led his crew, single file, up the apartment building's basement steps, out the back door, and across the moonlit lawn. He made them stay in the backyard as he jogged down to the end of the driveway and made sure there was no ambush waiting for them, then gestured for everyone to come and join him in front of the house. As they all walked together toward their final destination, the joking and horsing around gave way to a brittle silence.

Nass walked up to the front of the column, next to Raphael. "Maybe we should skip the next one," he said quietly, and Raphael looked at him.

"You think something really bad is going to happen?"

"I don't know," Nass said. "But *something* is going to happen—to one of us, anyway."

"Who? Do you know?"

Nass hesitated.

"Nass, if you know something tell me."

"I don't know—that's the problem. I only *think* I know."

"Remember the Wu-de," Raphael said. "There can't be any secrets between us. I'm the leader here. If there's something I need to know, then tell me."

"I'm not sure," Nass warned. "But I think it's Beet. He's going to get hurt."

Raphael nodded and clapped a hand on Nass's shoulder.

"Beet," he shouted, and Beet lumbered to the front of the line. "We're going to need a getaway car. Get the Beetmobile and bring it over to the house. Wait for us in front of the green apartment building two doors down."

"Man," Beet grumbled. "It's my turn to pee in the toolbox."

Raphael laughed. "You can pee on something next time. Now get the car. That's an order."

Beet obediently hustled off in the opposite direction.

"Thanks," Nass said, visibly relieved.

And there was no more time for talking. They'd made it to the house, a tiny, rundown place with dingy white siding and sagging black shutters. There were no lights on inside, and all was quiet as Raphael led the guys up the driveway to the back of the house. Clarisse had the door open in no more than thirty seconds.

Raphael paused on the threshold and addressed his crew.

"Okay, listen up," he said. "We're not here to fight—but if we run into Zhai again, we may have to. We've seen how dangerous he can be. He almost took us all out last time, me included. So if anyone shows up, even Zhai by himself, I want you to run. Scatter, all of you. And don't look back until you get home. Got it?"

He looked at them until they had all nodded, even Clarisse, and then he led them inside.

The smell in the house made Raphael gag. The place was completely empty; there were no boxes, no furniture, nothing but matted, orangey-yellow carpeting. But whoever had lived here must have been a chain smoker, because the air had a dizzying, ashy stink to it. Raphael covered his nose with his sleeve as he tried the first door he found. The room was filled with dirt.

The third door Raphael opened revealed the basement staircase, and he led the way down the creaking steps, raking the darkness ahead of him with his flashlight, and listening for any hint of an ambush. All they found was another big hole in the basement and more tools left scattered around. He paused at the bottom of the stairs.

"There's not a lot of space down here," he called up. "Emory, Clarisse, Benji, you guys stay up there and keep watch. Nass and Josh, come on down and help me trash these tools."

When Nass reached him, Raphael asked, "What do you think? Any treasure here?"

Nass tilted his head slightly, as if listening for something. Then he shook his head.

"All right," Raphael said. "Let's get this done."

At first, he thought there wasn't much down there to sabotage. There were a couple of shovels (he showed off by breaking them both with kicks) and three plastic buckets, which Josh ruined with a few well-placed stomps. The guys were about to head up the stairs again when Nass noticed two cases stacked in one corner.

Raphael felt his heartbeat quicken as Nass opened the smaller one. Inside was the silver divining rod he'd seen the mysterious men using in the backyard of Emory's vacant building.

"Sweet," Josh whispered as the thing glistened in the glow of the flashlight.

Nass picked it up. "It's so light," he said in wonder.

"Put it back in the case," Raph said. "We'll take it with us. What's in the other one?"

The other case was much bigger, somewhere between a briefcase and a crate, actually, and so heavy that it took two of them to move it. After a moment, Nass figured out how to get it open. He smiled as he gazed down into it.

Raphael shone his flashlight into the shadows and saw what he was smiling about. It was one of the high-tech scanning devices they'd seen the strangers using.

"This is awesome," Josh said.

"Close them up, we'll take them both," Raphael said. His anxiety was increasing by the moment and he wanted to get out of there. From the way Nass fumbled with the latches on the cases, he also seemed to be strung a little tightly.

Together, Nass and Josh grabbed the larger case while Raphael picked up the smaller one. Just as they turned to head for the stairs, they heard the sound of screeching tires outside.

Clarisse's voice shouted down to them. "Guys, you better get up here—fast!"

∞

"What's going on?" Raphael shouted as he thundered up the steps.

"I'm not sure," Clarisse said. "We saw somebody run by the window and then heard a scream."

Nass and Josh were still on the stairs, struggling with the heavy case.

"Leave it," Raph shouted down to them. "Let's go!"

Benji hurried in from the living room, looking rattled. "I just saw Beet pull up out front—he jumped outta the car and ran into the backyard."

Without hesitation, Raphael handed Benji the divining rod case and ran out the back door, with the rest of his crew right behind him. The minute he stepped into the dark backyard, he froze. Beet was lying in the middle of the driveway, his face covered with blood.

"Hello."

The voice was somehow both familiar and foreign. Raphael looked up to find Zhai standing atop the roof of the ramshackle garage—and he had Emory's little sister.

Raphael's mind spun with confusion, until he realized what must have happened: Haylee had followed them, and after Beet got injured trying to protect her, Zhai had grabbed her. Now he had one arm clamped around her neck, choking her. Her face was red, and strands of her hair were plastered across it by her tears. She managed to wheeze out a little scream, but Zhai squeezed harder and choked off the sound.

"Let go of her, Zhai. Now!" Raphael commanded. "What the hell is wrong with you? Have you forgotten the Wu-de completely?"

Zhai's laughter was strange. "The Wu-de," he said at last. "The *law*. It is a quaint notion. But this is the new me, *Si-dai*. I have no use for the law."

"What do you want?" Raphael asked. As he spoke, he scanned the garage, looking for some way to get up to the roof where Zhai was. "We'll do anything—whatever you want. Just don't hurt her."

"If I only threaten, you'll keep meddling in our business. But if I kill the child . . . " His eyes took on an unnatural light. "Yes, the child will serve as a sacrifice . . . as an example of what happens when you interfere . . . "

Raphael wasn't waiting to hear more. He hurled himself forward, jumping at the rickety fence that ran along one side of the garage. He grabbed the top of it, then pushed off, twisted in midair, grabbed the edge of the garage roof and pulled himself up. In seconds, he was on the rooftop with Zhai.

"Impressive," Zhai said. "But the only way to make me let go will be to kill me—and I'll take the child with me."

It occurred to Raphael that Zhai had gone truly and completely crazy, but Raph wasn't worried about him; all that mattered now was Haylee. Out of the corner of his eye, he could see Emory following him up onto the garage roof while the other Flatliners stayed below, some of them hurrying to help Beet and others watching the drama unfolding above them.

He couldn't wait any longer. Haylee's face was a dangerous shade of red that bordered on purple.

"No more talk, Zhai. Let her go and fight me."

Zhai only laughed, and Raphael attacked. But Zhai managed to jerk Haylee in front of each strike Raph threw, and Raphael was forced to pull back in order to avoid hitting her. He threw five more punches, and each time Zhai used Haylee as a shield. Finally, Raphael grabbed Zhai's forearm and tried to pry it away from Haylee's throat. It was impossible. Zhai was always strong, Raphael thought, but never like this.

Emory was on the roof now, too, and he charged Zhai. "Let go of my sister," he shouted, but Zhai spun around and caught him in the right temple with a kick. Emory's knees buckled beneath him and he slid down the roof on his stomach, coming to a rest with his face half buried in the eaves trough.

Zhai's spin had also pulled him free of Raphael, and as Raph hurried forward to grab his enemy's arm again, Zhai swept Raphael's feet out from under him. Raph landed in a kneeling position, with one knee hitting the shingles hard. He was instantly on his feet again, but it was too late.

Zhai tossed Haylee over his shoulder and leaped from the roof of the garage onto the low porch roof of the next house, then scrambled up the slope toward the two-story portion of the house. As Raphael went after him he heard Emory cursing. The jump was too much for him.

"Don't worry!" Raphael called over his shoulder. "I'll get her back!"

Ahead, he watched Zhai leap from the peak of the house's roof onto the gable of the apartment building next to it. Raph sprinted across the rooftop after him and launched himself off the edge. He hit the gable of the roof next door chest first. The impact knocked the wind out of him, but he managed to pull himself up in time to see Zhai running away under the bright winter moon. He struggled to his feet, cursing, and gave chase.

Raphael thought about trying one of the fingertip lightning blasts of Shen power he'd used to defeat Oberon, but there was too big a chance he'd hit Haylee, or send her and Zhai tumbling off the roof—from three stories up. His only hope was to catch them on foot, but that prospect was looking more unlikely.

Zhai leaped to the rooftop of the next building and Raphael followed him across it, and across two more roofs. Finally, Zhai ran out of running room. They were on top of the highest building in the Flats, five stories up, above a gravel parking lot on the corner of Golden Avenue. Cornered, he turned and waited for Raphael, a wicked grin on his face.

Breathing hard, Raphael approached slowly, careful not to make any quick movements as he balanced on the peak of the sharply pitched roof.

"Zhai," he said, his voice calm, soothing. "I know you, man. I've known you since we were kids. Maybe we have our differences, but I know you'd never hurt a little girl."

Zhai's strange smile only widened.

"Well, people change," he said. "And who knows what a person is like when no one is watching? There's only you and me here, no witnesses. So imagine, if this little girl were to fall off the roof now—who do you think the police would blame? The son of a billionaire, or the son of a dead loser?"

A searing anger lashed Raphael's heart at the insult to his father, but he forced himself to remain calm. Haylee's life depended on it.

"You wouldn't do it, Zhai. I know you."

The terrible smile on Zhai's face disappeared. "Forget the treasure," he said harshly, in an unnatural voice unlike his own. "It will never be yours."

And before Raphael could take another step, Zhai turned and threw Haylee from the rooftop.

Raphael's mouth opened in a silent scream as he saw her body fall. Unable to contain his horror and fury, he rushed forward to attack Zhai. Before he could reach him, however, Zhai stood stiff and straight, like a soldier at attention. His eyes met Raphael's for an instant before he closed them and let himself fall backward, off the rooftop.

Raphael reached the spot where Zhai and Haylee had been only seconds before and fell to his knees. Anguish and frustration wracked his whole body, and he collapsed, his fists balled up and trembling, his forehead pressed against the grit of the shingles, his teeth on edge and grinding. He had failed. Zhai was gone. Haylee was dead.

CHAPTER 19

It seemed like hours passed, instead of just seconds, by the time Raphael got the courage to inch his way forward and peer down, over the edge of the roof. First, he saw black pavement stretching off to his right and his left. Then he saw a lone figure on Golden Avenue, running away and heading in the direction of downtown. He recognized the runner's gait immediately; it was Zhai. Somehow, he'd survived the fall. Apprehensive, Raph lowered his gaze to the shadows below. At first, he saw nothing but a few gnarled bushes. Then, he heard approaching footsteps and saw two figures running around the side of the house. After a moment Benji and Emory rounded the corner and stopped.

"Haylee!" Emory shouted joyfully.

"No way," Benji said quietly.

Raphael followed their stares into the shadows below him and he made out something he'd missed before. He could see the blue and white of Nass's L.A. Dodgers cap, and Nass was holding something in his arms. As Raphael watched, it squirmed. Nass set it down, and it ran toward Emory.

Haylee.

"Raph, you up there?" Benji shouted.

He scrambled to his feet. "I'm here. Coming down."

After a quick survey of the roof, Raphael found a rickety wooden staircase stuck to the far side of the building as a makeshift fire escape. He hurried down it, and then jogged around to his comrades.

Emory was locked in an embrace with his tearful sister. "I saw you fall." His words were muffled as he pressed his face against the top of her head. "I thought you were dead."

Wearing a strange, dazed grin, Benji was shaking his head in wonder. Nass stood rooted in place, staring up at the edge of the roof.

"What happened?" Raphael asked, still too much in shock to piece it all together. "When Zhai dropped her I thought . . ."

"I caught her," Nass said, still a little stunned by the fact.

"You caught her?" Raphael repeated, sure he must have misunderstood.

"When you and Zhai took off across the rooftops, something made me run to this spot. I knew she was going to fall. And I caught her."

Benji cackled. "That's freakin' awesome!" he said.

Raphael looked up at the rooftop, then down at Nass. It was a good fifty feet from there to the ground. If Nass had been two feet to the right or the left, Haylee would be dead.

"It's a miracle," Emory said, blinking away tears as he turned to Nass. "I can't thank you enough, man."

Nass replied with a solemn nod.

"So what happened to Zhai?" Benji asked.

"He landed in those bushes over there," Nass said. "He just rolled out of them and shot off down the street like some kind of alley cat, not even hurt." Nass shook his head. "Hey, I know those Toppers are douche bags, but I never expected something like this from Zhai."

"That bastard—I'm going to kill him. Seriously," Emory said as he stroked Haylee's hair. Her arms were still clamped around his waist.

"What about Beet?" Raph asked.

"He's coming to. Josh is with him," Benji said. "He wasn't hurt that bad—all that blood came from his nose. I think he broke it."

"We better go check on him," Raphael said. "Come on."

He led his troops toward the sidewalk. Benji followed first, then Emory, one arm still around his little sister. Bringing up the rear, Nass stopped for a moment and took one last look at the moonlit rooftop before he turned and hurried to catch up with them.

"So, are you loving Shen yet?" Raphael asked as Nass came up beside him.

Nass laughed. "Do I love Shen?" He tipped the brim of his ever-present Dodger's cap. "I'm going to trade in my hat and get one with *Shen* written on it, that's how much I love Shen."

හ

Chin felt himself rising toward consciousness. It was the feeling of ascending a black, spiral staircase from some deep, dark primordial basement. His head throbbed with pain at each step he took.

When at last his eyes opened, the light that spilled into them felt like slivers of glass. Still, he forced himself to sit up. The room was spinning, but at least he was still in his barn; Zhai hadn't dragged him away somewhere. Nausea came to him then, and he felt his mouth filling with saliva. He rolled onto his hands and knees and spat twice on the gnarled, blood-speckled floorboards of his kwoon, and then sat back again, closed his eyes, and called upon the power of Shen to restore him. Soon he felt the energy wicking up from the floor like water up a tree's roots, and spilling down from the heavens like sunlight on a tree's leaves. The throbbing in his head diminished to a dull ache, and the nausea boring into the pit of his stomach shrank and then disappeared. When he opened his eyes again he still felt pretty awful, but it was getting better. He stood on shaky legs and ran his fingers over his brow. They came back bloody. He could feel a goose egg over his left eye and a sizable gash near his hairline. He had been lucky, he knew. The Order of the Black Snake could just as easily have snuffed out his life. The question was, why hadn't they?

Walking gingerly through his dizziness, Chin took his coat off a hook in the corner and pulled it on as he stepped out of the barn, shutting the door behind him. A frigid wind blasted across the fields and seemed to cut right through his flesh to chill his very soul. Large snowflakes swirled in the darkness, like stars that had come unmoored.

As he made his way up to the house, he thought of Zhai's strange transformation, just at the moment the boy was about to remember something important. Something—*someone*—had taken possession of Zhai's body and mind.

Truly, the Order of the Black Snake had made him their slave, and that was something Chin would not stand for. He would find Zhai, even if it took him all night. He would capture him, subdue him, and free him from the Order's spell.

And do you think you can find him if they don't want you to? The voice that echoed through Chin's head was familiar, as was the laugh that followed it. He looked around.

Chin couldn't see him, but he knew he was there; he could feel him—that strange, mischievous, malevolent presence. Chin turned and walked out of the barn, past the corral and into the barren field, stumbling over furrows of desolate, frozen earth. The trees that surrounded the field were like charcoal marks against the shroud of the sky, black on black, but soon the snow was falling more heavily, blotting the darkness out with swirling, blowing flecks of white. Chin felt himself shivered by another blast of wind, and before him, coalescing out of the blizzard, a tall, imposing figure approached. His face was ancient, timeless, his beard dark and wispy, his eyes filled with ferocious mirth, and his fingernails long, black and sharp. It was the Magician, and this time he was clothed in robes of the lightest blue, so pale it was almost white.

"Why do you torment me?" Chin asked, his head throbbing. "You offer me no help, no wisdom, only suffering. I don't have time to waste with you." Chin turned away. But there was a sudden gust of wind, and the Magician stood in front of him again, closer this time, and again coalescing out of the drifting snow.

"What will you do, then?" the Magician demanded. "Seek your student? At this late hour, don't you think his work is already done?"

"I'm not going to sit back while the Order uses him."

"And *you* can defeat them?"

The question was simple enough, but it hit Chin like a lead brick. Images of the dark days before he left China flooded his mind. With some effort, he forced them out. Perhaps the Order had been too powerful for him back then. Perhaps they were too powerful now. But if he had to die to keep the treasure out of their hands, then so be it.

Because if the Order got their hands on the treasure, all would be lost.

The Magician seemed to comprehend Chin's thoughts, for he smiled and nodded.

"Your willingness for self-sacrifice is very noble, Chin, but will it be enough?"

"It will have to be," Chin said simply. His fingers and toes were freezing, and his cheeks ached with the cold.

"Are you so full of pride you think you can fight them alone?" There was a hint of tenderness, even compassion in the Magician's voice.

Chin thought of Raphael. There was so much he'd concealed from his students. At first, because they weren't ready to hear the truth about Middleburg. Then, he was afraid they were too young to accept the part they must play in its destiny, and to bear the terrifying burden he had carried all these years. Ignorance, Chin knew, truly was bliss. Those who know the rules must be accountable when they break them. Those who know about an impending tragedy are duty bound to try to avert it— even if their efforts may prove futile. Still, Raphael—and Zhai—were just as important to Middleburg's destiny as Chin was. More important, in fact. Perhaps it was time to put more responsibility on his pupils. Besides, the Magician was right. There was no way he could fight the Order on his own.

"I will consider your words, teacher," he said.

"The nectar of wisdom is not always sweet," the Magician declared. "But it is always nourishing." And with a bow, he became a million fluttering snowflakes that scattered on the wind.

Chin trudged back across the field toward his house, his feet, his hands, and his mind completely numb. Like a sleepwalker, he entered his home, climbed the steps to his little bedroom, undressed, and slipped into bed.

Whatever the Order was using Zhai for, it was done for tonight, so Chin would rest. He would recover and prepare for what was to come. Perhaps it was time to tell Raphael the truth. He would, he decided. As soon as they got Zhai back, he would tell both of them everything. How strange it would be, after all these years, to have companions on this harrowing journey.

He thought of Raphael's request to be allowed to train the Banfield girl. Could it be that the All was recruiting more soldiers for the Army of Light? Or were they all just snowflakes in the wind, being blown and buffeted and finally melting to nothing when spring came at last?

So many questions without answers—but as urgent as it was for Chin to reason through them, he was falling, plummeting fast, into the dark chasm of slumber, toward dreams of a mighty, black snake waiting and watching, ready to wrap all of Middleburg in its deadly, coiled embrace.

෨

Aimee sat on the couch, watching MTV and crunching down the last of her Lucky Charms when the doorbell rang. She was already so tense about her first training session with Raphael—not to mention the fact that she would have to sneak into the Flats to get to it—that she nearly spilled milk all over herself when the doorbell rang.

Annoyed, she put her bowl and spoon in the sink and went to answer. It was probably one of Rick's stupid friends, but he was downstairs working out with this music cranked up so loud he'd never hear the bell. As she pulled the door open, a frigid wind blasted her, slicing straight through her clothes and chilling her to the bone. Orias stood on the stoop, smiling at her.

"Uh, hey," she said. "My dad's not here. He had a meeting in Topeka with a senator or something."

"I'm not here to see him," Orias said. He stepped inside, shutting the door behind him.

"Rick's downstairs pumping iron, if you want to. . ." she began, but he was already shaking his head.

"I'm not here to see him either," he said softly, staring at her with those eyes of his. "I'm here to see you."

She didn't know how to answer that, and she felt a vague panic, standing so close to him. She was oddly aware of the driving music blasting on Rick's stereo and the floor beneath her vibrating with the beat.

"Well," she said at last, ending the silence. "I . . . have somewhere I need to be."

"I'll give you a ride then," Orias said pleasantly. When she hesitated, he laughed. "You'd rather walk in the freezing cold than ride with me? Am I really that horrible?"

Aimee shook her head. "You're not horrible," she said quietly. "I just don't think—anyway, I could really use the exercise," she finished.

"Well . . . have a nice afternoon, then." His eyes became veiled, as if he was suddenly self-conscious. *As if he's used to being refused*, she thought, and again she felt bad for him, as she had when she heard his talk on career day. "I didn't mean to intrude."

He started to leave, but Aimee stopped him. "Wait."

He turned back to her.

"I guess you could give me a ride downtown," she said, and his radiant smile gave her a warm rush of unexpected pleasure. She grabbed her purse and yelled down to Rick in the basement:

"Hey! Rick!" The volume of the music suddenly decreased.

"What?" he yelled back.

"I'm going out with Orias!"

Over the music, she heard his grunted, "Whatever."

As Aimee rode down the hill with Orias, she realized what a stroke of luck that he had dropped by. Rick thought he was beyond cool—and he was the only person who could get her out of the house without a full-scale interrogation from her brother.

Orias stopped his Maserati at the corner in front of the Dug-Out, and she smiled and thanked him. As his car roared away, she feigned going into the coffee shop, then turned around, crossed the street, and hurried toward the Flats.

∞

It was all Aimee could do to keep herself from fidgeting and biting her nails as she waited, just as Raphael had instructed, for her first kung fu lesson. She was in the backyard of his apartment building where no neighborhood gossips or stray Toppers could see her if they happened to pass by on the street. After a few minutes, she heard footsteps coming up the driveway and then Raphael came around the corner of the building.

He wore one of those black jacket-shirt things with the weird buttons that kung fu guys always wore in movies, and baggy black pants, and he had tied a plain strip of black fabric around his head to keep his hair out of his face. On anyone else, she thought, that getup might look a little cheesy. On Raphael it looked perfect . . . *right*. Even sexy.

"Hello, teacher!" Aimee flirted, and hurried in for a kiss, but Raphael stopped her, pressing a gentle finger to her lips.

"None of that until after the lesson," he said gently but firmly. He was smiling, but he seemed serious, too. "It's important to stay focused. If you're really going to come with me to look for your mom, this stuff might save your life one of these days."

"Fine," Aimee teased. "But that doesn't mean I can't think about it."

He took his keys out of his pocket and went over to a set of peeling, half-rotted cellar doors that angled out from the foundation of the house. He unlocked the padlock and threw them open, then ushered Aimee inside.

Giving him a skeptical glance, she looked down into the dimness that waited at the bottom of the crumbling concrete stairs, but Raphael reassured her with a smile.

"It's okay," he said. "There's nothing scary down there, I promise."

"Right," Aimee replied dubiously, moving down the steps as bravely and quickly as she could. "Except spiders and rats."

"And cockroaches," Raphael added. "Don't forget them."

At the bottom of the steps, Aimee stopped while Raphael slipped past her and waded into the darkness. After a moment, there was a heavy click and an overhead bulb came on, along with several strings of Christmas lights.

"Wow," Aimee said, surprised. The basement was actually pretty cozy. There were a few old, worn rugs laid over the bare concrete floor, a couple of plush reclining chairs in the corner, and a host of posters on the wall: Jimi Hendrix stood shoulder to shoulder with Bruce Lee and Dave Matthews. There were also a lopsided floor lamp, a stack of old water-stained books, and a dusty set of free weights. In one corner of the room, a rusty, potbellied furnace churned away, filling the place with nearly tropical warmth. The Christmas lights cast everything in an inviting glow, and Aimee felt comfortable immediately.

"My buddy Joe has been the maintenance guy at our building for a few years now," Raphael explained. "He used to hang out down here sometimes. He let me copy the key."

Aimee was ready to kick back in one of the easy chairs and relax—but Raphael was already getting down to business.

"We always start with a bow," he said. "Make a fist and press it against the palm of your hand, like this." They bowed to each other. "Good. Now let's begin with our opening stance."

Aimee studied Raphael's posture as his knees bent and his hands went up in front of him in a defensive ready position. She tried to copy him.

"Stay there," Raphael said, and he walked over to her, put a hand on her shoulder, and gave her a little push. She stumbled a few steps back.

"Hey," she said, kidding but also mildly embarrassed.

"Try it again," he told her, and she again assumed the opening position. "Widen your legs, bend your knees more. Sink down. Good. Now tilt your pelvis forward."

Aimee felt a little thrill as Raphael put his hand on her hip and guided it into the correct position, but she tried not to smile.

"Back straight, shoulders back. Get your hands out farther. Good. You want both hands to be straight up and down, like shark fins. These are going to protect your center line. That's where all the most vital parts of your body are—your nose, jaw, eyes, solar plexus, stomach. With your hands up like this, it will be harder for your enemy to strike you in those spots."

In the slightly squatted position, Aimee's legs were already beginning to ache and tremble. "It's not very comfortable," she pointed out.

"No," Raphael agreed. "Not at first. But your legs will get stronger. Plus," he stepped over to her and pushed her again. This time, she barely moved. "It's a much stronger position. This is called the horse stance."

Once she had the stance correct, Raphael showed her the first part of the form, a series of choreographed movements that she was to practice every day in order to perfect the mechanics of her technique. She performed the movements along with Raphael, and they seemed simple enough at first—aside from the persistent trembling in her legs—but the second time they went through it, he made about a dozen corrections in her form. She felt a little discouraged, but he assured her it was normal.

"It's a bit like learning to ride a bike," he said. "If you don't have the mechanics exactly right, you're going to tip over. But once you have it down, it just feels right."

Once Aimee had written down the different parts of the form so she could practice it at home, three times a day as Raphael had instructed, he showed her a simple block—the *Pak Sau*—used to deflect straight punches.

"Make sure your energy is going forward," Raphael warned. If it's going to the side, you'll overextend and leave your center line open."

Next, he showed her the *Biu Sau* block. To Aimee it looked like the salutes Nazis gave one another in one her history class videos.

"It's for blocking haymakers," Raphael explained. "Ready?"

Aimee nodded, a little frightened, but when Raphael threw a big, powerful punch toward her head, she surprised herself by blocking it.

"Whoa. I did it!" she exclaimed, laughing.

"You did," Raphael agreed. "Nice work."

Next, he taught her the basic strike, a quick but powerful series of jabs that she was able to throw fast, one after the other. It felt almost as if she was paddle-wheeling her arms, but in reverse.

"These punches don't generate quite as much force as a haymaker," Raphael explained. "But they can be thrown much faster. The power comes from the speed. You can deliver four or five punches this way in the time it takes for most people to punch once."

After he'd shown Aimee these basic moves, he made her drill them over and over and then put them together in combinations until her shirt was drenched with sweat and her legs were trembling so much she could hardly stand. But she didn't complain. In fact, she felt amazing. For the first time in a while, she felt like she was really working toward something—something that would not only allow her to get her mom back, but would help her become a stronger person, too. Plus, it was fun.

"You're a natural," Raphael said, and the pride that showed in his smile made her heart swell with joy. Actually, she thought she was terrible; all the movements felt awkward and foreign to her, but when she watched Raphael performing the same techniques, she saw how they could be fluid, even graceful. Of course, she reminded herself, he had been doing it since he was seven years old. But maybe if she worked hard enough she'd be good too.

Finally, Raphael had Aimee sit cross-legged on the floor with him.

"Now I'm going to teach you to meditate," he said. "This was the last thing Master Chin taught me, but I think it's important for you to begin cultivating your use of Shen now. That way when you need it, it'll be there."

"Shen," Aimee repeated the strange word. "That's what you blasted Oberon with, right?"

Raphael nodded. Unbidden, the memory flashed before Aimee's eyes: Raphael and the strange, black-winged form of Oberon doing battle on the top of the temple in that bizarre, ancient Middleburg. Just when it looked as if Oberon was undefeatable, Raphael had pointed a finger at him and some kind of magical power had lashed Oberon in the face, causing him to stumble backward and tumble off the temple summit. It still seemed too crazy to be real, like something out of some cool fantasy movie, except she'd seen it with her own eyes.

"You're going to teach *me* to use Shen?" she asked. It was still hard for her to believe Raphael had been able to do it. She couldn't imagine herself shooting magical blasts at people.

"I'm still learning about Shen," Raphael admitted. "Master Chin is always vague when he talks about it, but it seems like it manifests differently in different people. The abilities it gives you might be different from the ones it gave me."

Yeah, Aimee thought. *It's not going to work for me, guaranteed.*

But she followed Raphael's instructions, lying on a mat on the floor, closing her eyes, slowing her breathing, and imagining a heavenly illumination filling her as she silently chanted the words he gave her.

Fill me, oh light.

And when Raphael finally told her to open her eyes, she did feel a little different. There was a slight tingle throughout her body, and she felt calmer, more centered, more balanced. More than that, she felt satisfied too, as if a thirst she didn't even know she had was now quenched.

"So," Raphael said, finally breaking his kung fu master demeanor and smiling at her. "Do the form three times, and meditate once, every day until our next class. Any questions?"

"No, Master, you're a very thorough and honorable master," she said with playful sarcasm.

Raphael laughed, also playful. "You don't have to call me master," he said. "Sifu will be fine."

And Aimee decided she had kept her hands off Raphael long enough. "Thank you, Sifu," she said, and crawled across the floor and kissed him.

It was only after she got home later that she realized she'd forgotten to tell Raphael about getting a ride with Orias. She'd meant to—she didn't want to keep any secrets from him. But, she told herself, it was no big deal. There was nothing wrong with it, and being with Raphael all afternoon had felt so right.

CHAPTER 20

CHIN WAS SWEEPING THE FLOOR OF HIS kwoon on Sunday afternoon when Raphael burst in, fifteen minutes early for his lesson.

"Sifu," he said, bowing to Chin as he entered the barn. "I—are you okay? What happened to your face?"

"Long story," Chin said. He tried to smile but it hurt, so he settled for a wink instead. It was easier, since his eye was swollen almost shut anyway.

"I need to talk to you." Raphael told him.

Chin was surprised; he was about to say the same thing to Raphael. Silently, he pulled the beanbags over to the wood stove and they sat down.

"It's Zhai," Raph began. "Something's wrong with him—I mean, more than usual." His attempt at humor fell flat. "Last night he almost killed a little Flats girl."

"But you saved her." A statement of fact, not a question.

"Nass did. He was in the right place at the right time. He just knew where to be."

"Ah, yes—Ignacio, your spirited second. He will serve you well," said Chin.

"Last night was the second time Zhai has attacked us—unprovoked." Raphael's indignation grew with every word. "If anything, we should be going after him. It's his father and Jack Banfield who are evicting all the families in the Flats—block by block—and digging holes under all the buildings."

"As I suspected. They're looking for the treasure."

"You know about it!" Raphael exclaimed.

"Of course," Chin said. "But how do *you* know about it?"

"Aimee. Her new history teacher has an old scroll that tells all about it."

Chin leaned forward, the beanbag chair scrunching under his shifting weight. "You are sure about this?"

"Aimee saw it."

Chin leaned back in the chair again. "Aimee's teacher must be warned," he murmured. "She is in grave danger. If the original scroll still exists, they'll stop at nothing to possess it."

"Who?" Raphael asked.

Chin hesitated for only a moment. He knew the time had come. "It's a secret Chinese brotherhood—the Order of the Black Snake."

"Who are they?" Raphael asked. "What do they want?"

"The treasure. They are formidable enemies, Raphael. Sorcerers. They practice a rare form of snake-style kung fu, blended with black magic. They're using the dark arts to control Zhai."

"This makes no sense," Raph said. "How did this hugely valuable treasure end up Middleburg? And how do they know about it?"

Chin was already on his feet and heading for the door, gesturing for Raphael to follow.

"No time to explain now," he said. "Come on."

As they rode in Master Chin's rusty old pickup truck on the way into town, Chin gave Raphael his instructions: "Keep an eye out for those men—you and your Flatliners. I must find Zhai and try to free him from the spell the Order put on him. As soon as you see them, call me. Do not attack until I arrive."

"We're going to fight them?" Raphael asked, and Chin could tell he was worried. He saw determination in his pupil's eyes, but there was fear, too.

"We cannot let the treasure fall into their hands, Raphael—no matter what. The result would be unthinkable. So, yes. We'll fight them—you, me, and Zhai, together."

"I don't think you should count on Zhai," Raphael replied.

Chin dropped him at the corner near his house and then headed for Hilltop Haven.

The heater in his truck had been broken for months, and his hands were so cold he was afraid they might freeze to the steering wheel. Still, the day was pretty enough; a pallid sun hung in a faded blue sky above the festering old apartment houses of the Flats. The world seemed serene as he headed up Golden Avenue, passing the stately old brick-front buildings of downtown. On a day like this, he could almost believe everything would be okay.

The guard at the gate buzzed him in immediately, and the Shao's front door swung open the moment he rang the bell. A maid ushered him into the living room. Cheung entered a few minutes later, clad in a gray suit and a red tie. He looked as put together as he normally did, but Chin could tell his old friend was a little frayed around the edges. The knot in his tie was loose, as if he'd been tugging on it, and there were bags under his eyes. He managed a stiff smile as Chin approached, but it quickly faded when he saw the bandage on Chin's head.

"What happened?" he asked urgently, without the usual courteous greeting.

"Even the most careful and coordinated of us will have an accident occasionally," Chin answered. Cheung was too wise to believe that explanation, but Chin knew he was also too polite to challenge it. "I have come to see Zhai."

"He is not here, Chin. He didn't come home all night." Cheung shook his head and his worry was evident. "This is not like him. I had my secretary call all his friends this morning. No one has seen him."

Chin nodded. He should have expected as much. He had been foolishly optimistic to think that his enemies would allow him any chance to wrest Zhai from their control.

"Listen, old friend," Chin told Cheung Shao quietly. "I need to ask you something, and you must be honest with me." He'd hoped it wouldn't come to this; he didn't want to dig into Cheung's carefully protected private life, but he had to get at the truth. Saying the name of the Order aloud, however, was a dangerous proposition.

Instead of speaking, he lifted his arm as if to shake hands with Cheung, and then made an undulating motion with it. The sign of the Order. Cheung's eyes grew wide and the color drained from his face.

"You know, I could use some air," Cheung said quietly. "Let's go out and finish our visit over lunch."

Chin nodded and silently followed Cheung into the foyer, where Cheung rang for the maid to bring him his coat. As she helped him put it on, Chin glanced up the stairs. Lotus was there, standing at the banister, looking down on them, her eyes devoid of emotion as they met Chin's. Then, without a word, she turned away and slipped back into the shadows of the upstairs hallway.

"Shall we?" Cheung said, gesturing to the doorway, and Chin followed.

ಇಲ

Aimee stood in front of her mirror, going over the kung fu form Raphael had taught her. Her legs were stiff and every muscle in her body ached, but Raphael promised that the more she practiced, the faster she would advance, so she had decided to push herself every day. When the knock came on her door, however, she was more than ready for a break.

It was her dad, with a stack of mail in his hand. He held an envelope out to her. As she took it he asked, "What are you up to?"

"Just practicing my . . . uh, my cheerleading," Aimee said, looking down at the envelope and wondering who it was from. "I'm going to try out next semester—I told you." She hadn't, but she knew he wouldn't remember.

"Well, that's good news," he said. "It's about time you got back to your real life." He continued shuffling through his mail. When she didn't say anything, he looked up and nodded at the envelope she was holding. "Aren't you going to open it?"

She wanted to say, "Why—are you suddenly interested in my life, for a change, instead of just trying to control everything I think and do?" But things were going so well lately; her dad was paying less attention to her than ever, Rick was busy with football, and she was able to sneak out and see Raphael or hang with Dalton once in a while. She didn't know who the letter or card or whatever was from and she didn't care. It wasn't from Raphael—he was too smart to do something so brazen. "Do you want to open it?" she asked her father quietly.

"Oh, don't be silly," he said, as if humoring a small child. "Go ahead, honey. See who it's from."

She tore the envelope open and took out a lovely, old-fashioned card. It was a pale violet and had a hand-painted bouquet of lavender and the words "You're Invited," on the front. She flipped it open and found, in neat, masculine, dark blue script:

You are cordially invited

To the home of Orias Morrow

On the afternoon of November 24th, at 4pm,

For High Tea.

Aimee stared at the card.

"Well?" her dad asked.

"It's an invitation. From Orias," she said, frowning. "He's inviting me to high tea, of all things." The whole idea was ridiculous—who had high tea, in Middleburg, in the twenty-first century, for heaven's sake? The fact that he was having a tea party seemed strange; the fact that he had invited her was even more perplexing.

"Do we have to go?" she asked, surprised to find that although she dreaded another encounter with Orias, she was also intrigued by the idea.

"Let's see the card," Jack said, and she showed it to him. "Nope," he said. "Not us. You. It seems neither Rick nor I are invited. Unless yours is a plus-one?"

She looked at the invitation again and shook her head. So he'd just invited her. *Great*. She shrugged and stuck the card back in the envelope. "I'll call and tell him I can't go."

"What do you mean?"

"Well, I'm grounded, right?"

Her dad flipped absently through his new issue of *Fortune* magazine. "Aimee, Aimee, Aimee . . . Orias isn't one of those delinquents from the Flats. Orias has class. He's smart, ambitious and richer than God. I think you should get to know him better."

"Even though his father kidnapped me?" she snapped, no longer able to control her mouth.

Her dad closed the magazine and looked at her. "You, of all people, should not want a kid to suffer for a parent's mistakes, not after your mother—well, never mind. Oberon is dead—he has to be, or he'd have made a move by now. He wouldn't let Orias take over control of his businesses and properties if he were still alive, believe me. Orias has done nothing to deserve being made to feel unwelcome—which is how he'll feel if you refuse his invitation."

Aimee held up the card. "So let me get this straight. You *want* me to go?"

"Yes, I do," he said. "It looks like I'm going to be doing business with that young man, and I don't think it will send a good message if you don't show up. Tell you what. Go and have tea with him, and I'll repeal your grounding. You'll be off the hook."

"Really?"

"Really!" He grinned, and he looked disarmingly like the doting father she remembered as a little girl.

"Okay, then—I'll go." She was stunned but it was a deal she couldn't refuse. An hour of swilling tea and eating cucumber sandwiches, and she'd have her freedom back. It seemed like an excellent trade to her.

"Good," her father said, and she tried to remember the last time she'd gotten his approval for something. "I'm having lunch with him tomorrow. I'll let him know you'll be there."

He left then, shutting the door behind him, and Aimee stared at the invitation. The prospect of seeing Orias was a little scary, but at least it was a party—she wouldn't be alone with him.

Because, as much as she loved Raphael, she was afraid of what might happen if she were alone with Orias for too long.

✍

Chin sat with Cheung in a private upper room of Spinnacle, one that was reserved for V.I.P. guests—which typically meant either Cheung or Jack Banfield. The room was comfortably appointed with a large, rectangular table of beautiful wood and several expensive-looking leather couches, most of them facing a large picture window that looked out across the rolling fields and forests north of town. It was a nice space. Chin could see why it was reserved for the most honored clientele.

Cheung sat with a glass of Cognac in front of him; it was the first time Chin had ever seen him drink. He stared down into the amber liquid for a long time before he finally spoke.

"Are you one of them?" Cheung Shao finally asked.

The silence sat heavily between them for a moment.

"I was once," Chin said, gazing out the window, across the bleak, barren fields. "A long time ago."

Cheung Shao looked up from his drink, directly into Chin's eyes. "But they kill anyone who leaves."

"They try," Chin agreed. "And they almost always succeed."

Cheung sighed, long and slow, and then sipped his drink again. "They will kill me for talking to you," he said.

"Maybe. But if you don't tell me the truth, Zhai may end up dead. Or worse . . . "

Cheung was silent for a long time, but when he started speaking again, he didn't stop.

"I've told you that my father was a simple fisherman—uneducated—but he always made sure I went to school. And I was smart. The best in my class. The best they'd seen in the school, for many years. When I was old enough, I moved to Hong Kong and became a stock trader, determined to make my fortune. I married, and we were happy, and soon Ming was pregnant with Zhai. Chin, I was never so happy, before or since. I was good at my job, but unlucky. When I lost the fortune I'd made, I was too ashamed to tell my wife. So I made one last try to get it back—at an illegal gambling parlor. I was losing—fast and big—but I was wearing an expensive suit, so they extended me a line of credit. The more I tried, the more I lost. At last, I gave up and went home. Still, I couldn't bear to tell Ming the truth. Every day I put on my suit and left in the morning, as if going to work. I did odd jobs—carrying wood, painting buildings—whatever I could find. But it wasn't enough. I couldn't pay my gambling debts, and one day I went home to find Ming—"

Here, Cheung paused for a long time, trying to steady his voice and stave off the emotion. Finally, he finished in a hoarse whisper:

"I found Ming dead. Zhai—he was only a toddler—had a note pinned to his shirt that said, 'Pay us or he's next.' So I took him and we fled. The Order found me three days later, living on the streets with Zhai. The man who approached me was wearing an old-fashioned derby hat—and a tattoo of a snake ran up both his forearms. He was kind, and he was charming. He bought lunch for me and Zhai, and I explained my situation to him. He told me he could take care of it. He could buy my debt from the owner of the gambling house, and all it would cost me was devotion to the Order of the Black Snake. I thought what he promised was impossible, but I swore if he could help me save my son's life I would do anything. He came back half an hour later with a letter from the leader of the Hong Kong Triad that said my life, indeed, had been signed over to the Order of the Black Snake.

"I had heard whispered stories about the Order—everyone had—but I never believed they really existed. I asked the man what I would have to do for them.

"'We've heard how smart you are, Cheung Shao,' he told me. 'We are going to put you in place for a very important job. You will live like a king, in a mansion. You will have a fortune at your disposal. You will have a beautiful wife. You will run our companies in America and that will give you great power. Everything under the sun that a man could desire will be yours. And one day, when it's time to do that very important job, we will come to you.' That's how Zhai and I got to Middleburg. Two members of the Order met us when we arrived and escorted me to the mansion they had waiting for me, and everything they promised came true. A large share of several companies, including Middleburg Materials had been purchased in my name. A few months later, I met Lotus. Everything was as they said it would be, and I was happy. They went away and I forgot about them. There was no contact as long as I submitted a profit-and-loss statement twice a year to their agent in Hong Kong. Most days, I could even forget that I belonged to them."

Cheung tilted his head back and downed the last of his drink. Chin's heart ached for his friend, but he knew there was nothing he could do to ease the pain of the past. All he could hope to do was bring Zhai home safely and help to avert a future tragedy.

"They've come back," Cheung said.

"I see." Chin finished his soda water. "What do they want you to do?"

"If I tell you any more, they will certainly kill me." He signaled the waiter for another drink and then looked at Chin, in agony. "Do you think they have my son?"

"I don't know," Chin answered. "But I will find him."

"If he's still alive. . . . When the Order is done with Middleburg, I wonder if any of us will be."

ॐ

Chin called Raphael as he drove away from Spinnacle. "Any news?" he asked eagerly. "Any sign of Zhai—or the Snakes?"

"Nothing," Raphael said quietly. "We covered the Flats—twice. There's no sign of the Shao Construction guys, either, or their equipment. It's like they vanished."

An odd, vacant feeling crept into Chin's soul as he stared out his frosty windshield. They hadn't vanished, he knew. They were Snakes and snakes were patient, coiled in their holes, waiting to strike.

CHAPTER 21

IT WAS THE WEDNESDAY BEFORE THANKSGIVING, and the energy in the Middleburg High cafeteria was manic as everyone went from table to table talking with friends, taking good-natured snipes at each other, and generally getting amped up for the long weekend. But the mood at the Toppers lunch table remained sullen.

"I bet he got mono," D'von said in his low, bass voice. "Cle'von, you remember when our cousin got mono and he couldn't leave the house for three months?"

Cle'von, chewing a huge bite of sub sandwich, nodded.

"I don't know," Dax said, drumming his fingers on the table. "You all know how responsible Zhai is. He'd have to be half-dead not to even call."

Rick managed to keep his temper in check, but he was losing patience with all this talk. No one had heard from Zhai since the weekend and he hadn't been in school Monday, Tuesday, or today. Rick and Bran had called his house, but the maid said only that Mr. Zhai wasn't home and no one else in the family was available.

But Rick wasn't worried about Zhai. What was pissing Rick off was that no one had thought to suggest that he should lead the Toppers—at least until Zhai returned. But he kept silent, biding his time. If there was one thing he'd learned from his father, it was how to do that.

"Well, there's one way to find out what's going on real quick," Bran said in his cool southern drawl. "We ask Li."

A few heads nodded in agreement and Michael Ponder said, "Oh yeah . . ."

Even though Li was one of the hottest girls at Middleburg High, there was an unspoken rule among the Toppers that their leader's sister was strictly off limits. And as difficult as it was, they studiously ignored her on the rare occasions that Zhai invited her to go with them somewhere, only stealing looks at her when they were sure he wasn't paying attention.

Li. It pissed Rick off that he hadn't thought of it first—but if Li could confirm that Zhai had gone out of town or something, that might prompt a vote for Rick to be their interim leader. And he had plenty of ideas about what he would do with his newfound power.

"What do you say?" Bran said to Rick. "Let's go ask her."

Rick nodded, swiped his mouth with the napkin and rose. He and Bran headed over to the table in the corner where Li sat with two girls who were only pretty enough to accent her exotic beauty, and the little wussy guy who followed her everywhere. Rick didn't remember his name.

When Rick and Bran stepped up to the table, the conversation ground to a halt. Li's friends blushed and the kid—Weston, that was it—sat up straighter. Only Li seemed unaffected by their presence. She looked up at Rick and he saw playful defiance in her dark eyes. It struck him again how beautiful she was. Like her mom, she was a total freaking fox. While Rick stared, Bran, always the talkative one, struck up the conversation.

"How's it goin', ladies?" he asked, and Rick noticed he really poured on the smooth Southern charm. The girls, except Li, giggled nervously. Weston stared resentfully at the intruders through his horn-rimmed glasses. Li studied Bran for a moment before her gaze drifted to Rick.

"It's going fine," she said. "How's it going with you guys?"

"Good, real good," returned Bran, taking his time. Li got right to the point.

"So what do you want?"

"Oh—we were just talking about your brother," said Bran. "We haven't seen him around all week. Is he okay?"

"I couldn't tell you," Li said.

"What do you mean?" Rick retorted.

"He hasn't been home. My mom said he went out of town for some training thing at Spike Ferrington's gym. My dad says he's been staying over at your house."

"My house?" Rick was surprised. "He hasn't been at my house. And he's not training with Spike. Spike is my trainer. He would have told me."

Li smiled up at Rick. She didn't seem too concerned about Zhai, or about the fact that her parents had lied to her. "Well, I don't know where he is," she said.

Rick and Bran exchanged a glance. They'd first thought maybe the Flatliners had done something to Zhai—but if the Shaos were lying about where he was, that couldn't be the case.

"You sure about that?" Rick demanded.

"Yes," she said sweetly, still looking steadily into his eyes. "I'm sure." Rick detected a strange undercurrent in her attitude, as if she were daring them to challenge her.

"She said she doesn't know," Weston, the little bespectacled blond kid, piped up.

Rick turned slowly to look at him, fully prepared to knock his head right off his shoulders, but Bran's laugh diffused the tension. He reached out to give the kid a high five, which, after a moment of confusion, Weston returned.

"Looks like you got yourself a knight in shining armor!" Bran told Li. To Weston he added, "My granddaddy has a sayin', kid. Don't poke sleepin' bears. You feel me?" He clapped Weston on the back, jarring his slight frame so hard his glasses almost fell off the end of his nose, and then he walked away.

Rick hesitated a moment longer, still gazing at Li. Yeah, she was hot, all right. If Zhai stayed lost, Rick might need to take more than just his leadership position. Li gave him one last radiant smile before he turned and headed back to the Toppers lunch table.

"Is it just me, or was Li playing with us?" he asked Bran.

"She knows more than she's letting on, that's for sure," Bran agreed, giving Rick a sly glance. "I think under the circumstances we should pick a temporary leader."

Rick only nodded, though inside he was shouting in triumph.

"I'll bring it up to the other guys, see if they want to vote on it." Bran stopped walking and looked up at Rick, who stopped, too. "Whoever gets picked, I hope he has a strong sense of honor. You know how bad I got dissed at that homecoming dance. I asked Zhai three times for permission to get back at Raphael Kain for it, and every time he said no."

"If I was the leader," Rick said quietly, "It wouldn't be a matter of permission. I'd *order* you to get revenge."

Bran smiled, "I knew I could count on you, buddy. Let's go," he said and started back to their table.

Rick looked up as the door opened and Raphael Kain walked in. Behind him, Rick saw Maggie passing by in the hallway. "Give me a minute," he said.

∞

Leaning against her locker, Maggie started shaking as soon as she heard his voice behind her.

"Where have you been?" Rick demanded, surly and threatening. She whirled around, her heart racing—but he still looked like Rick.

"What do you mean?" she said.

"You've been avoiding me for days, and you haven't sat with me at lunch all this week," he said. "What's going on?"

"Nothing's going on—I've just been busy."

"Well, get unbusy," he ordered. "You're making me look bad. Everybody's asking if we broke up or something." Behind him, she could hear the noise of the crowded lunchroom. "Come on, before lunch is over. Sit at my table with me."

As she reluctantly followed him inside to the Toppers' table, she noticed Raphael sitting a couple of tables away. He looked up and saw her come in with Rick. She cast a desperate look in his direction and, picking up on it, he moved one table closer.

"Come on," Rick told her. "Sit down."

"I don't think so," she said.

"What?" He looked incredulous. "Don't be stupid. Do as you're told and we won't have any trouble." He looked around at his jock friends, smug.

"No. I . . . I think we should break up."

His eyes narrowed. "Oh, you think so?" He glared at the other Toppers, and Bran rose and picked up his tray. The other jocks followed suit and filed toward the doors, leaving Rick and Maggie alone.

"What the hell do you think you're doing, Maggie?" Rick demanded. "You *never* want to embarrass me in front of my friends. You ought to know that by now."

"I don't think we should see each other anymore," she said.

"Even if it means you'll never date in this town again?"

"Yes. I don't care about that anymore."

A red flush of anger inched up from his neck to his cheeks. "Hmm," he said as if giving it consideration. "No," he finished calmly.

"You don't own me, Rick," she said, getting angry now. "Anyway, we're not in love. We never were. You're not even nice to me. So we're done."

Rick sniffed and cracked his neck. "Nope," he said evenly. "Not even close. I like having you around. I even like it when you get all pissed off like this. It's a turn-on." He moved closer, leaned in, and added quietly, "Besides, you need to think of your mom, with no man around the house to protect her. Accidents happen all the time. She might . . . I don't know . . . fall down the basement stairs or something. Wouldn't that be tragic?"

At the mention of the stairs, the blood in Maggie's veins turned to ice. She looked up at Rick, trying to keep the horror from showing in her face. Did he know where the stairs in her basement led? He was some kind of a demon, after all. . . .

At the edge of her vision, she saw Raphael slowly rising from the next table. Rick glanced over and saw him too.

"What are you looking at, rat?" he snarled.

"You, getting dumped on your ass," Raphael said calmly. He was leaning casually against the table now, watching Rick, his eyes glittering with all the hatred Maggie felt. She had never been more attracted to Raphael Kain than at that moment.

Rick took a quick step toward Raphael, but suddenly, Principal Innis approached, walking up the aisle between tables and passing right between Rick and Raph, with three teachers behind him. They all sat down at the table right next to Rick, oblivious to any kind of confrontation going on. Rick looked at them with disgust as they started chatting about curriculum changes, and then he turned to Raphael and cracked his knuckles.

"That's all right, ghetto boy," he hissed. "But watch your back. You don't want to let me get you alone."

Raphael smiled at him. "I look forward to it, Rick," he returned evenly. "Every time."

Rick looked down at Maggie. "We're done when I say we're done," he whispered, and leaned in to kiss her. Before she could pull away, he bit her bottom lip, hard.

Maggie watched him leave, trembling with fury.

Raphael was standing next to her now. "Well, that went well," he said. He sounded amused. "You think he got the message?"

"Not likely," she whispered, thinking about her mother tumbling down the cellar stairs. Rick, she knew, did not make idle threats. "But don't worry," she added. "It'll all work out. Thanks for backing me up."

"Any time, Maggie," Raphael said, walking away.

She reached up and touched her lip, and her fingertips came away bloody.

Maggie sat in her darkened bedroom, leaning against the foot of her bed, staring into the shadows. She heard a crash downstairs—her mother, no doubt looking for art supplies. She'd been a bit more lucid lately, and although she still spent sleepless nights obsessively working on the design for her new tapestry, the manic edge that dominated her behavior had softened a bit. But Maggie was getting worse. It was as if, when Maggie was finally crowned homecoming queen, some of her mother's craziness had passed on to her.

Because she *was* going crazy. She no longer denied it. It started when she saw her boyfriend's face transform into something demonic and she'd progressed from that to stairways to hell, floating cell phones, and books full of invisible writing. Now, for an encore, she'd decided to go ahead and starve herself. After a few days of indecision, she'd started her fast on Monday. She was fine all morning—half the time she didn't eat breakfast anyway. But by lunchtime, she was ready to jump somebody for a french fry. Her stupid friends assumed she'd forgotten her daily yogurt and kept offering to share their lunches—raw carrots, string cheese, apples, containers of pudding, handfuls of potato chips. It was torture. By the end of the next period, she was really hungry. She went into the bathroom, locked herself in a stall, and leaned against the door, fighting the dizziness she guessed was from low blood sugar. Then she remembered what Lily Rose had told her. Meditation instead of starvation. Spiritual nourishment. *Yeah, right*, she thought. *I'd like a spiritual pepperoni pizza and a spiritual Diet Coke, please.*

But with nothing to lose, she closed her eyes, slowed her breathing, and tried. First, her mind kept drifting to Chips Ahoy. Then a group of loud Flatliner girls came in, talking about how cute the new kid Ignacio was, which shattered her tranquility. When they finally left, she managed to fall into a stupor that was half meditation, half midafternoon nap. When the class bell roused her, her hunger had diminished somewhat.

At home when dinnertime rolled around she heated up a frozen meal for her mom and took it to her in her breakfast-room-turned-art-studio. To Maggie's amazement, her mother actually put down her sketchpad and watercolor brush long enough to pick up her fork and try a bite.

"Where's yours?" she asked Maggie.

"I grabbed something at the Dug-Out after school," Maggie lied. Even the smell of a disgusting TV dinner was making her ravenous.

The next day—Tuesday—hadn't been as bad. She woke up dizzy and she was pretty spaced out for most of her classes, but her breakfast and lunchtime meditations really did seem to be tamping down her hunger. During her dinnertime meditation, she fell asleep and didn't wake up until Wednesday morning.

When she sat up, her stomach was cramping, and she really felt for the first time like she was starving to death, but by the time she got to school a new clarity seemed to have seeped into her consciousness somehow. She actually listened to her teachers and she was taking notes even faster than they were talking.

Bobbi Jean and Rhonda noticed a change in her too.

"Are you wearing different eye shadow or something?" Bobbi Jean asked as they picked up their trays.

"No, why?"

"Your eyes look weird."

"Thanks a lot," Maggie shot back.

Rhonda was staring at her too. "Well, they don't look *bad* weird," she said. "Just *weird*."

When Maggie stood in front of the mirror in the girl's bathroom gazing at her reflection, she could see what they were talking about. There was something about her eyes. Not a light or a glow exactly, but a certain animation; a *vitality* that wasn't there before. There was a new sheen to her skin, too.

All the same, she was dying for a cheeseburger. As she washed her hands, she fantasized for the millionth time about Thursday when she'd be able to eat again. All she could think about was Thanksgiving—and turkey, stuffing and biscuits smothered in gravy.

She splashed water on her face, dried it with a paper towel and looked at herself again. Yes, there was definitely something different. Her senses were heightened too. There were dozens of conversations going on out in the hall and she could hear and follow them all. Li's dweeby little friend Weston was bragging about his calculus grade; that fat Flatliner Beet was talking about movies with the annoying Flats cheerleader Natalie. The new history teacher—Miss Pembrook—was walking by with Mr. Brighton, talking about some History Channel special. She heard them all at once, and every conversation individually. It was amazing.

The bell rang. It was time for her to go back to class, but she wasn't ready—not yet. She dug her phone out of her back pocket and held it in the palm of her hand. She stared at it hard, concentrating like the psychics she'd seen on TV and in movies.

Nothing.

She took a deep breath, shook the tension out of her neck and shoulders, and tried again. This time, she relaxed, and the same weightless, tingly feeling she got during meditation came over her. Instead of trying to make the phone rise into the air, she imagined herself untethering it, releasing it, *letting* it float away. A moment later, it left her hand and hovered a good six inches above her palm.

"Holy crap," she whispered, staring at it in wonder. She let out a wild little laugh, and it dropped into her hand.

Now, she turned her attention to the mirror in front of her. Relaxing, letting that magical feeling work through her, she raised her arm and pointed at the mirror.

"Bam!" she said—and it shattered.

Maggie took a little step back, startled. Then she giggled. "I know magic," she whispered. "This is so freaking awesome."

On Thanksgiving, Maggie ordered dinner from Spinnacle for herself and her mom and drove down to pick it up. When she walked back into the kitchen with the heavy paper bag full of food in her arms, she was shocked to see her mother pouring sparkling grapejuice into two crystal flutes. Her hair was up and wet from a shower, and she was dressed presentably for once. Maggie peered through the doorway into the dining room. The table was set with their good China and silverware and candles were lit.

"Well, look at you," she said as she unloaded the bag. It was still a little weird to see her mom looking almost normal.

"I didn't want to stop working this morning," Violet admitted. "But this is such an important holiday."

"Yeah, I'm dying for some turkey, too," Maggie agreed, but her mom gave her a strange look.

"It's not the food that's important," her mom said.

It was to Maggie. She gave a sarcastic little shrug as she carried the turkey into the dining room. It smelled amazing. After they sat down to eat, something else happened—something weird. Maggie's mom said a grace of sorts.

"We humbly thank you for the food you've set before us, the family you've placed among us, for the world you've set beneath us and the sky you made above us. You keep evil from us, and raise us when we fall. For these and all our blessings, we thank the mighty All."

Before her mother even said amen, Maggie was ladling gravy onto her massively stacked plate, as fast as she could with trembling hands. As she chewed the first bite, her eyes closed in ecstasy. She'd never known heaven could exist in a single bite of food, so deliciously mind-blowing it was almost divine—and perhaps for the first time in her life, she was truly thankful for it.

As she plastered butter on a dinner roll something else happened. She thought about all the people who weren't going to have Thanksgiving dinner—and it bothered her. It had never bothered her before. She'd never given it a thought—not even when the cheerleaders were leading the food drive at school.

Oh, yeah, she thought. *No doubt about it. I'm going to be stark-staring, bug-eyed loony tunes, just like my mother.*

∽

Laughter rang through the dining room of the Torrez's apartment.

"And my stupid brother laughed so hard, *horchata* shot out his nose!" As Clarisse finished her story, Ignacio's mother roared with laughter and his dad chuckled. Nass was smiling too (it was kind of a funny story), but his heart wasn't in it. He was thinking about Dalton.

It was too bad he couldn't just love Clarisse, he lamented to himself— his life would be so much easier. She was best friends with his mom, she was already like a daughter to his dad, and although she had a bit of a wild streak, she was crazy about him. No, he corrected himself, Clarisse was just plain crazy—no one in their right mind would rip off a bad dude like Oscar Salazar. But she was hot. Hot in Los Angeles and even hotter in Middleburg where the local guys didn't quite know what to make of her. But she still wasn't Dalton.

"Hey, Dad, you mind if I take the truck out?" he asked suddenly.

"It's Thanksgiving! You should be here with your family," his mom chastised him.

"What for?" his dad asked. "Let them have fun. You and Clarisse want to go to the movies or something?"

"Nah, I talked to Raph earlier. We're taking some food over to Emory and his family."

"You're a good boy. I'll put some of our leftovers in containers for them," his mom said as she gathered up the dessert plates.

"Great," Clarisse said. "Let me grab my jacket."

"No," Nass said, so quickly his mom looked up in surprise. "Raph wants to talk to me about something. I think it's kind of personal. I won't be long, but I have to do this alone."

∽ 303 ∾

Clarisse's expression darkened, but she said nothing. She picked up the rest of the plates and followed Amelia into the kitchen. He knew she'd make him pay later for leaving her behind, but he had to get some downtime—away from her.

Ignacio's dad took the keys out of his pocket and tossed them over. "Be careful," he said.

"You know I'm a good driver."

Raul Torrez smiled at his son. "Who said anything about driving?"

ဢ

Lily Rose's house was the place to be on Thanksgiving. She took great care to make every holiday special by decorating and cooking and inviting as many people over as their little house and tiny budget could accommodate. So when Dalton told her grandmother that Emory and his family had no place to go that day, she invited them over immediately. Knowing that Lily Rose couldn't afford to feed four extra people, Raphael quickly devised a plan. On Thursday afternoon the Flatliners convened at Lily Rose's, each of them bearing food. The result was the most awesome pot-luck Raphael had ever seen.

The kitchen counter was spilling over with casserole dishes, pie pans, platters of turkey and ham, and bowls of vegetables and gravy and fruit. Basically, everything Raphael knew a Thanksgiving feast should have was there, and the house was stuffed with people, too. Emory's mom stood in one corner, wiping tears away, overwhelmed by the kindness of her neighbors. Emory's dad was next to her, his arms folded and a grateful smile across his face. Haylee, shy with so many people around, was quiet for once. Since her near-fatal experience with Zhai, her attitude toward Emory had changed, and she followed him around like a shadow.

Nass had arrived last, with a bag full of Mexican delicacies. He was standing right next to Dalton, but Raphael noticed they were pointedly ignoring each other. It seemed there was nothing Nass could do to patch up the rift between them, though Raph knew he had tried. She still wouldn't return Nass's calls and she avoided him at school.

Kate was there too, wearing jeans and a colorful sweater, probably borrowed from Dalton, Raph thought. She had on a little makeup and she looked really pretty. She was also staring at the counter, her green eyes wide with wonder, as if she'd never seen so much food in one place in all her life.

When Kate saw Raphael, she hurried over. "So kind of you to arrange this for your friend," she said with a smile.

Raphael shrugged. "We help each other out. That's how we do it in the Flats," he said. "We make do with little and share what we have."

"Well, no one could be having a finer holiday meal, not even in Hilltop Haven," she said. "And 'tis a lovely tradition—giving thanks."

"Yeah," he said and wondered why it seemed like such a revolutionary idea to her. "I guess it is." But her enthusiasm was contagious and he started to cheer up, even though he was missing Aimee like crazy.

"How's your friend, Zhai?" she asked. "Did you call a truce to your feud yet?"

Raphael shook his head. "No chance of that."

"But I guess you see him at school," she replied, a shadow of concern crossing her face.

And suddenly he got it. She was fishing—she was interested in Zhai.

"No, sorry—I haven't seen him at school at all this week," he said. *Not since he tried to kill Haylee, jumped off a rooftop, and disappeared up the street.* "How do you know Zhai?"

"Oh—it was the day after Halloween," she told him. "The ghosties and goblins were still runnin' amok and he came by the *Celtic Spirit*. He needed something for some kind of scavenger hunt." She paused, Raphael thought, to see how he would take the news that she was consorting with his enemy. "He seems a good lad," she added. "'Tis a great shame you can't be friends."

"Like I said, no chance." He looked at the time on his phone. It was getting late and he'd promised his mom he'd be back as soon as he'd delivered the food for Emory's family. Even though Raphael's dad was gone, his mom went all out for Thanksgiving. It was a good thing her unemployment checks had kicked in, in time to pay for the food she'd been cooking all morning. Maybe Jack Banfield was helping her—if he was the big man he thought he was, Raphael thought, he would be.

Everyone was chatting happily, but as soon as there was a lull in the conversation, Raph said to his crew, "Okay—we should get a move on and let these guys eat."

They said their good-byes and started filing out of the crammed kitchen amid a chorus of thank-yous from Lily Rose, Dalton, and Emory's family. Raphael was among the last to leave, and as he passed Ignacio, he saw his friend lean close to Dalton.

"Hey, Dalton," Nass whispered. "Can I talk to you? Just for a minute."

Dalton didn't smile, but she nodded and led Nass down the hall toward the back of the house.

෨

"Wow!" Nass said as he stepped out the back door and into Lily Rose's garden. A multitude of beautifully colored flowers stuck up in rows from the thin layer of frost on the grass.

Even that tiny three-letter word made Dalton's heart ache. Ignacio got so excited about everything, just like a little kid. It was one of the things she loved about him, and one more painful reminder of how miserable she was without him.

"You've never seen my grandma's backyard before, huh?" she said, trying to keep the emotion from creeping into her voice.

"They have to be fake, right?" Nass asked, bending down to examine one of the flowers.

Dalton shook her head. "I know—it's weird. But they're real."

"It's more than weird," Ignacio said. "Does she come out here and put heat lamps on them, or what?"

"No—she says all they need is her special fertilizer. Love."

His laugh sounded, to Dalton, a little nervous. There were a few other amazing things she could tell him about her grandma—things she would like to share with him—but now it felt hard to trust him.

He sat down on an old swing (just two old ropes with a weathered board between them, tied to a big tree branch), and leaned against the ropes halfheartedly.

"So," Dalton asked. "What did you want to talk about?"

"Anything. I just miss talking to you."

"Ah . . . desperate to hear my voice, eh?" she said cynically. She was determined to be cold and aloof with him, but all she wanted to do was run into his arms.

"Yeah," Nass said, serious. "I do want to hear your voice—all the time. I miss you."

"And does Clarisse know you're over here, missing me?"

Nass winced, and Dalton almost felt bad for ruining the moment. But, she noticed, Nass didn't answer the question. "She doesn't know you're here, does she?"

Still, he didn't answer.

"Nass, what are you doing?" She was no longer able to push her anger down. "Maybe things work a little differently in L.A. Maybe out there, you can be living with one girl and have something going on with another one, but guess what—you're not in L.A. anymore. This isn't the hood. You're not in a rap video. And if you think I'm going to just let you string me along while you make up your mind—then you don't know me at all."

"I guess I deserve that," he said quietly, staring down at his shoes. "Look, the last thing I'd ever want to do is hurt you. But Clarisse—she's almost like family. I mean, we were best friends for years. And yeah, we did go out for a few weeks before I left L.A. but—it's not like I'm in love with her or anything. When I'm with her I don't feel . . . " he hesitated, swallowed hard and continued. "When I'm with her I don't feel like I do when I'm with you. And when you won't talk to me—when you see me at school and you walk the other way—man, that's cold."

"What did you expect, Nass? If you'd told me about her from the beginning—"

"I know," he broke in. "I should have. But what you need to know is that my mom and her mom have been close for years—closer than sisters—and Clarisse is going to be around for a while. She's got some personal stuff going on that I can't talk about. The bottom line is that I have to help her out right now—but I don't want to lose you. If you think that makes me a player or something and won't hang out with me, I understand. But it won't change how I feel about you."

Nass finally looked up at her, and his pain was unmistakable. He was telling her the truth—even if he wouldn't tell her the whole truth.

"So she got into some trouble in L.A.? That's why she's here?"

"I really can't talk about it, Dalton," he said gently. "I'm sorry. It's a bad situation, but there's nothing I can do to change it for now."

She could see that he was just as miserable as she was. He was hurting and she wanted more than anything to put her arms around him and comfort him. Whatever trouble Clarisse was in, Nass was going to stand by her—another reason Dalton loved him.

"Okay," she said. "I just want to know one thing."

"What's that?"

"Are you sure she's not playing you?"

"I'm sure," he said. "I wish it were that simple."

She didn't say anything for a moment. "Then it sounds like the last thing you need is another complication in your life. So we have to stay away from each other until you figure this out or she doesn't need you anymore."

"I don't think I can stand it."

"Neither can I," she agreed, and she realized that the moment they were sharing in the frosty garden might be their last.

"Close your eyes," she said.

"Why?"

"Close them."

He obeyed and she pressed her lips softly against his. He opened his eyes, just for a moment, and then he gathered her in his arms, closed them again and kissed her more deeply. When at last she pulled away he asked, "Does this mean we're okay?"

"It means good-bye—for now."

ഇ

Clarisse stepped back from Lily Rose's fence, her eyes trained on the cold, blank whiteness of the snow at her feet, but all she could see was the image of Ignacio kissing Dalton.

The helpless rage swirling inside her head seemed to coalesce into something darker, colder, and it sank into her chest like a stone. Her first impulse was to fight for her man, to climb the fence and kick Dalton's ass and take him back. Her second idea intrigued her more. There was a better way to get her revenge . . .

If she played everything just right, she might be able to solve her money problems too. She could get back at 'Nacio and have some fun. A wicked excitement coursed through her veins as she hurried away, the details of her plan already forming.

CHAPTER 22

RAPHAEL WATCHED, AMUSED, as his mom pushed a strand of hair out of her face with one hand to make way for the forkful of turkey she shoveled into her mouth. He didn't see much of her these days; he was always at school, training with Master Chin, working at Rack 'Em, hanging out with Aimee or doing something with the Flatliners.

His mom was still looking for a job. Word had spread quickly in the Flats that Oberon's son and heir was about to create jobs in Middleburg, and Savana Kain, like almost everyone else in the neighborhood, was eager to line up for an application. Raph didn't know if she was still spending time with Jack Banfield. He hoped not. She hadn't mentioned him lately and that was a good sign. Whatever was going on with her, she seemed happier than she'd been in a long time.

Every day, she looked more radiant than she had the day before. Even though the whole situation made Raphael uncomfortable, it seemed like being pregnant agreed with her. She was more like her old self than she'd been since his dad had passed away. Today, she'd made the whole turkey dinner from scratch—well, almost. Raphael had helped out with some instant stuffing and Pillsbury crescent rolls.

"So, how are things going with Aimee?" she asked.

Raphael tried to suppress a smile. "Fine. She's learning kung fu now."

"Ah, just what you need. A girl who can kick your butt," Savana joked.

"Yeah," Raphael said. "But you can't tell her dad. He still doesn't want us together."

He hadn't meant to bring up Jack; they had sort of an unspoken agreement about that. His mom frowned.

"Did he say why—or did Aimee?"

"He doesn't think I'm good enough for her," Raphael said with a shrug, and scooped a big bite of mixed-up mashed potatoes, stuffing, turkey, and gravy into his mouth. His mother's frown deepened.

"No," she said. "It's not like that. It's just that the situation is so complicated. You know—me and him, you and Aimee."

Raphael looked into his mother's eyes and saw that she was completely serious. She really didn't think Jack Banfield would look down on him just because he was a poor kid from the Flats. He wondered how Jack had made her think he was such a nice guy instead of the two-faced shark he really was. Raph was simultaneously angry at his mom for being so gullible and furious at Jack for using her—because he was sure Jack had no serious, permanent interest in the widow of a blue-collar worker from the Flats who had been reduced to working at a strip joint after her husband's death. But he didn't want to ruin the wonderful dinner she'd prepared, so he swallowed his anger along with the turkey and said nothing.

"Ohhh!" Savana winced suddenly, and both hands went to her abdomen.

"What is it?" Raphael asked, alarmed.

"Ow . . ." she groaned, clearly in pain.

"What? What's going on?" He put his fork down and pushed back from the table. Often, since he'd found out he was going to have a little brother or sister, he'd imagined himself rushing her to the clinic in Benton to have the baby, like some comic, addled dad in a movie—but she wasn't due for months. He was afraid something was wrong.

Savana exhaled and opened her eyes. There was a sheen of sweat on her forehead, but otherwise she looked okay.

"That was strange," she said, and then she winced again. She lifted her shirt and looked at her bulbous belly and he wondered if it should it be so big, this early in the pregnancy.

Raphael could see something moving, twitching slightly beneath her skin. That seemed weird, too. He stood up from his chair, unsure what to do.

Savana tilted her head back and closed her eyes, still in pain. And then he saw a white glow coming from within his mother's belly, like somebody shining a flashlight on the wall of a tent from the inside. He stood frozen, staring at the moving, glowing light. It blinked twice, shifted positions, and then went out. His mom relaxed, rubbed her abdomen, and pulled her shirt back down, took a few deep breaths, and wiped the perspiration from her forehead with her napkin.

"Are you okay?" Raphael asked, his heart racing.

"Yeah—fine." But her smile was weak and she was pushing her plate back. "Just indigestion, I guess. It's over." And she laughed, that wonderful sound Raphael always associated with his happy, carefree childhood. "What's wrong with you? You look like you saw a ghost."

Raphael shook his head and then slowly sat back down. "I'm just worried about you," he mumbled. "Is . . . is that supposed to happen?"

"Aw, Raphy, you're so sweet. Don't worry though, really. You'll find out some day when you're having kids of your own that a pregnant woman is a strange and mysterious thing."

"No kidding," he said. And they both laughed loudly—maybe a little too loudly. Beneath the laughter, though, Raphael was worried. On top of everything else that was going on, he had to worry about his mom. He didn't know much about pregnancy, but he knew there was something bizarre about the baby she was carrying—something unnatural. Babies moved, at some point, inside the mother—but they didn't *glow*.

⁊

On Saturday at the appointed time, Aimee's dad pulled up in front of Orias's house. She was wearing a dress under her overcoat, along with a pair of high-heeled boots her mother had left behind. She felt totally awkward and entirely too grown up in her outfit.

Most of all, she dreaded seeing Orias again . . . but she was looking forward to it also, with a funny feeling that was almost like *longing*. That not only puzzled her; it made her feel disloyal to Raphael. As her dad put the car in park, she appealed to him one more time.

"Do I really have to do this?"

"I honestly don't understand what the big deal is," he griped. "Orias is a family friend and a business associate and he's having a get-together. It's called networking, Aimee. You go in, sip tea, make some small talk, and when you're done, call me and I'll pick you up. What's so hard about that?"

"I just feel weird. I hardly know him."

"I'm sure there will be other people there you do know."

"Like who?"

She could tell he was starting to lose patience with her. "Look, I've got my fingers in just about every pie in town," he told her. "Except the businesses Oberon controlled. Now, Orias owns them and he seems willing to play ball with me. If we act quickly, I can own a piece of every bit of commerce that happens in Smith County."

Aimee sighed. "I don't get it. Why is it necessary for you to own every business and every piece of land in sight?"

"You're right," Jack said. "You don't get it. Neither did your mother. If you were a man, you'd see things differently. But you don't have to understand, Aimee. You just have to do what I tell you. Now go in there and try not to say or do anything that will reflect badly on me. You think you can handle that?"

"Sure," Aimee said, her voice barely more than a whisper. "I'll call when I'm ready to leave."

She got out and shut the door carefully. She wanted to slam it, but she knew how particular her dad was about his stupid cars and that would just be one more thing for him to be pissed off about. The engine growled behind her and the car tore off down the street, leaving her to stand alone on the sidewalk. As she headed up the walkway toward the old house, a gust of wind whipped her skirt around her. Pausing to straighten it, she glanced up at the dilapidated Victorian structure. There was an overwhelming stillness about the place; the windows were as black as chalkboards, and one shutter creaked in the breeze and thumped against the siding.

Great place for a party, she thought cynically. *Too bad Halloween is over.*

An odd mix of apprehension and anticipation assailed her, but up the steps she went, into the shadow of the porch roof, across the rickety decking. She reached up to knock on the door, but before she could, it swung slowly open. She expected to see Orias standing there to greet her, or another guest, maybe. But there was no one. It was as if the door had opened by itself, like something out of a horror movie.

She hesitated then, standing there on the threshold. If this were a movie, she would be rolling her eyes, thinking how stupid the heroine was to go into a creepy house right after the door opened on its own. But this was real life, and there was no way she could call her dad and tell him that she refused to go into a house where doors opened by themselves. He would ship her off to Mountain High Academy in a New York minute. Anyway, Orias had probably started making improvements on the place and simply had an automatic door opener installed. At least, that's what her father would say.

Tentatively, she stepped into the house and into the entry hall, wondering who else would be there—Cheung Shao, maybe. But then, since her dad wasn't invited, probably not. Maybe just some kids from Hilltop Haven.

"Hello?" she ventured, trying to sound cheerful rather than frightened. She walked a little further into the hallway and through an arched doorway on her left, she saw Orias sitting on a beautiful, antique Victorian couch in the living room, in front of a blazing fire. A shiny silver tea service sat next to what looked like a fancy bottle of red wine on the coffee table in front of him. No one else was there.

He looked up and saw her standing in the doorway. "Hello, Aimee." His voice was warm, tranquil.

"Hi," she said, trying to keep her tone as bright as possible. "Am I the first one here?"

He gazed at her, his hypnotic eyes probing deeply into her own as he rose to greet her. "The first . . . the last . . . the only one," he said softly.

∞

It was Saturday afternoon, and Raphael had invited his crew over to hang out. Beet, Josh and Benji all had to work, but Emory, always eager to get out of the family garage, had come, and so had Nass—with Clarisse tagging along. Savana had gone to visit Lily Rose, leaving them all to do their homework together, but they quickly gave up on that idea, deciding instead to watch a movie. Raph and Nass were on a mission to watch every martial arts movie in Master Chin's sizable collection. This week, Raphael had borrowed *Ip Man 2*.

Now, they all sat around, eating generic-brand microwave popcorn and watching the movie. When it was over and the credits were running, Nass made a joke.

"That's going to be you one of these days, man. We're going to be old guys, all going to the movies to see *Flatliner: The Legend of Raphael Kain*.

Everyone laughed and Nass did too, but Raphael noticed that his smile faded fast. There was a weird vibe coming from Clarisse as well. She was being nice—nicer than usual, actually, but to Raph it seemed a little forced. Maybe he was being paranoid, he thought as he stuffed the last of the popcorn into his mouth. He headed to the kitchen for another glass of Kool-Aid.

"So when are we going out treasure hunting again?" Clarisse called from the living room.

Raphael dumped the unpopped kernels into the trash as he considered the question. After what had happened to Haylee, he'd been a little concerned about leading his guys into danger again, especially since Zhai hadn't turned up yet. When Zhai was sane, he was a fairly predictable adversary. Since he'd gone off the deep end and gotten mixed up with this Order of the Black Snake business, there was no telling what he might do. Still, Raph knew, Emory and his family couldn't live in a garage forever. Ignacio's family was running out of time too, and he'd noticed a new rash of eviction notices posted on doors around the neighborhood. If they didn't find that treasure soon and use it to buy their apartment buildings back, or hire a lawyer to stop the evictions, they'd all be living on the street. They had to get the treasure before Jack Banfield and Cheung Shao found it—that was the only way. But with Zhai and the Order running around, he couldn't risk his crew getting attacked again. He'd have to figure something else out.

"Soon," he said, going back to join them.

"I hope so." Emory said. He'd been patient so far, but Raphael knew his current living arrangements were wearing on him.

Raphael nodded thoughtfully. "Well. . . I guess . . . Friday when we get off work," he said at last. Maybe Zhai would turn up before then.

Clarisse smiled eagerly. "I'm in."

"You're worried about the Obies, huh?" Nass asked Raph, ignoring her.

"The who?"

"Order of the Black Snake," Nass said with a grin. "Obies."

Raph chuckled. Leave it to Nass to give them a name that wasn't such a honking mouthful.

"Obies? What's that?" Emory asked.

"The dudes in the hats," Nass explained.

"Guys we don't want to mess with," Raphael added. "Until we figure out how to deal with them, it's too dangerous to go treasure hunting."

"What do you think the treasure is?" Clarisse interjected eagerly.

"I've been thinking about that a lot," Raphael said. "Kate found a valuable coin in the train graveyard when she first came to town. At first

I thought that was part of the treasure. And from the things Aimee told me, it sounded like it might even be precious gems—diamonds or something. But I think it's more than that. Like maybe it's got something to do with the Wheel and the Magician and everything."

Besides Aimee and Master Chin, Nass was the only person Raphael had fully shared his supernatural experiences with. Emory and Clarisse looked mystified.

"What Wheel?" Emory wanted to know.

"And who's the Magician?" Clarisse asked.

"Long story," Raphael said. He still hadn't figured out exactly how to explain all that magic stuff to the Flatliners. They all understood that Nass's saving Haylee's life came from the knowing, which came from Shen, and they had all experienced some weird stuff on Halloween night. But despite all that, he knew most of them were still struggling to accept the whole idea of magic.

"What he means is that the treasure isn't just a bunch of gold or something," Nass explained. "It's something more special than that. Something rare and unique."

"Like . . . maybe a priceless ancient artifact?" Emory suggested.

Raphael nodded. "Maybe."

"Well, when you go out looking again I want to go too," Clarisse said. Nass gave her a look, and she added, "What? I want to see the treasure!"

"Okay, guys," Raph said. "As much fun as this has been, I've got to get ready for work. My mom's gonna be home soon, anyway."

After they left, Raph tried to call Aimee. It went straight to voice mail. He went through his kung fu form and daily meditation and tried calling her again. Voice mail.

With his friends and his mom gone and Aimee not answering his calls, the apartment felt lonely, he thought as he changed for work. And in the silence, all the other crazy, frightening things he'd experienced lately came creeping back in. Bloody images swam through his imagination—the strange samurai . . . the creepy sail-board guys he'd killed. He saw Oberon's one glowing red eye staring at him from the depths of every shadow. By the time he locked up and started out on his evening walk to Rack 'Em, he was feeling so anxious he jogged all the way there.

ℴℴ

"Why would you have a party and invite only one guest?" Aimee asked. But she knew why and her heart did a funny little riff.

Orias walked slowly toward her, holding her gaze in his. "I don't recall mentioning a party," he said.

"Your invitation—"

"Was to you, for high tea." He was standing in front of her now, close, and looking down at her, his expression unreadable.

"You couldn't just call?"

A smile teased at his lips, and it annoyed her that he found her so amusing. "My romantic nature," he told her. "I'm old-fashioned that way."

She knew she should be furious with him for tricking her—she wanted to be. Only he hadn't—and she was actually *flattered*, of all things. And that made her angry with herself. She studied him for a moment.

"Does my dad know I'm your only guest?" she asked.

"I believe I was quite clear about it."

Oh, yeah, she thought. *Daddy dearest.*

Her first instinct was to get the hell out of there, until it hit her that her father had no problem with her being alone in a house with a really hot guy, as long as it was a guy he chose and it suited his purpose. She wondered if he had ever put her mom in this position.

Well, okay—fine, she projected in her mind, with contempt. *Be careful what you wish for, Jack.*

Anyway, if she left too soon he would make her pay and she'd never see Raphael again.

"Will you come in, then?" Orias urged softly. "And let me take your coat?"

"Sure. Why not?"

Her voice was harder than she meant it to be. She turned and when she shrugged out of her coat, his hands brushed her shoulders as he caught it. He let them linger there a moment before he went and hung it on an ornate rack near the door. She didn't resist when he took her elbow and ushered her through the arched doorway into his large, elegantly furnished living room.

The house might look rundown on the outside, but the interior was magnificent. Everything was very old—centuries old, it appeared—the furniture, the drapes, the big chandelier that sparkled with what looked like hundreds of flickering candles, thick Persian rugs that covered gleaming oak floors. Her mom loved antiques and Aimee knew a little about them. These were the real deal, and everything was in perfect, pristine condition. She felt almost like she'd stepped back in time.

"Why?" she finally said it out loud as he steered her to the sofa. "Why invite only me?"

"I want to get to know you."

"Okay, look," she told him. "This is important to my dad, so I'll play along. We can have some tea and polite conversation and then—"

"This has nothing to do with your father, Aimee," he said smoothly as he sat down next to her. "Oh, I'll do business with him, certainly. But this is about you."

"But why?"

His smile grew wider—and she saw it again, as she'd seen it when she'd looked through the window of Morningstar Inc. It was like he knew some kind of wonderful secret, and he hadn't decided whether to tell her or not. Finally, he spoke.

"Because I *am* interested in you . . . that way."

"Oh."

That really did surprise her, but strangely, she didn't object to the idea—and she hated that she didn't object. She closed her eyes for a moment and imagined Raphael's face, and all the love she saw in his eyes when he looked at her. When she opened them again, Orias was watching her calmly, waiting for her to go on.

"Well, then you should know I have a—" She stopped herself, just in time. If Orias reported back to her father that she claimed to have a boyfriend, Jack would know who she meant—and that would be bad for Raphael.

Orias picked up a saucer with one delicate teacup balanced on it and reached for the teapot. "This is a blend from my plantation in India," he said. "It has an exquisite bouquet. I suggest no cream and just a touch of honey."

"Fine."

He poured the tea and passed it to her, with a lace-trimmed linen napkin. She couldn't believe how light, how fragile the dishes were. They were made of some kind of eggshell porcelain so light it felt like they might dissolve in her hand.

"What's transpiring here, Aimee, has nothing to do with the Kain boy," Orias said.

She wondered how he knew about Raphael, and she remembered that Myka was working for him now—but would she have told him? She decided to change the subject. "So what's New York like?"

His expression was instantly more alive, more animated. "New York is amazing," he said. "Whatever you need or want is at your fingertips, whether it's three in the morning or three in the afternoon. I'd love to show it to you."

Well, that's not going to happen. The words formed in Aimee's head, but for some reason, she didn't say them.

On a silver tray next to the tea service, there was a cold fruit compote swimming in rich, red syrup, a plate of the prettiest petit fours she had ever seen and another heaped high with finger sandwiches cut in the shapes of stars and crescent moons. He picked up a plate and the silver serving tongs and asked, "Cucumber or watercress?"

She hadn't intended to eat anything. She wasn't even hungry—or at least, she hadn't been. Suddenly she was famished. "Both," she said.

He laughed. "A girl with a healthy appetite. You've stolen my heart already." He loaded her plate with sandwiches and pastries and placed it on the coffee table in front of her, along with a small dish of fruit. She had never tasted anything so incredible. Not even Lily Rose's cooking could compete. And he was right about the tea. It was delicious. She thought it was even making her a bit lightheaded—or maybe it was a sugar rush from the little cakes. He drained the dull metal chalice he was holding and poured himself more wine, from the fancy bottle.

"What's that?" she asked, not really meaning for it to sound sarcastic. "Wine from the family vineyards?"

"It is," he said simply.

"You're really that wealthy?" she asked.

"You can't even begin to imagine."

"What I can't imagine, Orias, is why you're still here." It was the first time she'd called him by name, and she was stunned at how natural, how *right*, it felt. "I mean, I know why you came—but why are you staying?"

"I told you during that assembly on Career Day," he said, watching her carefully. "I fell in love."

"And I told you. There's someone else."

"Yes," he agreed. "You did. But that's no reason we can't be friends."

"I'm sure you could have a million friends if you wanted. My brother thinks you're awesome. I think he'd jump off a bridge if you asked him to."

"Do *you* want me to ask him to jump off a bridge?"

"Maybe," she said, and laughed. "I'll let you know."

"In any case, we're going to be more than friends, you and I. Much more."

"I don't think so." Why did she say *that* when she meant, *no way*? What was wrong with her?

"You know what?" she said. "This was a really bad idea. I don't want to do this anymore." She put down her cup and got to her feet.

He stood in front of her, blocking her exit. "How do you know, Aimee?" he asked languidly. "How do you know you don't want something before you even try it?"

As she looked up into his eyes all she could think about was how his lips would taste, flavored sweetly with the wine from his vineyard. She tried to think about Raphael, to form an image of his face in her mind, but she was having trouble remembering what he looked like. The place in her mind where the memory should have been was scrambled, like a static-filled TV screen.

Abruptly, she turned away from Orias and went to the other side of the room, to look out the window and onto the street below. To put some space between them, because his presence was overwhelming her, driving every other thought away. She wondered how he could have such an effect on her.

"Please stay, just a little longer," he said.

She looked at her watch. Only half an hour had passed. If she left now her dad would never let her hear the end of it. "Okay," she agreed. "But no more of this polite-conversation bull crap. I'll stay—if you answer some questions for me. About your father."

"Whatever you want to know." He went to stand beside her again.

"For one thing, what kind of person—" she began, and then started over. "He didn't just abduct me, you know."

At that a flash of pain shot through Orias's eyes, so sharp it surprised her. "What did he do to you?" he asked grimly.

"For starters, he took me to this really weird place—somewhere inside a big, ginormous tunnel—or at least you have to go through a tunnel to get there. Then he shot a boy right in front of me. Killed him and made me dance in his blood. What kind of person does that?"

"Someone who is insane, clearly."

"Insane?" she repeated, incredulous. "How does that explain the rest, Orias? How was he able to sprout wings—big, black feathery wings—and fly right up into the sky like some kind of demented angel?"

The contempt Orias felt for his father was obvious. There was no mistaking it. "I can't believe he let you see that," he said.

"Well, he did," she told him. "So what was he? And what does that make you?"

Disgust showed in his face at her final question—a loathing so strong it was undeniable—and she wondered if he might actually hate Oberon as much as she did. He walked back to the table, poured more wine into his chalice, and drank it down quickly.

"You wouldn't believe me," he said at last. "And you could never understand." There was anguish etched in his face and she felt sorry for him. But she wasn't about to let it go.

"Try me," she said. "After what I've seen and struggled to understand in the last few months, you'd be surprised at what I'd believe. So tell me, like you promised, or I'm out of here."

"All right." He put the chalice down and went back to her. "My father was an Irin. A Watcher. He was an angel, Aimee. A fallen angel." He waited a moment, she thought, for it to sink in. "Surely you know about his kind, from going to Sunday school when you were a little girl?"

"Kind of," Aimee answered Orias. "Is that what you are?"

His sigh, though shallow, was so full of despair it almost brought her to tears. "No," he said patiently. "I am Nephilim. My mother was human. She made the mistake of loving him and it killed her."

Nephilim. Aimee had heard the term before, after her mother had taken a Bible study course at Middleburg United Church, during what her dad called Emily Banfield's "angel phase." For a long time, it was all her mom talked about. She'd become so fascinated with angels that she'd sent away for lots of books—some of them rare and some that she said had been left out of the Bible in use today. She'd had pictures and paintings and ceramic figurines of angels all over the house. Most of them were beautiful and graceful, but the fallen angels were dark and frightening, and the Nephilim were horrendous. When her mother had gone away on one of her frequent vacations, Aimee's dad had taken them all down and packed everything away.

"My mom told me some people think that's what Goliath was but—I mean, you're tall, but so are a lot of pro basketball players. You're not a giant."

He uttered a short, sardonic laugh. "We've evolved, Aimee," he said. "We're still giants—but now of industry and commerce. It would be very inconvenient for us, in your modern world, to be as we were in the beginning. Every species evolves, does it not?"

"I guess. Do you have wings too, like your father?"

"That I won't know for a couple of years—not until my twenty-first birthday. Some Nephilim do get them, but only the most powerful."

"So you have powers?" she asked.

"I think that's why my father didn't want me around," he said. He went to fill his chalice again and came back to stand beside her. As much as he was drinking, she noticed, he wasn't getting drunk. It was like he was swigging down grape juice. "I have the power of an angel and the heart of a human. That could make me very dangerous, indeed," he warned and looked at her darkly. Her heart did a somersault into her stomach.

"So you're part human. Does that mean—you have a soul?" she asked.

"My human half does. Half a soul, anyway."

Aimee frowned, confused. "Does that mean angels don't have souls?"

"A soul is the part of a being that is eternal," Orias explained. "And that which is eternal is a part of God. When the Watchers fell, the eternal part of them—the soul—was revoked and taken back to heaven. Now, though they retain their terrible power, the fallen are only soulless shells. And the Nephilim are even worse. We're burdened with all the want, the need, the aching love that humans possess, but our withered spirits are trapped forever in the banished husks of our bodies. Our souls are wretched, broken, exiled things—half souls." He was trembling now, and tears welled in Aimee's eyes as she saw the painful emotions coursing through him. She wanted to do something to comfort him—take his hand, give him a hug—but she restrained herself.

"That's really sad," she said. "But I still don't get it. With all your so-called supernatural power and all your money, you're happy to settle for life in plain old boring Middleburg?"

"From what I've heard, it's not so boring. And you're here."

"You've really got to stop talking like that," she told him, but she was feeling a little more comfortable with him. "I'm taken."

"So you've said." He reached out and brushed her hair away from her face, and again she wondered what his lips would feel like on her own. "You're very special, Aimee." He took her hand and drew her closer to him. "It's time you realize that. You can do anything you want to do. This world can't hold you." His voice was low, almost a whisper. "You can slip through its fingers, any time you want. Be anywhere you want. Tell me, where would you be at this moment, if you could be anywhere in the world you wanted to be?"

Looking for my mom was the first thing that came to her mind, followed by, *anywhere, as long as it's with Raphael*. But what came out of her mouth was, "I don't know. I'd have to think about it."

"Think about it, then," he said softly. He put his wine down and reached out to gently caress her cheek with his fingertips, which then moved lightly, barely touching her, up to her temple, until his warm, broad hand was resting lightly against the side of her face.

Stop letting him do this, she told herself; *stop letting him touch you.* She should step away from him but she couldn't. She didn't want to.

"Close your eyes and think about where you would like to be, in the most secret place of your heart—where you want to be more than any place else in the world," he whispered. "And you'll be there."

Something told her it would be dangerous to obey him, but she couldn't resist. She wanted to be with Raphael, of course, wherever he was at that moment—hanging out with his friends at Rack 'Em, watching TV with his mom, or walking along the old train tracks with Nass—and Orias seemed to think he could take her there. So far, the only magic she'd seen had been negative and destructive. It might be cool to see it do something positive for a change.

She closed her eyes.

And she shot through space and time, traveling at light speed through some kind of brilliant, multicolored wormhole, surrounded by exploding starbursts of bright, white light... spinning, falling, rolling, and then drifting... slower and slower ... until she felt solid earth beneath her again.

But she wasn't with her mom. Or Raphael.

She was in the red tent—the tent that Oberon had intended as a bridal tent—and she was sitting at a vanity in front of an ornate mirror brushing her hair. A maid was turning down the covers on a giant satin pillow as big as a king-size bed—but it wasn't one of those horrible antler women that had served Oberon. This maid was pretty, neatly dressed in some kind of shiny, flowing red gown and a simple red cap. When her task was done, she bowed and left the room. It was *right*, Aimee knew, and she wasn't afraid as she had been the first time she'd seen the red tent. She was waiting for something... or someone ... and it was the happiest night of her life. She rose from the mirror and realized she was wearing a beautiful gown that shimmered with all the brilliant colors of a peacock, and she knew it was her wedding night.

The curtain parted, and Orias walked in. Her husband. She looked at her left hand and saw that there was a wedding band there. But she didn't feel the sick dread she'd felt when Oberon had kidnapped her and announced that he was going to marry her. She felt love. Warmth. Satisfaction. Contentment. And she yearned to have her husband's arms around her.

Orias drew her to him and she went willingly, arching up on tiptoe to meet his kiss.

"No!" she opened her eyes and backed away from him. She was still in his living room. The vision had been so powerful, so real—but she was still there, standing in front of his window. And he wasn't even touching her. She noted absently that it was starting to get dark outside and a gentle snow had started to fall.

He laughed softly, and she could see how pleased he was. "Now that we've got that out of the way," he said. "Let's try something more practical."

"How did you do that?" she demanded.

"I didn't do it, Aimee. You did."

"But that's not where I wanted to be," she protested. "You—you hypnotized me or something."

"I did no such thing. Your mind took your body where you wanted it to be. You teleported, Aimee, which is a rare gift for a human to have. And we just teleported together. You were *there*—in some future time, of course—but you were really there." He grinned. "And so was I."

"That's impossible."

"Want me to prove it to you?"

She nodded.

"All right. There's a chair at the top of the stairs," he said. "A wooden chair with red velvet cushions. Close your eyes again. This time, I want you to aim your energy and do it slowly. Feel yourself falling gently . . . but this time you're falling up, through the ceiling. The ceiling can't hold you back. Time . . . space . . . can't hold you. You can slip through, if you want to, and be in the red velvet chair."

Aimee closed her eyes. Instantly, she felt a tingling in her body, even more intense than when she meditated. The tingling increased and for an instant she felt like every cell in her being was vibrating wildly and she jerked slightly—like a person nodding off to sleep who suddenly catches herself and wakes up.

Then there was a sound: footsteps, coming up a flight of stairs.

She opened her eyes, completely disoriented. She was no longer in Orias's living room. She was in a hallway, looking at a banister. A large, wooden staircase arced off to her left, leading downward. The footsteps drew closer as Orias came up the stairs and walked across the landing to her. She looked around and realized that she was sitting in the chair with the red velvet cushions.

A moment later, he was pulling her to her feet, holding her close against his broad chest. "You did great, baby," he said gently, his voice low and soft. He touched her face and she realized he was wiping her tears away. She was crying.

"I'm really confused," she said.

He shook his head. "No you're not. You understand perfectly. Deep down, you've always known there was something special about you. Something unique. Powerful. This is it."

"So what?" she said, pulling away from him. "What good is it? What can I do with it?"

"Find your mother, for one thing."

"How?" She wasn't so sure she should believe him, after the way Oberon had tricked her.

"I can show you," Orias said.

She looked up into his eyes and for a moment she feared she would be lost in their depths forever. She couldn't get the image of them together, in his red tent, out of her mind. And she couldn't believe that had really happened.

"Why would you help me?" she asked.

"Because you are also going to help me. There's something I need you to get for me, and you're the only one who can do it."

"What is it?" she asked.

He shook his head. "I can't tell you," he whispered. "All I can say is that it's wonderful, and if you get it for me, I'll share it with you. Do we have a deal, my beautiful traveler?"

"Deal," she said, although she'd barely heard his words. She was falling, spinning, dizzy . . . gone. But not through the magic wormhole this time. This time, it was his eyes.

Orias leaned closer, and she didn't pull away when his mouth touched hers. His strong, gentle hands moved down her cheeks, down her neck, along her collarbone, and she trembled in his arms. Then one word cut through her mind, like a flashing, fiery meteor:

Raphael.

She struggled against Orias for a moment, but he was strong, too strong—and too gentle, too beautiful. Her arms went around his neck and he lifted her, drawing her closer. A final, desperate wave of panic lashed through her, and she felt her whole body vibrating once more. The closer he pulled her to him, the closer she wanted to be. Her body hungered to stay there with him and her mind lacked the will to leave but her *soul* needed to escape. A shiver went through her whole being, and when she opened her eyes, she was no longer in Orias's upstairs hallway; she was sitting on his front lawn, and her skirt was wet with snow. Big, white snowflakes drifted down from above, looking like tiny plummeting ghosts in the glow of the streetlights.

Completely numb, Aimee reached into her pocket, took out her phone, and called her dad. Her throat felt dry, and her voice sounded strange in her ears.

"Hey, Dad. You can come pick me up. I'm ready. Yeah, it was great. . . . Okay, bye."

She stood on shaky legs. As she brushed snow off her skirt, the front door opened, and Orias stepped out onto the porch. Her coat was draped over his arm. He leaned against the rail and smiled at her from the shadows.

"Well done," he said. "You got all the way outside that time. You're even better than I thought."

"Thanks," Aimee responded, although she was having trouble getting her head around it. Had she really teleported herself from the living room upstairs to the red velvet chair, and from upstairs outside into the snowy front yard? It seemed impossible.

"All the stories are true," Orias said. "You really are the one. No one can get it but you."

She didn't understand what he was talking about, and she didn't care.

A warm, dreamy feeling enveloped her and she opened her hand and watched snowflakes drifting down onto her upturned palm, each one instantly melting and disappearing against her skin. That's what all these crazy experiences were like, she thought—Tyler's death, Raphael's battle with Oberon, her newly discovered special teleporting trick—as soon as she tried to touch them with her rational mind, they seemed to disappear. But she knew with all her being they were real.

When she looked up, Orias was standing in front of her. Carefully, he helped her into her coat. Looking into her eyes, he slowly buttoned it and then he leaned down and kissed her once . . . slowly, gently. She no longer tried to pull away. She didn't want to pull away. He gazed at her for a moment longer.

"I'll see you soon," he whispered. And then he turned and strode back up the steps and onto the porch.

They stood there like that, in silence, him on the porch staring at her and her on the sidewalk, watching the snow fall, until her dad's car pulled up to the curb. She waved at Orias. Silently, he raised his hand to her. When she was safely in the car, he waved to Jack and went back into the house.

Aimee nestled into the leather of the car seat and shut the heavy door. The blast of the heater felt amazing, and she realized she was freezing.

With a sudden urgency she took out her cell phone and looked at it. Two missed calls, blocked number. Raphael. She quickly shoved the phone back into her pocket. No way she could call him back tonight.

"So," Jack said. "How'd it go? You think we're in business with Orias?"

She looked at him for a moment before she answered, no longer shocked or surprised at the raw greed that showed in his eyes.

"Yeah," she said tonelessly, as she turned to stare out the window. "I think we are."

CHAPTER 23

"Hey, Raphael—can I talk to you?"

He looked up from the table he was clearing to see Maggie Anderson, looking glamorous in an elegant white winter coat with a fur hood. She always looked beautiful, but there was something different about her tonight . . . something hopeful, radiant, and it made her even prettier. She was smiling at him.

"Sure. I guess."

"I mean—when you take a break," she said. "So we can sit down."

Without a word, he led her to a table in the corner. "Give me a couple of minutes," he said and then took the full bus tub back to the kitchen. When he returned, she'd slipped off her coat and made herself comfortable. He approached her warily.

"Come on," she said. "Sit down."

He pulled out the chair across from her and sat, looking at her expectantly.

"Thanks again for helping me out with Rick."

"You came all the way down here to tell me that? Come on, Maggie—what's up? He bothering you again?"

"Not really. No more than usual, anyway. I've got it under control." She hesitated for a moment and then plunged ahead. "Okay, look—you said we're friends now, right?" He nodded, still silent. "So I came here as a friend. It's about Aimee." Her expression was strange, he thought—a mixture of smug satisfaction and sympathy.

"Look, Maggie—you need to stop right there," he warned her. "You know I like Aimee—everyone knows we're together. It's not a secret anymore. And even if her father sends her away to that school again, or gets me arrested, or has everybody in the Flats evicted, we're still going to be together. Got it?"

"Oh, I get that you're with her," Maggie said seriously. "But I think you should know she's not with you . . . at least, not exclusively."

And she took a camera out of her coat pocket, turned it on, and handed it to Raphael.

He looked down at the screen. The photo was of Orias Morrow. He was standing on the front porch of the big, old house on Church Street— Oberon's house—while a girl stood out on the snow-covered lawn, looking up at him.

Raph moved to the next picture. Now, Orias was standing right in front of the girl, who looked a lot like Aimee. With a growing sense of dread, Raphael clicked to the next picture. Orias was buttoning her coat and looking down into her eyes. In the next photo, they were kissing. He felt a sickening constriction in his chest. This couldn't be real. There had to be some mistake. Maybe the picture was Photoshopped or something. In the next image, the girl had glanced over and was gazing up the street. It was Aimee. No doubt about it. He could see her face clearly. In the next picture, she was getting into a car; he could even see the license plate: BNFLD 4.

He turned off the camera.

"Nice try," he said, a tremor in his voice. "But you can tell Rick I'm not that gullible. You should go now. I'll walk you to your car." He needed to be alone, needed to assimilate his thoughts. *Aimee . . .* and Orias. *Oberon's son.* The guy everybody in town was saying would save Middleburg with all his new business ventures. The guy all the girls at Middleburg High couldn't stop talking about. What in the hell was Aimee doing with him? *Kissing him?*

"Rick doesn't know anything about this," Maggie said quietly. "Only that Orias invited Aimee over and she decided to go. That's how I knew she would be there. But he doesn't know about the pictures. No one else knows—just you and me."

It's a trick, he thought. *Don't believe her.*

But the crosscurrent raging though his mind taunted him: *Why wouldn't Aimee be with Orias? He's rich, tall, good-looking, buff. He's older, sophisticated, self-assured. No matter what I do, I'll never be anything to her but a troublemaker from the Flats. Something she can throw in her father's face.*

Deep down, Raphael had always known it wouldn't last. It was just a dream, and now it was over. She was better off without him anyway. What did he have to offer her except a life full of stuggle?

He tried to return the camera to Maggie, but she pushed it back to him.

"Why don't you keep it for a while," she said. "Look at the pictures on a bigger screen if you don't believe me."

"I believe you," he said, still staring at the camera in his trembling hands. He didn't want to believe her, but he did. He could tell it was true by the way his soul ached. He picked up Maggie's coat and purse and handed them to her. "I need to think about this, Maggie," he said. "And I've got work to do. Come on—I'll walk you out."

"Friends tell each other the truth, Raphael," Maggie said as she allowed him to steer her toward the door. "You said we could be friends."

He was silent until they reached her car. "Okay," he said. "Do me a favor—as a friend?"

"Sure."

"Keep this between us for now. It's got to be some kind of misunderstanding. I'm sure she can explain—" but he stopped abruptly. How could you explain away a kiss in which you were participating, and obviously enjoying? "Anyway, just don't tell anyone else for now, okay?"

"Okay," she agreed. She looked at him for a moment and then added, "You've helped me, Raphael—twice already. I can help you, if you let me."

"I don't think I'm ready for anything like that—"

"That's not what I mean," she interrupted. "I can do things, too."

"What are you talking about?"

"Lift the camera up—in your palms. Don't hold on to it. Now, watch." She looked around as if making sure there was no one else in the parking lot.

Intrigued, he did as she asked and watched as she focused her attention on the camera. She gazed at it serenely, and after a moment it jiggled on his outstretched palm, then it jerked. And then it slowly rose into the air and hovered two inches above his hand, then five inches, then ten. He looked at Maggie, stunned. She was still staring at the camera.

"No *way*," he breathed.

"It's easy for me now. I can do other things, too. *Lots* of things." The way she said it—seductive, inviting—left no doubt about what she meant, but he had no intention of getting into that with her. He still couldn't trust her. And he was still trying to get his head around the images in the camera. Images of Aimee and Orias . . . *together*.

When he didn't respond, Maggie looked away from the camera, at him, and the camera suddenly dropped. He caught it and then looked at her again. He'd thought there was something different about her tonight, and he'd thought he was just imagining it, but now he could see it was really there. A glow. A light. A *power*.

"Where did you learn how to do *that*?" he asked.

"Cheerleading camp—where do you think?"

"Seriously," he said.

"I don't know," she told him, and he thought he detected a shadow of fear in her eyes. "After Homecoming night . . . well, I'm sort of different now. I don't know where it comes from, exactly. And I don't know why, but I know it's important. I can *do* things." Her voice got softer for a moment. "So—if I can ever help you, Raphael, you'll let me know? Magic or no magic—as a friend?"

She *was* different. It was obvious. The hard, bitchy edge she'd always had was fading, diminishing. Their eyes met.

"All right," he said. "Thanks."

"And you know, not that it matters, but I didn't relish the idea of telling you about Aimee and Orias. I just don't like to see my friends getting taken advantage of." He was glad she didn't say "being played for a fool" because that's what he was beginning to feel like.

"Okay."

She smiled, and Raphael flashed back to his middle-school days when he, like every other guy there, was madly in love with Maggie. She leaned over and kissed him on the cheek.

"I'm sorry about Aimee," she said, and she sounded like she really meant it. "If you ever want to talk about it . . . and you know, all the supernatural stuff that's been going on . . . I'm here."

"Maybe," he said. "Things have been a little overwhelming—with all the supernatural stuff." He didn't want to talk about Aimee. "You too, Maggie. You can talk to me anytime."

She looked at him another moment and then reached out and gently touched his hand. "Bye, Raphael," she said.

She got into the car and drove away without looking at him again, leaving him alone in his confusion—and with her damned camera and the mocking images of Aimee in Orias's arms.

෨

Zhai awoke with a start. He was shivering violently in spite of the thick, scratchy blanket someone had thrown over him. He lay on a concrete floor and the cold that radiated up from it seemed to have seeped all the way into his bones. As he sat up, his breath caught in his throat. Every muscle in his exhausted body ached, as if he'd been training for hours. Above him and to his left, a big window composed of many small square panes of glass let in cheerless gray morning light. Looking around, he realized he was in an old, abandoned warehouse or factory. Off to his right sat a row of hulking machines, sheathed in dust and draped in cobwebs. Occasionally, a drop of water fell from the ceiling and patted down nearby. Somewhere, an unseen animal scratched around in dead leaves that must've blown in through a broken windowpane. Ahead, perhaps fifty yards away, he could see several men sitting in front of what looked like an old kiln with a fire burning in it. Two of them were the men with the derby hats—from the Order of the Black Snake. The rest were wearing jackets emblazoned with the Shao Construction Company logo.

When Zhai stood up, he heard the jangling of chains and discovered he was unable to move more than a foot or two. He looked down to find manacles around his wrists and ankles. He was chained to a set of thick, steel loops secured to the concrete floor.

The snake men exchanged a few words and then one of them, noticing Zhai was awake, came walking over. He held a blue plastic plate in his hand.

There was an expression of mild amusement on his face as he held the plate out to Zhai. It was piled high with white rice and some kind of strangely spiced meat—pork maybe, and broccoli. Zhai's first impulse was to slap it away, but as soon as the scent reached his nostrils, he realized he was starving. He took the plate and started shoveling the food into his mouth. He ate so fast he almost choked.

"Slow down. No rush," the man said in his thick Chinese accent. He sat down in a battered old wooden chair nearby and folded his arms over his chest, watching Zhai eat. Zhai glanced at him again. It was the same man he'd fought in the train graveyard. He acknowledged Zhai's recognition with a smile.

"You did well for us," he said. "Jumping across rooftops with a little girl on your back—that's not easy."

"What the hell are you talking about?"

"It's a shame you don't remember. You were tossing that kid around like a bag of rice." He pointed a finger at Zhai and nodded approvingly. "You're very athletic."

"A little girl? I didn't hurt her, did I?" Zhai cleared his throat. It was so dry it burned. The man stood up from his chair, went to a cooler near the wall, pulled out a bottle of water, and tossed it to Zhai.

"You did everything we told you to do."

Zhai didn't know what that meant, and he was afraid to ask. "So then . . . are you planning to let me go?"

The man laughed. "I just said you did well. That means no—not ever. You belong to us now. To the Order."

Zhai shook his head, which made his neck ache even more. "I'm not your slave," he said with contempt. "You may have control over me for now, but you don't own me."

His tormentor laughed. "You've been in America too long—where they believe in freedom for everyone," he said sarcastically. "In the Order of the Black Snake, we know that some were born to be slaves—and others deserve to be, like those we take. What we take, we keep. That is the rule we live by. And for now, we're taking you."

"And what if I don't agree?" Zhai asked.

Instantly, a huge switchblade appeared—out of nowhere—in each of the man's hands. He spun them both expertly for a moment, enjoying himself. Then he stopped spinning the knives and held one of them to Zhai's throat.

"I can release your soul now," he said. "But your body stays with us."

He laughed as if he'd just made the greatest joke in the world. Zhai imagined himself snatching the dagger from the man's hand, but discarded the idea instantly; his opponent was far too fast for Zhai to disarm him. Zhai's eyes scanned the room looking for any means of escape, but that was pointless too—at least until he figured out how to get the chains off his wrists and ankles. And that looked pretty impossible. They were made of half-inch-thick steel and were so new they were still shiny.

As he gazed down at the chains, he noticed that his clothes were filthy. He wondered how long he'd been gone and if anyone, especially Kate, had missed him.

The man put the weapons back into the inside pockets of his overcoat. "The truth is, you are most fortunate," he said. "The Order has been working for years—for centuries—to bring about this day. Now, you will be here to share the glory as the Era of the Black Snake dawns. The strong will take, and what we take we keep—and you will be one of the strong. All the earth will be laid before you. Women. Money. Power. More women. Whatever you like, you take." He made a gesture, as he spoke, as if picking fruit from an invisible tree. As he moved, Zhai noticed marks on the back of the man's hands, fading from black to a sort of rusty brown. When he saw Zhai looking at them, he raised both his fists up for a closer examination.

"Oh, yes," he said quietly. "I began like you. We all did. Everyone resists at first, like your father. But he grew to love the power, as you will."

"You're lying," Zhai said. "He isn't one of you."

The man laughed softly. "The Snake is long. You'd be surprised how many are wrapped in his coils."

"Not me," Zhai said. "I'm not a slave."

The man laughed again. "I said the same thing, two hundred and four years ago," he tapped the mark on the back of his hand with his index finger. "But the mark changes you. Each time the Snake moves within you, he changes you. And when you eat snake, he changes you even faster."

Zhai looked down at the plastic plate, now empty and discarded at his feet, and his stomach suddenly roiled with nausea.

The man laughed at him, "Yes. Snake. What is it they say? You are what you eat," he laughed again for a moment, and then grew serious. "The truth is, Zhai Shao, you have no choice. We take what we want, and we want you. The less you resist, the less painful it will be. We will give you long life, and teach you the greatest style of kung fu on earth: Venom-of-the-Fang. And soon, when we have what we seek, you will be very glad indeed to wear the mark of the Snake. Now get your rest. We will have another mission for you soon enough."

He turned away from Zhai and walked back to his comrades, his footsteps echoing eerily on the gritty, bare concrete. Zhai glanced down at his tattooed hands.

It was true. He was a slave. The question was, what was he going to do about it?

ɛɔ

Aimee's body ached. Her muscles trembled. Her shirt was soaked with perspiration. Every day since her lesson with Raphael, she'd locked herself in her room and practiced the kung fu moves and the form he'd taught her until she could hardly stand up. She'd found some kung fu videos on the Internet and tried to learn a few more moves that way. Already, her work was paying dividends. At first, she could only maintain the horse stance for a couple of minutes before her legs started shaking; now, she could do it for more than an hour. Her shoulders and legs, which had ached terribly the first few days, now felt stronger, and she could tell her strikes were getting faster. The more comfortable she became, the more she relaxed—and, as Raphael had promised her, the more she relaxed, the faster she became. Sometimes, she could even hear a slight whistle of wind as her fists shot through the air. It made her feel like a total badass.

The ringing cell phone on her dresser interrupted her drill, and warily she crossed the room to check the caller I.D. The peace, the serenity, the feeling of wholeness and inner strength she'd gotten from her kung fu practice dissipated, replaced by a sickening twisting feeling in her stomach.

Ringing.

The I.D. was blocked so it was probably Raphael. She picked up the phone, then set it back down, then picked it up again and pressed it to her forehead and sighed.

Ringing.

She wanted to talk to him. She needed to hear his voice, but what could she say? She wouldn't lie to him, but there was no way she could tell him that she had kissed Orias.

Ringing.

When she thought of Orias, a flood of emotion filled her, full of pity and a longing that she didn't understand. Sweat ran down her body as she set the phone down on her desk and stared at it, feeling strangely, terribly empty.

The ringing stopped. The call went to voice mail.

৪১

Thursday, Raphael stood in an alcove in the school's courtyard. Middleburg High was caught up in a frenzy of fight songs and pep rallies and plastered with painted banners in preparation for the Phoenixes's upcoming state championship bid, and he was glad to be outside where it was peaceful. Still, it was freezing, and as he waited he huddled against the brick wall, trying his best to stay out of the biting wind and blowing snow.

If this is any indication, he thought, *Middleburg is in for a brutal winter.* As he gazed out at the forest that bounded the school grounds, he could hardly see the trees in the haze of falling, drifting white. It was the first big snowfall of the season, which meant more than flurries and some actual accumulation. They usually only got one or two significant winter storms each year—and this one was early.

Watching the drifts cover the trees and bushes and buildings, it was as if the entire world was being erased; as if creation was being reduced to emptiness, a blank page, and everyone would have to start over from scratch. Raphael felt like everything in his heart had been erased too. Maggie's camera sat on his bedside table at home, a constant reminder of his misery. It was five days since she'd brought it to him, and he'd been calling Aimee ever since. She hadn't picked up or returned his calls. This morning, he'd slipped a note into her locker asking her to meet him during lunch; now, lunch was almost over and she still hadn't shown up.

Just then, the door opened and she emerged, leaning forward at a slight angle to counter the blasting wind. She glanced at Raphael, but her hair was lashing across her face, and it was impossible for him to gauge what emotion, if any, waited for him in her eyes. As usual, she trudged to the other side of the courtyard, brushed some snow off the picnic table, and sat down, while Raphael punched in her number.

"Hey," she said, her voice sounding as hollow as the wind.

"Hey," he said. Silence hung between them then for a long moment, and in that silence, Raphael heard all the confirmation he needed. The pictures were real. Everything Maggie had told him was true.

Finally, Aimee spoke. "I'm . . . I'm sorry I haven't called you back. I've been really busy. But I've been practicing the kung fu you taught me. I've been practicing hard every day. I think I'm starting to get pretty—"

"What were you doing with Orias Morrow?" he interrupted. He was only slightly satisfied at the shock that registered on her face.

"I—" she began, and then she looked away from him. It broke his heart. "My dad made me go over there," she said. "They're doing some business deal together."

"That doesn't answer my question," he said quietly. He wanted her to tell him about the kiss—and to explain it, if she could.

"Raphael, I had no choice." She looked at him again, but her gaze didn't linger. It was like she *couldn't* look at him. "If I didn't go, my dad would have kept me in the house forever. At least I'm not grounded anymore."

"So now you can see me and we can hang out?"

"Not . . . exactly. But I can hang out with Dalton, which means I can see you more."

"And that's why you went to visit Orias?" he persisted, giving her another opening. "To buy your freedom—so you could see me more?"

The bell rang then. Lunch was over. They both had to get to class—especially Aimee, he knew. They couldn't afford to let Rick, or anybody, get suspicious.

"Yes," she said as she got up and turned to go. "Can we talk about this later—tonight, maybe?"

"Okay."

"I love you, Raphael."

His heart felt like ice in his chest. "Tonight," he said. "I'll wait for your call."

He put his phone back into his pocket and watched as Aimee turned away. Without a single glance at him, she went back inside.

Raphael closed his eyes, steadying himself against his hurt and frustration. It didn't take Shen or the knowing for him to realize that she wasn't going to call him.

The sting of it grew suddenly overwhelming, so much so that he couldn't bear to stand still, and he walked away too, in the other direction, trudging into the blinding white.

Let him get grounded for skipping school. Let him freeze to death in a snow bank. He didn't care anymore.

∞

"Rick Banfield."

Classes were over for the day. It was time for what Rick loved best—smashing into other players as hard as he could, with the intent of doing as much damage as possible, even to his own teammates. He told them it was to toughen them up, but that was only part of it. He just enjoyed the look on a person's face when he caused them pain.

He barreled out of the locker room, heading toward the glass doors and the walkway beyond that led to the football practice field. He had his full practice gear on and his helmet tucked under one arm. Completely psyched up and focused for his last practice before the big game, he found the interruption a little jarring. Still, he stopped, his cleats skidding to a halt on the smooth tile of the hallway floor. He looked over and saw a hot, dark-haired Latina girl leaning against the wall in a casually seductive pose. She smiled at him.

"Yeah," he said. "Do I know you?"

"No, you just wish you did," she replied with a teasing little smile.

Rick couldn't help but laugh. This babe was bold. He liked her style. He walked to her and stood very close, looking down at her with interest. "Yeah," he admitted. "I've seen you around. What's your name?"

"Clarisse," the girl said, her voice all soft and breathy, just the way Rick liked. This close to her, he could tell she was even hotter than he thought at first glance. She had delectable curves in all the right places, and from the sultry way she was looking at him with her big brown eyes, he could tell she knew how to use every single one of them. But she was a Flats rat—cousins or something with that little Mexican punk Ignacio.

"Well, it's really nice to meet you, Clarisse," he said. "But I don't date girls from the Flats. Sorry."

There was something dangerous in her laugh. "Who cares?" she said, grabbing the front of his jersey and pulling him, dragging him, partway into a little alcove, away from the prying eyes of his teammates. He was amazed at her strength. As soon as they were concealed in the shadows, her lips were on his, her hands groping him. He kissed her back hungrily, pushing her against the wall and pressing his body against hers. She responded with a soft moan before she pushed him away. There was a slightly sinister smile on her lips that appealed to him.

"Just a taste for now, football star," she whispered.

"Oh, I see," Rick said. "It's like that. You're a tease."

"Not me, baby," she replied, gazing seductively into his eyes. "But I have something you're going to want even more than what you want right now."

Rick grunted out a laugh. "Yeah?" he said. "What's that?"

"Information," she whispered. "You know all those holes your old man and his partner are digging under buildings all over town?"

Automatically, Rick went on guard—and his resentment toward his father flared briefly. He knew they were looking for something; he'd overheard enough of his dad's phone calls to know that much. But the one time he asked about it, all he got was a terse, "Mind your own business." It pissed him off that his own father didn't trust him enough to tell him what was going on.

"Yeah—what about it?"

She moved a little further away from him and put her hands on her hips. "The Flatliners know what they're looking for," she said smugly. "And they're going to find it first, unless you and your crew stop them."

"Really?" Rick said. "And why would you tell me that?"

"Because I'm getting a little sick of sitting home alone while my boyfriend is out half the night with his little search party." She tilted her head and smiled up at him again. "As you can tell, I'm a girl who doesn't really enjoy spending time alone."

"That's too bad," he said. "What do you expect me to do about it?"

"Why are you asking me? Man, if your so-called gang was back in South Central, you'd know what to do." Rick was pretty sure she was insulting him, but he didn't mind. Coming from her, even that was kind of hot. When Rick didn't say anything, she finished, "Like I said, you've got to stop them. Unless your dad and his partner don't care if someone steals the treasure right out from under their noses."

"The treasure . . . do you know what it is?" Rick asked.

"Don't you?" she countered.

"Of course I do," he lied.

"So—you gonna to stop them?"

"You got that right," he blurted, then paused. "Wait a second. "What do you get out of all this?"

"That depends on how valuable it is. But if you find it first, you cut me in. We got a deal?"

Rick shrugged. If his dad and Mr. Shao were putting this much effort into finding something, it had to be worth millions; it would be no big deal to throw her a few thousand bucks. Not that he'd actually pay her anyway.

"Sure," he agreed.

"Okay," she said, evidently satisfied. She held her phone out to him. "Put your number in. If you get a call from me, you better pick up because I'm only calling you once."

It still seemed too good to be true, Rick thought as he entered his number. "Maybe you're setting me and the Toppers up for an ambush," he said. "How do I know this isn't a trap?"

She moved close to him again. "You don't," she said. "There's only one way to find out. But if I give you a tip and you act on it and put an end to the Flatliners' little treasure hunt—" She paused then, and leaned closer so that her body was touching his, her head tilted up just beneath his chin. Before she spoke again, her lips traced a sensuous pattern on his neck. "Well, who knows how I'll show my gratitude?" she finished.

The longer he stood there with her, the more aroused he got. She was good, he thought—damn good. If it was a trick, this girl was going the extra mile to pull it off, that was for sure. She stood on tiptoe and kissed him once more.

"All right," Rick said, stepping back. One more minute that close to her and he was going to lose control. "You got a deal. Where are they going next?"

"The train graveyard, tomorrow night. I'll call you with a time. And I'm riding with you—that's part of the deal."

"I'm playing in the championship game. There's no way we'll be back in town before eleven p.m."

"That's about the time they're gonna roll," Clarisse said. "I'll send you the exact location as soon as I know."

"If the Flatliners see you with me they'll run you out of town."

"I know—so you're going to drop me off near the action, where they won't see me."

Rick couldn't believe his good fortune. With Bran backing him, his move to get himself elected temporary leader of the Toppers, at least until Zhai turned up again, had worked. And if this little Flats bitch was telling the truth, he would have an opportunity to put an end to the Flatliners for good. If the Toppers could get the upper hand in a surprise ambush, they could hurt those punks so bad they would flatline for real. It was going to be awesome. He would win a state championship and demolish his enemies all in the same night.

"Well, I guess this is my lucky day," he said, already smiling at the thought of all the Flats rats he was going to crush.

"Later, football star," she said with a wink, and she took off down the hall.

Rick stepped out of the alcove and watched appreciatively as she hurried away. She looked as good going as she did coming, he thought. He and the Toppers would check out her little piece of intel, he decided—and even if she was lying (especially if she was lying) he *would* get lucky with her. One way or the other that little bit of fine, hot stuff was going to give him the reward she'd promised.

He heard someone approaching behind him. "Rick!" Bran called. "I been looking everywhere for you, man. Coach is freaking out." Rick was still staring down the hall, watching as Clarisse disappeared around the corner. "Who was that?"

"An angel," Rick said, unable to repress a grin. "A sexy little angel of death. Come on." He clapped Bran on the shoulder pad. "Let's go out there and bust some heads."

☙

"You did what?" Dalton looked stricken and Aimee rushed to explain.

"It wasn't like a real date," she said. "It was my dad's idea. They're putting some kind of deal together."

"Well," Dalton said. "To be honest, I don't understand why your father would want to go into business with the son of the guy who kidnapped you. But I get it—it was just one of those social things you Hilltop Haven types have to do once in a while. So what's the big deal?"

"He's . . . he's interested in me," she said. "You know—like, *interested.*"

The last class had just finished and they were in Miss Pembrook's room, waiting for her to bring some research materials in from her car. Aimee didn't know exactly why she had decided to tell Dalton about her evening with Orias—maybe for some kind of absolution, she thought glumly. Confession was supposed to be good for the soul. But it wasn't working—she still felt guilty.

"So you told him about Raphael, right?" Dalton asked.

"He already knew about Raphael."

"So like I said—what's the big deal?"

"He kissed me, Dalton. And . . . I kissed him back."

Dalton's mouth dropped open in shock. For a moment she was speechless, and then, "Girl—what is wrong with you?"

Aimee put her head down on the desk and closed her eyes. "I *know,*" she said miserably. "But I felt—I almost felt sorry for him. He's nothing like his father—he hates Oberon as much as I do."

Dalton responded with her trademark, squinty-eyed, *you-gotta-be-kidding-me* stare, and Aimee wanted to tell her all of it—how she'd teleported up Orias's staircase and then out onto his front lawn—but she knew it would sound crazy. She'd never told Dalton everything about the day Oberon abducted her—she and Raphael had decided after her rescue that they'd keep the supernatural elements of the story to themselves.

Raphael.

Thinking of him now made her so sad. As if reading her mind, Dalton asked, "What about Raphael?"

"I love him," Aimee said quickly, and in her mind she knew that was true. But even as she said it, a deeper, darker part of her was crying out for Orias.

"If you love him, then what are you doing kissing someone else?" Dalton asked, as Aimee had already asked herself a dozen times.

She sat up and looked at Dalton. "I don't know. When I'm around him, I just feel so..." Aimee struggled to continue, but there was no word for how she felt around Orias. Intoxicated, alive, terrified, free, trapped: all accurate descriptions, but somehow insufficient. "But it won't happen again—that I *do* know." She finished.

But when she tried to remember Raphael's face, all she could see was Orias bending to her, his lips parted, getting closer and closer...

Miss Pembrook came in then, pulling a suitcase on wheels. Dalton whispered to Aimee, "You *know* this conversation is not over."

The teacher hoisted her suitcase up onto one of the desks, opened it, and started unpacking books, periodicals, and folders, which she placed on the table in front of them.

"How's it going, girls?" she asked, looking from one to the other when they both remained silent. "Aimee—everything okay?"

Absently, Aimee looked up and forced a smile. "Oh, yeah—sorry. Everything's fine."

"Okay, good. Then let's get to work."

Aimee knew that Dalton was still looking at her as if she'd lost her mind, but Miss Pembrook didn't seem to notice. As she put another stack of books and a cardboard box in the center of the table, she said, "All right, girls—dig in."

They both reached for the box at the same time, but Dalton pushed it toward Aimee and grabbed a big, cloth-bound book instead. Aimee opened the box and looked inside, relieved to see it was full of pictures instead of old, musty manuscripts. Today of all days, looking at pictures was probably all her brain could handle. She pulled out a big stack and started to sift through them.

"I borrowed those photos from an archive at the Middleburg Library," Miss Pembrook said. "See if there's anything interesting in there. Especially pictures of the church or the tunnels."

Aimee nodded and turned her attention to the photographs. The first was a portrait of a family that looked like it was taken a really long time ago—like right after photography was invented. The next image was an old farmhouse. The next was a big, old city hall building with a clock tower that, according to the caption, had burned down sometime in the late 1800s. The next one was an old, faded sepia picture, printed on thick card stock. In it were seven women. The one in the middle was taller than the rest, and she was beautiful, with shoulder-length blond hair styled in a more modern fashion than the others. Aimee leaned closer and blinked, unable to trust her own eyes. The photo was grainy and faded, even a little water-stained along one edge, but there was no mistaking it.

The woman was her mother.

But it couldn't be. She flipped it over. On the back, she found an inscription, written in a graceful hand:

Middleburg United Church Women's Club, March 9th, 1877. Gertrude Hennig, Rebecca Brown, Constance Buchwald, Emily Banfield, Peggy Emerson, Bernice Beuller and Lilly Thorpe.

Aimee flipped the picture back over and stared at it for so long her eyes began to water. When Dalton left to use the restroom and Miss Pembrook was busy at her desk, Aimee slipped the old photograph into her pocket. It couldn't be an ancestor, a coincidence, or a simple resemblance. It was impossible, unthinkable, ludicrous, but there was no doubt about it: somehow, her mom was in the year 1877.

CHAPTER 24

RAPHAEL WAS SPRAWLED ON THE COUCH in his living room, the curtains drawn, his face buried in pillows, an old quilt pulled up over his head, when the knocking woke him. He prayed that whoever it was would go away, but they didn't. They knocked again, and then he heard the doorknob twist and the door swing open. Tentative footsteps crossed to his bedroom and then came back to the living room. Any other day he would have been up in a heartbeat, ready to beat the intruder down—but not today.

Just go ahead and kill me, he thought. *Just put me out of my misery.*

"Hey—I thought kung fu masters were supposed to be vigilant."

At the sound of the familiar voice, Raphael sat up and pulled the quilt off his head with a soft groan.

Nass sat on the arm of the couch, watching him. "I didn't see you after lunch. What's up?"

Raphael shook his head. "I had to get out of there. I've got a lot on my mind."

He wondered if Maggie was keeping her promise not to tell anyone about Aimee and Orias, and if anyone else in Middleburg had seen them kissing. *Middleburg*, he thought with contempt. *Where gossip travels at the speed of light.*

He wondered how long it would be before word got back to him that Aimee had dumped him. That would give the Toppers something new to laugh about over their filet mignons.

"Want to talk about it?" Nass asked.

Raph considered. After he'd seen Aimee and decided not to go back to class, he'd left school and wandered around in the cold until time lost its meaning, until every part of him—his toes, his cheeks, his fingers, and finally his heart—was numb. He walked around downtown, up River Road, across the Flats, until he felt at one with the snow: blank, white, empty. It wasn't coming down hard anymore, just slow and steady and several times in the swirling flakes, he heard (or imagined) the Magician's shrill laugh, and his mocking questions:

Did you think she would love you forever?

Did you think you deserved her love?

Did you think you could really keep her happy?

Foolish boy, all things corrupt.

When at last Raphael could no longer bear the cold, he had made his way back to his apartment, climbed the stairs, and passed out on the couch, hoping never to wake up. His mom was out, probably lined up to fill out an application to work for Orias Morrow, like everybody else in town.

"What time is it?" he asked Ignacio, rubbing his eyes.

"Almost four. So what do you want to do? You got any more of those kung fu flicks?"

Raphael smiled. He felt miserable, but maybe it was better to be miserable with a friend than miserable alone. At least it was a distraction, until he could figure out what to do about Aimee. Besides, sitting around his apartment waiting for a phone call that wasn't going to come would only drive him crazy.

"Actually, I think we should do some treasure hunting," he said. "You and me." The thought occurred to him just that moment, but it felt right. It was better to be out there, *doing* something. If he could find the treasure, get lots of cash, and solve the eviction problems for everyone in the Flats, that was way better than moping around on the couch.

"What about the Obies?" Nass asked.

Raphael shrugged. "Whatever. I'm not worried if you're not."

Nass grinned. "I thought you might say that." He reached behind the sofa and pulled out the black briefcase he'd concealed there when he'd walked in. He put it on Raph's lap and clicked the latches. It popped open to reveal the silver divining rod inside.

"Wow," Raphael said. "You came prepared."

"Yeah," Nass agreed. "I had a feeling we'd need it tonight. Let's do this."

෪

Chin walked slowly down the hallway, gazing at each tapestry as he passed, with Violet Anderson trailing in his wake. He thought she seemed a little calmer these days but there was still a strange, heartbreaking gleam in her eyes that was far too close to madness. She kept glancing at the basement door.

With some effort, Chin wrested his attention from his beautiful hostess and forced it back to her creations. As many times as he'd viewed her tapestries over the years, he still noticed new things whenever he came here—new themes, new symbolism. No matter how hard he tried to commit the images to memory, whenever he returned to them he discovered details that had eluded him before—almost as if the tapestries were changing.

Today, he was searching for clues about where he might find Zhai Shao, but the tapestries were not cooperating.

"What's wrong?" Violet asked, her hands clutched together in front of her. "Is it the portal? Is something going to break through?"

Chin shook his head as he stepped up to the next tapestry and gazed at it.

"No," he said. "Not at the moment, anyway. The imminent danger is from the Order. I fear they are close to finding what they have sought for so long."

He wished he could offer her more comfort, but he and Violet always spoke the truth to each other—always. While she fidgeted behind him, he remained rooted in place, staring intently at the tapestry before him. It seemed to change even as he looked at it, providing sharper detail than he'd seen before. The image was of a beautiful woman holding a quill pen in one hand and a scroll in the other. Her face was downturned and her eyes closed, which, Chin knew, could mean impending death. Even more interesting was the shadow on the wall behind her. At first he thought it was her shadow, but on closer examination he realized that it couldn't be. It was too big, for one thing, but there was something else bothering him. The arm of the shadow fell across one spindle of a chair back, which made it look like the tattoo of a snake ran up the shadow's forearm. Through the doorway of the room in which the woman sat, Chin could see three figures coming up a flight of stairs and heading through the darkened hallway, but their faces were indistinct.

There were interesting symbols, too. A painting hung on the wall of the woman's room, depicting a blond-haired girl in a silver dress. In the center of her chest a heart glowed, like a religious painting depicting the sacred heart of Jesus. The golden halo surrounding her head was covered in flecks of black, as if it were corroding. The frame of the picture was made up of gears and springs that looked like clockwork and at the bottom of it was a plaque bearing the words: *La Princesa del Viento*. He had no idea what it meant.

Frustrated, he scanned the images again and again. Shen was calling his attention to this particular tapestry, like an unseen child tugging at his sleeve—but why?

Then he noticed the title Violet had stitched at the bottom: *The Teacher*.

He'd already spent a good amount of time watching the teacher Raphael had told him about—Miss Pembrook—to make sure she was safe. So far he'd seen no sign of any Order members following her. The tapestry, however, told a different story. He glanced again at the figures in the shadowy hallway. Now, one of them had distinct facial features— Chin's features. It was him, running up the stairs—too late.

"Thank you, Violet," he said, already turning to leave. "I have to go."

"That boy—Raphael—take him with you," she said. Chin turned to look at her. The faint, golden aura that became visible to him whenever the power of Shen came on her enveloped her now. When she spoke again, it wasn't just Violet giving him advice, he knew—it was the voice of the All, speaking through her.

"You'll have to fight," she said. "And you can't win on your own."

Chin nodded once, as someone entered the hallway behind Violet. It was Maggie.

"I'm going too," she declared.

Chin mustered a smile, trying to be kind even as the urgency of the situation drove him. "I'm sorry, Maggie," he said. "It's too dangerous, and I'm in a hurry." He started for the door, but she stepped in front of him, blocking his way.

"No," Maggie said again, standing firm. "I heard what my mom said. If you're taking Raphael with you to fight someone, I'm going too. He's my friend—yeah, I know," she added impatiently as Chin raised his eyebrows. "Flatliners, Toppers, *blah, blah, blah*. But Raph and I are friends now, for real. And I can help you."

Chin turned back once more to study the tapestry. Three people going up the stairs: himself and two others. Their features were clearer now and one of them, he could see, was Raphael. The other was still indistinguishable. Then there was the portrait depicted in the scene: *La Princesa Del Viento*. Maggie was blond and she had a hereditary claim to extraordinary power—and she was the new Harvest Queen (*Homecoming Queen*, he reminded himself) and wore the crown. Perhaps she was the princess in the tapestry.

"All right," he decided. "But we have to hurry."

Maggie followed him outside but stopped in the doorway when she saw his beat-up old truck. "Ah . . . no offense, Mr. Chin, but if we're in a hurry, we'd better take my mom's car," she said.

"Good—let's go," he agreed quickly.

Maggie clicked a remote control on her keychain and the garage door rose, revealing Violet's red Mercedes. They hurried into the garage, and Chin climbed into the passenger seat as Maggie fired up the engine. By the time he got his seatbelt on, they were halfway down the hill, sliding around corners in the slushy snow and roaring through the straightaways. They would definitely get to Miss Pembrook's apartment faster with the Mercedes, Chin thought—if Maggie didn't kill them first.

∽

It wasn't long before Raphael started to question the wisdom of going out treasure hunting in the middle of a blizzard. Well, it wasn't a blizzard, exactly—but it was steady and the snow was getting deeper by the minute. Where it drifted, it came almost up to his knees.

By the time they reached the tracks, his socks were damp, his feet were cold, and his legs were aching with exertion—but Nass pressed on like a dog on the scent, and Raphael trudged along behind him. Somewhere in the back of his mind, the sound of a train whistle registered—far off and mournful.

He stopped walking. "Nass—wait. You hear that?"

Nass froze, listening. "I don't hear anything. Probably just the wind."

Yeah, Raph thought. *It had to be*. No trains had run through Middleburg for decades.

They kept going, hiking up the embankment on the far side of the tracks, and wading into the woods that ran between the east side of the locomotive graveyard and River Road. Then they turned northward, pushing their way through the brittle, frozen underbrush. At the top of a small rise, Nass paused, gazing out across the barren winterscape of black tree trunks and white snow.

"Are we getting close?" Raphael asked, but Nass held up a hand to silence him. He closed his eyes briefly and then opened them again.

"Yeah," he said. "It's not far now."

He cracked open the briefcase and took out the silver divining rod. Raphael picked up the empty case. Nass held the two ends of the Y-shaped rod between his thumb and forefinger, just as they'd seen one of the Obies do, and they started off down the rise.

About ten minutes passed as they hiked north, weaving among trees and crashing through thickets, mostly pressing forward but sometimes veering to the left or right or even doubling back. The more they walked, the more uneasy Raph became. The snowfall had abated somewhat, but he realized now that they shouldn't have come out alone. His tension growing, he scanned the trees. There was no one in sight, but he couldn't help feeling like someone was watching them.

He was about to ask Nass if he wanted to head back, but then he saw that Nass's eyes were closed as he moved confidently ahead, the divining rod out in front of him. They walked for another thirty yards, and Nass never opened his eyes once. Obviously, he was getting something, and whatever was happening, Raphael didn't want to interrupt it. Even when the feeling of being followed got worse, he didn't say anything. He didn't want to mess up Nass's psychic flow.

Half an hour later, as the sun waned toward a bleak, gray twilight, they were still wandering. They had made their way to the base of the mountain the Middleburg Tunnels passed through. As far as he could tell, they were skirting the foothills about halfway between the south and east tunnels. Worried, he looked up at the darkening sky.

"Hey, man," he said. "Maybe we should go home—" but Nass stopped abruptly in front of him. Raph saw the divining rod twitching wildly in his hands.

Ignacio opened his eyes and looked down at the rod, just as surprised as Raphael was. Slowly, he took one more step forward and the rod trembled so violently it became a blur of motion. Then, suddenly, it shot out of Nass's hands and stabbed itself into the ground, vibrating there for a moment like a giant tuning fork.

"It's here," Nass said quietly, his voice full of awe. He fell to his knees and started clearing snow away from the earth where the rod had pierced it. Raphael knelt too, and helped him. Soon they had moved enough aside to reveal a rose-colored stone about twice the size of a manhole cover. Miraculously, the rod had penetrated the solid rock and was firmly embedded in it. Nass pulled off his gloves and sat with his hands pressed to the pink stone.

"It's under here," he whispered. "But deep. Maybe thirty or forty feet down."

"Can you tell what it is?" Raphael asked. "Is it gold? Diamonds?"

Nass only shook his head.

Raphael cleared some more snow away, revealing the line of weeds and dirt that surrounded the stone.

"This is rose quartz," Raphael said. "Just like on top of the tunnel mound. The mountain must be full of it. But this thing is huge," Raphael said. "How are we going to move it?"

"It's going to take all of us," Nass said.

Raphael nodded. "Tomorrow night," he said. "Once everyone's off work we'll bring the tools and meet here."

They stared down at the big, pink stone for a moment, then turned and headed through the forest, back the way they came. Raphael thought about taking the divining rod with them, but decided to leave it there to mark the spot where they would search tomorrow. He thought chances were slim that anyone would be wandering around in the woods before then. Besides, something told him it was like King Arthur's sword— Excalibur—and they wouldn't be able to pull it out even if they tried.

In the stillness of the falling snow, Raphael's ringing phone gave off a strange, muted sound. It was Master Chin.

"I need your help with something," he said. "Where are you?"

"I'll be at the corner of First and Golden in ten minutes." Raph answered.

"I'll pick you up." And Chin abruptly ended the call, which wasn't at all like him. Raphael looked at his phone for a second, perplexed, then shoved it back into his pocket.

"Everything okay?" Nass asked.

"I'll find out in a minute," Raphael said. "Master Chin needs a favor. You in?"

"Nah," Nass said. "I gotta get home."

"Okay—but start spreading the word. Make sure everyone brings whatever equipment they can. Tomorrow night at Rack 'Em. Eleven o'clock."

☙

Zhai stood atop the tunnel mound, perfectly still, gazing down on the woods below, where Raphael and Ignacio were tromping off through the snow and disappearing among the trees.

It was different this time, Zhai thought. On every other occasion when he'd gone into the trance of the Snake, he'd blacked out and when he'd come to, he didn't remember anything that had happened. This time, he'd been awake and aware the whole time. He still was—he just couldn't control his body. It was as if they had unplugged his brain from his body and hotwired their controls into his musculature. He was aware of something else, too. A presence inside his mind, watching through his eyes, listening to every sound he heard, taking note of his every thought.

Oh yes, I'm here, came a silent voice inside his head—the voice of the member of the Order he'd fought with, Zhai knew. *You wouldn't expect me to wander around in a snow storm when I can send you? Why do you think no one has ever been able to prove our existence? We have slaves like you to do our work for us. But soon we will come out of the shadows and rise, and every person on earth will know our names.* And then his tormentor's tone changed, colored with subtle amusement: *Stay where you are. My brother and I are taking care of a little business now, but we'll be there shortly with enough equipment to dig to the center of the earth if that's what it takes. Before the night is over, the Heart of the Eagle will be ours.*

But Zhai wasn't listening to the voice anymore. He was looking at the divining rod stuck into the round slab of rose quartz in the forest below, trying to will his body to move in the direction his mind wanted to go.

☙

Raphael squinted up the street as the red Mercedes blazed toward him. He knew exactly who was behind the wheel, and she was the last person he wanted to see right now. But when the car glided to a smooth stop in front of him, he was stunned to see Master Chin in the passenger seat beside Maggie.

"Quick, let's go!" Master Chin said, tilting his seat forward. Obediently, Raphael slid into the back.

"Hey, Raphael," Maggie said sweetly and he could see she was enjoying his surprise. She smiled at him and jammed on the gas, sending his head bashing into the headrest.

☙

Anne Pembrook opened her apartment door expecting to find the pizza delivery boy on her stoop—one of the benefits of her little apartment above Middleburg Couture was its proximity to Little Geno's—but instead, she found an Asian man wearing a derby hat.

"Hello, Anne," he said serenely. In spite of his thick Chinese accent, she understood every word. "We have been looking for you."

Warning bells went off in her head, and she tried to slam the door in his face, but he was too fast for her. He blasted the door with a kick that sent it flying open and launched Anne halfway across her apartment.

"Stay away from me!" she warned as she scrambled to her feet. Showing no concern, he casually turned and locked the door behind him. By the time he turned back, Anne had the pistol out of her desk drawer. Her hands were trembling, but she brought it up, squeezed one eye shut, and aimed at the intruder's chest.

"This is for Donovan," she said through clenched teeth, but before she could pull the trigger, the man had somehow crossed the ten feet that separated them and snatched the gun away from her. As she watched, he deftly disassembled it, jerking the barrel away from the grip, and dropped the two pieces of the now useless weapon to the floor as she backed away.

"Was that too fast for you?" he said with a wild grin. "You want me to do it again in slow motion?"

He laughed gleefully. Desperate, Anne tried to run past him, making a break for the door, but she didn't get far before he was on her again, tripping her so fast she didn't know what happened. One minute she was running for the exit, the next she was on her back with the intruder on top of her, his face an inch from hers.

"You're almost too pretty to kill," he whispered. "Maybe we'll do it slowly . . . keep you around for a while."

"You won't kill me," she said, defiant. "You don't know where the scroll is."

The man laughed and jerked her roughly to her feet. "I must say, you did very well giving us the slip in Chicago. Such cunning from an insignificant little teacher. And what a bold move—coming to Middleburg. We never expected that. But you are not as clever as you think. There is no creature more cunning than the snake. The scroll is here—I can feel it. You wouldn't let it out of your sight, not after your precious Donovan died for it. I *will* find it and then—"

Suddenly there was a loud knock at the door. Anne took a big breath, getting ready to scream, but the vile man clapped his hand over her mouth and pressed a huge switchblade that seemed to appear out of nowhere against her throat. His breath was hot on her face, and his eyes sent her an undeniable message: *make a sound, and you die.*

So she sat there, frozen, one of the man's hands holding the knife to her throat, the other covering her mouth. Soon they heard footsteps walking away and the hall outside her door was silent. She was overwhelmed with despair. Whoever it was had gone.

When her attacker's eyes came back to hers, there was an unmistakable glint of pleasure in them. *He's excited*, she thought with disgust. *He's going to kill me slowly, and he's going to* enjoy *it*.

But just as she closed her eyes, preparing to feel the blade bite into her throat, there was a loud crash and the door flew off its hinges.

Instantly, the man was off her, standing and facing the doorway, brandishing his two large blades in front of him like something out of a martial-arts movie. Anne sat up, eager to see her rescuer—but the sight didn't give her much hope. It was an older Asian man with a wispy white goatee and a placid smile.

"Chin," the intruder sneered. "We should have made your student finish you with that chair."

"Too late now," said the Asian guy—Chin—and he charged into the room.

They were on each other at once. Anne expected Chin to get chopped to shreds, but he also had a weapon—and he moved it so fast, snapping it against the blades of his opponent's knives, that it looked like nothing but a brown streak.

Suddenly, Anne remembered her gun and she crawled across the floor toward it. She found the grip right away, but the barrel part was nowhere in sight. She looked under the chair and then under the coffee table as sounds of battle raged. When she looked up at last she saw that another person had entered the fight—a young man. He stood on one side of her attacker, defending himself with two long, metal candlesticks from Anne's upturned dining table, while Chin barraged the intruder with kicks, occasionally parrying a thrust with what she now realized was a leather belt. Despite being outnumbered, the man in the derby seemed to be doing fine—he even smiled, as if enjoying the ferocious contest.

Anne got busy looking for the rest of her gun. There was a crash as her assailant tossed the young man into her china cabinet. So much for her grandmother's crystal.

She stuck her head under the couch again, searching for the gun barrel, when a flash—like a blast of lightning—illuminated the room. She looked up to find the young man's arm outstretched toward the intruder, and a sparkle of what looked like electrical energy on his fingertips. The blades of the intruder's daggers were sparking with power too.

"The blades of the Snake can diffuse your Shen power, boy!" the intruder snapped, but Chin lunged at him again.

Anne had no idea what was happening, but she knew whatever it was, she'd feel better with her gun reassembled. She reached under the couch again to look for the barrel, but a movement to her left caught her eye and she saw someone else. Someone she recognized from class. Maggie Anderson stood quietly in the doorway with her eyes closed, as if concentrating hard on something. Then, she opened her eyes and looked at Anne's china cabinet. It jerked and skittered a couple of inches—and then it lifted slowly off the floor, hovering about three feet in the air before it flew across the room, straight toward the intruder. He dodged out of the way and it crashed to the floor. Maggie raised her arms and pointed both hands at the man and a ripple of pink fire shot out of her fingertips, blasting him backward, into the wall, as one of his knives skittered away. When he slid to the floor, he left a cracked indentation in the shape of his body in the plaster.

And there goes my security deposit, Anne thought.

The young man turned toward Maggie, his eyes wide. "Did *you* do that?" he demanded.

She seemed just as stunned as he was, but she nodded and gave him a little smile. "I told you, Raphael," she said. "I can do lots of things."

But there was no time for her to gloat. The man was on his feet again, his look of pleasure now turned to rage. He glared at the girl for a moment and adjusted his hat.

"Okay," he said, his tone menacing as he spun his remaining knife. "No more fun."

Raphael rushed him and was immediately brought down with a brutal kick. Chin must've snatched up the intruder's other knife because he charged forward with it now. The two blades spun and clashed against one another in a blur of sparking silver, so fast that Anne couldn't follow their movements; all she knew was that one of them was bound to end up dead. She glanced over at the doorway. Maggie was leaning against the wall now, looking a little pale. Whatever crazy power she'd used to levitate the china cabinet and shoot the pink flames seemed to have drained her.

There was a final clatter and flourish of steel, and one of the long knives skittered to a rest next to Anne.

She looked up in time to see Chin spin his knife upward to leave a long slash on the side of the intruder's face and knock his hat off. The man backed away from Chin, snarling in fury.

"You got lucky today, old man. But your luck will run out."

Chin had him backed up nearly to the wall now, but just as he lunged in for the final strike, the intruder hurled himself through the window in an explosion of shattering glass. Anne hurried to the window in time to see him sprinting down Main Street amid the stares of baffled pedestrians.

Chin stepped up next to her and threw the derby out the window.

"You forgot your hat," he shouted. He pressed a button on the handle of the knife to retract the blade, and then he spun it with a satisfied flourish. After he turned and surveyed Anne's ruined apartment, he called out, "Everyone okay?"

The young man—Raphael—was on his feet now, cracking his neck.

"Fine," he grumbled.

Maggie was no longer leaning against the wall and a little color had come back into her face. "Better," she said. "Miss Pembrook?"

The teacher was still a little dazed. "The three of you just saved my life," she said. "I think it would be okay if you call me Anne."

Chin nodded, satisfied. He was slipping the brown belt back into the loops on his sagging pants now; it looked pretty knicked up. "Nice work, both of you. Not many people can say they faced down a Black Snake and lived." He turned back to Anne and offered his hand. "I'm Chin," he said.

Bewildered, she was still thinking about the belt. "That guy had two knives—and you fought him with a *belt*?"

"We use what we have," he said simply. "We need to get out of here quickly, Anne, before more of them come. Bring the scroll. You will be safe at my house."

She was about to protest that she didn't know anything about a scroll, before she realized it was foolish to lie. Whoever this man was, he'd saved her life—and if he wanted to take the scroll from her, he'd have done it already. Besides, he was right. She couldn't very well sit around and wait for the man who'd assaulted her to come back. She had no choice but to trust Chin, whoever he was.

Someone else stepped into the doorway now. He was tall, with a shaved head, and wore a T-shirt that had *Little Geno's* emblazoned across the chest. "Somebody order a pizza?" he asked, with an accent that sounded straight out of Italy. He looked, with childlike curiosity, around the demolished apartment.

Suddenly, Anne laughed. The whole thing was just so unbelievably absurd. Raphael laughed too and then Maggie joined in.

"Yeah," Anne told the giant holding the pizza box. "The pizza is mine."

Chin was the only one who remained serious. "All right," he said. "But we're taking it to go."

∞

The snow had almost stopped by the time Jack pulled up in front of Spinnacle. "Go ahead," he told Aimee. "I'll park and be right in. If Orias is here already we don't want to keep him waiting."

Absolutely not, she thought. *Heaven forbid*. She opened the door and started to get out—it would do no good to argue with her father, or protest—but he caught her hand and stopped her. She looked back at him.

"Don't think I haven't noticed the change in you since you started seeing Orias," he said pleasantly—more pleasantly than he'd spoken to her in a long time.

"Really?" She hadn't thought it showed—in fact, she thought she had been covering it pretty well. "What do you mean?"

"You're like the sweet, cooperative little girl I used to know," he said indulgently. "You're making your old man pretty happy."

"Oh . . . good," she replied vaguely, thinking as she went inside how he'd always been too busy to notice that little girl hadn't been around since she was about eight.

Orias *was* waiting, already seated, but he rose as the maitre'd led her to the table—and she smiled up at him. She would never get used to his old-fashioned, old-world manners, she thought.

No, she wouldn't—of course she wouldn't. She wasn't going to know him that long, certainly not long enough to care about his manners. All she needed from him was a little more information on how to use that teleporting thing so she could go back to 1877 and find her mother. If she could teleport into the future, she reasoned, then she should be able to travel into the past—not that she was ready to admit that she *had* teleported to a future that had Orias's red tent in it. A wave of unexpected euphoria washed over her briefly as she remembered those few blissful moments with him, when she thought he was her husband.

Spinnacle was crowded and several heads turned when he bent to kiss her cheek and then held her chair as she sat. Fortunately, there was no one in the place who would be likely to tell Raphael.

Raphael. She struggled often now to remember his face, when she thought about him at all.

As other customers turned their attention back to their own tables, it dawned on her that her father wanted people to see her with Orias. That's why he'd suggested going out to eat when Orias had called to reciprocate for (as he put it) the enchanting dinner at the Banfield home.

Jack came in then and announced that he was just going to have a quick drink and be on his way. "You young people don't need an old dude like me hanging around," he quipped, and patted Aimee's hand.

But Orias, ever the gracious host, insisted that he stay.

The two men discussed business throughout the meal—business in general and some specifics about Orias's plans for Middleburg and Jack's desire to be involved—although Jack still insisted he was not at liberty to discuss the real-estate deal in the Flats.

"But I will tell you this," he admitted. "Cheung Shao mentioned the other day that the project he's working on in the Flats will be wrapping up soon, and he's going to give me free reign to spearhead new development there when he's finished. Times are changing, and Middleburg has to change with them. So much of the Flats is just wasted space, what with all the abandoned buildings and half-empty tenements. I say purge the place—tear it all down and start over. That's what I say."

You would, Aimee thought bitterly. *You would toss people out like trash to get whatever you're looking for,* and again she had the strange sensation that she was forgetting something—something about the Flats, and about doing something to help Raphael find . . . *something*. But as she struggled to bring it up from her memory, Orias looked across the table at her and smiled. Her dad droned on and on about percentage profit points and bottom lines and she forgot what she'd been thinking about.

After the men had coffee and dessert, Jack thanked Orias for a pleasant evening and said to Aimee, "Shall we, honey?"

"I'd like Aimee to take a short walk with me, around town," Orias said smoothly. "With your permission, Jack, naturally. I haven't had a chance to see much of Middleburg yet, and it's such a charming old place. I want her show it to me."

"Well . . . " Jack hesitated. "If she wants to go and you'll have her home early . . . "

"Within the hour," Orias promised. "Aimee?"

I don't want to go, she thought. *At least, I don't* want *to want to go*.

But she did. She wanted to be alone with him. She wanted (*craved was more like it*) the forbidden thrill that took over when his eyes . . . and lips . . . met hers. Thinking about his lips, she looked up at him, her gaze steady. "I wouldn't mind," she said.

When her father had gone, she asked Orias frankly, "What do you really want?"

Delighted, he gave her a broad grin. "I love it—that you can stay a step ahead of me, most of the time," he said and signaled the waiter for the check. "You're quick, Aimee. Indeed, you are." She thought it interesting that he only signed the check but provided neither cash nor credit card. "The fact is," he continued, "I want to see Middleburg through your eyes. I told you. I want to know everything about you." When they stood to leave, he brushed a stray curl away from her face and lightly traced the line of her jaw with his thumb. "But we won't be doing much walking," he finished, and he steered her out into the crisp, cold air.

CHAPTER 25

RAPHAEL, MAGGIE AND ANNE PEMBROOK were at Chin's kitchen table, eating pizza and watching Master Chin work. He sat upright in his chair, with the scroll laid out at his left hand and a legal pad on his right. Every minute or so, his gaze would shift from the scroll to the legal pad and he'd write a word or two. Often he crossed out what he'd just scribbled and turned back to the scroll. At last, when he had filled a page, he put his pen down, sat wearily back in his chair, and rubbed his eyes. He looked exhausted.

"It is done," he said, and gently pushed the pad toward the teacher.

She dropped her pizza crust onto her plate and grabbed it eagerly, scanning the lines.

"Well," Maggie asked. "What does it say?"

Raphael hadn't gotten a chance to ask his sifu how he'd come to be riding in Maggie Anderson's car, and he hadn't asked Maggie how she'd been able to blast the Snake with a shot of pink fire, either. But neither event really surprised him. The more crazy stuff happened, the easier it became to accept it. He was more curious about what the scroll said.

"I'll just read the last section of what Donovan translated, so we can get the context for Chin's new translation," she said, and began:

> "... This is the treasure that wise men have sought,
> Since the day that the earth came to be,
> With this treasure alone are you rich beyond words,
> With this treasure alone are you free..."

Then she flipped the page and, her eyes scanning Chin's meticulous writing, she read aloud:

"... *In depths of the earth, beneath sentries of stone,*
In an impregnable tomb it sleeps,
The power of ages protects its rest
Only one may disturb its long peace,
A princess who ne'er has lain with a man,
From exile she shall return,
Like the great queen before her
She walks with the winds,
Transcending the bonds of the earth,
As a diver through water she will pass through the stone,
For no matter or magic may bind her.
The heart of the Wheel she shall pierce with her steps
To retrieve its celestial fire.
But woe to those who grasp for the sun,
The brazen and selfish shall fall.
Live by the sword, by the sword you shall die,
These are the words of the All."

As Anne's voice fell silent, everyone looked up at Chin, who sat back in his chair now, thoughtfully drumming his fingers on the table.

"What does it mean?" Raphael asked.

Master Chin looked at him, a lifetime of compassion and worry brimming in his eyes, but he didn't answer.

"How were you able to translate this?" Anne asked. "Donovan said that form of Cantonese is ancient—so rare that hardly anyone knows it now."

Chin smiled at her. "I first learned to speak and write in this dialect," he told her. "The man who wrote this scroll was my great-grandfather."

Anne, Raphael noted, seemed stunned by the revelation. He would have been, too, if he hadn't known his sifu for so long.

"Who was he?" she asked soberly.

Chin stared at the table in front of him for a moment, deep in thought. "He was a prophet. A seer," he said. "And a martial-arts master. Like most prophets, he was revered by a few and hated by many. He angered the Qing Dynasty. They claimed that theirs was the greatest kingdom on earth and that the emperor was the greatest man, but my great-grandfather taught his followers about a greater kingdom—the celestial kingdom of the All."

"Did the emperor have him killed?" Raphael asked. That was how those situations generally played out, he knew, but Chin only shrugged.

"Some said he died when the famous Shaolin Temple was burned— but at least one survivor wrote that he climbed an invisible staircase and disappeared into the clouds, never to be seen again. Still others claim he wasn't at the temple at all. In any case, his followers kept up the traditions he taught them for many years after he was gone. His teachings gave his initiates special abilities, so he was always very selective about who he allowed into the Order. When my great-grandfather was gone, my grandfather made a mistake. He allowed a man named Feng Xu to join.

"Members were required to live simple lives. They could not use their abilities to accumulate wealth, or seek political power. Feng Xu was a good student and a gifted martial artist who possessed a powerful spirit. But he was ambitious and greedy. He began using his abilities to accumulate power and riches and persuaded other members to do the same. Feng Xu was also jealous of my grandfather's spiritual gifts, and his jealousy grew into hate. By the time my grandfather realized how dangerous he was, it was too late. Feng poisoned him. My father was still young, and no match for Feng, so my grandmother helped him get away before Feng could kill him, too.

"With them out of the way, Feng remade the Order as he saw fit. He changed its name from the 'Order of the All' to the 'Order of the

Black Snake.' He communed with demons and became a skilled sorcerer. Anyone who opposed him, he murdered. Soon, he was one of richest, most powerful men in Southern China, and feared by all. Only one thing evaded his grasp—the Heart of the Eagle—and he was obsessed with my grandfather's prophecy about the city where it would be found."

"Middleburg," Anne said.

Chin nodded. "The center of the contiguous United States, in the heart of the nation whose symbol is the bald eagle."

"And they're here for the treasure," Raphael said.

"Treasure?" Maggie asked, her eyes wide.

Chin nodded again.

"But why?" Raphael asked. "Is it really worth so much that they'd come all the way from China to look for it?"

"The treasure is not money," Chin said.

Raphael drew a breath, prepared to tell Master Chin about his mission with Nass earlier in the day, when they had found the spot where the treasure was supposedly buried. But then he remembered the corral behind Master Chin's house, and the four beautiful horses Zhai had given him after their last adventure. Zhai was always outdoing Raphael when it came to honoring their sifu, but if Raphael could surprise him by capturing the treasure, Master Chin would really be proud of him. Even if the treasure wasn't money, it had to be worth something. He had the chance to save the Flats and bring honor to his sifu, all in one night. It was settled—he and his crew would retrieve the treasure tomorrow, secretly.

"If the treasure isn't money, what is it then?" asked Maggie.

Chin didn't answer immediately. He merely took a bite of cold sausage-and-mushroom pizza and closed his eyes as he chewed. When he'd finally swallowed he said, "We'll never know what it is. It's locked away where no one can reach it. If the treasure is safe, the world is safe. That's all you need to know."

The snow had abated by the time they got outside, and the air was fresh and cold. Aimee liked the familiar crunching sound their boots made on the ice-crusted sidewalk. "So where do you want to go?" she asked Orias.

"Show me the Middleburg of your childhood," he said softly. "Show me your memories, Aimee . . . all the places that have touched you, or that you have touched. Places that are special to you."

"That should be really fascinating," she said skeptically. "But okay—if that's what you want." She started walking, heading south. "The library's not too far from here. They have evening hours tonight, if you want to go in."

"Yes. I love books."

She loved books too and as soon as they entered, the smell of the place retrieved a warm memory for her. Orias pulled her into a quiet corner between the historical romance and experimental fiction shelves.

"Your mother brought you here when you were six," he whispered, "to get your very own library card. As soon as you were able to write your full name."

"How did you know?" She was surprised. "Did my dad tell you that?"

"I'm sort of telepathic, when it's something or someone I care about."

"Oh, that's really fair," she protested. "You get to know everything about me, without even asking?"

He leaned closer. He hadn't kissed her yet, and she was anticipating it with dread and with longing. Every time she was near him she had the same terrible feeling of helplessness—like the feeling she got whenever she dreamed of falling from the top of a building or from a bridge, plummeting down . . . falling . . . falling . . . and reaching out desperately to grab something—anything—to hold on to. His strange, smoky scent, almost like incense, assailed her (but now she found it comforting), and it seemed to anchor her in reality again.

"The other night, at your house," she said quietly. "It was a mistake."

"Was it?" he asked, his voice even, but she was surprised at the hurt she saw in his eyes.

"It never should have happened. I can't get involved with you," she told him, trying with all her might to remember why she couldn't get involved with him. She finally grasped it—or the *idea* of it. "There's . . . there's someone else."

"So you've said. Why are you here, Aimee? You could have gone with your father."

"You know why." She moved away, to what she thought was a safe distance, and turned to face him. "One reason only. You said you would show me how to use that teleporting thing to find my mom. And now I know exactly where to look. I just have to figure out how to get there." Because she knew if she could find her mother and bring her back, everything would be okay again and she would remember everything she needed to remember. "So I want to ask you—can I teleport into the past? Like, over a hundred years? You said I went into the future. Can you help me go back in time?"

"Going back is a little trickier," he said.

"Would it help if we used the Wheel?" she asked, suddenly remembering the strange device that she—and *someone*—had used.

"You know about the Wheel. I *am* impressed," he told her. "But that's only part of it, Aimee. And you have to work to get ready for that part. But yes. With practice, it can be done."

"Then teach me."

He smiled that lazy, delicious, inviting smile she was starting to look forward to as he went to her and put his arms around her. "That would give me immense pleasure," he murmured against her ear. His nearness, the heat of his breath on her cheek—all of it—was making her dizzy with a strange yearning she couldn't describe.

"If you'll help me find my mother, Orias, I'll gladly get whatever it is you need me to get," she said. "And then everything can go back to the way it was." A name—*Raphael*—rose to the surface of her consciousness for a second or two, like a fisherman's cork bobbing on the water, before it sank again into the depths of forgetfulness.

"Things will never again be the way they were," Orias told her, his voice low and enticing. "Not for me—and not for you. I won't give you up, Aimee. I'll never give you up."

Each word he spoke drove deeper and deeper into her brain, like a hammer driving a nail into a piece of wood. Even as she thrilled to them, she knew there was something about the whole thing that was so wrong—and all she wanted to do was escape the fierce pressure of his intractable will.

And suddenly, she was shooting through the dazzling, star-splendored wormhole—the brilliant white light—but this time it was little more than a momentary spark, a brief sensation of falling. Then she was outside, across the street from the library. An old woman inching along the sidewalk, leaning on a walker, almost bumped into her. The woman blinked, stared at her for a couple of seconds, and blinked again.

"Sorry," Aimee said. "I slipped." That was the only way she could think of to explain it. The old lady shook her head and continued on, muttering something about ill-mannered, inconsiderate juvenile delinquents. A moment later, Orias was standing next to her.

It took her less time to recover from the experience than it had before. "So that's how it works?" she asked him. "Some kind of strong emotion can just send me flying off into space and time?" And as she spoke, she was thinking, *but I* don't *love you—I don't.*

"You don't have to love me, Aimee, in order to help me," he said as if she'd spoken it aloud. "But you will. Before this is over you will love me and need me as much as I need you."

She turned away from him and started walking downtown, toward the Starlite Cinema. He caught up with her and fell into step beside her. After they'd gone about half a block, she asked, "What for? You have all this money—and magical powers. You're hotter than hot. You could get any girl in this town to fall at your feet. What could you possibly need me for—after I do your little errand, that is?"

Laughing softly, he stopped walking and made her face him again. Lightly caressing her cheek with one fingertip, he said, "I am a wretched, soulless creature, Aimee. So you will be my soul."

"Hang on," she responded. "You *do* have a soul—sort of. You're half human, and half a soul is better than none, right?"

"I'm afraid not. It doesn't work that way."

"Well, how does it work? I don't see how I can help unless you tell me."

They were at the park now, where Aimee and her mother had gone to collect specimens of leaves and acorns for her third-grade science project. He took her elbow and guided her to a bench near the sidewalk, brushing enough snow away to make room for them to sit down. Then he opened his great, leather overcoat, drew her down next to him and enfolded her against him, in its warmth. When he was satisfied she was comfortable, he spoke again.

"Humans," he said and there was no rancor in his voice, only envy. "You just don't get it, do you?"

"Then explain it to me."

He shook his head, as if in wonderment. "You get chance after chance after chance with God, or the Creator or the All—whatever you want to call the supreme *It*. And there are so many loopholes in the deal that it makes my head spin. You humans wallow in iniquity night after night and repent daily and still He forgives you. My father and his kind got one chance. *One*. Make a choice for all eternity. No second chance. No do-overs. Sentenced for all time to a living hell. And hell, dear Aimee, is not fire and brimstone. Hell is never—*ever*—being able to go back to the light. My father's choice—and my mother's—doomed me to live in that hell forever. There is no place for me anywhere—I am unfit for human companionship and my father's kind consider me a mongrel. I am banished from heaven, despised in hell. And in this world—I will never belong in this world."

His pain was etched clearly in his face, and she wanted to comfort him somehow, but it was all she could do to comprehend what he was telling her.

"When the mighty Oberon learned of my . . . inopportune. . . existence," he said bitterly, "he told my mother I would be an abomination—not angel, not human—and he insisted that she abort me. She refused and he left her."

"That's awful," she said.

"So, Aimee—my fate is decided. I'm going to live for a very long time and then I'm going to die an unimaginably horrible death. But until then, I intend to have everything I want—for as long as I want it. And I have decided, my sweet little innocent, that I want you."

"Like I said—for what?"

"To reign with me. What else? If I am to be trapped here, I fully intend to make the best of it." He laughed, a cynical, hollow sound.

She thought about it a moment, considering what her mom would say—or maybe Lily Rose—because they were the only truly religious people she knew. "But there must be a way around it," she said at last. "The half-soul thing, I mean. It hardly seems fair to punish you for the choice your parents made."

He laughed now, really laughed, as if enjoying the most supreme joke the universe had ever told. "So incredibly guileless," he whispered. "And so human—already looking for the loophole. You are such a fascinating creature, Aimee. Never before have I seen . . . or touched . . . such *goodness*."

He kissed her again and she felt like she would lose herself in the sensation. It reached down into the depths of her soul and drew her to him, into his melancholy sweetness, into his undeniable spell. She felt warm and tingly and lighter than air. He looked into her eyes, and she wanted to disappear into them.

And she realized she wanted stay with him forever even though she knew in the end he might find nothing but eternal damnation. Eternal darkness. Absence—*forever*—from the light.

But not if she could help it, she decided. *Because it wasn't fair.* There had to be something that could save him, something that could change his destiny. After all, it wasn't through his choice, and he did have half a soul. There had to be a way. And after he helped her bring her mother home, she would find it.

"Would you truly stay with me?" he whispered, reading her mind again. He seemed moved to tears by the words she hadn't even spoken aloud. "And will you comfort me when I am denied?"

"I'll help you," she said. "I told you—any way that I can. If you help me." She opened her purse and took out the old sepia photograph of her mother. "This picture was taken, here in Middleburg, in 1877." She pointed at the woman in the center. "That's my mother. And that's where—or when—I have to go to find her. So when can we get started?"

"One more day," he told her, smiling again. "Only one more day. In the meantime, we'll practice and improve your ability to control the teleport, so you'll be ready."

"So what are you going to do—just kiss me silly until I've got the hang of it?"

He bellowed with laughter as he stood and pulled her to her feet. "As much as I'd like that, it won't be necessary," he said. "Strong emotion creates endorphins that act as a trigger for a true teleport. You must learn to use the trigger at will, when you're alone—because you're going part of the way without me. But yes. Any strong emotion—it doesn't have to be love—can trigger it. It could be hate, disgust, desire. And all you need is the trigger. When you learn to recognize it, you'll be able to reach deep down inside yourself and pull it up at will."

"And you think I'll be ready by tomorrow?" she asked doubtfully.

"Yes—if you stay with me tonight. I want to show you the world that could be yours, just for the asking."

"But my dad—you told him you'd have me home within the hour."

"Don't worry about your father," he said. "He'll go along with whatever I suggest."

The blast rattled the entire train car and sent Kate to her knees. While she was down there, she crossed herself and muttered, "Jesus, Mary and Joseph, protect us!"

A profound silence followed the explosion: the snowdrifts muffled every sound. After a moment, she was able to make out distant voices sifting through the wind. The workers had been absent for several days, but today she'd seen them around again, moving equipment through the forest. Now, there were explosions.

Her time in Middleburg had been sometimes frightening and often confusing, to be sure, but she had managed to remain reasonably content as long as she was safe in her little train car—and (more and more) as long as Zhai was around. But now strange men were stamping all about the place and Zhai was nowhere to be found. She wished once again that she was at home—her real home, living the simple life she'd known before. She missed her family terribly. But, she knew, wishing would do no good.

She got to her feet and made her way tentatively to the window, expecting another blast at any moment. She peered out into the night and caught sight of a figure moving through the broken-down rail cars, and crossing the tracks that ran between her and the tunnel. He disappeared behind a car again, and she thought she had to be mistaken. But when he came out from behind it, she saw him clearly. It was Zhai.

Her heart leaped in her chest and she felt several conflicting emotions—she was worried about him, furious that he had just disappeared without a word, and desperate to be close to him, all at once. She grabbed her heavy coat, pulled it on over her sweater and jeans, and bolted out the door. Soon she was jogging up the tracks toward him.

"Zhai!" she shouted as she drew close. "Zhai!"

He turned to face her, and she stopped running and stared at him. It was Zhai—there was no question about that—but it *wasn't* Zhai, too. His hostile energy, the cold, blank expression on his face, the utter lack of recognition in his eyes as he looked at her—even his posture—were nothing like Zhai's. And his clothes were dirty and wrinkled, as if he'd been sleeping in the woods.

"Are you all right?" she asked quietly.

Her first impulse, as he began walking toward her, was to run, but she stopped herself. It was Zhai, after all. No matter what strange, evil spell he was under, she knew he wouldn't hurt her. By the time she saw that the Chinese markings on his hands were glowing red, it was too late to run—but he was looking at her with such rage that she was starting to doubt the wisdom of staying where she was. But behind the rage, she could see a reasonable, intelligent struggle going on, as if he were trying to regain control.

"Run," he said, his voice hoarse and distorted—not like his own.

"What?"

"Run!" he repeated. "Get as far away from me as you can, Kate!"

He knew who she was, then—Zhai was still in there somewhere. "I only want to help," she said.

"There's nothing . . . you can do." His face contorted as he spoke, as if he was in great pain. "Now go! Run!" And he turned and moved away from her, deeper into the forest.

After watching him for a moment, she said aloud, "I've never run from anything in my whole life, Zhai. I'm not about to start now." And she took off after him. "Zhai, wait!" she called.

If he heard her, he gave no indication, but she soon caught up with him. Together they ran into a clearing in a ring of towering pine trees. One of the Asian men she'd seen poking around the train graveyard was sitting cross-legged against a tree trunk, his eyes closed. The marks on his hands were glowing, just like the marks on Zhai.

A shadow fell over her, and she looked up to see another man in a matching hat, standing over her, a thin smile on his face.

"Well, look what the slave dragged in," he said in a thick Chinese accent. He grabbed Kate and clapped a pair of handcuffs on her wrists and ankles, his hands moving so incredibly fast she hardly knew he was doing it. "Sorry—no witnesses," he explained politely. "You understand."

Then he approached Zhai, who meekly offered his wrists and with no resistance allowed the man to shackle him next to Kate. When Zhai's bonds were secure, the man pushed him down into the snow beside her.

"Sit," he said, as if commanding a dog, and laughed.

"Whatever it is you're doing, you'd best watch yourself," Kate said. "He won't be your slave forever, and when he's free he'll have your hide!"

He laughed at her and then turned to his friend who was still sitting beneath the tree. He was stirring now, and the red glow was fading from the back of his hands.

The taller man helped him up, and Kate wondered at how much alike they looked.

"Our slave caught a pretty intruder," the shorter man said, glancing at Kate with lascivious interest.

"Forget her," his companion said. "Any sign of the fallen ones—the *duo luo tian shi*?"

"Nothing. I'm sure they're biding their time. You know how patient the immortals can be."

"Any sign of the *what*?" Kate asked, unable to contain the question.

The shorter guy gazed at Kate, looking amused. "What, you don't know the *duo luo tian shi*?" he joked, approaching her. "Well, you will know them when you see them. They will fly in on invisible wings and try to make trouble for us, and the Snake Lord will eat them. That's what *duo luo tian shi* is," he chuckled. "Snake food!"

"Quit messing around," the other man groused. "The explosives aren't working. We need something more powerful."

And the two walked away together, further into the circle of pines.

Kate could see it wasn't a natural clearing. They'd cut down several trees to give their work crew enough room to maneuver, and a large, yellow machine with a big scooper on it sat nearby, next to a huge, rose-colored stone that looked like it had been just been pulled out of the ground. A few workers stood around with their hands on their hips, shaking their heads. Two of them glanced over at Kate and Zhai and then quickly looked away. The two men in the derbies walked over and stared down into the hole where the stone had sat. The taller one shook his head. After a moment, they headed back toward Kate and Zhai and she caught a bit of their conversation.

"That much C4 should have at least cracked it. Did you see the markings carved into the stone? It's protected by magic," the smaller man said. "It has to be."

"We're too close to give up now. The new explosives will arrive tomorrow night. We'll try again then. Magic or no magic, we're getting into that chamber. For now, let's get everyone back to base."

"Kate?"

Kate glanced around to see Zhai looking at her, a dazed expression in his eyes. She felt incredibly relieved to have him back; she couldn't stand to be alone with these strange men a moment longer. In her joy she would have hugged him—if it weren't for the manacles binding her wrists.

"What are you doing here?" he asked, and then he looked around. "Where are we?"

"We're together," she answered. She wasn't trying to be clever; it was just the only thing she understood at the moment—and, she realized, it was the only thing that mattered.

❧

Maggie drove Raphael home from Chin's, and they were silent for most of the ride. When she stopped the Mercedes at the curb in front of his apartment house, she asked, "Hey—you okay?"

"Yeah," he said. "I'm cool."

"You want to talk about anything?"

"Like what?" he asked, but she only raised her eyebrows. She wasn't going to say the name, but she was dying to know what happened. He said it for her. "You mean Aimee?"

"I don't know if you broke up with her, but if you want to talk about it—"

"Not yet," he cut in. "I would break up with her if she'd return my calls or talk to me at school for more than five seconds. You were right. But you already know that," he finished bitterly. "You have pictures."

"I'm sorry." And she really was. She didn't want him with Aimee, but she didn't want him to hurt, either. Tentatively, she leaned toward him. He didn't back away so she kissed him—very gently, on the lips. He still didn't back away, but he didn't kiss her back. Maggie was smart enough not to push it. "Whenever you're ready, we can talk about it," she said. But she meant more than talk—and she knew he understood what she meant.

"Yeah," he said. "When I'm ready—I might just take you up on that. You okay from here?"

"Fine," she said. "You don't have to worry about me, Raph. I can take care of myself."

He broke into a grin. "I guess you can. What you did at Pembrook's place was awesome."

Maggie laughed—and it felt good. "Yeah," she agreed. "It was. And I have a feeling that was only the tip of a very big iceberg."

He looked at her tenderly, she thought, like they had shared a real moment, before he got out and headed up the rickety stairs of his building. As she drove home she realized she was happier than she had ever been—in her entire life—really, truly happy.

CHAPTER 26

At dusk on Friday evening, Orias sat at his dining room table, feasting on lobster, mashed potatoes, salad, pan-seared asparagus and rich, buttery rolls he'd ordered in from Spinnacle. Every few bites, he took a hearty swig of his special drink—the libation of the Dark Territory, an elixir made with the black roots of mandrake known to grow only on the banks of the River Lethe, mixed with sweet red wine made from his own grapes. It was the potion of forgetfulness, and it filled him with a delicious black fog that dulled the constant ache in his soul. Many days it seemed that nothing else would get him through the misery of his existence. Nothing—until he met Aimee.

At the thought of Aimee, the image of her blue eyes looking up at him—eyes as dark and deep as the waters of the Lethe itself—flashed through his mind. Since the day Orias turned thirteen and realized what he was, he had lived as a spider lives: spinning webs of seduction to entangle his hapless admirers, draining them until they were wasted husks and then casting them aside—sometimes for money, sometimes for lust, sometimes for influence, and sometimes just for fun. But in all this time, he'd never encountered anyone like Aimee Banfield. When he looked into her eyes, he saw himself reflected there. All his wickedness, his unmitigated selfishness, his crushing loneliness were laid bare before her innocence. And when he kissed her, he'd *felt* something . . . strange. There was no use denying it. He'd felt a stirring of *hope*—and it was terrifying.

Traveling with her—teleporting—all through the night had been amazing. First, they went to New York, and he left her for an hour to soak in a bubble bath in his penthouse on Manhattan's Upper West Side while he went out and bought evening clothes for her. When she was dressed, he brushed her hair, wriggling his fingers through the strands until it draped, as if by magic, into a stylish updo. And bare-chested, in bare feet, wearing only his tuxedo trousers and suspenders, he'd applied her makeup and painted her fingernails and toenails blood red. When she expressed surprise at his cosmetological prowess, he'd told her his ancestors had been the ones to teach women how to adorn themselves with face paint and jewels. He'd heard the stories often—even read them in scholarly texts—but now, for the first time, he understood why they'd done it. It was, even in his wide experience, the most intimate interaction he'd ever had with a female.

He took her to a party, where he was the guest of honor, and those who'd already chosen him over Oberon bowed to him (and to Aimee) and gave offerings of wine and gemstones. Then, when everyone left, he took her to the rooftop restaurant where, enclosed in the establishment's giant retracting Plexiglas bubble to protect them from the winter wind, they danced under a brilliant canopy of twinkling stars. As they'd looked down on the magnificent view of Central Park and the city surrounding it, he'd kissed her with renewed passion and instantly they were in Paris, standing atop the Eiffel Tower. In Venice they shared a gondola in the moonlight. Next they went to Rome, but he'd had to explain to her that they couldn't go inside Vatican City because he couldn't stand on hallowed ground. Another of the curses his father had bequeathed him.

It was no wonder he hated his father, Orias thought now, staring out the dining room window at the last few straggling snowflakes drifting down in the deepening gray twilight. The hate was part of his father's legacy—and his mother's. The bitterness of his existence stabbed at his soul again.

They had done this to him. They had bequeathed to him the biggest curse of all. To despise what you love and long eternally for that which you despise—that was the way of the fallen, and that was his heritage. To have all the mortality—eventually—of a human being, with none of the blissful ignorance.

At first, his feelings for Aimee had terrified him. For love, he knew, was weakness, and weakness was death. How could an insignificant human female give him even the faintest glimmer of hope? There was no hope—and there certainly was no love—for him.

He would allow no one to corrupt him with weakness, especially some foolish little high-school girl who had the audacity to be concerned about his soul—what there was of it. All the lines he'd fed her had started out as so much romantic drivel, designed to seduce her into bending to his will so that she would retrieve the treasure for him. But somewhere along the way, it had changed. He had started to care what happened to her. That was not only weak—it was futile.

If he loved her, all the more reason to destroy her. So, after Aimee had served her purpose, he would dispose of her as he had all the others.

Unless, he thought absently . . . unless he decided to keep her around for a while, just for his own amusement. And as he thought of her now, sleeping on the old couch in the parlor after eating a fruit cup steeped in a teaspoon of his libation, he realized how much he *wanted* to keep her. Even if he soon would have no need of her.

Soon, she would place it in his hands—the treasure Oberon had spent eons searching for, preparing for. How ironic that his despised half-breed son was going to step in at the last minute and claim all the glory. The prospect of his father's coming rage made Orias chuckle as he took another sip of his wine.

A loud knock came at the door, and Orias glanced at his watch. Uphir was right on time. He drained his chalice and, after looking in on Aimee for a moment, he closed the door to the parlor and went to greet the demon doctor.

He recognized the man on the stoop immediately. It was the bald attendant from the gas station down the street; Orias had seen him several times when he'd gone to fill up. But when Orias looked into his eyes, the man blinked—and his eyes were no longer human. The pupils were elliptical, like a cat's, and they were orange. A roiling black steam emanated from the top of his head and hung above him and, superimposed over his face, nine sets of eyes and nine snarling mouths slowly coalesced into one set of arched eyebrows, one matching pair of cunning, dark human eyes and one pencil-thin mustache set over thick, moist lips the color of raw liver.

"Dr. Uphir," Orias said and extended his hand. "How nice to see you."

The doctor bowed from the waist and kissed Orias's ring. "And you," he responded pleasantly.

"That's a nice vessel you've got there," Orias mocked, eyeing Uphir's large, gas-station attendant gut as he led him into the parlor. "Will you be giving it back in time for me to fill up my car tomorrow morning?"

Uphir laughed. "Fill it up with piss, for all I care," he sneered. "Cars—damn filthy means of transport." He looked down at his wrinkled button-up shirt with the name *Don* stitched over the pocket, his tattered denim jacket, and his protruding stomach. "And this is a disgusting mantle," he added with distaste. "Most undignified. I shall enjoy being rid of it."

There was a strange dissonant harmony to his voice, as if eight other people were also talking.

"I see you brought friends," Orias observed.

"Well, restoring the sight of a fallen angel is no simple matter—even for the greatest of demon physicians. Where is he?"

"In the tower. But before we go up—will you have him unconscious for the procedure?"

Uphir shrugged. "It doesn't matter to me—he doesn't need to be. It will be painful, but your father's a creature of pain. He can take it."

Orias reached into the interior pocket of his sport coat and took out two thick packets of one-hundred dollar bills. "Here's your fee," he said, giving Uphir the first packet. When he held out the second, he added,

"This is to make sure he's unconscious until we leave the room. You'll see why when you get up there."

Uphir grinned as he took the money. "It sounds like there's trickery afoot in the House of Morrow," he said, his amusement evident. "I *adore* trickery. But your father and I go way back, *boy*, and he's the one who sent for me. Why should I take orders from you?"

Orias closed his eyes for a moment, gathering his strength. Then he raised both arms out to his sides, level with his shoulders. When he opened his eyes, an unearthly, red glow emanated from them and a dark, foggy mist filled the hallway and swirled around the now cringing demon. Everything in the hallway rattled: the paintings on the walls, the hutch by the door, the chairs along the walls, the crystals in the chandelier. Orias snarled and the rattling became more violent, until at last a whimper of fear escaped the doctor. Satisfied, Orias took a deep breath and closed his eyes. When he opened them again, the red light was gone and the fog dissipated. He lowered his arms.

"My time is coming, Uphir," he said, grasping the devil doctor by the throat with one powerful hand and lifting him about three feet. "Oberon's power is waning and mine is growing stronger. Align yourself wisely, demon, if you know what's good for you."

"Oh—certainly. Certainly," Uphir choked out nervously and then, as Orias lowered him to the floor, his face split again, into nine leering grins. Nine pairs of eyes squinted with silent glee. "Like father, like son," all nine voices said in unison. Then they became one, and Uphir added, "We have a deal. Now, if you will take me to him, we can begin."

෴

Oberon was sitting on the bed when Orias and the doctor entered the small, round tower room.

"Uphir," Oberon growled. "You're late."

"And you're ugly," Uphir replied. "Uglier than ever, if that's possible."

"Save the jokes. Let's get this done."

"You'll have to reveal yourself," Uphir said. "You know the drill. But first—your absence at the conclave was sorely felt. Azaziel wanted me to deliver that message *personally*. I think he means you should be at the next one, no matter what."

"I know what he means," growled Oberon.

"Hey—I'm just saying," Uphir told him. "Don't shoot the messenger. Okay—go ahead. Whenever you're ready."

Oberon took a deep breath and when he exhaled his true form became visible—those glorious black wings, the onyx-like skin covered with glistening scales. *Truly*, Orias thought, with the same awe he'd felt as a child, *my father is terrible and beautiful to behold*. The only flaw was his eyes; their sockets were still jagged, empty craters.

"Will you give yourself over to my ministrations?" Uphir asked.

"I will," Oberon replied.

Uphir placed one of the gas station attendant's grease-stained hands on Oberon's head. "First, you will sleep," he whispered. Instantly, Oberon's body relaxed. Uphir guided him backward, easing him down on the bed and gently folding his wings beneath him. When he was satisfied that Oberon was unconscious, Uphir took a moment to glance around the room at the writing that covered every inch of the ceiling, walls, and floor. Even the door was covered, now; Orias had finished it.

"Well, well," Uphir said smugly. "It is rare indeed that a half-breed gets the drop on a prince like Oberon. I'd love to see the look on his face when he opens his new eyes and sees what you've been up to . . . "

"Sorry," Orias reminded him. "We'll both be on the other side of that door, with it locked securely behind us."

"Betraying a fallen angel is a tricky business, Orias," Uphir warned. "And dangerous—especially for so small a fee."

"Yes," Orias agreed coldly. "My father and his kind are dangerous—but so are their sons."

Uphir's expression darkened. "I'd need more money—at least twenty thousand. I want to put *distance* between myself and Oberon before he wakes up, just in case. I'll have to hide and I want to hide in comfort."

Demons, Orias thought with contempt. *Their obsession with human money was pathetic.*

"Agreed," he said impatiently. "Now get it done, before he wakes up and destroys us both." As the doctor turned back to his patient, Orias retreated to a chair in the corner to watch.

Uphir began by chanting. It was a horrible language—it sounded more like he was vomiting than speaking—but all the languages of the Pit were like that. It was the worst part of the Dark Territory, a place, Orias knew, where not even one as powerful as his father would venture. But the incantation was working. Slowly, Oberon levitated off the bed.

Now, Uphir opened his mouth wide, unnaturally wide, and eight demons in their spirit forms—as ethereal as shadows—emerged from the gas station attendant's mouth and whirled around Oberon, spinning faster and faster until four of them were holding him up, one at each arm and each leg. Another grabbed his torso from above and another from below, all of them clutching him at once, gouging him with their fearsome black claws, until Oberon's mouth snapped open, and, even unconscious, he shouted in agony. The remaining two spirit-demons shot down his throat, and Uphir reached over and forced Oberon's mouth closed. Orias saw the glow they cast through the cracks between the scales that covered his father's skin: two points of red light, rippling back and forth within his body like fire. Uphir, meanwhile, continued chanting, swaying, moving, as if performing some kind of primitive, terrifying rain dance.

Finally, both sparks of red fire moved upward, into Oberon's head. Lights the color of flames shone from his nose, his ears, his blasted eye sockets and, when Uphir released his jaw, from his screaming mouth. The light intensified, and from the way Oberon was bellowing and writhing, Orias knew it was incredibly painful—but he took only a little satisfaction from that. The best was yet to come.

"The pain is normal," Uphir told him. "My little friends are rewiring his brain to function with his new spirit eyes. It's all part of the process."

"I don't care," Orias shot back. "Hurt him all you want."

Uphir raised both his hands over his head and finished with a guttural shout. Six of the demons swarmed back into his mouth, and Oberon fell back to the bed, already reverting to his human form. He looked terribly mortal, terribly frail. Cautiously, Orias approached the bed.

"His eyes still look the same," he said. It was true: his father's eye sockets remained empty, livid red holes filled with shiny scar tissue.

"The fleshly damage was caused by the All," Uphir said. "There's nothing I can do about that. But look again."

Orias looked, and this time he saw two ghostly, transparent eyes floating in Oberon's eye sockets. One looked vaguely reptilian, the other round and blue and somehow feminine. "The demon spirits will see for him. Believe me, his sight will be better than the sight of any human. Much better."

Orias chuckled. "Won't win any beauty contests though, will he?"

Uphir fished into the station attendant's pocket and came out with a pair of black sunglasses. "No charge," he said with a cackle as he handed them to Orias.

Orias placed them on the bedside table. "All right. Let's get out of here before he wakes up." He led Uphir into the hallway, shut the door behind them and locked it.

"Are you sure that spell will hold him?" Uphir asked, one eyebrow quizzically raised.

"Are you questioning my abilities, doctor?" Orias looked at him sternly. "Would you like another demonstration?"

"Oh, no—no," Uphir said quickly. "Not necessary."

Without another word, Orias led him down the stairs and to the study where he opened his father's safe and took out a heavy canvas bag. "Twenty thousand," he said. "It's all here—in gold coins. Enjoy it."

"Yes, indeed," Uphir said. Orias walked him to the door and when he'd opened it, Uphir went on. "This is always my favorite part," he said with a grin. "Watch this."

Uphir walked down the steps and to the curb. Just then, a large moving truck came barreling down the street. The demon doctor suddenly lurched forward and leaped out in front of it. The truck hit with a sickening thud, a crunch of bones and then a screech of brakes as it came to a halt. Blood flowed across the pavement from the station attendant's head, like the yolk from a broken egg. Orias could hear laughter as nine shadowy forms swirled around, circling the body like buzzards.

Their laughter grew louder as the driver jumped out of the truck's cab and ran around to look down, with horror, at the dead man, and they shrieked with amusement as he made the 911 call.

"I need help! A man's been hurt. I hit him. He just ran out in front of me. I . . . I think he might be dead."

"*Catch you later*," Uphir's voices whispered to Orias in unison from beneath the streetlights, and then the demon doctor's wispy, shadowy form shot straight down—right through the blacktop, with the eight other screeching, screaming demons following. A second later, the white bag full of gold sank through the surface of the road, also disappearing.

The truck driver was pacing back and forth next to the body, getting more hysterical by the moment. Orias shook his head and stepped back inside, closing the door behind him. *Demons.* Of course it was occasionally necessary to kill someone in order to achieve an objective, but did they really have to enjoy it so much?

"*Orias!*"

The deafening roar shook the whole house, and Orias stopped in mid-stride, frozen for a moment, every sense alert. He looked up at the ceiling and waited.

"You did this, boy!" his father raged. "I'll skin you alive! I'll roast your kidneys and eat them! How dare you betray me? Orias! *Orias!*"

In the tower, Oberon pounded on the door of his bedroom-turned-prison-cell until the windowpanes rattled. Orias waited, scarcely breathing, for the sound of the door splintering and his father thundering down the stairs, but seconds passed and all he heard was more screaming and pounding. Orias broke into a smile. The spell was holding.

"You just wait, boy!" his father bellowed. "The train is coming! And when it does everything is going to change! You hear me? Everything!"

Orias pointed up the stairs and made the sign he'd learned from a very old book he'd discovered in the basement of his mother's home. Immediately, the roar of his father's rage went silent, as if he were imprisoned in a soundproof room.

CHAPTER 27

"YOU ALL RIGHT, *PAPI*?" Clarisse asked as she and Nass crossed the parking lot of Rack 'Em Billiards Hall. "You look a little sick."

The truth was, Nass wasn't okay, not really. The knowing had been dogging him all day, nipping at his psyche. Something big was going down tonight, and the crushing weight of anticipation was so strong he felt like it might buckle his knees. The knowing had told him something about Clarisse, too—something he didn't want to believe. He hadn't planned on bringing her along, but she'd stopped by as his shift at Little Geno's was ending. He'd told her she could go with him as far as Rack 'Em.

"I'm fine," he said. "I've got some stuff to take care of with my crew tonight. You can wait for me at home, or you can stay here with Dalton and the other girls, but you can't come with me."

"Yes, sir, *jefe*," Clarisse said. She was always sarcastic, but he'd noticed a new, more acidic edge to her jokes the last couple days, and it was really getting on his nerves.

As they approached the old Western saloon-style doors, Beet and Benji came out with Josh and Emory, and finally Raphael. Raph didn't look so good either, Nass thought, but he was still firmly in charge. He led his crew out to the far end of the parking lot for a conference, his stride as quick and determined as ever.

"Okay—listen up," Raph said when everyone was huddled around. "We're gonna do this. Beet, you got the gear?"

Beet nodded. He still had a bandage across the bridge of his nose and purple rings under both his eyes, but he had recovered from Zhai's previous attack nicely. "Yep—in the trunk. Shovels, a pickax, some rope, flashlights—everything you asked for."

Raphael nodded. "We have to be careful, guys. These Obie dudes are dead serious. We get in, get the treasure, and get out as fast as we can. No joking around. And if you have a cell phone, shut the ringer off. We're going ninja-style here—quietly."

"You think Zhai might show up again?" Benji asked. He looked worried.

"Yeah," Raphael said. "And some other guys might show up with him so keep your eyes open—stay alert. Whoever they hit first, shout so that everyone else knows we're under attack. Try to hold them off for a minute to give everybody else time to escape and then run like hell."

"You don't want us to try and regroup and fight them off?" asked Josh.

"Trust me, none of you guys can fight the Snakes," Raph replied. "Even I can't fight them. We've got to work as fast as we can. There's more snow moving in later tonight and we don't want to be out in it trying to dig."

"Where are you going to be?" Clarisse asked. Nass whirled around. He shouldn't have been surprised to see that she was still there. He glared at her. She added placatingly, "Just in case something goes wrong and I need to send someone to look for you."

Nass hesitated, suddenly uncomfortable about giving her any information, but before he could figure out what that was all about, Raphael answered her.

"In the woods, just southeast of the tunnel hill," Raph said. "We'll park the cars in that stand of old pines out on River Road and then hike in. Everybody ready? Let's roll."

Nass turned and pointed at Clarisse. "Stay here," he told her again. "I mean it, Clarisse."

"Yeah, yeah, mijo. I heard you."

"And how come you followed me out here when I told you to wait inside? How come you can't do anything I ask?"

Her smile was as enigmatic as it was beautiful. "I just can't stay away from you, baby," she said. Behind him, a car honked.

"Yo, Nass! You coming or what?" Josh shouted.

He gave her one last warning look and then jogged across the lot to the waiting car. As he got in, he looked back to see her standing alone under the streetlight, pulling her cell phone out of her pocket.

❧

Except for Zhai, the entire Toppers crew was gathered in the Banfield basement. Dax Avery and D'von Cunninham were playing pool, but the rest of the guys were slouched in the large, leather reclining couches in various poses of frustration.

"Man, I can't believe we lost," Michael grumbled.

"Shut the hell up," Rick barked. His eyes flicked from his wide receiver back to the cell phone sitting on the table in front of him.

The Middleburg Phoenixes had lost the state championship by twenty-one points. Rick had thrown three interceptions, Bran had fumbled twice, and the Cunninham brothers had allowed five sacks. They'd been humiliated in front of the whole town, and there was only one way Rick could think of to take out his anger. All they were waiting for now was the call from Clarisse.

"You sure your ringer is on?" Cle'von asked quietly.

"Of course it's on. I'm not retarded," Rick snapped. "Be patient."

His words plunged everyone into silence once again. When his phone rang at last, Rick looked at the caller ID and pressed the talk button.

"Hello?" It was Clarisse. Bran and the others all sat up, at full attention now.

"Hey," she said quietly. "They'll be in the woods by the tunnel hill, between the south and east tunnels in about twenty minutes. I'm at Rack 'Em. Swing by and pick me up. I'll wait for you out back. Don't worry. I'll make sure no one sees me."

"I'll be there," Rick told her. He ended the call and stood. "All right, boys," he said. "We're going to war."

Raphael knew something was wrong the minute the rose-colored stone came into view. Someone had dug it out of the ground and it sat a few yards away, the silver divining rod still protruding from it. A yellow backhoe was parked nearby, next to a massive mound of dirt.

"Aw, man. You think somebody got the treasure already?" Benji asked.

Raphael moved forward cautiously. "There's only one way to find out," he said.

He stopped at the edge of the hole, and the other Flatliners gathered around it with him, shining their flashlight beams down into a pit so deep they couldn't see the bottom. The Flatliners could have toiled all night with their shovels and they wouldn't have made this much headway. He had a sinking feeling in his gut. If the Snakes already had the treasure in their possession, that meant the Flatliners would have to take it from them. He looked at Nass, the question in his eyes.

"No, man—it's still here," Nass said as if he'd asked it aloud. Raphael scanned the woods again. No one was around but them. Whoever was digging here must have given up. Either that, or it was a trap.

Raphael looked at his comrades. "Benji, Beet, Josh, Emory," he said. "You guys keep watch in a twenty-yard perimeter around the pit. You see anyone, shout—but until then stay quiet, okay? We don't want anyone to know we're here if we can help it. Nass, grab the rope and help me tie it to that tree. You're going to spot me as I go down."

But Nass was shaking his head.

"What?" Raphael asked, slightly annoyed that his second-in-command was questioning his orders.

"If the Obies show up, it's going to get crazy," Nass told him. "You're the only one who might be able to fight them. If you're down in the hole, we don't stand a chance up here. Why don't I go down instead?"

That's what made Nass such a good lieutenant, Raph realized. He was always thinking.

"Right. Okay, you guys—hit the perimeter. Nass, you're going down."

The four sentries all strode outward from the pit and took their places, staring out into the forest, while Raphael and Nass tied the rope around the trunk of a stout maple tree. Rather than taking the end of it straight toward the pit, though, Raph headed for a smooth-barked birch tree that stood a few yards from the maple and passed the rope around it before helping Nass tie the end around his waist.

"Why'd you do that?" Nass asked.

"It'll act as a pulley," Raph said. "That way, lowering you down and pulling you up, I'm not taking your whole weight."

Nass gave Raph a thumbs-up. "Cool," he said.

Raphael took hold of the slack rope between the maple and the birch and pulled it taut. "Okay—now lean back slowly. Good."

Raphael started lowering Nass into the pit, deeper and deeper. Several times he thought Nass had to be close to the bottom, but he was still feeding out rope. Finally, when Raph's arms were aching and his hands stinging, the rope suddenly went slack.

"Okay, I'm here," Nass shouted, only his voice was so distant it sounded like it was coming from another galaxy.

℠

Dalton stared at the nachos on the table in front of her, but she couldn't eat a thing.

"So what are we doing?" Natalie asked. "Just sitting around here and waiting for them to get back from their stupid treasure hunt?"

Dalton was sitting with Natalie, Myka and Beth in a back booth at Rack 'Em. "That's what *I'm* doing," she said. Clarisse came in then and waved at them on her way to the ladies room. All the girls at Dalton's table exchanged looks. None of them really liked Clarisse, for Dalton's sake, but they tolerated her for Ignacio's.

"How can you just sit there so calmly while she's walking around breathing air?" asked Natalie resentfully.

"Believe me, it's not easy," Dalton said. "But anything else I do would only make it worse. Maybe she'll go back to Los Angeles soon—and stay there."

Clarisse came out a few minutes later, her hair neatly brushed and a fresh layer of gloss on her lips. Zipping up her jacket, she ambled over to their table. "Evening, ladies," she said with insincere, sugary sweetness.

"Hey," was the halfhearted response from Dalton and Beth. Myka and Natalie gave her the silent treatment.

"Well, okay then," Clarisse quipped. "I guess I won't be breaking any hearts if I blow this joint, right?"

When none of them replied to that, she snorted her cynical little laugh and walked away, heading for the back door. Dalton thought that was unusual. If she was going back to Nass's apartment, all she had to do was go out the front door, turn left, and walk a couple of blocks.

"What's wrong with this picture?" she wondered aloud.

"Huh?" Natalie said.

"Never mind." Dalton got up, went to the window, and eased the blinds a little to the side—just in time to see Clarisse getting into Rick Banfield's SUV.

"Oh, no, she didn't!" she exclaimed.

"What is it?" asked Myka.

"I don't know—but it's not good. Natalie—you got your cell?"

"Yeah. Right here."

"Okay—come with me. We've got to find Nass and Raph and the guys." A simple gut feeling told her she would find them faster if they followed Rick and Clarisse. They climbed in Lily Rose's old Woody and before they headed out, Dalton used Natalie's phone to try Aimee again, on the outside chance she would know what her brother was up to. It went straight to voice mail. She'd been trying to reach Aimee since their unfinished conversation about Orias kissing her, but Aimee hadn't answered or returned her calls.

"It's time," said Orias.

"I'm ready." Aimee was awake now, and incredibly refreshed. The amazing night she had spent with Orias, traveling through space and time, had awakened within her a world of new possibilities.

With each slip, she got stronger, more focused, and better able to control her ability. Although Orias stayed beside her, he touched her less and less, letting her find the triggers within herself. By the time they returned to Middleburg, shortly before dawn, he wasn't touching her at all. He'd last held her hand as they'd settled softly on the thick Persian carpet in his parlor.

He'd prepared a sandwich and some kind of fruit cup for her, and after she ate she had fallen, exhausted, into a deep sleep on his antique Victorian sofa. She had slept all day. She wondered vaguely if anyone had missed her at school and if her dad had even noticed she was gone, but those thoughts slipped away as fast as they had come. In one night, she'd seen so much. Everything from her old life seemed trivial.

Now it was night again. Time to do Orias's little errand. And then he would show her how to use the Wheel to slip backward, into the past, and find her mother.

She was wearing the same clothes she'd worn to dinner with Orias and her father just last night (it seemed so long ago), and Orias was buttoning her coat. A sudden recollection of how he'd helped her get ready for that bizarre party in Manhattan, his fingers curled in her hair, and how he'd knelt before her and painted her toenails, filled her with a warm rush that made her a little dizzy. She reached out to him.

"Steady now," he said. "Not yet."

She moved to the window and looked out on the street, feeling suddenly shy with him. There was something else bothering her too, but she couldn't quite remember what it was. Her thoughts felt pleasantly soft but tangled, like a jumbled ball of yarn. Since the past seemed to be eluding her, she decided to focus on the journey ahead.

"What if someone sees us?" she asked. "I mean, it didn't matter in New York or those other places where no one knows us, but here in Middleburg—I don't think we want people to see us appearing or vanishing right in front of them."

Orias's laugh was short, cynical. "They'll assume their eyes are playing tricks on them, or think they must've looked away just as we left or arrived. They will assume any number of things—but not that we are travelers, dropping through the fabric of materiality. Never underestimate a human being's ability to turn the incredible into the ordinary, Aimee. Humans witness miracles every day—and then proceed immediately to explain them away. But not you—not anymore. You are becoming one of the enlightened ones. It will change you . . . forever."

It already has, she thought. *I'm stronger, calmer, more peaceful now, more . . . in tune with things.* And she suddenly knew: she was ready. Ready to do Orias's errand, ready to find her mother. "Let's do it," she said.

He smiled and looked at her with that same longing she'd come to recognize and respond to, but he still didn't touch her.

"Okay," he said and she basked in the approval she saw in his eyes. "You know the mountain the tunnels run through?"

Aimee nodded.

"There's a beautiful clearing at its peak," he said. "Close your eyes and picture it. It's completely silent now, washed in moonlight, covered in snow. Can you see it?" She nodded and he went on. "At the center of that clearing there's a smooth, flat slab of rose-colored stone. There's no snow on it; it's the only thing up there that's bare. I want you to take us there."

She looked up at him. "And then you'll tell me what it is I'm supposed to get for you?"

"You'll know soon enough," he said patiently. "Now, close your eyes. When you feel it, take us there."

She put her hand in his and closed her eyes again, and suddenly they were soaring through an endless, sparkling, silver tube filled with a brilliant luminescence. When they stopped, they were standing in the very spot Orias had described to her, with the sparse lights of Middleburg twinkling in the distance below them as a few gentle snowflakes started to fall.

Orias was looking at her with wonder. "I never imagined you would be like this," he said quietly. "So beautiful. So vibrant. I knew you would be powerful, but I never imagined . . . I never *thought* I would find someone like you. Someone who could rule beside me. Someone who could be my equal."

And, at last, he kissed her, and she thought her soul would drown in the bliss. When he opened his eyes and looked at her again, she was stunned at the deep emotion she saw there.

"One more slip, and it's done," he said. "But this time, you must travel alone."

଼

Zhai and Kate sat next to one another on the floor of the old factory, chained to a piece of machinery near the only source of heat in the place—a huge old furnace that, Zhai assumed, was once used as a part of the manufacturing process. At first, they had been left in a distant, frigid corner, but Kate had complained and, after some discussion, the Snakes had decided to move them closer to the heat.

"We don't want our slaves getting pneumonia," the shorter one had said to Zhai as he led them across the floor and rechained them to a piece of heavy machinery near the furnace. "Especially this pretty one," he added, leering at Kate. "She'll be even more useful than you."

Once they were both secure, he'd gone into a glass-walled room on the far side of the factory that, Zhai guessed, had originally been the foreman's office.

Kate had dozed beside him, off and on through the night. They sat there all the next day, too, through a breakfast of cold rice and overcooked vegetables. Sometimes, he and Kate would chat, but more often there was an easy silence between them as they sat shoulder-to-shoulder in the warm firelight. As much as he wished Kate were somewhere else—somewhere safe—he found her presence comforting.

The two Snakes were standing in the foreman's office now, staring at what Zhai thought was a map—or a section of scroll, perhaps—laid out on the table, while their workers sat in chairs that lined the wall, waiting for further instructions. From the few conversations he'd overheard, Zhai had surmised that they were waiting for a shipment of more powerful explosives to arrive.

He had given up trying to think of an escape plan; it was futile. The chains and padlocks were unbreakable, the machine they were chained to was unmovable, the shackles around their wrists were too tight to slip out of—and even if they had somehow managed it, the Snakes kept them under constant surveillance through the glass wall. There was only one way they might be able to get away, Zhai thought, and he wasn't sure he could do it. If he could get centered, if he could focus his energy, perhaps he could use Shen to break the manacles. But each time he tried, his mind went all fuzzy, like a radio picking up nothing but white noise, and the marks on his hands ached. Somehow, he guessed, the spell that made him a slave to the Order was also blocking his ability to harness Shen.

He turned to Kate. "I don't know how I got you into all this," he said, "but I'm going to get us out of here, I swear. I just have to figure out how."

Kate was staring thoughtfully into the fire. "Are you sure it's the marks on your hands allowin' them to control you?" she asked.

"Yeah, I'm sure. Why?"

She pulled her eyes away from the dancing flames and looked at him, hesitating for a second before she spoke, as if she didn't want to say what was on her mind. "When Raphael was chained to that burning train car, the hot metal touched his wrist and left a scar."

Zhai nodded. "Yeah . . . "

"If he'd had a tattoo on his wrist, it would have been ruined," she finished, and she looked back at the fire. Now, Zhai finally understood what she was saying, and why she hadn't been eager to say it. He might be able to burn the marks off his hands—but it would be incredibly painful, and it might not even work.

He followed her gaze to the furnace. Behind a door with heavy, iron bars across its face, the fire raged, its flames lashing against the metal. The door had to be hot, there was no question about that. But would it be hot enough to destroy the tattoo?—or just hot enough to cause him a lot of pain?

Either way, Zhai decided, he had to try.

With a wary glance at the foreman's office, he inched closer to the furnace, but Kate grabbed his hand.

"Wait," she said. "Maybe it's a bad idea."

"No," Zhai replied, resigned. "It's a good idea." He looked down at her hand in his and couldn't repress a nervous smile. She smiled back at him, looking truly stunning in the firelight. If only they were in a mountain cabin someplace, or in her little train car, Zhai thought wistfully, instead of chained up in a dingy old factory. He squeezed her hand, steeling himself for what had to be done. Then he quickly crawled forward and pressed the back of his right hand against the furnace door.

For a second, he felt nothing—the door even felt cool against his skin—then a sudden stinging ignited all the nerves in his hand at once. Still, he kept it pressed to the door. He was trembling now, forehead drenched with sweat. The pain ebbed for a second, then came back tenfold, as if a million wasps were attacking him at once. The world went blurry as his eyes teared up, and he felt suddenly sick as he caught the odor of his own burning flesh. A tendril of black smoke went up from his hand, and there was sound like bacon sizzling in a skillet. Finally, he couldn't take it any more and jerked his hand away, falling back onto the concrete. It was cool against his back and he instinctively pressed his hand against it, his mouth gaping in a silent scream. Kate was there, running her hands through his hair.

"Zhai! I'm sorry," she whispered, distraught. "Aw, lad—I shouldn't have said a word. Not a word." He was hurting too much to answer.

Finally, he'd recovered enough to turn his hand over and look at it.

There were three parallel, crimson gaps in his flesh, each one singed black at the edges. But, he thought with a sense of wild hope, it had worked: the mark was hardly visible now. He was about to repeat the process with the other hand when he heard footsteps and looked toward the office. The two Snakes were approaching.

"On your feet," the taller one said.

"What's going on?" Zhai asked, not really expecting an answer.

"A disturbance at the site," the shorter Snake replied. As he unchained Zhai and Kate from the machine, Zhai hid his mutilated hand, covering it with his uninjured one.

"Time for you to earn your keep," the short Snake said to Zhai as he hustled him and Kate toward the door.

Maybe they can't control me with only one mark, Zhai hoped. *I guess I'll find out soon enough.*

✑

Maggie sat staring at the red-and-white-checked tablecloth in Rosa's Trattoria, sipping the last of her Diet Coke and waiting for the dinner she'd ordered for herself and her mother. Even though it was late for dinner, her mom was back in the groove of working on her tapestry, and Maggie was once again subject to her strange whims.

She sighed as she lifted her eyes from the table and gazed out into the night. It was bitter cold outside and snowing lightly, but the wind had abated, leaving Middleburg in an eerie state of suspension. She replayed the events of the evening before and how, after all the excitement, she had kissed Raphael goodnight—and he hadn't resisted. And he'd said he was going to break up with Aimee.

In spite of all the bizarre things that had happened, hanging out with him had been awesome. Maggie took refuge in the fact that, with Raphael in her life now (sort of) and with her new power, she didn't have to be afraid of Rick anymore. And once she figured out a way to keep her mom safe from him, she would dump him like he deserved to be dumped. She was so deep in thought she didn't notice Anne Pembrook sitting nearby with Master Chin until she rose and walked over.

"We need to talk to you," said the teacher, and Maggie jumped. "Sorry," she added. "I didn't mean to startle you. Come have dinner with us."

"Oh—no thanks," Maggie said. "I just ordered takeout. But I can sit for a few minutes." She followed Miss Pembrook back to her table where Chin was waiting. As soon as they sat down, Chin gazed calmly at her. He cleared his throat and then spoke:

"A princess who ne'er has lain with a man,
From exile she shall return,
Like the great queen before her
She walks with the winds,
Transcending the bonds of the earth,
As a diver through water, she will pass through the stone,
For no matter or magic may bind her
The heart of the Wheel she shall pierce with her steps
To retrieve its celestial fire.

"Do you remember those words?" he asked.

"Some of them," Maggie said. "They're from the scroll."

Anne leaned across the table toward her. "Maggie, Chin thinks they were written about you."

Maggie's eyes widened. "Me?"

"It refers to a princess, the daughter of a queen," Chin explained. "And you were just crowned harvest queen—or homecoming queen, rather—by your mother, who wore the crown three times. The scroll alludes to this princess having magical powers, which we know you do. Also, there was a portrait in one of your mother's tapestries, of a blond princess wearing a crown. I think that's you."

Maggie could see the similarities but what bothered her was the "ne'er lain with a man" part. She had a pretty good idea what that meant and although she wasn't sure if the things she and Rick had done out at Macomb Lake really fell into that category, it didn't exactly make her pure and untouched. Still, the way Chin and the teacher were looking at her, it was pretty clear they thought she was the one.

"So what if the scroll *is* talking about me?" she asked. "What does it mean?"

"It means that someone—or something—is going to use you to retrieve a very special, sacred object," Chin said. "But—and this is very important, Maggie. No matter what happens, that object is not to be disturbed. It must stay where it is. It contains a power that mortals are not yet ready to possess. If it were to fall into the wrong hands, it could mean the end—of everyone and everything."

Maggie nodded solemnly. Her life was getting weirder by the minute. "So what am I supposed to do?" she asked.

"I think it's best if you stay with us," Chin said. "Only the princess in the prophecy can pass through the enchanted seal and retrieve the treasure. If I'm right, then someone will try and force you to do it—tonight. We can make sure that doesn't happen."

"Okay," she said. "I can hang out with you guys after I take some food home to my mom and get her settled in for the night." Maggie was gratified at the relief in Chin's face.

Miss Pembrook smiled at her. "It's just for tonight," she said.

"I've translated a little more of the scroll," Chin said. "If it's right, the danger will diminish after tonight. But it may not be easy. There were other warnings too, and I fear we will fight more than one enemy before it's all over. There's great danger coming—especially for Raphael—but he's not answering his phone."

"Then I'm in," Maggie said. "I'll go and get my mom squared away. I can be back here in less than an hour."

Her takeout was ready then, and she grabbed the bag and waved to Mr. Chin and Miss Pembrook as she left. She had to get something from home and she had one more stop to make after that.

§

Raphael was staring down into the pit when the attack came.

"You sure there's no way to dig around it or smash it or anything?" he'd just called down to Nass.

"No," Nass called back, sounding like he was a thousand miles away. "It looks like a big slab of stone with some kind of hieroglyphics on it, and it's all scorched. Looks to me like someone tried to blow it up, but it's not even cracked."

Raphael stared down into the darkness for a moment—the hole was so deep he couldn't even see Nass's flashlight beam. That's when he heard the warning shout.

"Guys!" Beet yelled.

Raphael turned to see the Toppers thrashing through the woods, Rick and Bran leading the way. They immediately overpowered Beet and took him to the ground and then charged onward, leaving D'von and Dax to continue kicking Beet. Josh, Emory, and Benji abandoned their lookout posts and hurried to Raphael.

"It's not the Obies—it's the Toppers!" Josh growled. "What the hell are they doing here?"

Nass's voice sounded faintly from the depths. "Hey, guys—what's going on? Guys?" But no one answered him—and there was no time to pull him up so he could help fight off the Toppers either, Raphael thought. They were outnumbered.

Rick was in the lead, sprinting toward Raphael, who was ready for him, but Emory leaped forward at the last second and tried to tackle him. Raphael had never seen such ferocity from Emory—his difficult experiences lately had obviously made him stronger.

With Rick tied up, Bran was on Raphael in an instant, throwing barrage after barrage of furious punches. His swing was so wide that Raph blocked the strikes easily with a series of *Biu Saus*, but Bran's power was another issue. He drove Raphael back until he was teetering on the edge of the pit. Seeing that he had the advantage, Bran lunged forward and tried to shove Raphael into the hole—but Raphael was quicker. He sidestepped Bran and delivered a spinning backfist to the side of his head as he lurched past.

With his momentum disrupted, Raph was sure Bran would plummet into the pit—and he could kill Nass if he landed on top of him. But somehow, Bran managed to regain his balance and leap away from the hole. He tumbled to the ground on the other side, rolled to his feet, and turned back to Raphael, angrier than ever.

"You love to make a fool out of me, don't you?" he yelled. He was skirting the hole, heading for Raphael, but Raph moved in the same direction and kept the pit between them. When Bran reversed his direction, Raphael did too. He could see the little game of ring-around-the-rosy was infuriating Bran, and that was good. The angrier he got, the more likely he was to make a stupid mistake.

Raphael glanced over to see how his guys were doing. It wasn't good. Emory was on his hands and knees in the weeds, coughing, as Rick kicked him without mercy. Michael Ponder had Benji down in the dirt and was punching him—until Benji managed to jab him in the eye with a fingerstrike Raph had taught him. Josh was holding his own with Dax, but as Raphael watched, D'von ran over and pancaked him to the ground. Beet, his already injured nose bloodied once again, ran over to Rick and crashed into him, knocking him off Emory. Rick recovered quickly, picked Beet up, and slammed him to the earth.

Snow was falling again, coming down faster by the second, so Raph's view of his comrades was almost obscured by white. This much snow in November wasn't just unusual, Raph thought with a growing sense of dread—it was unnatural. Like the lightning storm that had happened on Halloween night.

Bran charged around the hole again, his fury reaching a boiling point, but Raph darted away from him. It was almost time for Raph to make his move. But before he could complete another circuit, Cle'von came stampeding through the blizzard toward him, and with Bran sprinting toward him from the other direction, he was no longer able to run.

Raphael backed up slowly. Between Bran's temper and Cle'von's size, he was in kind of an awkward situation. Then, another figure appeared through the veil of falling snow.

Rick.

"What's up, Flats rat?" he taunted, taking his place between Bran and Cle'von. "I've been waiting a long time for this."

And all three of them charged Raphael at once.

CHAPTER 28

"THERE IS A HUGE UNDERGROUND CHAMBER beneath this mountain," Orias explained to Aimee. "Envision yourself slipping through the mountain, past the train tracks, through the earth itself, and then on into the chamber. It's a perfect cube, a mile in each direction, and its walls are made of rose quartz and carved with elaborate symbols no living mortal can read—the celestial tongue. Because of those carvings, the chamber is sealed. The only one who can pass through it is you."

Aimee opened her mouth to ask why she had to be the one, but Orias continued. "Close your eyes. See yourself slipping down through the earth, through the wall, through the energy barrier, and into the chamber. Don't be afraid. If you need me, just talk to me. I'll be able to hear you. Once inside, you'll move to the exact center. You will find the treasure there. Don't worry," he added in answer to her unspoken question. "You'll know it when you see it. Go now, Aimee. Time is short."

He kissed her gently on the lips and then stepped back.

Quickly, before tension had a chance to creep all the way up her spine, she closed her eyes, made herself relax, and focused her energy. The next thing she knew, she was traveling. When she stopped falling and opened her eyes, she was in total darkness. She pressed her back against the cool stone of the wall behind her and gradually, her eyes adjusted. She could see a faint, blue illumination bleeding through the tangle of looming shadows before her.

"Okay, I'm here," she said aloud and Orias answered her inside her head.

Good. Tell me what you see.

"The chamber—it's just like you described it. The wall behind me and the floor where I'm standing now are carved out of some kind of pink stone—that must be the rose quartz."

Perfect. Do you see anything on the quartz?

"Yeah . . . it's covered with hieroglyphs."

Look up. Can you see the ceiling?

"No—I guess it's too far up. What is this place?"

The chamber was filled with hundreds of impossibly large gears—some of them had to be several stories tall and all were carved out of some kind of dark stone. They crowded the room from the floor to the ceiling—or until they were lost in the darkness above.

She'd read a couple of steampunk books while she was in Montana, and that's what this reminded her of—a crazy scene out of a steampunk story. But this was *her* story, she reminded herself, and she wasn't in some outlandish fairy tale place. This was Middleburg. Why in heaven's name was something like this buried beneath their ordinary little town?

Nothing about Middleburg is ordinary, Orias assured her.

"So what is all this stuff?" she asked.

Don't you know?

And then, she did. There was only one explanation for all the machinery. It had to be the mechanism that operated the Wheel of Illusion. The thought filled her with awe.

That's right, Orias said. *The treasure is the wheel's power source.*

"But if I take the Wheel's power source, how can I use it to find my mom?"

Don't worry. It contains all the power of the Wheel, and then some. With the treasure, you can travel without the Wheel, anywhere in the universe, anywhere in the future, the present or the past. But you have to hurry!

By then her eyes had adjusted and she moved away from the wall and walked forward, through the labyrinth of gears and switches, chains and pulleys.

Remember, what you're looking for is in the center of the chamber.

"I know—I'm going there now," she responded.

Although the maze of stone gears looked ancient, there was not a speck of dust on them or a spider web anywhere. The longer she walked, gaping up at the gigantic mechanisms suspended overhead, the more she got the feeling that she'd somehow been shrunken down to the size of a dust mite and had wandered inside somebody's wristwatch. The whole idea gave her an odd, jittery sense of vertigo that made her pick up her pace. The place was also filled with a strange vibrating, pulsing energy that Aimee found unsettling. The silence was so thick she could almost swim through it—but it was more than silence. There was substance to it as well. And then she heard a single, barely audible note that sang out endlessly until everything around her seemed to tremble with its resonance.

She moved between the teeth of a massive gear, through a gap almost the size of a garage door, and that's when she saw it:

Formless, wrapped in seething shadow, its teeth like sabers and its eyes like burning coals, it was waiting for her. She had seen Tyler impaled on those teeth; now, it was her turn. The Middleburg monster opened its great mouth, reared up until its head was twenty feet above her, and hissed.

Aimee, run! Orias shouted in her mind—but she was already moving.

She backed out the doorway as the creature's jaws snapped shut in front of her, then she turned and ran parallel to the huge gear she'd just passed through. On the other side of it, she could hear the legs of the beast scratching their way across the stone floor.

You are not worthy of this great treasure, Aimee Banfield, it hissed in her mind.

"Maybe not," she shot back as she ran. "But I'm going to get it anyway and no crappy shadow creature is going to stop me! My *mother* is waiting for me!"

She will be waiting forever, the monster whispered. *Flee now, or we shall bleed you to a husk.*

Aimee, are you okay? What's going on? Orias asked.

"Not now!" she yelled. "I need to focus!"

The edge of the gear she was running next to was just ahead, and as she approached, the creature swung around it with a blood-chilling roar.

Aimee skidded to a halt. She turned to run back the other way and then stopped dead. There were two more red eyes, coming toward her. Another monster. There were two of them, and there was nowhere to run. Fighting panic, she looked around and spied a gold lever sticking out of the floor. Next to it, a massive chain with gigantic links ran from a hole in the floor upward, into the blackness above.

She had no idea what the lever might do, but instinct and adrenaline told her to grab it and pull. Instantly, the entire room groaned around her and, with a shuddering rumble, the machinery began to move. The chain next to her started traveling upward, moving from its hole in the floor toward the ceiling. She grabbed it, passing her arm through one of the huge links. The chain jerked her upward and she looked down to see the two shadow-worm beasts almost collide with one another as they rushed to the chain and leaped upward, snapping at her toes as she rose out of their reach.

She was suddenly thirty feet from the floor and rising fast. If she fell, she would die from the impact, even if the monsters didn't get her. Carefully, she slipped her leg through the chain link directly below her, which made her feel a little safer. But where was the chain taking her, and how would she get off of it?

The massive clockwork clattered and clacked and whirred and groaned around her, and the clamor was deafening. Above, she spied what looked like a catwalk, and she was speeding toward it.

Jump. Orias's voice, inside her head. *Don't think—just do it.*

And just as she reached the catwalk, she did. It was almost a deadly decision. Her hands slipped off the top rail, and she barely managed to snag the lower one with one hand and the crook of her other elbow, leaving her legs dangling like bait for the giant snake-worm monsters below. Grunting with effort, she pulled herself up and clambered over the top rail. She landed on the catwalk on her hands and knees and paused a moment to catch her breath. Then she glanced up at the chain again. A few yards above the catwalk, it disappeared into a small hole in the ceiling. If she'd still been holding on to it, she'd have been knocked off—and down into one of the gaping mouths below.

Shaking off the grisly thought, she rose to her feet and jogged down the catwalk. It was made of what appeared to be bronze, and it clanged with every step she took—but unfortunately, she saw, it wouldn't take her where she needed to go. From up here, she could tell that the blue light that had illuminated her way was coming roughly from the chamber's center, but the catwalk cut diagonally from one side of the cube to the other. It didn't go anywhere near the center.

How would she get down? There didn't seem to be any ladders or stairs. And once she was down, how would she get to the center without becoming dinner for the shadow monsters?

Slip to the center, Aimee. Orias again. Of course. The solution was absurdly simple. All she had to do was teleport.

"Oh, yeah—right. Okay, here goes."

She stared toward the source of the light (she couldn't see it directly; several churning gears blocked her view). She closed her eyes and slipped, and suddenly the light was before her, maybe a hundred yards away. It was small and round, suspended in midair like a captured star, and it glowed so brightly she couldn't look directly at it.

Aimee laughed, triumphant, and started toward it, but one of the monsters suddenly reared up in front of her with a vicious hiss, plunging her into shadow. Another one rose up on her right and another on her left. She glanced over her shoulder and—yep—there was one behind her, too. She was surrounded. They circled her, their hissing turning into eager roars, as if they were already savoring their victory.

But this time, Aimee wasn't scared. She assumed the kung fu ready position, as if she would fight all four of them at once. "All right, you wormy bastards," she said. "Come and get me." And she could have sworn she heard Orias chuckle.

As the first one shot toward her, she slipped to another spot. "Hey, you looking for me?" she called. She was twenty yards away from the four beasts now, outside of their circle. They hissed furiously, all of them turning and lurching toward her at once. She glanced to her left and saw two large gears whirring together near the floor. She slipped again—just a blink this time—and reached the grinding gears.

"Here, wormy-wormy!" she called, and they turned again, all of them charging toward her. Closer . . . closer . . . so close she could smell them. They gave off the foul, musty odor of rot and decay. Closer now, their fangs bared, they shrieked in triumph. She let them get just a little closer before she slipped again.

From a safe distance, she watched as the first and second monsters shot between the whirring teeth. She heard twin shrieks of pain as the gears ground them up like pieces of lumber hacked by a giant buzz saw. Flimsy tatters of shadowy, scaly skin fluttered into the air for a second or two before they disappeared completely. The other two monsters stopped short of self-destruction and turned back toward Aimee—but they were too late.

It was so easy now—almost as easy as walking or breathing. She slipped from the ground up to the altar.

The glowing blue object was suspended, and now it was directly above her—a spinning, glittering ball of blue-white radiance—and as it spun, it emitted one perfect note.

Oooooooooooooooo . . .

And she wanted with all her soul to open her mouth and sing with it, to be a part of it. But the worm thingies were coming fast, and she had to slip again, but just a fraction, to where that perfect, radiant ball of light hung. This time she popped out of the atmosphere at eye level with the shining blue light—and once she was close to it, she could see that its source was a perfect blue-white circle, a ring, about a foot across. She was hanging in midair, right in front of it and she knew she had to act fast, before she fell.

For an instant, she believed it would burn if she touched it. Maybe it would even disintegrate her, turn her into ash or something. She knew that this thing, whatever it was, was powerful enough to destroy her if that's what it wanted.

But she reached out and grabbed it anyway.

It held her aloft, as if she were standing on a cloud of air. Then it gently lowered her back to the altar. As her feet touched the stone, she studied the treasure. It was a ring, made of some sort of perfect, flawless crystal, and it still glowed so brightly Aimee could hardly look at it.

The two remaining giant worms were coiling and uncoiling and she knew they were getting ready to charge her again but she was no longer afraid of them. The light from the ring was inside her now, inside her mind, filling her soul, her thoughts. It was a glorious illumination that would allow no fear.

The monsters sped closer, and when they rose up before her, their fangs dripping thick, smelly venom, she looked at them and said one simple word.

"No."

The single word reverberated through the entire chamber; even the massive clockwork seemed to slow down for a second. The crystal ring pulsed in her hands, the blue light cycling fast around its circumference. And then, before her astonished eyes, the shadow beasts exploded—both of them. But instead of blasting into fleshy bits and pieces, they exploded into nothingness. There was no debris, no fire, no heat. They simply ceased to exist.

"Sweet," Aimee said quietly.

And Orias responded. *And that, my darling, is how you conquer your demons. Now—bring it to me.*

As she stepped away from the altar, the huge gears around her all chugged to a halt, and she understood immediately that Orias was right; the beautiful object she was holding had to be their power source.

But what *was* it, she wondered. And if it could run the Wheel of Illusion, what else could it do?

∞

Chin pulled his truck over to the shoulder of the road and slumped toward the steering wheel, panting.

"Chin?" Anne asked. "Are you okay?"

There was a sheen of sweat on his forehead, and his eyes were squeezed shut as if he was in pain. "The Wheel has stopped," he whispered, his words barely audible.

"What?" asked Maggie, who was sitting between Chin and the teacher, her backpack on her lap.

Anne reached over and touched his arm.

Chin straightened up and looked at Maggie. "I was wrong," he muttered. "The girl in the tapestry—it's not you. We've made a terrible mistake."

He hit the gas and cranked the steering wheel around. Kicking up a rooster-tail of snow, the old truck made a U turn and shot back up the road, toward town.

∞

Aimee reappeared on the summit of the tunnel mound, right in front of Orias. During her time in the chamber, the snow had started coming down more intensely. The sky was almost solid white with churning snowflakes.

"You did it!" he said, his pleasure unmistakable. "Here, give it to me."

"Not until you tell me what it is and what it's for," Aimee said, backing away.

She saw a hard glint in his eyes—anger, maybe, or impatience—but it was gone in an instant, and he nodded.

"Very well," he agreed quietly, his gaze boring into hers. There was a strange, disquieting light in his eyes. "With the treasure, I can pierce the veil, which will throw open the door to the Dark Territory."

"Okay—and what will that do?" she persisted.

Orias didn't answer. There was a flash of lightning, and in its harsh glare, Aimee saw an army stretched out behind him. Each dark tree seemed to become a hideous soldier in a vast militia. Wearing heavy black armor, they brandished strange weapons and held their red banners aloft. Just as quickly as the flash came it was gone and the trees were merely trees again. But Aimee knew what she'd seen was real. And she remembered the half-buried tank in the horrible, barren desert Middleburg had become when she and . . . *someone* . . . had used the Wheel to go there. A wasted, war-torn, devastated Middleburg . . .

"No," Aimee whispered. "Orias—you can't."

"I can and I will."

"But why?"

"You haven't figured it out yet? Middleburg is where it all began for me. Where I was conceived. Where my damnation was created and sealed for all time. So I will destroy it . . . I will bring it down and bury my father beneath this miserable place for all eternity. And I will have all his power, and I will reign over all his holdings."

"I won't do it," she said, holding the ring further away from him. "I won't be part of it."

"Aimee—don't you understand? The world will be ours. And if you choose me, you will rule beside me. And we will travel . . . oh, how we'll travel . . . anywhere in the world—in the universe—that you want to go."

"I'm not choosing anyone," she said, stepping away from him. "Not until I get my mom back—and I'm starting to think I could probably figure that out on my own. But this—what you're planning. How do you know it will stop at Middleburg? How do you know it won't destroy the world?"

His laughter was bitter and full of contempt. "This world is already destroyed. Look at the pain, the misery, the injustice, the greed. It's a world of bitter lessons, abandoned by the All. But you and I, we can make it a paradise again. And even if it were to be destroyed, with the ring, time is our playground. We'd have years—eons—to play and love and slip. Come with me, Aimee. *Choose me.* Do this one last thing for me, and I'll make you a queen. The world will be yours."

"I don't want the world," she said. "I want—" but she stopped. She couldn't name what she wanted. She couldn't remember the name. "I want to help you, like I promised. You know—to find that loophole we were talking about. To save your soul."

The hand that gripped the ring fell to his side.

"You would do that for me?" he asked, a heartbreaking vulnerability in his eyes. "You'll stay with me until I find salvation?"

"Yes," she said. "But you can't destroy Middleburg, Orias—or anything else. That will only make everything worse."

"So you're choosing me, then?"

She sighed. She didn't know exactly what that meant, but if it would stop him from going through with his plan to destroy Middleburg, she would let him think so.

"Yeah," she said. "I guess I am. I'm choosing you." She held the ring out to him.

"Damn my mortal heart," he whispered softly. He took a deep breath, as he took the ring from her hands. "Come, then," he said. "Let's go home."

He took her hand as if preparing to slip with her and then he stopped, lifting his face as if sniffing the air. He was looking down, in the direction of Middleburg but the blizzard obscured the view.

"They're coming for the treasure," he murmured. "Slaves of the Snake. I shall enjoy destroying them." He took her hand and led her down the wooded hillside. "You're mine now, Aimee," he said. "And so is the ring, to use as I see fit. But I swear to you: as long as you stay with me, Middleburg—and the world—will be safe."

The crystal band pulsed again, as if sealing their union.

☙

Raphael stood perfectly still as Cle'von, Bran, and Rick attacked. Cle'von was so big, he crowded the other two out and Raph knew he would have to defend himself against Cle'von's attack first.

His mind took a backseat, merely watching as his body performed the necessary movements. First two blocks, then switching hands with a *Chun Sau*, now grabbing his forearm with a *Lap Sau* and pulling Cle'von forward, off balance. Now trap the arm, twist the hips and—snap—break the arm. With a cry of anguish Cle'von fell to his knees, clutching his elbow.

When Bran saw that, he pulled up in fear, but Rick barreled forward. Raph blocked his punches, *Pak Sau, Tan Sau* and then slipped to the outside with a *Lau Sau*, peppering Rick with three quick punches before he could step out of range. Raph didn't give him time to regroup. He shot forward, blocked Rick's arm and cracked him right in the forehead with an elbow. Dazed, Rick fell on his back in the snow. Bran hesitated a second longer and then stampeded, but Raph was in his groove now. Bran leaned forward, overextending in his attack. Raph simply sidestepped and hit him with a palm-strike in the back of his head, causing him to slam into the snow with his arms spread out like a face-down snow angel. He didn't move, and Raph knew he had to be knocked out.

Cle'von was rolling on the ground, holding his arm and crying like a little girl, and Rick lay on his back, still dazed. *Not bad work*, Raphael thought.

He turned to see how his crew was doing, but the snow was falling so fast there was zero visibility. Crunching through the deepening drifts, he looked to his left, then his right.

"Guys?" he called, but a sudden gust of wind swallowed his words.

Then he saw someone moving toward him through the blizzard. The man was wearing a blue robe, so pale it was almost white.

Come on!

Raphael heard it clearly, but he wasn't sure if the man was shouting at him or if the words were coming from inside his own head. He hesitated only for an instant and then plowed forward into the blasting wind. He'd gone perhaps a dozen yards before he could get a good look at the man. He knew him immediately—long black hair, narrow, cunning eyes and sharp black nails. It was the Magician.

"Hurry!" the Magician shouted before he turned and plunged forward again. Raphael struggled to keep up. He heard footfalls and shouts as people followed him through the snow—either his friends or the Toppers, he didn't know which and didn't care.

"Where are we going?" Raph yelled, barely able to hear his own voice in the wind.

Your si-dai needs your aid. The treasure has been stolen. Your moment of testing approaches. Run!

Raphael's si-dai—his spiritual brother—was Zhai. Aside from that, he had no idea what the magician was talking about. But he knew it was urgent, and he flung himself headlong into the blinding storm.

ॐ

The two Snakes had been dragging Zhai and Kate through the woods for about ten minutes. As far as Zhai could tell, they were nearing the entrance to the West Tunnel, but it was difficult to tell with the snow coming down so hard and fast. Kate had stumbled and fallen twice, and for a while, Zhai tried to slow his pace to make it a little easier for her, but as soon as they noticed, the taller Snake pulled one of his long knives from of his jacket, spun it and pressed it to Kate's throat.

"You play games with us, slave? Any more games, I cut her pretty little neck open." He looked at Kate and barked, "Keep up."

The blade retracted and he whipped the knife back inside his coat and pressed on; Zhai gave Kate an apologetic glance and followed. Soon the woods gave way to a clearing. Zhai tripped on something and looked down to see that he was standing on one rail of the train tracks. They were near the tunnels, just as he thought.

Here, both Snakes stopped. As Zhai watched, Tall Snake pressed the palms of both hands over his eyes and the marks on his hands began glowing. Short Snake turned to Zhai.

"Time to earn your keep, slave," he said. He clenched both his fists and pressed them together, and the marks on his hands began to glow. The mark on Zhai's left hand ignited with heat as it also started to glow— but the other hand, where he'd burned off the tattoo, didn't light up. So far, his captors hadn't noticed he'd destroyed some of their handiwork.

He felt control of his mind slipping away from him, but it wasn't the same as before. Now he could resist it. Suddenly, his left side went numb. It was a bizarre sensation, as if someone had painlessly chopped his body in half and thrown the left half away, and Zhai understood what it meant: the left half of his body belonged to the Snakes, but the right half was still his.

Short Snake removed Zhai's handcuffs and turned to his comrade, who lowered his hands from his face.

"What did you see?" Short Snake asked.

"The half-breed has the treasure," the other replied gravely. "I don't know how, but he has it."

"So, we take it from him."

"It won't be easy, now that he has its power to combine with his own."

"We must summon our lord," the short Snake said. "It is the only way."

His companion nodded. "Let's prepare our ambush. You and the slave on one side of the tracks, me on the other. And our lord will wait in the center."

Zhai glanced at Kate, trying to figure out how he could get her handcuffs off. He didn't see how he could get hold of the keys that Short Snake carried on a ring on his belt, especially with control over only half of his body.

When he looked back at his captors, they were facing each other, holding hands, their eyes closed. Their tattoos were glowing—but now the light was a deep burgundy, and it pulsed with malevolent power. A shudder went through both men at the same time and something changed. The air grew suddenly warmer, and there was a smell, as if someone had dredged the ancient muck from the bottom of some deep, dank cave.

A hissing sound pierced the wind, low and brief and frightening, but when Zhai looked around, he saw nothing but the falling snow.

Then, they were moving. Tall Snake headed to the woods on the far side of the tracks and Short Snake took his place on the near side. Zhai felt his body jerk and realized that the left side of his body was trying to move toward Kate. He stepped with his right foot, too, trying his best to keep both halves of his body in sync. For now, he knew, it would be better if the Snakes thought he was entirely under their control. His left hand grabbed the chain that ran between Kate's cuffs, and yanked her along, toward the ravine beside the tracks where Short Snake now crouched.

"Zhai?" Kate asked, worried. He knew she couldn't tell if he was himself or not, but he couldn't risk saying anything to her now.

"Hurry, slave!" Short Snake shouted.

And Zhai dragged Kate to the ravine. The Snakes didn't seem to notice his jerky movements as he tried to make the half of him that was under his control move smoothly with the half that was still enslaved. Their attention was focused completely on the West Tunnel.

Zhai had no idea what was going to be coming at them from that direction, but he had a feeling whatever it was, it would be deadly.

Still holding hands, Orias and Aimee crossed out of the woods and onto the snowy railroad tracks. The tunnel loomed ominously behind them and she tried not to look at it. Orias pulled her onward, away from the tunnel mound. The snow was falling so hard now that she couldn't see more than a few feet in front of her.

"Wait," Orias said, and he stopped walking. He held the crystal ring above his head and it lit up. A spark of light shot around its circumference, penetrating the falling snow like a giant searchlight and giving them greater visibility as they continued forward. Still, she didn't see their attackers until they were almost on them.

Two men wearing black overcoats and derby hats were standing near the tracks in front of them, one on the left and one on the right—and they both had two wickedly long knives each, which they twirled threateningly. A moment later, Zhai Shao appeared behind one of them, but somehow, he didn't seem like Zhai. His movements were strange . . . lurching . . . and something on the back of his left hand was glowing red.

"You're outnumbered, half-breed," the taller man told Orias as he moved moved slowly toward them. "Drop the treasure."

Orias laughed. "Says who? The mighty Order of the Black Snake—a bunch of petty demon worshippers?" He gripped the ring tighter and held it up in front of his chest. It flashed with power again, seething with bright blue-white energy just as it had inside the chamber. The two men hesitated, and in that moment, a blast of deep blue lightning shot from the disk, crackling through the air and sending them tumbling backward into a snow bank.

Aimee was glad to see Zhai still standing and unharmed, except that his body was strangely twisted and he seemed rooted in place. "Orias— wait," she said. "That's Zhai. He's a friend of mine—and he's no threat to you."

Orias looked at her, his expression guarded, and then he said, "For your sake, then—I hope that's true." He started to pull her onward, but the Snake men were already rising.

"Big mistake," the taller one snarled, his coat steaming from the heat of the blast and the snow it had melted.

Aimee heard a deep hiss and looked up. She couldn't see the beast that rose above them, perhaps thirty feet into the night sky. Only its outline was visible as the creature displaced the flurrying, drifting wall of white with its massive body. It was incredibly long, incredibly thick, and coiled in huge loops. There was a wide hood around its head. And then she saw it through the lashing snow. It was a giant black cobra.

Orias saw it too, and Aimee heard what he was thinking.

The god of the Black Snakes.

Orias released Aimee and held on to the ring with both hands, and the energy within it grew brighter. But it was too late—the cobra struck.

And suddenly Aimee was standing several yards away from the tracks, at the edge of the forest. It took her a second to realize what had happened: in her fear, she had automatically side-slipped. Flashes of blue lightning blasted across the snowy sky and she could see Orias over on the tracks, battling the massive snake.

A frightened voice came from behind her: "Help me—please!"

She whirled around to see a slight, pretty red-haired girl chained to a tree, her hands cuffed together. Aimee hurried to her. "What's going on?" she asked.

"I'd tell you if I knew," the girl said. "I have to help Zhai. I'm Kate—his friend. Can you get me free?"

Aimee looked at the handcuffs, which were made of steel and looked pretty solid. She glanced around for a big stone or something to smash them with, but everything was covered with snow. *But wait*, she thought. *I don't need to break the cuffs, do I?*

She took both Kate's hands.

"Close your eyes," she said. "This might feel weird, but it won't last long," Aimee warned. And before Kate could protest, they slipped. Half a second later, Kate stood next to the tree she had been chained to and they watched as the empty handcuffs fell to the ground.

"How did you—?" Kate began, but Aimee was already racing back toward the tracks, tugging Kate along with her. She had to help Orias. She knew it would be bad if the giant snake got a hold of the treasure.

At the tracks, a major battle was raging. Orias had levitated and was hovering ten feet above the earth, his legs trapped in the snake's coils. Each time the beast struck at him with its fangs, Orias managed to blast it with the treasure, which only seemed to stun it momentarily. Meanwhile, the two Snake men were trying to climb up its coils to slash at Orias with their knives—but each time they came near, Orias blasted them back into the snow.

As Aimee and Kate approached, the short Snake man turned angrily to Zhai.

"Slave, attack!" he shouted. Zhai lurched in place, but didn't move. The Snake grabbed his right hand and looked at the back of it. "I see." His eyes narrowed. "You have defaced your mark. Then you have ceased to be useful. Slave, kill yourself."

He threw one of his long knives to Zhai, who caught it in his left hand. Aimee was dumbfounded to see Zhai spin the knife expertly, and then plunged it toward his own chest.

"No!" Kate screamed, running to him. Just in time, she caught his arm and stopped him. He looked down into Kate's eyes, as if trying to take in the love and concern he saw there.

"You are useless!" the Snake man screamed. Zhai didn't see the blade flying out of the Snake's hand but Kate did, and she threw herself in front of it.

"Kate!" Zhai's agonized cry slashed through the wind.

Then Aimee saw it. Kate's coat was already dark with blood as she slumped into Zhai's arms. Her face was pale, her eyes unfocused.

"No!" Zhai shouted. "No!"

CHAPTER 29

MAGGIE CHARGED UP THE TRACKS through the storm, next to Mr. Chin, her backpack slung over one shoulder and bouncing against her hip. Anne Pembrook followed a few paces behind. Ahead, flashes of blue-white light sparked through the drifting flurries, and the shouts of combatants drifted on the wind.

With each step, the ghost crown grew heavier on her head, until she was certain that if she reached up and touched her forehead, she would feel its metal there beneath her fingers. With each flash of supernatural lightning it throbbed, and with each throb she felt another shot of adrenaline rush through her bloodstream. She felt energized enough to run two marathons back-to-back. She had no idea what waited ahead of her, but whatever it was, she was ready for it.

As they approached the fray, Maggie took in the sight as if there was nothing unnatural about it. Orias was hovering, somehow suspended, above the railroad tracks. Two men wearing old-style hats and brandishing daggers leaped up and slashed at him, but he was holding them off with shots of lightning from the glowing ring he held in his hands. They deflected the blasts with their daggers, but the force of Orias's attack was driving them back. And there was something else. The snow itself seemed to be attacking Orias, too. Or, she corrected, something displacing the snow—something shaped like a huge, coiled snake.

"I'll distract the Snake men!" Chin shouted to Maggie through the cutting wind. "Orias has the treasure—he cannot be allowed to keep it. You know what to do."

"What do you want me to do?" Anne shouted.

"Over there!" Chin pointed to where Aimee and Zhai were bending over Kate. "Go see if you can help them," he said, and then he turned to Maggie, concerned. "Are you ready?"

Her stance wide, Maggie could feel the solid presence of the railroad ties beneath her feet, and the ground beneath that, and the searing, swirling molten core of the earth below that. She felt the whisper of the snow and the humming of the wind. She felt the All, rising within her. And she felt the ghost crown on her brow, its energy circling insistently around her head.

"I'm ready," she said.

Master Chin ran with surprising speed toward Orias and his attackers. He hit the short Snake from behind with a flying kick, and knocked him face first into the snow. Chin snatched up the weapon he dropped and, dodging the sizzling, snapping blasts of lightning that Orias was aiming at the cobra and its followers, he charged the tall Snake with the dagger. They met in mid air, their spinning blades clashing together, a dervish of deadly steel.

"He's amazing," Anne whispered breathlessly, but Maggie paid no attention. The power of the universe was filling her, and it was about to erupt.

ॐ

As Raphael plunged ahead through a world of blinding whiteness, a ring of blue-white light burned ahead through the blizzard.

That is the treasure, the Magician whispered through the wind. *Take it.*

Raphael's legs pounded through the deep snow with renewed energy, but as much as he felt drawn to the prize ahead of him, he was also repelled by a mortal terror that infected every fiber of his soul.

If I touch it, I'll die, he thought with a horrifying certainty. *But if I don't get it, the whole world will die.*

He didn't know exactly how he knew this; the revelation seemed to come from everywhere—the snowflakes around him murmured it, the wind shouted it. Even the crunching snow beneath his feet grumbled out a warning.

He was at the tracks now and while his mind told him that what he was seeing could not be true, his soul knew it was. Master Chin, looking kind of battered, was fighting blade to blade with the two Obies. A little further in the distance, the Toppers and Flatliners were mobbed together pummeling each other. But what was really astonishing was the giant black cobra rising up in the center of the tracks—and it had Orias Morrow suspended in its monstrous coils. The snake-beast's hooded head was as big as a boxcar, and it swayed above them all, its fangs bared and dripping venom. And then Raphael saw someone else running toward Orias and the deadly cobra.

It was Aimee.

ಎ

Nass groaned in pain and frustration. Over and over again he'd tried to scale the walls of the pit, and each time he'd slid back down, his fingers raking painfully, uselessly, across the sheer walls of crumbling rock and earth. When he heard the fight starting above, he'd immediately tried to climb up the rope, but before he'd gone more than a dozen feet, it had either come untied or been cut and he'd fallen back to the bottom. He'd listened to the sounds of the battle above him, desperate to get to the surface and help his friends, but it had been impossible. He'd even turned his phone back on and tried to call for help, but it kept losing the signal. He was pretty sure he'd be stuck down here forever. Then, miraculously, it rang. He looked at his caller I.D.

"Natalie?" he asked, puzzled.

"No, it's me," Dalton said. "Where are you?"

"In a hole," he said. "Where are you?"

"At the Eastern Tunnel, near the tracks. You're breaking up a little, but I could swear you said you're in a hole."

ಎ 431 ಇ

"Yeah—and I'm close by. Take your ear away from the phone for a second. I'm gonna yell—see if you hear me." They heard him loud and clear, and in another few seconds, they were at the edge of the pit. He turned his flashlight on and off a couple of times to signal them. "You see any of the crew around?" he asked. "I need someone to pull me up."

"You got a rope?" Natalie called down.

"Yeah."

"Throw it up," she told him. "I'll get you out of there."

"Maybe you should get one of the guys," he suggested.

"Oh, give me a break," Natalie shot back. "Toss me up the rope."

Nass tried, but it was soon clear that it wasn't going to work. It was too light and the distance too great. If it was a baseball, he would have no problem lobbing it up there. That gave him an idea. He needed something to tie it to. He shone his light around the pit and found a half-buried stone—about the size of a baseball. With his bare hands, he dug it out of the dirt and then tied the rope to it.

"Stand back," he shouted when he had it ready. "It's coming up now."

The first time, the stone hit the wall and fell back down, almost beaning him in the face. The second time his throw wasn't powerful enough. It bounced off the edge of the pit and fell again. But on the third throw, all those years of baseball paid off.

"Got it!" Dalton called.

"Okay," he yelled back. "If you'll tie it to a tree, I can climb up—"

"I got you covered," Natalie shouted. "Jump on, and start climbing!"

Five minutes later, Nass was standing at the edge of the hole, looking down into it with contempt.

"Thanks, guys," he said. "How'd you know to come here?"

"You're not going to like it," Dalton said.

The knowing hit him in the gut, full force. "Clarisse?"

Dalton nodded. "I saw her get in Rick's car and we followed them. So what's going on? Where is everybody?"

A sudden flash of lightning ripped through the trees, coming from the far side of the tunnel mound. All three of them turned and looked in that direction. Nass didn't need the knowing to realize it wasn't normal lightning. Something major was happening; he could feel it.

"Let's go find out," he said, and together, the three of them set off toward the battle.

જ

Clarisse watched Dalton and Natalie pull Nass out of the pit, and then she followed them through the snowy woods to the edge of a clearing. What she saw there made her drop to her knees. She clung to the trunk of a pine tree, desperate to steady her shaking body.

"No," she whispered. "No, no, no..." but she couldn't tear her eyes away.

Strange people battled each other savagely, and in the weird flashes of light, she could see a huge, writhing snake. It couldn't possibly be real.

"No," she groaned again, and tears started running down her cheeks. She'd just wanted to teach 'Nacio a lesson, she thought. She'd just wanted to get the money she needed to pay Oscar S. But it was too late now. It was too late for everything. There could only be one explanation for what she as seeing: she was going insane.

જ

"Aimee!" Raphael called to her. Lightning flashed, and he looked over her head. Orias was grasping some kind of shining ring that was emitting a blue glow, and the closer Aimee got to it the bluer and brighter it became, as if it were emitting more and more energy. It looked like Orias was having trouble keeping a hold on it.

"Aimee!" Raph yelled again. He was standing on the tracks now. "Aimee—stop!"

And she did. She came to a complete stop and slowly turned to face him.

"Aimee?"

She stared at him, a strange, puzzled look on her face. Keeping his eyes on the giant snake, he hurried toward her. Behind her the snake lurched forward, its head hovering only a few feet above her. Raphael froze, terrified that any movement would cause the monster to strike.

"Aimee—listen to me," he said. "You've got to walk back to me, okay—slowly."

Her head was tilted and her eyes slightly narrowed, as if she were trying to place him.

"Come on," he begged. "It's me. Raphael."

And then Orias's voice cut through the storm. "Aimee!"

At the sound, Aimee smiled. She turned and started moving toward Orias again, unmindful of the snake that watched her hungrily, its massive head drifting along beside her as she walked.

She doesn't know me, Raphael thought. *She looked right at me, and she didn't recognize me.* And then he got it. *Somehow Orias, son of Oberon— some kind of dark, supernatural creature—had put a spell on her.* Raphael had to get her—and the treasure—away from him.

As Aimee halted near the lowest coil of the enormous snake, the glowing ring Orias was holding sparked brightly. It suddenly jerked out of his hand, spun straight up into the air and hung there for an instant like a sapphire moon, then started falling back down, heading for Aimee.

It landed directly in front of her, a bluish arc protruding from the snow at the center of the tracks. She looked down at it for a moment. Everyone stopped and looked at it. Orias quit struggling with the snake, the Obies lowered their weapons, the Toppers and Flatliners ceased their fighting.

Everyone froze, dreading what might happen next.

The cobra's head swayed and dipped above Aimee, its keen eyes locked on the treasure. Raphael held his breath.

Take it, the Magician whispered over his shoulder.

Take it, the universe urged.

Slowly, as if sleepwalking, Aimee stooped and reached for the crystal band.

In a blur, the cobra struck—and Raphael struck, too, launching himself over Aimee's head in a spectacular aerial kick. His heel caught the massive snake right between the eyes and knocked it backward before it could touch her. As he landed in front of Aimee, Raphael could see its coils relaxing, releasing Orias, who floated safely to the ground a few feet away. Aimee ran to Orias.

Take it! the magician screamed in his mind. The glowing ring was stuck in the snow at his feet, where Aimee had dropped it. Raphael reached down and grabbed it, clutching it to his chest. Immediately, it began vibrating so violently that the earth seemed to shudder beneath his feet. Trees quaked. The tracks trembled. Incredible crosscurrents of power slashed through him, scattering his thoughts on the wind.

The snake reared back to strike at him again, and he was vaguely aware of Maggie charging into the scene like a beautiful, modern-day Joan of Arc, heading fearlessly straight for the beast. As she ran, she was reaching into her backpack, which she tossed aside when she pulled out—*a crown*. The homecoming-queen crown.

so

As Maggie stood beside the tracks looking up at the horrific cobra beast, she'd had a strange moment of clarity. Only a few weeks ago, she had been a normal high-school cheerleader—worried about boys and clothes and being popular. Now, somehow, she was a warrior. And it was time to fight.

So she had pulled the homecoming queen's crown out of her backpack and put it on her head. She felt it merging with the ghost crown, and their combined heat entered her brain and coursed through her body, filling her with . . . *splendor*. That was the only word for it.

An invisible wave of it came up through her feet, down through her head, then out through her fingers, and when she saw the cobra's fangs descending toward Raphael, she raised her arms, pointed at the snake and said, "Stop!"

And the single clear, crystal stone in the center of the crown—*the real crown*—shot out a beam of pure, white light.

It flared into the huge, hideous, green-black snake like a detonating star and the ensuing explosion flung the beast away into the woods with a crackling electric charge, where it snapped tree trunks and branches with the force of its passage.

∽

When Maggie blasted the huge snake demon, Raphael hardly noticed.

Instead, his heart breaking, he stared at Aimee as she clung to Orias.

And then, he realized, something else was happening. The ground vibrated ferociously beneath Raphael's feet, and the rumble became deafening. A low, lonely-sounding whistle cut through the storm and he turned toward the sound, already knowing what he would see. A massive train, glowing a ghostly blue-white, sped out of the tunnel, toward him.

A phantom train.

"Raph, look out!" he heard Nass scream.

But he didn't move. He stood frozen in place as it bore down on him. It whistled again, the sound cutting through every atom of his body, a divine, eerie howl that made him shiver with excitement and . . . anticipation. The sound was pure Shen. It was the treasure. It was death, and life. It was unstoppable. It was the All.

Raphael felt himself smiling despite his terror as the train sped inexorably toward him.

∽

Nass watched in horror as the train struck his best friend.

In the instant it hit, there was an explosion—not a fiery one, but an explosion of energy—that sent a massive shockwave blasting outward from the point of impact. He felt like he was sitting on an atomic bomb as it exploded—the light, the heat, the roar of the blast were all too much to handle. One second he was experiencing everything at once, senses completely maxed out. And then there was nothing.

The next thing Nass knew, he was lying on his back in the snow, staring up at the sky as the last few snowflakes fluttered down. The silence was so profound that he thought for a second he'd lost his hearing. *I blacked out,* he thought. But how much time had passed? Minutes? Hours?

Then, he remembered Raphael.

He struggled quickly to his feet and, despite his dizziness, jogged over to where Raph had been standing when the train struck him. The knowing was flooding his mind now, overwhelming him with a fear and sadness he'd never experienced before.

"Raph! Hey, Raph!" he shouted. But there was no sign of him, or of the train. Nass glanced around, looking on both sides of the tracks to see if he'd been thrown into the woods. Nothing.

The trees that surrounded them, for a radius of about a hundred yards, had all been snapped by the blast and their remaining branches stripped bare.

"Raph!" he called out again, but there was no answer.

He looked down at his feet and he saw, scattered in the center of the tracks, the shards of the crystal ring. The blast—or something—had shattered it, and the light that had glowed within it was gone.

He knelt and picked up one of the pieces. It was still hot.

Dalton and Natalie were standing beside him, and the rest of the Flatliners joined them. One by one, they all stooped to examine the shattered ring, each of them picking up a shard, turning it over in their hands in wonder. For an instant, Nass thought he saw a wink of light within the piece he held, but it disappeared so fast he figured he must have imagined it.

The Toppers, who all seemed a little dazed, came walking up to stare at the empty space on the tracks where the train, and the cobra, had been.

First Bran picked up a crystal shard, then Dax, then Michael. The Cunningham brothers each took a piece too, and stuck it in their pockets.

It was strange, Nass thought, but it made sense, too. Even if it was broken now—who wouldn't want to have a piece of something so beautiful—a souvenir of something so amazing it was impossible to understand?

Only Rick seemed unconcerned. He sat on a snowdrift, absently staring at the slow-falling snow.

Suddenly Orias Morrow shoved his way into the little circle to stare down at the broken crystal ring.

"No." It was an agonized whisper. He grabbed a piece in each hand, looked at them a moment and then cast them back to earth. Aimee came up beside him and knelt to pick up a shard.

"Maybe we can fix it. . ." she suggested. He looked at her blankly and then he took her hand and walked away with her, into the swirling snow.

Slowly, Rick got up. "I'm outta here," he declared. The rest of the Toppers fell in behind him.

"Where we goin'?" Bran asked absently. "Spinnacle?"

"Nah, I gotta hook up with someone," Rick told him. "Someone who owes me big time. And believe me—I'm gonna collect."

As the Toppers disappeared up the tracks, Chin, with Anne Pembrook at his side, approached the little gathering, his expression somber. Just as the rest of them had done, he knelt and picked up a piece of the ring and gazed at it thoughtfully.

"What happened to the Obies?" asked Nass.

"Driven away by the Shen blast," Chin said. "We should leave, though, before they come back."

"But . . . where's Raph?" Benji asked.

Finally, someone had voiced the terrible question aloud. Nass looked immediately at Chin, desperately hoping for an answer, but the old man said nothing; he only glanced at the broken crystal shard in his hand, then slipped it absently into his pocket.

"Raphael?" Beet shouted, and some of the other Flatliners took up the call, looking around. Nass looked again at Master Chin, but the old man's expression was unreadable.

"Raph! Raphael!"

The only answer was a distant, mournful train whistle, fading away into the night.

Raphael Kain was gone.

෨

Kate was resting comfortably in Lily Rose's big old feather bed. Sitting up, in full control of the TV remote, she was happily channel surfing with the sound muted. Dalton sat on the bed beside her and Nass sat in a nearby chair. They dug into the plate of homemade cookies Dalton's grandma had just brought in.

"I'd offer you another one," Dalton said playfully to Nass. "But you've probably got to rush home so Clarisse won't get mad at you."

"Don't worry about that. Clarisse will have enough problems to deal with when my mom gets a hold of her," Nass said with a grin. "Miss Clarisse never came home last night and Amelia Torrez is pretty steamed, let me tell you. Anyway," he assured Dalton. "Clarisse is no longer a problem. You're my girl and that's that."

Dalton beamed at him. "Okay, then. I'll ask my grandma if you can have some milk, too."

As if on cue, Lily Rose stuck her head in the door. "You up for another visitor, honey bun?" she asked Kate. "I've got a very anxious young man out here, just champing at the bit to get in here and see you."

"Aye, that I am!" exclaimed Kate and her face lit up like a Christmas tree when Zhai walked in. Both his hands were bandaged.

"Now listen, all of you," said Lily Rose. "Flatliners, Toppers, Armies of Light or Armies of Night—I don't care. You all remember that this is *my* house and it is, always has been and always will be, neutral territory. You got that?"

"Yes, ma'am," came back meekly from all of them.

"All right then. I'll get you a pitcher of milk to go with those cookies."

Zhai nodded to Nass and Dalton as he moved to Kate's bedside. "How are you?" he asked her, a little shy in front of the others.

"As fine as the mornin' sun," she told him with a big smile. "Thanks for bringing me here. Miss Lily has fixed me up fine. She said it looked a lot more serious than it was. The herbs from her garden work wonders. I'm right as rain, Zhai—and I think I'll be goin' home tomorrow. Well, to my little train car, anyway."

"Come on," Dalton told Zhai. "Sit down and relax. Neutral territory, remember? We're not gonna bite you."

Zhai smiled and took the place Dalton vacated, next to Kate. Nass passed the plate of cookies to him.

"Thanks, man," said Zhai.

They all took another cookie and started munching away, and after a moment Dalton spoke up again. "Well," she said. "Are we going to talk about the elephant in the room, or are we going to bury our heads in the sand and ignore it like most everybody else in this town?"

"You mean like all that weird stuff that happened at the tracks last night?" Nass asked.

"For one," Dalton said. "And for another, what about Raphael? He couldn't have just vanished into thin air."

"No," Nass agreed. "He couldn't. We've got to find him. Beet and I spent half the night trying to explain to his mom what had happened. She just looked at us like we were crazy or high or something. She's convinced he ran away."

"And what about Aimee?" Dalton added. "She acted like she didn't even know him. Something's wrong—bad wrong—since she's been hanging out with that Orias guy. We've got to find out what that's all about, and get her away from him if we can."

"We will," Nass said. "But first, we find Raph. The crew and I are putting together search teams and going two-by-two, and starting this afternoon we plan to comb the woods."

"I'll help," Zhai offered.

"Cool," Nass said. "We'll need every man we can get." He turned back to Dalton. "We'll drain Macomb Lake if we have to—but we'll find him. That train couldn't have taken him far—it wasn't even a real train."

"What kind of train was it?" Kate asked quietly.

"Some kind of ghost train," Nass said. "One minute it was there, bearing down on Raph, and the next minute it was gone."

"Then I'm sorry," Kate said. "But you're not likely to see him anytime soon. I've had a bit of experience with that train, you see."

∽

Aimee stared out the window of her bedroom, down at her father's perfect lawn, his new, perfect car parked in their perfect driveway, and on to their perfect, pristine street beyond. She couldn't get over the nagging feeling that she was waiting for someone . . . someone besides her mother. Orias had brought her home last night, after they'd recovered from the shock of the explosion at the tracks, and after he'd promised they would begin looking for her mom soon. And he'd kissed her passionately, sweetly, at the door of her father's house, with whispered promises of a bright future together.

She'd thought her dad would be furious that she'd been with Orias for two days—and one whole night—but he seemed actually pleased with her. Orias was right. Jack Banfield would go along with whatever he suggested. *Daddy dearest*, she thought again.

Feeling like a stranger in her own skin, she realized she didn't belong in her father's house anymore. And she certainly didn't want to go back to Mountain High Academy. She was like Orias in that way—there was no place for her. There was no place that she felt like she really belonged—except with him.

Only, she couldn't get rid of that nagging feeling that she was waiting for someone else. Someone she'd known before Orias came into her life. Someone who had been important to her.

If only she could remember who it was.

BOOK DISCUSSION QUESTIONS

1. Ignacio faced a difficult situation when his ex-girlfriend Clarisse showed up in Middleburg. Would you have handled the situation differently than Ignacio did? If so, how?

2. Do you think Dalton should stick with Ignacio after what happened with Clarisse, or should she stay away from him?

3. Maggie develops her magical powers through meditation and fasting. Why do you think the authors chose these activities as the means for her spiritual development?

4. Orias is banned from heaven because his father is a fallen angel. Do you think that's fair? Why or why not?

5. Do you think Orias really loves Aimee? Why or why not?

6. Who should Aimee choose to be in a relationship with, Raphael or Orias? Why?

7. Who is your favorite character and why?

8. How do you think Emily Banfield (Aimee's mother) ended up in the past?

9. How (and why) do you think Kate Dineen ended up in Middleburg?

10. If you had to choose, would you rather be a member of the Flatliners or the Toppers? Why?

11. Why do you think the magician wore a red robe in Book One, but a bluish-white robe in Book Two? What do you think the colors symbolize?

12. In this book, Master Chin decides Aimee isn't ready for his

kung fu training yet. Do you think that was a fair decision on his part? Why or why not?

13. Do you think Raphael is alive at the end of the book, or dead? If he's alive, what do you think happened to him?

14. What do you think the ring (the treasure) symbolizes?

15. Oberon is a fallen angel, and his son Orias is a Nephilim. Can you pinpoint any other characters in Middleburg as otherworldly? Who? What was your first clue?

16. What is Violet hiding in the basement and why does she keep the basement locked? Are all the bolts and locks on her front door to keep something from coming in or to keep something from getting out? What do you think it is?

17. Now that Maggie is becoming a warrior of the light, do you think she has a better chance of getting Raphael to fall for her?

18. How can Maggie overcome her destiny, so that she doesn't end up like her mother?

19. If you could get your hands on Lily Rose's Good Book, what would you want it to show you and why?

20. What is it about the little town of Middleburg that makes it a portal for the supernatural?

21. Aimee believes that since Orias is half human, he must have at least half a soul, and she's determined to help him find a way to beat the curse of being born a nephilim. How do you think she can help him and why?

ACKNOWLEDGMENTS

My heartfelt thanks to: Charlene Keel for being such a wonderful creative partner; Peter Vegso, Carol Rosenberg, Kim Weiss, Kelly Maragni, and everyone at HCI for their unwavering support; and Peggy and Wendell Gates for kindly donating such excellent office space. Thank you to my sifu Robert Vahovick and everyone at Battle Creek Traditional Wing Chun Club for your exemplary kung fu instruction. Rest assured that everything that is correct in these books regarding kung fu comes from sifu Bob's excellent instruction, while any inaccuracies should be attributed solely to my own fallibility! Thanks to my wonderful language consultants, Judith De Los Santos and Wu, Yu-I. Finally, I owe an eternal debt of gratitude to my parents, grandparents, and other incredible family members who have never, ever failed to believe in me.

—*J. Gabriel Gates*

It's virtually impossible to express my gratitude to all those who have inspired me over the years, but I continue to be thankful for my patient and understanding family—my daughters and granddaughters—for putting up with me when the voices of the people in Middleburg are louder and more insistent than their own. So this is for Rachel, Sarah, Allie, Francesca, Melody, Olivia Valdes, Omar Valdes, my best friend Philece Sampler (who now holds the title of Number One Fan), with great appreciation for all the laughter and encouragement, and Paul Wineman for his continued faith in me. Thanks to my TV and film agent, Susan A. Simons, Debbie Dangerfield for being the best "twin sister" a girl could ever have, Wendy Jackson and Robbyne Kaamil for being so *totally* Dalton, and my other sister, Jordan Giovanni, for giving me the sweetest dog in the world, and with love to Lugene Lewis, my very own Lily Rose. A special thanks to my coauthor J. Gabriel Gates for his grace, talent, and open mind throughout our creative conflicts (that sometimes rival the kung-fu throwdowns in our books), and to our publisher, HCI, and all the wonderful people there who made this series happen.

—*Charlene Keel*

ABOUT THE AUTHORS

J. Gabriel Gate is the nationally acclaimed coauthor of *Dark Territory*, Book 1 in The Tracks series and author of the horror novel *Sleepwalkers* and the soon-to-be-released sci-fi novel *Blood Zero Sky*. A native of Marshall, Michigan, Gates discovered his passion for writing and performing at a young age. He received his bachelor's degree in theater from Florida State University and relocated to Los Angeles, where he acted in several television commercials and penned several screenplays. These experiences laid the groundwork for his career as a successful novelist. When Gates is not writing, he can usually be found reading, working out, hanging out with his friends, or watching college football. He is an advocate for social justice and participated in the Occupy Detroit and Occupy Lansing protests in 2011. His lives with his dog and faithful writing companion, Tommy. Visit him online at www.jgabrielgates.com.

Veteran journalist, author, and screenwriter **Charlene Keel** read *Little Women* when she was in the third grade and decided then and there to become a famous author. By the time she was in fifth grade, she was sitting at her mom's typewriter, hammering out what she knew would be the next bestseller (yes, that was in the dark ages before anyone had a computer at home). In high school, Charlene started sending stories to magazines and getting encouraging comments from editors, scribbled on rejection slips.

At twenty-one, while working as a flight attendant for a major airline, Charlene sold a short story and a two-part serial to *Teen* magazine, and a few years later Leisure Books (now Dorchester) published her first five books and her flying career came to an end.

Her next job as a publicist for Columbia Pictures Television put her in touch with producers who hired her to write episodes of *Fantasy Island* and the popular daytime drama *Days Of Our Lives,* and even turned one of her books (*Rituals*) into a series that ran five nights a week for a year in the United States and for two additional years in France. She also produced the first annual "Mr. Romance Cover Model Pageant" for *Romantic Times* magazine.

Charlene enjoys turning other authors' books into film scripts, and she has done screen adaptations of Patricia Hagan's *Love and War,* Rebecca Brandewyne's *The Jacaranda Tree,* and Peggy Webb's *Where Dolphins Go.* She has worked as editor or managing editor for several national and international magazines. She also ghostwrites books and scripts for celebrities, doctors, and corporate moguls.